OPERATION PEACEMAKER

Jennifer Haynie

To those who seek peace with God and others.

Blessed are the peacemakers, for they will be called
children of God.
—Matthew 5:9

THE TEAM

Victor Chavez (call sign One) — Team leader, former Special Forces captain and Secret Service agent, currently part-time sheriff's deputy and owner of Sentry Securities, Flagstaff, AZ

Suleiman al-Ibrahim (call sign Two) — Sniper/observer, former Hezbollah sniper, currently a waiter, Flagstaff, AZ

Sana Jain (call sign Three) — Breaking-and-entering specialist, former Olympic gymnast and cat burglar, currently a barista at Starbucks, Flagstaff, AZ

Shelly Wise (call sign Four) — Computer and security system specialist, former research and development specialist, currently with a defense contractor, Phoenix, AZ

Butch Addison (call sign Five) — Mechanic and escape-and-evasion expert, former Special Forces soldier, currently owner of an auto mechanic shop, Flagstaff, AZ

Diana Kasem (call sign Six) — Doctor, former Army cardiothoracic surgeon, currently practicing cardiothoracic surgery, Phoenix, AZ

Fiona Mercedes (call sign Seven) — Pilot, former Army helicopter pilot and CIA contract pilot, currently a charter pilot, Las Vegas, NV

Skylar James (call sign Eight) — Procurement officer and disguise specialist, former CIA agent, currently owner of Regions Restaurant, Las Vegas, NV

Supporting Team

Deborah Chavez — Wife of Victor Chavez

Anna Fields (14) — Oldest daughter of Deborah

DJ Fields (12) — Only son of Deborah

Gracie Fields (8) — Second daughter of Deborah

Marie Fields (6) — Youngest daughter of Deborah

Tuesday, June 23, 2015, 1530 hours local time, off the coast of Somalia

The sudden push of acceleration meant trouble—maybe.

Crouched over her duffel bag, Doctor Tori Walters paused from gazing at a photo of her and her fiancé.

It didn't repeat, so she shrugged and returned to packing. Two more days. Then she'd be off the South African hospital ship *Peacemaker* and in his arms. She placed the picture in her duffel and reached for another one.

She rose and pulled several books from the shelves above her desk. Most went into a cardboard box. A few would go into her other duffel. She gathered several more photos. Mom with her as a child. Had she lived, Mom would have been so proud of her. With her brother, George, when he'd visited her while in college. Dad and her stepmother, Elizabeth, at her graduation from medical school.

Her phone chirped.

She snagged it from her desk and resumed her crouch as she read through the text. "Sweetie, just got off the phone. Will be unable to travel with E and J to Cape Town due to closing on a business. Will see you when you arrive in Charleston. Dad."

"Figures," she muttered. "Business once more supersedes daughter. Why should I be surprised?"

Jesus's words regarding serving God or money flew through her mind. She reached up to put her phone on the desk.

The ship made a hard turn to port. The floor tilted, and she grabbed the edge of the desk to keep from tumbling face first onto her bags. What was going on? It evened out. She shrugged and picked up another picture, this one of Jake and her from the night they'd gotten engaged almost nine months before. Both wore wide smiles. Then came ones of her with her half-sisters. She placed her Bible on top and left it unzipped before turning to her clothing.

The ship rolled again, this time to starboard.

She lost her balance and fell onto her rump. Pain blazed up her spine. "Ow!"

What on earth? She hauled herself to her feet, threw open the door to her cabin, and stumbled into the hall. As the ship came back to port, she staggered into a wall. Somehow, she pushed through the crowd and made it to midships where the main stairs and elevator were.

Klaus, one of the radar men, bolted up the steps from the level below and nearly knocked her off her feet. "Sorry! Sorry!"

"Easy there, little brother." The ship heaved toward starboard, and she grabbed the railing to avoid running into some of the crew who dashed downward. "What's going on?"

The klaxon that suddenly blared overhead and the words that followed told it all. "Code Black. Code Black. Enact protocol."

Pirate attack.

The hallway came to life as the crew and medical personnel began running to their assigned stations.

"Come with me!" Klaus shouted.

At least that's what she thought he said over the electronic shriek.

He grabbed her arm and dragged her up the steps to the next level. He bolted into the hot afternoon.

Even from where she stood, spray splashed across her face and left in its wake the sharp taste of the beach on her lips. Her eyes watered in the bright light.

He turned to her. "I need your help. Get the hose."

"The what?"

"The hose!" He yanked open a cabinet outside the door leading to the main deck. "Unwind it. Hurry!"

Tori grabbed the wheel of the spool and cranked it until its entire length had come loose from the spindle.

Klaus snatched up the nozzle. "Turn the water on. That red wheel there. Now!"

Tori spun it to the left.

Like it gained mythical life, the hose filled and threatened to come out of Klaus's hands.

She hugged it to stabilize it. Now she realized their precarious situation. A speedboat had pulled to within yards of the ship's port side.

Pirates.

Klaus aimed the stream in their direction. It seemed to work by keeping them away.

Temporarily.

Yellow points of light flashed from the boat. Bullets pinged around them.

Klaus flinched "Get down!"

Tori fell to her knees but refused to relinquish her grip on the bucking canvas tube.

Men shouted above the noise of gunfire and the water spurting out.

Klaus cried out. He dropped the hose and fell to the deck with his hand covering his chest.

The hose jerked free and writhed like a sea snake.

"Klaus! No!" She crawled forward and cringed as more bullets popped and sparked against the metal. The fusillade ceased. She risked an upward glance.

"Oh, no."

Grappling hooks clanged against the railing. Then came the bang of an aluminum extension ladder as their attackers bridged the chasm.

She reached for the hose.

"Tori, it's too late." Using the wall of the dining hall, Klaus hauled himself to his feet and left a streak of scarlet along the white paint. "We must get inside. Hurry!"

They dashed into the shadow of the ship's superstructure. She shrieked as more bullets bit into metal behind her.

Wheezing, he collapsed. "Tori, the gate."

"What?"

"Get the gate!"

Inklings of the drills they'd run after leaving South Asia flew through her mind. She snatched the padlock from where it hung on the gate's hasp. With a great heave, she yanked the grate of iron bars from its clip and slammed it across the doorway leading to the outside. She shoved the padlock closed before yanking on it. Secure.

She fell to her knees.

Gasping, Klaus slumped against the wall. Blood had seeped between his fingers and stained his white uniform shirt. Blue tinged his features, and he panted as if he couldn't get enough air into his lungs.

"Klaus!" She crawled to his side. Panting. Pain. Pneumothorax. Those words swept through Tori's brain. "Your lung is collapsing. If we don't do something about it, you'll die. I need to get you to the OR."

"Get…to…your cabin," he wheezed. "Go!"

"No, I—"

"Go!"

A shadow crossed them.

Her stomach dropped. Two pirates, both armed with rifles, blocked the afternoon sun. One of them rattled the gate. "Undo lock!"

"We… don't have…" Klaus's speech faded.

"We don't have the key." Tori raised her hands.

"Open!"

Would they not understand? "No key! No key!"

The first one jabbered to his buddy in another language. He shouted something.

Tori cringed. Maybe she could escape to the operating room with Klaus. She'd lock the door, then stabilize him. She took his arm.

"No move!" the first one ordered.

She froze.

More yammering followed as another pirate handed them bolt cutters.

She couldn't let them cut the lock. Tori lunged for their tool.

The first one laughed and jabbed her hard in the chest with the muzzle of his rifle.

Pain exploded in her sternum as she stumbled over Klaus and fell heavily onto her side. Whimpering, she pushed herself to a sitting position and stared.

The lock plunked onto the steel deck. They pushed the gate open.

They were toast. Captured now by the pirates. Three hundred souls. Tori's heart sank as the first one spoke in English into his radio. "We are in."

She clutched Klaus's arm as she rose to a crouch. Rubbing her sternum eased the pain.

Their captors muttered among themselves as they kept their rifles trained on the two hostages.

Silence fell except for the throb of the engines and the hiss of the ship's hull as they cruised through the water.

A fourth man joined them. This one? The way he carried his shoulders told it all. Arrogance. Pure and simple. He wore bandoleers across his chest like a mantle and the turban with its end trailing down his shoulder like a crown. His dark eyes glittered in features that seemed to be carved by God only for those of royalty.

The leader.

He raised his radio to his lips. In precise English, he said, "Captain, we have breeched your defense and have two hostages. You have one minute to open bridge and tell crew to stand down. Starting now."

Lord, this is not how it's supposed to end. The thought raced through Tori's mind. She had so much she wanted to do. So much! She and Jake were supposed to marry in October. She was supposed to start her practice after Labor Day and—

"Forty-five seconds, Captain."

Don't do it, Captain Jameson, she pleaded in her heart. *But do it.* The two sides warred within her.

"Thirty seconds."

She stared at the leader as the words whispered from her heart into her soul blurred too much for her to recognize.

"Fifteen seconds." The leader drew a pearl-handled pistol.

"I will." Those two words, spoken in a crisp, British accent, sealed her fate. The klaxon ceased.

The leader barked orders into his radio.

Klaus moaned and sagged completely onto his side.

Tori's attention immediately snapped to him.

The blue had spread across his normally ruddy features.

Like a beta dog, she avoided looking directly at the leader. "Sir, with all due respect, he is wounded. I'm a doctor, and I—I need to operate on him. Otherwise, he'll die."

The leader pointed his pistol at the radar man. "Then I help."

"No!" Tori scrambled over Klaus and shielded him. "Let me stabilize him." She focused on the leader's feet. "Please, sir. I will stabilize him. That is all."

"Then we go." The leader gestured with his pistol.

He snapped something at his men, who nodded and withdrew.

"Hang on, little brother. I'll help you." Tori carefully helped Klaus sit up before looping his good arm over her shoulders. She rose, but her knees buckled under his nearly six-one frame. *Lord, please.* They stumbled further into the dim recesses of the ship. Their footfalls echoed as they descended the steps.

Once on the first level belowdecks, Tori's shoulder where Klaus leaned began hurting. She could have asked the pirate for help. No way, no how. She'd rather collapse in the hallway than appear as a weak and scared hostage to this man.

The leader said something to one of his men, who joined them.

Immediately, the smell of no hygiene and body odor filled her nostrils. Ick. Stinky. What a totally perfect name for him.

She shut out that and their chatter as she hit a button. The door to the prep area for the OR opened. They passed through that and into the OR itself. Her shoulder screamed for relief, and now her knees trembled. Finally, she eased Klaus onto an operating table. She took his hand and brushed a lock of hair from his forehead. "We're here. Your lung has collapsed. I need to release some of the air in your chest cavity so you can breathe."

He nodded.

Without wasting any time, she undid his shirt and cut away his undershirt. After donning surgical gloves, she sanitized the skin and injected a local anesthetic. "I'm sorry. This is going to hurt, but it'll save your life."

"Do…do…what you must." Klaus winced.

Get needle. Insert into chest cavity. Stabilize needle. Stop blood from bullet wound. Her mind flew through the steps of the procedure as she gathered the instruments she'd need.

The leader grabbed her arm. "I told you no operate!"

"If I don't, he dies! It's a procedure not—"

He drew his pistol and pointed it at her forehead. "Do not defy Abu Waheed!"

Heart pounding, she glared at him. She drew herself up to her full five-foot, seven-inch height and hissed, "This is *my* operating room. In here, *I'm* in charge, not you."

She braced herself for a fatal bullet.

Something like a smile crossed Abu Waheed's lips. He took a small step backward.

Skirmish won, she resumed her work until she secured the last bit of tape over the gauze and checked Klaus's blood pressure. Stable, it seemed. Good enough for now. Maybe later, she could convince Abu Waheed to let her operate.

"I'm finished." Heart pounding, she stepped back.

He came closer. "Then I take you to quarters."

She slipped away and shucked her gloves. As she did so, she noticed her engagement ring. No way would she let Jake's most precious gift to her fall into their hands. She put her body between the ring and the pirate as she slid it from her finger and into the upturned hem of her jeans shorts.

Abu Waheed grabbed her arm. "Where are your quarters?"

"Same level at the bow on the right. Klaus needs someone to monitor him. Ow!" Tori winced as his fingers tightened on her arm. They passed through the central area, where Stinky remained as Abu Waheed dragged her toward the bow. She thought she heard whimpering coming from behind some of the doors.

He didn't slow his steps. "I will consider after I get into safe."

"A woman named Nattie and I can be the two people to do so. She…she is on the second level belowdecks." Tori flinched as he slammed her into the wall at the end. A flag of fear began unfurling inside of her.

He shoved open her door. "Get in there."

He pushed her so hard that she stumbled across the cabin and caught herself on the porthole.

Tori whipped around. The adrenaline began leaking from her body. With its departure came trembling and pure, raw fear. What had she done by standing up to him? But, she'd lived, hadn't she? And so had her friend. That knowledge shored up her fast-waning courage as she eased onto the chair at her desk. She had to hide the ring. But where?

Her gaze fell on the Bible in her duffel. She opened it toward the middle and almost laughed. The Book of Job. How fitting for the situation in which she suddenly found herself. Using a small bit of scotch tape, she secured the ring to one of the pages. Surely God would forgive her if it ripped when she removed it. She clung to that idea because if she removed the ring, it would mean they were free.

She was about to shove her duffel under her desk when she froze. Her father, Norm Walters, was Chairman and CEO of Walters Enterprises.

And a billionaire.

What would happen if Abu Waheed found out? She wouldn't let herself go there. She pulled out the frames holding the pictures of her father and her family. After popping the porthole open, she removed the photos and released those into the wind. They fluttered away.

Now to her computer. She turned it on. Maybe they'd forgotten about the ship's Internet access. Hah. Fat chance of that. Leave it to her to assume that they weren't sophisticated enough to figure out their e-mail system. She tried to log into the Internet. Already severed. Who cared? She could still access her e-mail. One click of a button highlighted all of her messages, which she deleted, first out of her in-box and then from her computer.

What else? Tori rose and eased onto the edge of her bed as she thought about that one. The captain's personal safe. In it lay not only her passport but also a listing of everyone's basic health and emergency contact information. Hers held her father's name and phone numbers.

Her breath hitched.

What could she do? Run screaming to the bridge and demand access? Hardly.

Since it was his personal safe, only Captain Jameson had the combination. No one else. And he was loyal to the crew. But loyal enough not to divulge that information? She thought about what she knew about him. Career British Navy. Combat veteran. Even before joining Mercy Medical Missions, he'd been to some of the most dangerous parts of the world. He took care of his people. It was his nature.

The thought eased some of the tension in her shoulders.

She was safe.

Tuesday, June 23, 2015, 1600 hours local time, off the coast of Somalia

As he finished his initial walk-through of the ship, Abu Waheed stuffed some *khat* into his mouth. Almost immediately, the stimulant coursed through his blood.

His chest puffed out.

He lifted his chin.

The world was his, including this ship.

He sneered at the sounds of weeping coming from behind a couple of the closed cabin doors. In Somali, he said, "A most excellent idea to place the hostages in their quarters with the threat of death if they stick their noses out. No one can leave, and they can't collaborate with one another. It takes less men to watch them."

Wasim, his second-in-command, matched him step for step. "What of the safe?"

"Have you found it?" Abu Waheed entered the central core and stepped onto the elevator.

"In the captain's quarters on the level beneath the bridge."

"Most excellent." Abu Waheed jabbed the appropriate button. "Bring him to me."

Once the elevator doors opened, Wasim nodded and headed up the spiral staircase that led directly from the quarters onto the bridge.

"I will not go!" a man shouted in a British accent.

"You will come with me," Wasim growled. Then came the sound of skin on skin. "Now! Or shall I shoot someone to get you to obey?"

Abu Waheed chuckled. The captain would either confess or pay with his life.

"Get down there!" Wasim shoved the tall Englishman down the steps.

When he reached the bottom, the captain lost his balance and fell to his knees. Grasping the railing of the spiral staircase, he hauled himself to his feet

Abu Waheed smirked. In English, he said, "My men have found your safe. What is inside?"

The captain clamped his jaw shut.

Hot anger burned in Abu Waheed's gut. He popped him across the face with the butt of his pistol. The blood that now poured down his captive's face only fueled his anger. "What is inside?"

"Nothing." The captain nearly spat that word. He glanced toward the bookcase with an ornate cabinet beneath a wall-mounted television.

"You lie. Wasim, show me where it is."

His lieutenant swung the door open to reveal a stout safe with a spin-combination lock.

Abu Waheed pointed to it. "Open."

The captain shook his head. "No. I will not endanger my crew further."

"What?" That burning anger returned, this time growing stronger as the high of the *khat* filled him. How dare this captain, his captive, refuse an order from him? "You are fool!" In a rush of anger, Abu Waheed grabbed his arm and kicked the back of his knees. The big man collapsed, and he dragged him to the safe. "You open safe."

"I will not."

Al'abalah! Idiot! Didn't he understand the dangerous game he played? Maybe. He seemed to be a battle-hardened man. Well, even those kinds of men trembled at his hands. He put his boot between the captain's shoulders and shoved him.

With an audible crack, the captain's face slammed into the hard metal. He moaned.

Abu Waheed grabbed his collar and twisted. The high in him increased as he growled into his ear, "Do as I say, Captain, or die. Now open safe."

The captain reached for the dial, then lowered his hand. "No. I will not."

Heat flooded Abu Waheed. Fed by the *khat*, the beast of his anger roared. He pushed him again.

This time, his hostage caught himself and spun around.

That fueled his rage even more. "You dare defy me? You are fool!"

Even with blood pouring down his face, the captain remained stoic. "I will not endanger my crew. They are my responsibility to—"

"Shut up! Open safe!" Abu Waheed drew his gun. "Now!"

"No." The corner of the captain's mouth curled in derision.

Red filled Abu Waheed's vision. He pounced, knocking the hostage against the cabinet. He pressed the muzzle so hard into the man's forehead that he groaned. "Do now or die."

"No."

Abu Waheed pulled the trigger.

In the small quarters, the gunshot nearly deafened him.

The captain's body sagged to the light gray carpet. His blood splattered all over the face of the safe and pooled on the floor.

Abu Waheed jabbed the body with the toe of his boot before turning to Wasim. "Take it and dump it over the railing for the sharks."

With that, he stomped up the spiral staircase to the bridge. Someone else would have the combination, and he would shoot the lot of them until he found out who did.

The crew stared at him with wide eyes. A tear rolled down the cheek of the woman at the controls. She stared out the windows.

Abu swung around and scanned the crew. "Who is first mate?"

"I am." An Oriental man with three bars on his shoulders stepped forward.

"Your name?"

"Commander Thomas Ching."

"Well, Commander Thomas Ching, congratulations. You are now Captain Ching."

"What...what of Captain Jameson?"

"He had a date with the sharks." Abu Waheed started laughing, and Wasim, and Asam, another one of his pirates, followed suit.

The woman sent visual daggers toward him.

He raised his hand as if to strike her.

She flinched and turned away.

Abu Waheed cut his laughter off. "Captain Ching, you will set a course for La 'Amal. And what is the combination of the safe downstairs?"

Commander Ching stared at him for a long moment.

"That was his personal safe, you dipwad. Only Captain Jameson had the combination," the woman hissed.

Abu Waheed didn't know what a dipwad was, but he was sure he'd been insulted. He struck her across the cheek. She cried out.

The commander's Adam's apple bobbed. "Madison, continue course." He turned to another member of the crew. "Ensign Shah, determine the appropriate heading to this La 'Amal."

"So tell me, Captain Ching. Does this whore," Abu Waheed hitched himself onto the high captain's chair and nodded in the woman's direction, "does she tell the truth?"

"She does. The ship's safe is behind me." Commander Ching nodded over his shoulder.

"Open it!"

The commander's fingers shook, but he obeyed and swung open the small door.

The safe was empty.

"So our access died with the captain. How clever of him," Abu Waheed muttered in Somali. Over his shoulder, he called, "Wasim!"

His second joined him. "Yes, Abu Waheed."

"We will sail under radio silence. Once we get to port, I want you to use your connections to find us a safecracker willing to come to La 'Amal. Do what you must, but I *will* have access to that safe. Do you understand?"

Wasim nodded.

"Good. Dismissed." Abu Waheed swept the bridge in one look. As if satisfied, the thrum from the *khat* eased away, leaving behind it a languid relaxation comparable to finishing a big meal. The smirk returned when he noted the arrival of Balam, another pirate, on the bridge. The crew now realized he meant business. He had several hostages, three hundred by his estimation. And a safe full of an undetermined amount of baubles. Once they got to port, he'd ransom the ship for fifty million as a starting point. Not bad for a day's worth of work.

1

Today, he would die.

Suleiman al-Ibrahim knew it in his heart as he clung to the underside of a rock that capped a climb called The Mushroom.

What was he? Crazy? Crazy to think that he was a rock climber at the same level as Sana?

No.

He'd wanted to be with her now that he had the summer free from classes. Today, being with her meant going rock climbing. And going rock climbing meant saying yes to acts that defied gravity. He groaned as the pain in his fingers increased.

"This is how you do it." Sana Jain's voice floated down to him like a blessing from heaven. "Is the lip a foot in front of you?"

"Yes."

"Reach with your right hand. There's a handhold about a foot above the lip. Do you feel it?"

He reached out. His aching fingers explored the rock. There! He grabbed it. "I found it."

"Good. Now here's the tricky part. You're going to reach with your left hand. About six inches above the lip and six inches to the left of where your right hand is, you'll find another handhold. When you grab it, your feet are going to come off their perch."

Suleiman shuddered. He'd surely fall to his death despite the ropes to which he was attached and Sana belaying him from above.

"What you'll do is immediately swing your left foot up. You'll find a foothold at the edge. Snag it with your left foot and power up. Use your left arm to help. Then, you'll find another handhold for your right hand and put your right foot where your right hand is now."

So complicated. It was too much for his overtaxed brain to handle.

"You can do it. I know you can. The key is to move quickly."

"Sana—"

"Go for it before you get too taxed where you are."

Oh, so true. With a deep breath, he reached with his left hand. His feet came off, and he dangled by his fingertips over a thousand feet above the trees.

Visions of his life flashed before him. He was going to see Allah soon, and he wasn't in any shape to do so, not when his bad works out-weighed—

"Move it!" the drill sergeant shouted from above.

Suleiman groaned as he swung his left foot up. He found the foothold and pressed his foot against it. Traction. So vital to him now.

"Now push! Hurry!"

He thrust upward. His glutes and left quad burned as he snagged the higher handhold with his right hand. He jammed his right foot onto the tiny ledge his hand had just vacated. At this point, the rock began inclining a bit more. Who cared? One small move in the wrong direction, and he'd have to repeat the whole torturous process.

Breathe. Breathe.

Gradually, his heart rate slowed.

"You did it!"

He peered upward.

His angel gazed at him. Her black, chin-length hair gleamed in the midday sun like a raven's wing.

"Just twenty feet more. It's an easy junket up because of the way the rock slopes."

"Only if you're not exhausted," he muttered.

She giggled. "Seriously. It's lunchtime, and I can't eat until you're off belay."

"Very funny." His stomach growled at the mere thought of food.

"Then come on up. The handholds are laid out perfectly." She disappeared.

Almost reluctantly, he resumed his climb. The rock tilted further, making his job easier. Finally, he crested the lip and clawed his way onto solid ground.

Sana hauled him to safety. Sana's dark eyes sparkled as she grabbed his hand and briefly squeezed it. "Good job."

He scrambled a few feet further, then collapsed onto his front with a loud groan. He rolled onto his back. Never again would he complain about lying on hard soil with a rock poking into him. "I...I don't have any strength left."

"Do you want some gorp?"

"Only if it's separated into dried fruit, nuts, and chocolate."

"You are so strange. Here."

A bag landed on his chest. Suleiman opened his eyes, raised his head, and pushed himself to his elbows as she unclipped him from the ropes. For some bizarre reason, his muscles had stopped screaming at him. In the wake of the pain came a feeling of euphoria. "I have to say, I enjoyed that in a twisted, demented kind of way. And the view?" He sat all the way up as he took in the forest and ranch land below. "Incredible."

"It's hard to believe, but we can see Last Chance Ranch a couple of miles from here." She turned his shoulders and pointed. "There. Can you see it?"

All he saw was forest, then a black ribbon, then more ranch land. "No. Not really."

"I'll show you in a minute." Sana opened her pack and pulled out her peanut butter and jelly sandwich and a baggie of potato chips. "So how can you eat peanut butter and jelly but not gorp?"

"It is difficult to explain." He pulled out his own lunch, which included an apple and a bag of M&Ms.

She raised a perfectly coiffed eyebrow as she uncapped her water bottle and took a swig. A grin curved her lips upwards. "That's okay. We all have our eccentricities."

"What is yours?"

"Who knows?" She shrugged. Then she grinned and cut her eyes toward him. "I can't chew gum and walk at the same time."

He laughed.

Sana dug into her pack and produced two small cylinders. "Vic loaned me his binoculars. You know which pair I'm talking about, right? The compact but really powerful ones?"

"I do."

"I figured we could search out the ranch." She lifted them to her eyes. "We're almost two miles away, and I can see the Big House. Wow. This is so cool."

"Let me see." Suleiman crammed so close that their shoulders touched.

"Eat some gorp, and maybe I will."

He chuckled and held up his M&Ms. "So sorry. I prefer pure chocolate."

She frowned. "It looks like there's a silver car out front, like he has a visitor. Did you talk to him at all this morning to see what was going on today?"

"At breakfast, he didn't look happy. I didn't want to ask him."

"Here." Sana placed the binoculars in his hands and began eating her sandwich. "I want to finish lunch and get everything pulled together."

Suleiman scanned the horizon. At first, he couldn't discern the landscape enough to find the Big House, which was what they called the main house at Last Chance Ranch. He spotted the road. From there, he followed the thread of black until he noted the entrance for the ranch. The contemporary "L" and "C" on the ironwork of the gate told him he'd found where they lived. A car sat in the circular drive next to the steps leading to the porch. Two men stepped onto the dark wood. He immediately recognized

Victor Chavez's tall, lean form. He shook hands with the shorter, stockier man, who climbed into the car.

What was that all about? He wasn't sure, and it wasn't any of his business.

Sana cleared her throat. "Shelly called me last night."

"What did she have to say?"

"It was what she didn't say that worried me."

He lowered the binoculars. "What do you mean?"

"She seemed down. Like at work, they were giving her a really hard time about her brains." She sighed. "I wish people would respect her for who she is."

"People can be envious. It is easy to envy what you do not have."

"I know. I guess I hurt for her. But she said she's committed to it." Sana heaved a sigh and set her water bottle down. "This is a change in subject, but we have about an hour's hike back to the car. And I promised Deborah I'd help her do some unpacking at the house."

Did they have to leave? He knew it would sound petulant, like a child. It was just that right now, he didn't want this time alone with her to end. "Before we go, could we perhaps take a picture together?"

"Sure."

Using that as an excuse, he crawled beside her. When he placed his left arm behind her, she leaned into him. Her black hair tickled his chin, and the olive skin of her arm brushed him. His pulse shot up. It would be so easy to nuzzle—

"Well?" She nudged him.

So much for seizing the moment. "My apologies."

He lifted his phone and centered them on the screen.

"One, two, three, selfie!" She giggled as the phone recorded their image. "Let me see."

He handed it to her.

"Good one." She returned it to him.

"Now, one of you."

She sighed. "Do I have to?"

"Please?" He gave her his best puppy dog eyes.

"Well, if you say so." She struck a pose, and he snapped another picture before she scrambled to her feet. "Help me with the rope?"

"Of course." As they began pulling the ropes upward, Suleiman's phone chirped. He frowned and stared at the text.

Victor had written, "Potential job. Be at the studio at 8 sharp tonight."

Sana's phone beeped as well. Her pretty features knitted. "What do you think this is about?"

Suleiman hoisted the coil and looped it over his shoulders. "Not quite sure. Maybe it has to do with Victor's visitor. I believe we will find out very soon."

2

Already?

Suleiman's shoulder muscles grumbled at him as he pulled on a fleece over his T-shirt. What had he expected after such a hard climb? At least ibuprofen would help. Stretching, too.

He popped a couple of pills into his mouth and took a swig of water. He'd stretch later, like after the meeting. Right then, getting to the outbuilding that housed Victor's office took precedence.

It was a quick stroll through the rapidly cooling evening. From the barn toward the back of the box canyon, one of the twelve ranch horses nickered. Another horse answered.

He smiled. What a pleasant evening.

He found the screened door to the studio open with Victor tapping on a laptop at his worktable. Suleiman softly called, "Victor, I'm here."

His mentor turned. "Hey. Come on in."

He stepped inside and scanned the interior. Granite slabs on the floor made it appear as if the only natural disturbances to the landscape were the glass walls and Navajo rug on the floor in front of the stone hearth. "I like this. It feels as if nature has moved inside from the outside."

"When Dad designed and built the ranch, he used this as his home office. I guess it's kind of like that for me." Victor rose. "You want something hot? It's cooling down pretty quickly out there."

"Please. Thank you."

Victor poured some water into a coffeemaker. "I'll be a bit more social when I get this finished."

"No worries." As Victor resumed his work, Suleiman studied the photographs littering the spacious interior. Several hung from fishing line in the windows and appeared as if they were floating. They portrayed different angles of the Chavez property. He noted one of the mountain he and Sana had climbed earlier, including the mushroom shape that gave the hellacious climb its name. Other pictures, those of friends and family, graced the sills.

He turned toward the fireplace. Another landscape, this one of buttes he recognized from Monument Valley, dominated the place of honor above the mantel. To each side were four photographs, those of each member of the Shadow Box Team. All of these photos were in black and white, which seemed to be Victor's favorite medium.

Immediately, he picked out Sana. True to form, she hung from a rock. He traced the definition of her arms, legs, and back, which the monochromatic medium highlighted.

Behind him, the printer began whirring. Victor joined him and crouched as he lit the pine cones and kindling in the fireplace. "How was your climb today?"

Suleiman groaned. "Very difficult. She did not tell me it was the hardest in this area. She did not want me to" —he struggled to remember the phrase— "to chicken out."

Victor chuckled. "You did The Mushroom?"

"How did you know?"

"Because I chickened out climbing that with her. You're a brave man, Suleiman al-Ibrahim."

"Or foolish." Or willing to do anything to show his budding affection for Sana. Suleiman gazed at the photographs occupying the mantel. These were of Victor's new family, especially from the wedding that had occurred only two months before. He noted each. Deborah and Victor in their finery. Victor with his two youngest stepdaughters kissing him on the cheeks. Deborah with Anna, her oldest child.

Then he saw one of the Shadow Box men, sans Skylar, who hadn't attended the wedding. A color photo of him and Sana that the photographer had taken at the reception caught his eye. His cheeks warmed as he gazed at her. That April evening, she'd worn a sari of deep, rich green trimmed in sequins and rhinestones. It looked as if he had his arm around her shoulders when in reality, he'd rested it along the back of her chair. One could hope the former would be true one day.

Another frame toward the back caught his attention. Like many of the others, this one was in black and white. It was of a woman. Dressed in what was most likely blue jeans and a white sweater, she sat amidst sea oats along somewhere along the ocean. Her eyes appeared pale, as did her hair. "Victor, who is this? Is she a relation to Deborah?"

"That one?" Victor came to stand beside him. Sadness filled his eyes. "No. That's a picture of my former fiancée. She died in 2012."

"I'm sorry." What else could he say? And why did the woman seem familiar to him? Had he met her somewhere? How could he have done so? He shrugged it off. Or tried to, but something bothered him about that picture.

Victor picked it up. "You know, it's not right that she's up there. Not when Deb and I have married." He stepped to the table and placed it in a small box beneath it. "Coffee's ready."

"Told you so." Sana's laughter drifted upon the currents of the breeze sifting through the screens. She pulled the door open.

"Told you, what?" Victor asked.

Butch Addison grinned and practically hurled his large frame onto one of the chairs. "Sorry we're late, boss. Gracie and Marie absolutely insisted that I get their fish tank set up before I came out here. Women. They can be so demanding."

Sana giggled. "Told you so about women."

Victor picked up two more mugs and placed them by the coffeemaker. "Get used to it. The girls love having Uncle Butch around."

"Not that I mind." Butch rubbed a hand across his bald head. "You got some coffee there?"

"High octane or unleaded. High octane's ready. I can brew unleaded."

"Oh, you know me. High octane."

"Sana, I've got some tea, too." Victor poured some more water into an electric teakettle and plugged it in. Immediately, it began hissing.

"You have a job for us, eh?" Butch rose, poured himself a mug of coffee, and returned to his place. The silver hoops in his ears glimmered in the firelight.

Suleiman seated himself on the couch. Would Sana curl up next to him? Fantasy. Complete fantasy.

She picked up her mug and settled on the other chair with her legs tucked underneath her.

He bit back his frustration.

"Yeah, it's a job all right." Victor took a seat next to Suleiman. "I so totally didn't see this one coming." He opened his folder and pulled out four sets of stapled papers. "The briefing sheet's on top with details underneath. Each of you take a copy."

Suleiman scanned the top sheet. Victor had titled the job Operation Peacemaker. "The *Peacemaker*? I do not understand."

"We're getting pulled into the *Peacemaker* thing?" Butch set his mug on a side table and leaned forward.

"Smart man." Victor smirked at his deputy. "Or psychic."

"Heard about it on NPR, at least until Gracie and Marie started bickering when we were coming home. I only put two and two together when at supper, Anna talked about some guy named Norm Walters showing up earlier today."

"Let me tell you, this isn't a good situation. Early this morning our time, Somali pirates seized a medical missions hospital ship. The organization is called Mercy Medical Missions, or MMM for short. They have works going on globally, but their flagship projects, pardon the pun, are two South African hospital ships, the *Hope* and *Peacemaker*."

"So they're of South African registry." Suleiman frowned when he noted the details. "Five hundred feet in length. Three hundred crew. Based out of Cape Town, South Africa. Visited some of the poorest places in the world. En route from Mumbai to Mombasa when they were hijacked."

"You got it." Victor gazed at the papers for a moment. "They got off a distress call, but that's it."

Sana's brow knitted. "Does this have anything to do with your visitor?"

Victor glanced up. "How did you know?"

A grin played about her lips. "You loaned us your binoculars. What else can I say? I saw the car here."

"It has everything to do with my visitor. The man's name is Norman Walters, or Norm for short."

Butch raised an eyebrow. "As in Walters Enterprises?"

"You know the name?" Victor asked.

He nodded. "I have stock in his company. Not much, but my financial adviser recommended that I invest in it. Believe me when I say I'm glad I did."

"For the rest of you, the details are there. Suffice it to say that whatever Norm touches turns to gold."

Sana cocked her head. "He's that good?"

"Yep. A smart investor, first in software, but he's gotten into international shipping and has holdings everywhere. In other words, he's a billionaire."

Suleiman laid the papers on the glass coffee table and studied them. "I do not understand why he came here today."

"His daughter's on that ship." Victor cracked his knuckles as if to emphasize that point.

Butch stroked his goatee. "Why do I have a bad feeling about this?" He cut his eyes toward his boss. "'Cause Somali pirates and a billionaire's daughter don't go together too well."

Victor shifted. "Or maybe they do if you're the pirate. Victoria Walters, or Tori to her friends, is a plastic surgeon on that ship. According to Norm, she could care less about the fact that her father has more money than a lot of developing countries. She's at the end of a two-year tour of duty on the *Peacemaker*, and she's engaged to be married in October."

Sana sipped her tea as her eyes darted across the page. She rested it on her knees. "And no one knows who she is, right?"

Victor nodded. "Right. Norm reported that only the captain and her three closest friends know that her daddy's a billionaire. But there is a catch."

"Which is?" Butch leaned forward as if anticipating a juicy piece of news.

"In his personal safe, the captain stores a crew manifest that lists the basic medical and emergency contact information in case the need arises. That's standard protocol. According to what MMM told Norm, the combination for his personal safe resides only with him. Though no one wants to acknowledge it, I think the captain might be dead."

Sana drew in a sharp breath. "Why do you say that?"

"Just a gut feeling. Somali pirates aren't the most sympathetic." Victor took a deep breath. "I have his bio. Norm got it from MMM. He's a combat veteran. Decorated for various acts of valor with the Royal Navy. He knew the dangers of sailing in that part of the world, and he insisted that each ship have a personal safe installed with the captain being the only one with the combination. He made it clear to MMM headquarters that he planned to store everyone's personal contact information and passports in it. But that doesn't guarantee that the copy at headquarters in Cape Town is safe. Matter of fact, they've told Norm that the media have been hounding the headquarters staff."

Suleiman's mind raced. He understood the urgency of the situation. How could he not when a father's worry drove him to travel thousands of miles to Last Chance Ranch? "Why us?"

"He's personal friends with President Badin. Let's leave it at that."

Something like a strangled cough escaped Butch. "As in, he contributed money toward Badin's campaign. Problem is, it's South Africa's territory. The president ain't gonna horn in on that because of his isolationist stance."

"Exactly." Victor fixed each of them in his stare. "But he told Norm about Shadow Box."

"Um, question." Sana raised her hand. "We were officially disbanded."

"Right. Somehow, Norm got the impression that we could help him. Then he offered up his fee."

"Which is?" Butch asked.

"Twenty million flat. Plus expenses and all the equipment we'd need."

Murmurs exploded across the room as Suleiman tried to digest the number. Twenty *million*? What? Had he heard right? What did that sum look like?

"He was sincere," Victor was saying as Suleiman tuned back into the conversation. "Each of you would get a million."

Again, Suleiman gawked. Forget twenty million. What would a million look like for him? Maybe going to University full time without working his way through? Even buying a house? He couldn't fathom it.

"I'd bring each of you on as contractors, so that's the mechanism I'd use." Victor closed his folder and set it on the table. "Thing is, I told him we'd take the job on two conditions. First, we get all of the hostages out, not just Tori. Second, we have to have the whole team together, or we don't go."

Forget that. Just as quickly as Suleiman's mood lifted, it deflated. It wouldn't happen. Not with having to convince Skylar and Fiona to return.

"Goodbye, twenty mil." Butch groaned. "No way you're going to get Skylar and Fi back here."

"I understand your concerns." Victor fell silent for a moment. He squinted as if seeing something that the others couldn't. "There's simply no way that we can do this without them."

Sana scowled. "Can you give Fi a personality transplant?"

"I wish. Look. We go and we ask. And we sweeten the deal."

"How?" Suleiman asked.

"We tell them it's a one-shot assignment." Victor rose and stepped to the fireplace. He turned. "Time's of the essence here. Each day we waste is another day that the press has an opportunity to get that crew manifest and that the pirates have to take everyone ashore. And I don't need to say what will probably happen when that news becomes public."

Suleiman knew all too well. He'd seen the results. Human trafficking. Tori would go for a high price. Then, she'd disappear, never to be seen again unless her body turned up floating in a river or something. Not to mention, he was sure there were other pretty ladies on that ship. During his few years in Marseille, he'd seen evidence of human trafficking in the form of prostitutes on the streets of Marseille. Their looks? Hollow. Drugged. Hopeless.

"Sana, Suleiman, call Shelly and Diana. Tell them you're headed their way tomorrow. Then use this information and all of your persuasive speaking skills to get them to join us."

"So who's going to handle Skylar and Fi?" Butch asked.

"I will. Butch, I want you to get that gate on the back part of the property up and running. I don't want to leave Deb and the kids unprotected. DJ will probably be glad to help. Go ahead and start working on collecting the food and water we'll need and a list of ammunition that Skylar would need for his contacts."

"If he comes," Sana muttered.

"Let's think positive. We'll talk before I leave in the morning about how much we'll need."

"Wilco, boss." Butch rose.

Both Sana and Suleiman followed him into the night.

Suleiman's steps slowed as he thought about everything that had happened. A ship hijacked. Three hundred souls, including the daughter of a billionaire, onboard. Her identity a secret that would be disastrous if released. Twenty million to free her and the other hostages.

Victor's goal was admirable, but could the Shadow Box team put aside their differences long enough to accomplish the mission? Impossible. Simply impossible.

Tuesday, June 23, 2015, 2100 hours Pacific Daylight Time, Flagstaff, AZ

"Talk about being in pain." Suleiman winced as he climbed the steps with Sana to the Women's Building. With each move, his thighs ached. His shoulders had already tightened, and all he wanted to do was lie down on the floor and moan.

Sana turned as she opened the door. "It can't be that bad. Or can be," she added when he hobbled inside. "I know just the solution. You want a back rub? When I was in my climbing group in Texas, that's what we did all of the time."

"Sure." He eased onto the floor and leaned against the couch as he rubbed his quads. It was almost like they sighed with relief at the motion.

In the kitchen, Sana pulled open the refrigerator door. "Water?"

"That would be nice." He leaned forward and rested his arms on his knees as he turned on the television. *Deadliest Catch*, one of Sana's favorites. He gazed at the program but saw nothing. Instead, his mind darted in all directions like a cat chasing a laser dot.

Victor's dead fiancée. The offer of twenty million dollars and one million for each of them from that. The fact that they were short half their team with two people most likely refusing to join them sent a tinge of desperation through him. Why? Because he'd envisioned an easy path for himself now?

A drop of water hit him on the arm.

"Suleiman!" Sana stood above him, her small foot tapping, two bottles of icy cold water in her hands. She must have caught him lost in his thoughts.

"I'm sorry." He shrugged. "I was thinking."

"Well, as you think, scoot forward so I can get behind you." She settled on her knees.

Fire and ice brushed the skin of his neck. Fire from her touch, and ice from her cold fingers. He jumped.

"Sorry. I know my fingers are cold."

Tingling spread from his neck outward. If she only knew what her nearness did to him. He let his chin fall to his chest.

"You like that?"

Oh, yes. He wiped suddenly sweaty palms on his jeans as he sought ways to distract himself. "Did Victor ever mention his fiancée to you?"

"Huh?"

"He had a picture up on the mantel with pictures from the wedding. It was of a woman who was his previous fiancée."

"No. I never knew he was engaged before he moved here." Her motions slowed. "Matter of fact, I don't think I ever remember him mentioning why he joined up, only that he was in California when Gary recruited him." She moved down his back. "Why so curious?"

"She seemed familiar to me. That is all." He leaned into her and tried to tell himself that it was to get maximum effect on his sore muscles.

"Maybe you've seen someone who looks like her."

"True."

Sana's phone pinged. She paused and picked it up. "It's Shelly. She said to come on down and that supper would be better than lunch because both she and Diana have stuff going on then. I wish we could go earlier. I mean, we need to get ready for the mission."

"You heard Victor. Butch will take care of what we need. So. We leave around two tomorrow, then."

"I guess." Her phone chirped again. "Huh? She says something like she hates it there. Seems that she's still at work. Man, I've got to talk to her in person since she obviously won't talk on the phone about what's bothering her."

She rubbed his shoulders. "Why don't we leave earlier to avoid rush hour? Maybe we could find a Starbucks so we can get free drinks and hang out. I need to do my Bible study."

"So says the barista." He smiled, especially as he realized what it would mean. More time alone with her. "We can do that."

She paused again as she tapped on her phone before setting it aside. "Done. She said that's fine. Now back to the important stuff."

"As in?"

"Hanging out with you." She massaged his delts.

The tension released, and he rumbled low in his throat like a big cat.

She giggled. Her fingers slid onto his biceps.

Every nerve jumped to high alert. Her jasmine scent filled his nose. Cheeks flushing, heart suddenly hammering, he covered her left hand with his right.

As if stung, she scrambled away and staggered to her feet. "I—I'm sorry. I didn't mean to hurt you."

"You didn't. Promise on that." Suleiman tried to follow, but he slogged through the mud of his aching muscles. By the time she darted to her bedroom, he'd made it to his knees.

"See you in the morning." With that, she shut the door.

Oh, great. His pulse slowed, leaving in its wake a bone-deep weariness. Why couldn't he voice those feelings for her without scaring her off? How did she view him? As a friend. That seemed to be it. Nothing more.

And he saw no way to change that.

Tuesday, June 23, 2015, 2130 hours Pacific Daylight Time, Flagstaff, AZ

"Are you sure you don't want to watch *Up* with us?" Anna Fields asked.

"You know animated movies aren't my thing." Victor Chavez gazed at his oldest stepdaughter.

She sprawled on the couch next to DJ, her brother.

"Even *SpongeBob*?" she grinned as she highlighted the day Victor had taken her younger sisters, Gracie and Marie, to see it.

Busted. Caught because six months ago, he'd been the then-fiancé who'd not only wanted to impress his beloved but the young ladies who came with her. "Okay. You convinced me. Let me say goodnight to your mom and the girls, and I'll be back."

He climbed the steps to the second floor of the Big House. At the top, he hung a right and strolled along the walkway to the bedroom his two youngest stepdaughters shared. The lamp between their beds lit the room, which contained two overflowing toy chests, stuffed animals piled into a corner, a play table, and one gigantic plastic dinosaur that was Marie's. The fish tank Butch had set up burbled on one of the dressers.

Marie, his youngest at six, had pulled a chair up to it and sat on her knees as she gazed at it. "Daddy, when can we get fish?"

"Uncle Butch said a couple of days." He leaned over and tried to see whatever she did. A pirate's chest spewed bubbles through the water.

"Can I get guppies?"

"We can do guppies."

"And an angel fish?" She implored him with those hazel eyes he'd come to love.

"Sure. And maybe some neons too."

She grinned. "Cool."

"Where's your sister?" Victor picked up *Charlotte's Web*, which they'd begun while on their journey from North Carolina to Arizona. He settled on Gracie's twin bed.

"She's brushing her teeth." Marie scrambled onto the bed and pressed into the crook of his arm.

As if on cue, the door swung open, admitting Gracie, Marie's sister eighteen months her senior, as well as the Colonel, the family's Belgian Malinois.

"Are your teeth brushed?" Victor asked her.

"Uh, huh." The eight-year-old climbed into bed on the other side of him. "What about the Colonel?"

"He's exempt." Victor opened the book to where he'd placed the bookmark.

"What's exempt?" Marie asked.

"It means he doesn't have to brush his teeth." Victor mussed her brown curls.

"Daddy, can we get guinea pigs again?" Gracie asked.

"Maybe."

"Or we could get hamsters. And gerbils." Marie glanced at her sister.

"Or maybe rats." Gracie emitted a sinister cackle.

Victor chuckled. "We could. I know your mom and I promised that. Now. Where were we?"

"Chapter five!" they chorused.

Victor began reading aloud to them. His heart filled as each girl snuggled closer. Blessed. That's what he'd told Deborah that first night after they'd returned from their honeymoon a couple of months before. He'd been blessed in ways he'd never expected only a year before. He wanted to freeze this moment and pull it out whenever he started feeling sorry for himself.

He couldn't. Not when he finished the chapter. "Okay, you two. Time for prayers."

All three slid out of bed and knelt beside it with him in the middle. On the other side of the bed, the Colonel did a trick DJ had taught him. He put his paws and muzzle on the sheets as if praying.

Victor put his hand on Marie's light brown curls. "Marie, you start."

"Thank You for today, Jesus. Thank You for Mommy and for Daddy and for Gracie and Anna and DJ. Thank You that we'll have fish really soon. Amen."

He smiled. "Gracie?"

"Thank You for Marie, for Mommy, for Daddy, for DJ and Anna. Thank You for dogs and cats and horses. Amen."

"And bless the sleep of these two munchkins," he added. "Okay. Into bed with both of you."

Once both girls had pulled the covers up, he made sure each had their respective stuffed animals, then kissed them on the forehead. The Colonel had settled on the rug between the beds. Victor scratched him behind the ears. "Keep an eye on these two."

As if he understood, the dog waved his tail back and forth in a brief wag.

Victor pulled their door almost closed. He paused and craned his ear toward the den. The movie DJ and Anna watched still ran strong. Maybe if he procrastinated, they'd be finished. Fat chance when it paused.

"Dad!" DJ called. "We're waiting on you."

Oh, well. He'd take one for the team—again. But first, he had someone he needed to see. After heading toward the back of the house, he took the second stairway to the small landing leading to the master suite. Once he pushed the door open, he announced, "I somehow got roped into watching another animated movie."

His bride of two months, one week, and four days flipped a page in her Bible.

A flush started in his cheeks. Deborah could make even a T-shirt and a pair of pajama pants with dog bones on it look sexy.

She grinned. "You set a precedent when you watched *SpongeBob* with Gracie and Marie."

A wince crossed her pretty features as she rubbed her calf.

He sat down beside her. "Tough run?"

"Tough but good."

"Gracie and Marie want to get their rodents."

"Well, we did promise them in May that we'd get them replacements for their guinea pigs."

"They want rats." He imitated Gracie's cackle.

Deborah giggled. "You're too funny." Then she sighed. "I've been thinking about Norm's offer."

"Me too. A lot. A whole lot." Victor ran some of her blonde hair through his fingers as he considered his next question. "Did I ever share with you my vision for Sentry Securities?"

She smiled as she shut the book and laid it on the mattress. "You want the company to grow into a national presence, if not an international one."

"Right." He considered all of the thoughts that had flown through his mind ever since Norm Walters had mentioned the fee he was willing to pay for Victor and his team to rescue Tori. "Do you think my dream is foolish?"

She remained quiet for a moment. Slowly, she shook her head as she interlaced her fingers with his. "I don't think so. I think it's good to dream big. I believe God wants us to do that."

"With this kind of fee, it's like I started having all of these strange thoughts. Like maybe I'm only interested in the fee. Like maybe I don't care about Tori and the crew at all. It's making me question my motives."

She drew her knees to her chest and wrapped her arms around them. "I do think you need to be careful."

"What do you mean?"

Deborah reached down and ran her hand along a wrinkle in the blanket. "Think of it this way. If Shadow Box were still together as a team running missions for the president and you could say yes or no, would you take this mission? Or better yet, if you were in the Army and your team was tasked with the mission as an optional project, would pay even cross your mind?"

"No." Some of the tension in his shoulders eased when he realized how his answer was instinctive, spontaneous. "Even if I didn't know who Tori was."

She smiled. "Then you heart's in the right place." She reached up and ran her hand down his face. "Maybe this is God's way of providing the tools you need for this dream of yours."

Love for his bride filled him. "Maybe so." He took her hand and kissed her palm. Then his heart sank when he realized everything that needed to happen before the team could even contemplate heading overseas. "Now I just need to convince Skylar and Fiona."

Her smile turned impish. "I never said it would be easy."

He laughed. As he said goodnight to her with promises to return for a nightcap within an hour, he realized that Deborah was right. A monumental task lay before him. He could only hope Sana and Suleiman would have better luck with Shelly and Diana than he probably would with Fiona and Skylar.

3

Heat blazed across the asphalt in the Phoenix suburb of Tempe, Arizona. It was so hot that the air shimmered as if the entire landscape were shifting constantly like in some alternative dimension. Inside the local Starbucks, tinted windows cut down on the glare, and cool air pumped from the vents overhead.

When under the tutelage of his half-brothers so many years before, Suleiman had learned the value of constant observation. He slouched at a table with his back to the wall so he faced the door. Some habits simply never vanished.

At a nearby table, Sana huddled with her Bible open as well as a notebook and a steaming cup of tea. She chewed on the top of her pen as she read something. Her brow furrowed as if contemplating a new concept.

He thought back to the night before. Something had startled her away from him. What? Had he come on to her? Wasn't that the term Skylar had used when describing the romancing of American women?

He thought about his conversation with her. No. That wasn't it. And it hadn't come up on the ride down to Phoenix. Instead, Sana had laughed and talked as if everything were normal.

He bit back his sigh. Women. He didn't understand them. Did Butch? Victor obviously did since he'd married. Should he go to him for advice? No. He needed to figure it out on his own.

After opening his book on English grammar, he began working through exercises on punctuation. Rather than focus on writing sentences, he considered the photo he'd seen in Victor's studio. Almost like a buzzard circling a dead animal, he couldn't leave it alone. He had to figure this out, had to lay it to rest once and for all.

When in doubt, Google it. He reached into his backpack and pulled out his laptop. Once connected to the Internet, he hesitated. What would he search on? He typed in "Victor Chavez" and "Secret Service."

No social media profiles popped up. Victor had been strict about that, and even though Shadow Box was no more, he'd remained off the grid. But an article appeared in *The Washington Post*. "Secret Service a New Career for Veterans." It detailed how several former soldiers had signed on with the Secret Service, including Victor. It ended by describing Victor's assignment to relocate to Raleigh and guard Maggie McCall, the First Daughter. As he reread that last paragraph, his stomach did a small flip on the hamburger he'd eaten for lunch.

He glanced at Sana. She turned a few pages in her Bible and scribbled something in her notebook.

He focused on his search. Another headline, this one from *The News and Observer* out of Raleigh, North Carolina, caught his attention. "Preliminary Results from Attempted McCall Kidnapping Released. Agents Forced to Resign." The subtitle read "Punishment as Reward for Valor? The Injustice of Government Service".

A sense of foreboding filled him. Could this be connected with his last assignment with his half-brothers? He clicked on the link.

It was a full-page article that began with a description of the events leading up to the attempted kidnapping of Maggie. Then it presented a full chronology of what had happened the night of April 10, 2012.

Suleiman didn't need to read it. He knew it all too well.

"They're coming out," Jibril, his half-brother eighteen years his senior, had whispered as he and Suleiman maintained the sniper's nest high above on the convention center's roof. Suleiman pressed his eye to the sniper rifle's night scope. In its green glow, a service door to one of the neighboring hotels opened. Five people stepped through, two women and three men with the brunette woman being Maggie McCall. The tall slender man had been pointed out as the whip agent and was to be the last. And the blonde? She'd not live to see the next day. He slowed his breathing and focused on the short, stocky agent scanning the buildings. His heart rate dropped. In his ear came the order from Jibril. "Now."

"Excuse me, sir." One of the baristas stood next to him with a small tray.

Suleiman jumped. He'd braced his elbows on the table and his hands against his temples as if he could shut off the flow of memories spilling into his mind and tainting his soul. He couldn't. He offered a polite smile. "Yes?"

"Would you like to try one of our complimentary cookies?"

He shook his head.

She shrugged and moved on to Sana as he returned to his memories.

"Track them," Jibril hissed as the two agents who remained alive, the whip agent and blonde, hustled Maggie down the street and toward the amphitheater. Suleiman guided their path with carefully placed shots until they were trapped. Makmoud, the leader of the team and his oldest half-brother, stepped into view. The blonde jumped in front of Maggie.

"Do it!" Makmoud hissed through the comms unit in his ear.

The gunshot again echoed off the nearby buildings.

His eyes snapped open as he sucked in a quick breath. No, he wasn't on some rooftop. He was in a Starbucks in Tempe that was a mile from where Shelly and Diana lived. Sana now gazed at him.

"Are you okay?" she mouthed.

He offered a weak smile and nodded.

She cocked her head as if doubting him before she resumed her study.

He stared at the pictures included with the article. One of Maggie McCall speaking at an event for women's rights in the Middle East. Another of—

"Not you, Victor," he muttered aloud.

His mentor stared at him from his official Secret Service portrait.

Sana glanced up. Softly, she murmured, "What's going on?"

"Nothing," he muttered. He tasted bile as his hamburger and the coffee he'd drunk tried to come back up. He turned his attention to the last picture. Similar to Victor's, it was an official portrait. The blonde wore her hair up, but it did nothing to mask the high cheekbones and facial shape of the woman he'd seen in the picture in Victor's studio. Now he saw that her eyes were a violet-blue. The caption listed her as Rachel Marina, fellow agent and Victor's fiancée.

What have I done?

Suleiman slammed the lid of his laptop. His heart pounded in his ears as he made the connection.

Three years before, he'd killed Victor Chavez's fiancée.

He pushed to his feet so fast that his chair toppled backward and clattered to the terra cotta.

"Suleiman?" Eyes wide, Sana stared at him.

"Lunch hit," he muttered as he righted it and rushed to the bathroom. He locked the door before bracing his hands on the sink. Chest heaving, he stared at himself in the mirror.

Dark hair worn short and slightly thick along the top as per the current style. Two-day growth of beard, due more to laziness than trying to look suave. Skin on the fairer side than olive during the winter. Gray-brown eyes. He liked to say he favored his mother—until he noted his other features. Heavy brows, slightly aquiline nose. Firm mouth. A deeper olive tone in his skin now that summer had arrived.

A person Sana would call an Average Joe.

No, a gifted and talented killer.

Just like his half-brothers, Jibril and Makmoud Hidari, both *Quds* officers embedded with a South American Hezbollah cell, men who were brilliant and had honed their craft to perfection.

He hung his head. Fool him for thinking he'd be able to forget his past. FBI Special Agent Gary Walton had recruited him for Shadow Box almost two years ago specifically because of his observation and sniper skills. With Shadow Box, he'd taken what he'd learned at the compound in Venezuela and used it for good. He'd sworn he'd walked away from the life he'd had under Makmoud.

"You can call me Suleiman al-Ibrahim," he'd told Gary when he accepted the offer to join Shadow Box. "You are never to call me Ibrahim Hidari again because I am no longer a Hidari. Am I clear?"

He'd been wrong. His past had caught up with him.

Dizziness assailed him. His pulse quickened. So did his breath. Oh, no. Panic attack, his first since moving to Arizona.

Leaning against the door, he sagged downward. The world tilted. He put his head between his knees and focused on the simple act of pushing oxygen into and out of his lungs. *Breathe. In. Out. Slow it down. In. Out.* Gradually, things stopped spinning. He risked opening his eyes. Still the same tile on the floor. Same toilet. The muted noises of the espresso machines. Everything remained the same.

Hah. He wanted to laugh at that.

Nothing was the same. Nor would it ever be again.

Grasping the cold porcelain of the sink, he hauled himself upright and risked another glance in the mirror.

His discovery had destroyed his inner peace.

New dread washed over him. Sana had no idea of what he'd done. He couldn't tell her. She'd hate him.

Someone knocked on the door.

"Out in a minute," he called.

First things first. He splashed water on his face, then took several more deep, calming breaths. Time to rejoin the real world.

Sana peered at him, her dark eyes liquid with concern. "Are you okay?"

He'd never be okay. Not with the knowledge he now harbored in his heart. But he couldn't tell her that, so he lied, "Just a bit of indigestion. Look. It's almost four. I think we need to get going."

She didn't move. Instead, she glanced her notebook, then at him. She drew in a breath. Finally, she nodded and began gathering her books into a tote bag. "I think you're right."

As they strolled into the hot Arizona afternoon, Suleiman did what he had to do. He took what he'd learned and stuffed it into the deepest, darkest corners of his soul, the exact same place where he'd relegated memories of his half-brothers and his time at their Hezbollah compound in Venezuela.

Never again would he revisit it.

Never. Not ever.

4

Victor shut the door to his white Jeep Commander and peered at the marquee of the restaurant located on the edge of The Strip in Las Vegas. The restaurant's deep blue awning had Regions Restaurant painted in an elegant, deep red and gold script with a white outline of the United States behind it. He squinted at it as he shoved his hands in his pockets. Finally, he turned away and ducked inside before the sun baked his brain.

To his left, a white tablecloth puffed as one of the staff began setting a table in the dining area. To his right, a bartender shoved adult beverage glasses into overhead racks. They clinked against each other. Chopping emanated from the kitchen.

"Hey, Monty!" someone called. "Looks like we've got a customer already. Why don't you give him the 'full' Monty?"

Laughter rippled among the waiters and waitresses.

Victor's cheeks heated.

"Guys, lay off. I've been expecting him."

Skylar James. He'd recognize that honeyed drawl anywhere. Footsteps echoed in a slate hallway that ran the length of the building.

Resplendent in a navy blue suit and deep red shirt and tie that had to be all silk, Skylar strolled into the foyer. "Vic, hey. Good to see you."

Deborah had reported that Skylar's slicked back blond hair and blue eyes could make any sane woman swoon. Of course. Master scammers were always good looking.

"How's it going, man?" Victor shook his hand.

"Most excellent. Can't complain." Skylar flashed a smile, another trait Victor was sure would make women follow him like they were lost puppies. "Come on back. We don't open for a little bit, so we've got plenty of time to talk in private. You like my digs?"

What could he say? No? He forced a smile to his face. "Nice. How long have you had this?"

"A shade over six months. Regions serves up cuisines from all over the country." A woman shouted something in the kitchen, and he grinned. "That's Fiesta. I kid you not. Rich recruited her from the Bellagio here in Vegas, and she rocks."

"What kind of food do you serve?"

"Fried chicken from the South. Cajun from Louisiana. Salmon from Washington. Lobster from Maine. We just passed the main dining room when you came in on the left and the lounge on the right. The lounge is now open until two in the morning." Skylar turned and led the way down a hallway of dark paneling with black and white pictures of various iconic landscapes of the United States. "First quarter, we hit a profit. We doubled it last quarter. And this one? Not too shabby so far."

Victor sucked in a sharp breath through his gritted teeth. Here he was with Sentry Securities over a year old and not turning a profit to the point where he worked part time as a sheriff's deputy to make ends meet. Even with the sale of Deborah's farm and counseling practice in North Carolina, they had to watch pennies until both his and her businesses were more established.

And Skylar? He seemed to have a way with money like he did with women. Of course, he'd skimmed cash from the profits made running an arms business for the CIA in Pakistan, which was why they'd burned him and dropped him in his hometown of Richmond, Virginia. Maybe he'd done the same here.

Something twinged deep within his soul. Deborah would chastise him big time if she'd heard those thoughts in his head.

"And here's my office." Skylar stopped and threw open the door to an elegantly appointed room of rich mahogany and gray marble tile. What looked like a genuine bearskin rug anchored a leather couch and two leather chairs.

"Nice," Victor choked. He cleared his throat as guilt assailed him.

"Thanks. Fool me. I forgot to offer you something to drink." Before Victor could open his mouth, Skylar settled behind his desk. He pressed a button on his credenza, and a door slid open to reveal a fully stocked wine cooler. Pulling out a bottle of white wine, he opened it and poured some into two glasses that had been in the rack above the cooler. He handed one to his friend.

Skylar slouched on his leather chair and took a sip before placing his glass on the blotter. "You said you have a job for me. At least that's what your text said."

"I do. I don't know—"

"No."

Victor blinked. "Pardon me?"

"Not interested. Not after the way you basically kicked me out of Flagstaff." Skylar kept his gaze level.

"Wait. *I* kicked you out of Flagstaff? I think *you and Fiona* left on your own terms."

"'Cause you threatened me."

"This is about those counterfeit tickets for The Pick, isn't it?" Victor asked as he referred to the Arizona State Lottery. "Look. All I asked was that you leave Last Chance Ranch if you were going to try and swindle people in Flagstaff."

Skylar rested his elbows on his desk. "No, what I remember is that when you found the equipment I planned to use, you threatened to arrest me."

"Because I'm a sheriff's deputy." Victor fought an eye roll. "What did you expect me to do? Turn a blind eye?"

"Well, yeah. Turns out all you cared about was the Chavez name."

Victor wanted to leave right then and there. At least until Norm's plea echoed in his ears. He couldn't. He wouldn't. "Actually, you want to know what I was thinking when I went into the storage shed for those painting tarps, which I found covering your equipment? My first concern was for you. I knew what you intended to do. Create counterfeit tickets for The Pick."

"Hey, I wasn't going to sell them to folks, okay? I was going to sell them to other dealers who would then sell them to the locals."

As if that had made it all right.

Victor wanted to scream. "And this isn't Pakistan. You can't run a scam and not get caught. I gave you an option when I could have arrested you."

Skylar leaned back in his chair and steepled his fingers as he assessed his former commander through narrowed eyes. "I'm not sure I believe you."

"Then I'll leave. Too bad." Victor left his glass on the edge of the desk and rose. "You could've made a million off this deal."

He headed for the door and put his hand on the knob.

"Wait!"

A small smile crept across Victor's face. He smoothed it away and turned.

Skylar had punched to his feet and planted his hands on the desk. "You said a million?"

"Got your attention, didn't I?"

"So talk to me."

Victor resumed his seat, as did the team's former procurement officer. "Have you heard about the *Peacemaker* getting hijacked?"

"I heard about it on the news yesterday when it broke. Bad stuff."

"Norman Walters, president and CEO of Walters Enterprises, has a daughter onboard. His oldest." Victor nodded as he sampled the wine. Though Chardonnay wasn't his thing, he had to admit it was exquisite. "According to him, the press is banging on the doors at Mercy Medical Missions trying to get that crew manifest. We're racing against time."

"Makes things more urgent, as if it weren't that way before. And he's hired Shadow Box to do the job?"

"Well, Sentry Securities." Victor didn't feel like indulging in how his company struggled due to lack of capital to finance what he really needed. "I'd bring all of you onboard as private contractors."

"What's the total fee?"

"Confidential." Victor fibbed. He hated feeling desperate, but he knew what twenty million would offer—a chance to fully fund Sentry Securities.

"Sorry, but I'm not sure I'm your man. I mean, I've got the restaurant and all and—"

"And that's one of the lousiest excuses you've ever used for anything." Victor clamped his jaw shut. He needed to stay calm. "Look. I know there's some not-so-good history between you and me. I get that. And I'm sorry things went down the way they did. But truth be told, we need your brains and talents on this mission. You don't have to relocate to Flagstaff." He leaned forward. "Think about it this way. Three weeks tops, and you can be back in Vegas for good with a million bucks in your pocket."

"No commitment?"

"Only for this job."

A smile finally twitched Skylar's lips upward. His eyes glittered with something. Greed. He straightened. "Hey, good for me. What do you know?"

"Precious little, I'm afraid." Victor tore his mind away from comparisons of success. "We have to act fast. Norm says he can get us what we need, or at least most of it. Some stuff? Well, you and I both know it comes through the not-so-legitimate channels, if you know what I'm saying."

"Completely. Not a problem there so long as Norm understands that."

"He told me he does. I just know that once—and it's once and not if—the press gets that manifest, we're out of time." Victor paused as he thought about a couple of trainings his Special Forces team had completed in Somalia years before. Hopeless. That's the one word that always passed through his mind. "It's not a happy place."

"Hah, that's one way to put it." Skylar took a gulp of wine as if he needed something to tame his memories. For a moment, he stared at the glass as if contemplating his distant past, then lifted his gaze. "Before I headed over to Southwest Asia, I worked a couple of jobs out of the embassy there. And yeah, I met some of the dregs of human society, even some who I knew were peddling women as prostitutes to the highest bidder. It's…ugly. So yeah, you can count me in on getting Tori out so long as it's an in-and-out deal." Skylar leaned back in his chair and took a sip of wine. "Your problem's going to be…"

"Fiona," they chorused.

"Don't I know it." Victor winced.

Skylar chuckled and swirled the golden liquid in his glass. "Yeah. She's already called me. I guess Diana texted her after Shelly set up their supper date with Sana and Suleiman. She told me she's on to you."

"What are your thoughts?" Victor's fingers tightened around the goblet.

"Thoughts are that it'll take a bit of work, but she'll go."

"You're sure?"

"Yeah. This is what you do." Skylar rose and paced, his brow knitted as if considering the next move on a chessboard. "Head to the airport. Her flight gets in shortly after sunset, just after nine. You talk to her. I'm sure she'll turn you down because you're you."

"Thanks, I think. I know—"

"Then when she comes over here for supper, I'll do the work on her and close the deal." Skylar grinned as if he'd hatched the best plan in the world.

As he considered the way Fiona had called him an a-hole to his face as she'd left the ranch, Victor doubted their abilities to persuade her. "And that'll work?"

"Yeah. It should. Look." Skylar leaned against the edge of his desk with his hands braced on it. "She's a patriot, just as much as you and I. And just like you and I, she's been to the hellholes of the world, both during her time in the Army and as a contractor pilot for the CIA. She likes money, too. Matter of fact, she's trying to save up to open her own air cargo business. She'll jump at a mil."

Hah. If only it would be that easy. He had no choice but to trust the least trustworthy member of the team. "All right." He rose and set his mostly untouched wine on the desk. "I'll take your word for it."

"I'll deliver." Skylar raised his chin. "So what are you going to do until then?"

"I figured I'd go check in at the hotel and grab a bite somewhere."

"You'll eat here. It's on the house tonight. Matter of fact, I'll join you."

Victor headed toward the door. With his hand on the knob, he turned. "Until then, you might want to warm up your contacts. I've got a feeling we're going to need their services. And quickly, too."

Wednesday, June 24, 2015, 1930 hours Pacific Daylight Time, Tempe, Arizona

Ninety degrees. Still. Sweat trickled between Suleiman's shoulder blades as he leaned against one of the posts supporting the portico over the duplex's patio. He lifted a cigarette to his lips and took a puff. Not good for his health, for sure. He'd actually tried quitting and had gotten as far as a day before something—a cross word between Sana and him, getting fussed at by a customer at the restaurant where he worked—would send him running right back to the slender white cylinders of comfort. His discovery a few hours earlier hadn't done him any favors in that regard.

Could he just forget about it? His chest tightened, and he wanted to bellow. Impossible. He couldn't hide from it, not like he had from his former life.

The sliding glass door opened, and a slender woman his height with frizzy brown curls and black-rimmed glasses stepped through. "Oh! I was wondering what happened to you."

"So sorry. I had to have a smoke." He offered a weak smile and held up the cigarette with smoke streaming from the tip. Perfect. Conversation would help him avoid his discovery.

"We decided to eat out here." Shelly Wise busied herself with setting the picnic table.

"Even in this heat?"

"Relax." She grinned. "It'll cool down. And besides, it's about the only time of day I even want to be outside. Gag. I hate this weather."

Suleiman grinned despite his mood. "Changing your mind about Phoenix?"

"Uh, yeah." She winked.

"What was that for?"

"You'll have to find out." She refused to divulge anything else. "Diana just got here. Sorry you're the only boy at the house tonight. At least human boy."

"What does Skylar say? I'm surrounded by three beautiful ladies?"

She giggled. "Aw, you're sweet."

Suleiman stubbed out his cigarette in the finger bowl Shelly had provided and followed her into the townhouse. He breathed a sigh of relief as the ceiling fan swirled down the cool, air-conditioned breeze.

"Hey, Suleiman." Diana Kasem, cardiothoracic surgeon and the doctor on the former Shadow Box team, grinned. She pulled him into a hug.

He wanted to laugh at the way she towered six inches above his five-foot, five-inch height.

"Shelly told me a little bit about what's going on." The tight coil of curls she'd pulled into a ponytail bobbed as she reached for a wineglass and opened a bottle. "Sounds like we have a lot to talk about tonight."

"Do we ever!" Sana glanced up from where she chopped some vegetables.

"Uh, huh." Shelly pulled a pack of tortillas from the refrigerator and placed them on a plate. She turned to where steak sizzled in a frying pan. "Food's about up. What to drink, Suleiman?"

He selected a bottle of water. "How do you say it? Stop keeping me in suspense?"

"Only a few more minutes." Diana's smile rivaled that of the Mona Lisa. "I've got silverware and napkins."

Sana dumped the vegetables into another fry pan. They hissed as they hit the oil.

"Someone tell me what's going on." He peered at the computer and security specialist for Shadow Box.

"Okay. Here goes." Shelly stirred the meat with a spatula. "You remember how I moved down here to work for a defense contractor?"

"Of course." How could he forget the way Sana had cried shortly after her best friend had moved? "We miss you."

"Things were great for, oh, about a month. Then it was like when I was teaching at NAU. You know. I'm smart. Sorry, but I can't help that. And it's not like I lord it over anyone." Shelly sighed as she ladled the meat into a green bowl with red chili peppers painted on it. "So, like, when I started finishing projects early, I guess I made people look bad or something. So they started rumors about me. Can we say toxic environment? This past week was really bad. Like last night, I didn't get home until close to eleven. Finally, my boss and I had a row today, and I quit. Like that."

She snapped her fingers.

He fought a smile. Only Shelly would say "had a row" when she meant arguing. With his best straight face, he said, "I'm sorry to hear that."

"Oh, I'm not. I'm ready to get out of this heat. I'd talked with my dad last night, and he suggested contracting. And lo and behold, not an hour after I'd packed my car and unloaded all of my boxes here, my old boss from Maryland called me up and wants me to contract with him. Talk about the Lord providing!" She giggled as if not bothered at all by her sudden decision to quit her one source of income.

"She's moving back to Last Chance Ranch." Sana nudged him in the side as if pointing out the obvious.

"I am." Sheer delight filled Shelly's eyes. "I've already called Butch, and he said that the upstairs of the Tool Barn is pretty much a blank slate, meaning I could have my lab and office there—if Vic approves, of course."

"Oh, I think he will. C'mon." Diana nudged her roommate in the arm. "I'm famished. Everyone, outside."

Once they'd settled at the table with more ceiling fans swirling, Diana said grace. As she spoke the simple blessing, Sana took his hand across the table. Heat flashed through him. He wanted to hang on—at least until she dropped it as quickly as she'd grabbed him.

Diana unfurled her napkin and laid it on her lap."So, I've got big news, too."

"You got into Kona Ironman?" Suleiman asked.

She chuckled. "Oh, do I wish. No, I'm moving back to Last Chance Ranch as well."

Across the table, Sana met his gaze with an incredulous one of her own. "Did I hear you right?"

Diana nodded. "When I started looking at medical practices last fall, I received an offer from Dr. Knowles in Flagstaff. But by that point, I was so ready to leave for a sunnier climate. And when the practice here made me an offer, I grabbed it and signed on for six months." She grimaced. "Except that it didn't take me but a month to realize that my partners were some of the most unethical men I've ever met. Two of the five are married but sleeping with their nurses. The third wants to sleep with me—ick—and the other two don't seem to be above-board financially. Last month, I called Dr. Knowles and asked if his offer still stood."

"It did!" Shelly's hazel eyes sparkled behind her glasses. "So yeah, we're both moving to Last Chance Ranch. The team's back together again."

"Except for Fiona and Skylar." Diana added sour cream and salsa to her tortilla before rolling it into a burrito with surgical precision. "Tell us about the *Peacemaker*."

Suleiman let Sana do the talking. He admired her skill. Not even once did she reference the briefing sheet residing in the back pocket of her shorts. Just the facts. That's all she delivered.

Diana's brow furrowed.

Shelly fiddled with her silverware.

And the food? Mostly untouched.

Finally, Diana picked up her burrito. "Oh, wow. That is not good."

"That's one way of putting it." Sana grabbed a tortilla.

"Thing is, we haven't trained together in a year. That worries me in terms of working together when the stakes are so high." Diana took a bite.

"Don't I know it." Sana added some meat and vegetables. "It does worry me. But what worries me more is what will probably happen if the pirates get their hands on Tori. I mean, they could—"

"Don't say it." Diana winced. "I get it. But do you think we can set aside our personal differences?"

"I hope so." Sana took a bite of her burrito and chewed for a few minutes.

"I'm more worried about the physical conditioning part," Shelly muttered. She sighed. "This lab rat will never be a gym rat without someone to whup up on me. I guess that would leave me as the weak link—again."

"And Fi's told me that she's not exactly been working out either. I'm not sure about Skylar." Diana glanced at Suleiman. "What about you two?"

Suleiman nudged Sana in the ankles with his foot. "She made me climb The Mushroom yesterday."

As if poking fun at him, his shoulders began aching.

"Ouch." Diana winced.

"He did well." Sana smiled at him.

His cheeks heated. "Victor has definitely been working out. And you know Butch. In the gym almost every day."

"Except for Sundays," Sana added.

"Even though the president says he's handling things, Norm Walters is worried." Diana polished off her burrito and reached for another tortilla. "I'm kind of surprised that the president's not all over this."

Sana shook her head. "It's South Africa's territory. And who knows what they're doing? From what Victor says, he has isolationist tendencies. Even though there are Americans on that ship, he doesn't seem in any hurry to intervene."

"Suleiman, you've been quiet." Diana focused on him. "What's your take on it?"

He paused. "I think we can do it. You know Victor. He plans well, thinks through everything. We must trust him—and each other. If we work together, we can do it."

Sana picked up a tortilla chip and dunked it into the salsa. "Do you two think you're in?"

Diana fell silent as she assembled her second burrito.

Worry nibbled at his soul. She was smart, totally rational. Did she see it as an impossible situation? He glanced at Sana.

Her brow had wrinkled.

Finally, Diana drew in a breath. "I've been following this on the news. And after Shelly told me you'd texted her, I started praying. I knew we wouldn't have much time to make a decision. I…I think we—I—need to do it. Shelly, I'm not going to speak for you."

"No thinking needed, even from this brainiac." Shelly straightened. "I'm in all the way, even if we weren't moving back to Flagstaff. But since we are, I don't see how we can turn this down. And honestly, I don't care about the money."

"Same here." Diana nodded. "Tori and the crew are in the worst kind of trouble, and I want to help get them out of there."

Elation filled Suleiman. Not that he'd ever worried about them. But they had only three quarters of the team together. "Still, we need Victor to work his magic."

Diana started coughing so much that he pounded her on the back. After one last hack, she cleared her throat. "Sorry. Fiona told me to stay far, far away."

"She would." Sana scowled. "But we have to have her and Skylar in order to go."

"Why?" Shelly asked.

"Because if we don't get everyone onboard, then we don't go," Sana replied. "It's an all-or-nothing proposition because we need Fi's piloting skills and Skylar's scamming skills."

At that bit of news, Shelly's eyes widened. "Uh, oh."

Her simple reply summed up Suleiman's feelings exactly.

5

"Mommy told me you went into town and got your fish," Victor said as he rested his foot on a bench at the General Aviation terminal of the Las Vegas airport. He leaned on his knee and pressed his phone to his ear.

"Angel fish, guppies, neons, and a big catfish." Marie's voice practically chirped with excitement. "And we got ro…ro…"

"Rodents?" Victor grinned.

"Yeah. Rodents. I got gerbils. Gracie got rats." She imitated her sister's rat cackle.

Victor laughed. "What are their names?"

"Cupid and Valentine because they have red eyes and white fur. Mommy said that was okay even if they're both girls. And I named my gerbils Woody and Buzz since they're both boys."

"Those are great names. Put Mommy on for me, okay?"

"Okay. Love you, Daddy."

Some of the tension in his shoulders released. "Love you back."

"Vic, hey." Deborah's voice filled his ear. "Yes, Marie and Gracie are going to have a hard time sleeping tonight. Also, Butch wanted me to tell you that he and DJ have the back gate in place. They'll get the motor up and running tomorrow."

"Good deal. Did Norm come by?"

41

"He did. He dropped off the contract and some tubes of mapping. I put both out in the studio and locked the door. And we have a ton of food and water now sitting in the storage building."

His thoughts swung to earlier that evening. Confession time. Freeing himself of the guilt over envying Skylar's success would give him more energy to do battle with Fiona. "Hey, I have a confession to make."

"You gambled?"

"Hah. Hardly." He explained all of the complex feelings that had bubbled to the surface when he'd met with Skylar. His beloved remained silent and let him talk it out. Finally, he wound down. "Am I that base? I mean, I thought the money didn't matter. Maybe it does after all."

"No, I think you're a normal person. That means that though you're forgiven by Christ, you still struggle. Just like I do. Just like Butch and every other believer you know."

He settled onto the metal and rested his elbows on his knees. "I thought I was bigger than that. You know, more focused on the fact that God has me in the palm of His hand."

"He does. And I know it's hard to look at what Skylar has and not envy him. I'd probably be doing the same thing if I were you." Her soft words eased the worry in his heart. "If it makes you feel any better, we all struggle with something."

"I know." He raised his gaze. In the rapidly dimming cloudless dusk, he noticed one set of lights amidst the others that seemed to be getting closer. "Looks like Fi's plane is arriving. I'd better go."

"I'll be praying."

"I need it. I'll be back by lunch tomorrow, okay?"

"I love you, Vic."

"Love you back." He smiled and signed off.

Some of his levity faded as the Cessna 215 landed and taxied toward the General Aviation terminal to one of the T-stripes, which indicated a parking place. Its engine cut off, and gradually, the propellers stopped spinning.

A woman, her long, loosely curled dark hair caught up in a ponytail, climbed from the cockpit and chocked the wheels before pulling out a set of low stairs. She helped her six elderly passengers from the plane. Several pressed what had to be cash into her hand. She pocketed it.

She and Skylar were perfect for each other. Money hungry. That's what they were. His conscience pricked him as he remembered his conversation with Deborah not five minutes before. Time to let it go. He tried.

He got as far as thirty seconds into his effort when the first couple passed him. Their remarks settled over him like a toxic fog.

"Such a lovely young woman."

"She was so gracious and loving."

"What a kind, polite person!"

Huh. Lovely? Kind? Polite? Those weren't terms he'd use to describe Fiona Mercedes. Hardly!

"So friendly and informative," said the female half of the second couple. She leaned on her cane as they shuffled past.

He folded his arms across his chest and raised his brows. Really? They talked about the woman who'd threatened to take Sana's cats into the desert and dump them. Gag.

"You gave her a good tip, right, Brewster?" asked the third woman of her husband.

Like maybe a tip on how to be nice to the ones who'd saved her life a little over a year ago.

He turned away, lest he tell them what he really felt.

And the pilot? She lingered at the plane as she scribbled something in her logbook. She leaned inside and removed her briefcase. After taking her time to shut and lock the plane's door, she moseyed around the Cessna as she tied it down and inspected it. As if he'd give up out of sheer frustration and leave.

Not going to happen. He was too stubborn. Maybe that was why they'd had clashes of epic proportions over the almost two years he'd known her.

Finally, she squared her shoulders and raised her chin. She marched toward him with her briefcase slung over one shoulder. Her heels clicked against the concrete apron and echoed off the metal and glass of the General Aviation terminal. As she passed him, she didn't slow. "No."

"What?" He cocked his head.

"Not interested." She yanked open the door to the terminal.

It nearly hit him in the face.

She let it go.

He grabbed it and hustled after her. "You haven't even heard me out." His voice bounced around the lobby of marble and glass.

"I don't care. Not interested."

"Fi!"

The lone attendant glanced up. His gaze swiveled from Victor to her. His eyes widened, and he slid down in his chair as he pulled a magazine in front of his face.

Victor wanted to rip it away and shout, "Can you believe her?"

She slammed through a door leading to a hallway marked Private Charter Pilots Only. It banged into the wall.

He stopped it with his hand. "Listen to me for a minute."

"Diana called me all excited and ready to go on this *Peacemaker* mission. I don't care." Fiona unlocked a small office for her charter company and tossed her briefcase onto a desk.

"Do you even know what happened?"

She swung her feet onto the blotter as she lit a cigarette despite the signs in the hallway that said No Smoking. Her sherry eyes narrowed. She blew a stream toward the ceiling, where it hung in a bluish haze "Somali pirates hijacked a ship off their coast. Big whoop. It happens all of the time over in that part of the world."

He perched on the arm of a cheap vinyl sofa. "It's more than that."

Fiona stared at him for a moment. With a sigh, her gaze followed the smoke. "And since you'll probably not let me leave until you tell me, start talking."

He did. Like he'd done the night before with the Flagstaff half of the team, he briefed her. As if she played poker at one of the many casinos not too far from where they sat, her expression remained blank while she smoked her cigarette. As he wound down, he said, "I told him we'd go in on two conditions. First, that we free the entire crew, not just Tori. Second, we go as a team or not at all."

Fiona smirked and leaned back in her chair. Her eyes bored into his as she began chuckling.

Oh, great. He'd erred. Big time If he'd been at the poker table with her, he would have just lost all of his savings.

"And I'm the missing link." Her feet slammed to the floor. She leaned forward, stubbed her cigarette into a small plate that had "I Heart Las Vegas" stenciled along the rim, and pointed a finger at him. "So guess what? You're not going."

He stared at the brick-colored nail that matched her lipstick. Courage. He needed to have courage since Skylar had warned him this would be an uphill battle of the worst kind. "It'd pay one million. Skylar said you were working on saving up to open your own cargo business. That would go a long—"

"*Skylar* doesn't know what he's talking about." She reached down, opened a drawer, and grabbed her purse. She pushed to her feet. "You stay out of my business, Victor Chavez."

Like a windstorm, she swept into the hallway.

He scrambled to keep up as they burst into the hot evening. "Fi, please. It'd be one mission and one mission only."

She rounded on him when she reached a white Nissan Maxima with darkened windows. The car door nearly hit him in the knee as she yanked it open. "I'm done discussing this. Got it?"

"Don't you care that Tori could very well be sold into slavery? That's a fate worse than death, and you know it."

She slid into the front seat and put her key in the ignition. "Then she shouldn't have gotten on that ship in the first place."

With that, she cranked the motor and reached to close the door.

He gripped the edge. "Fi, please!"

"I'm. Not. Interested. What part of that don't you understand? Now I'm going to go and get comfortable. And when you call Skylar to whine and complain, tell that little traitor I've headed straight home. Goodbye, Vic." Fiona yanked the door from his grip. She backed out of the spot and nearly ran over his toes in the process.

Victor jumped back. As her tires chirped when she made the turn onto the road, he grabbed his hair. "Grrrr! Fool! Who were you to think she'd join up?"

With jaw clenched, he paced in small circles when what he really wanted to do was smash his hand through the window of the nearest car. Deborah's words from the night before about his heart being in the right place rang in his ears like an out-of-control bell. He truly wondered if he was upset simply because he wanted the twenty mil in fee.

His phone chimed "Wasting Away in Margaritaville," and he glanced at the caller ID. Skylar. Slowly, he brought the phone to his ear. "She didn't go for it. Not at all."

"I didn't expect her to. Don't worry. You just softened her up for me. I'll go in for the kill when I get home tonight. We'll be at your hotel at eight tomorrow morning. That much, you can count on." His procurement officer's voice rang with confidence.

Victor could only hope he was right.

6

Suleiman opened the door to the bathroom and stepped into less steamy air on the upstairs landing. As he laid his towel across a drying rack, he noticed the rise and fall of a conversation. It came from the room where Sana bunked for the night in Shelly and Diana's guest room.

"Suleiman…good time." Sana was speaking. She chuckled. A few more words, then a snort from Shelly that elicited more giggles from them both.

Curious, Suleiman drifted over for a closer listen.

"Want to join girl talk?" Diana stood not five feet from him. How had he missed her bedroom door opening?

His cheeks flamed. "Um, no. Perhaps I will go to bed. It is getting late." No, it wasn't, but he didn't want to reveal to Diana the depth of his feelings for Sana.

She laughed. "Well, they're waiting on me. Listen. While you were showering, Shelly put a set of sheets and a pillow on the couch in the study. Sorry it's a mess down there, but there wasn't any other place to put our boxes from work. What time do you want to leave in the morning?"

"Nine is fine. Well…" His gaze shifted to the door. "Good night. I will see you in the morning."

With that, he beat a hasty retreat downstairs. Upstairs, a door closed. More laughter reached him. For sure, they were talking about him. He shrugged. That was okay. It was good to see Sana smile. Laugh, too. She'd done both at supper, and he knew it continued during their girl time. With a start, he realized she'd not done a lot of either after Shelly had moved to the Phoenix area six months before.

He stretched out on the cushions. Ugh. Couch sleeping wasn't his favorite. It wasn't like he could request to bunk with Sana, though the idea pleased him. He shifted. Better. Once he closed his eyes, his body relaxed beneath the comforting bulk of a blanket.

Flickers of his past played on the screen of his mind as it drifted to several years before. His learning French the hard way when he started sweeping floors at a piercing shop in Marseille. His dyed green hair and numerous piercings. Moving in with Olivia, his girl. His surprise encounter with Makmoud near his apartment one hot night in June 2010.

"Ibrahim, it has been too long."

Suleiman froze at the baritone, a voice he'd never forget even though he hadn't talked to his half-brother in years.

He swiveled.

Makmoud, clad in a pair of jeans and a light windbreaker over a black T-shirt, stepped into the pale glow of a streetlight. His thumbs hooked in his belt and pushed the windbreaker back enough to reveal a gun peeking from underneath the jacket.

"What are you doing here?"

Makmoud's dark eyes remained unreadable. "I've come to bring you home. You've disgraced the Hidari name too long."

Suleiman shouted insults at him, which yielded only a smile. He walked away, but as soon as he turned the corner, he ran to his apartment.

Then came that night a week later when he dined with Olivia before going clubbing. Her laughter sprinkled the evening like the rain shower that had come through while they ate. Her perfume teased him with what would come later. And the way she snuggled up to him? Most likely, they'd see the sun rise. With his arm looped around her shoulders, they stumbled toward their small apartment.

The memories jumbled from there. Shouts from Olivia. A rag pressed over his nose and mouth. Coming to on the cold, reverberating floor of an ocean freighter. Makmoud threw him fully clothed into the shower. From there, he stripped his half-brother naked and scrubbed him down, all the while lecturing him about the stink of the cigarettes, alcohol, and hookah he'd consumed.

Suleiman landed on the hard floor again, this time wet and shivering. Clippers hummed. Clumps of wet, green hair fell to the floor.

Makmoud planted a knee between his shoulder blades.

One by one, Suleiman's piercings tinkled to the metal.

His half-brother hissed into his ear in Farsi, "You try to bite me, and I will beat you senseless."

Then, Makmoud reached into his mouth and removed the last piercing in his tongue. The pressure between Suleiman's shoulders released. Something soft landed on his back. "Get dressed, you disgrace to the Hidari name."

"No! I'm not!"

His eyes snapped open. No throb of a ship's engines. No grumbling from Makmoud. Suleiman was safe at Shelly and Diana's townhouse. Had he shouted those words like he had years before? It didn't seem like he did since no one burst inside.

Forget sleep.

He couldn't do that now that his mind raced faster than a Formula One car. He sat up. After reaching for his T-shirt, he pulled on his cargo pants and crept to the door.

"See you guys in the a.m. Leave at nine?" Diana's voice came from the landing upstairs.

"Nine works." Shelly had joined her. "Night, Sana. It was great catching up."

Sana said something he couldn't distinguish.

Their bedroom doors shut.

Suleiman stood there. He should probably get some sleep. How could he now? He couldn't avoid what he'd done three years before, and now, even his time under Makmoud's tutelage haunted him. It was like he'd built a wall to house all of his memories from years before. With the one crack of knowing the identity of the woman he'd shot in 2012, others had appeared, all of which stole any semblance of peace he'd had.

He slipped into the living room and eased onto the couch. LED lights from the microwave, television, and stereo cast a soft glow. He rested his hand on the arm of the soft leather. It'd be so easy to turn on the television and drown the memories with nothing but noise. He couldn't do that. He might wake the ladies, and besides, those memories would only stalk him later.

A step creaked. A petite silhouette crept downward, made her way into the kitchen, and opened a cabinet door. Sana. He'd recognize the grace with which she moved anywhere. Despite his worry and fear, a smile spread across his face. He drank in her image.

"Before I scare you, I'm here," he softly said.

She squeaked. A plastic cup flew from her hands. She dove for it, but her fingers only brushed it before it bounced against the kitchen island's granite and landed on the floor with a clunk. It rolled across the tile until it came to rest at his feet. "Suleiman! You scared me."

"So sorry." He leaned down, picked it up, and offered it to her. "M'lady."

Rather than take it, she scowled at him. "Shouldn't you be asleep?"

"Perhaps I should be asking you the same question."

She shrugged. "I guess I'm jazzed about today."

He smiled at her terminology. "Jazzed? I have not heard that before."

"Just…excited." She plopped down beside him. "What about you?" A smile crossed her pretty features. "Are you jazzed?"

"Perhaps." No, more like terrified and confused. Could he share his past with her? No. She'd only known the abbreviated history of why he'd joined Shadow Box—his revelation of the location of Hezbollah's Venezuelan compound to the Americans—and his new identity under WitSec. But maybe she could help him. "May I ask you a question?"

"Of course."

"Have you ever…" —how could he phrase it?— "Have you ever done anything you deeply regret?"

"That's a tough question."

"Have you?"

She cocked her head at his insistence. "Haven't we all?"

"I'm serious." He crossed his arms.

"And I'm being flip. I'm sorry." She drew her knees to her chest and wrapped her arms around them. "I told you about before I joined Shadow Box, right? I mean, I was a thief. A darned good cat burglar. But it took getting two years in prison for me to realize I needed to mend my ways and quickly. Ever since I got handed that sentence and…and dishonored my parents, I've felt regret."

How could he forget the story she'd shared one cold winter's night when they'd gone stargazing? "So you felt…sorry?"

She glanced at him. "Absolutely. What's this all about?"

He couldn't say anything. She'd hate him. "I was curious."

She blew out the smallest of sighs. "You mind if I hang out with you? I've still got adrenaline in my system after you scared me."

"Did I?"

"Yup. I kid you not." She smiled and unfurled from her tuck.

Did he detect a slight lean into him?

"But I don't want to watch television. I just want to…be."

He wouldn't argue with her. Besides, television would wake them up. Her jasmine scene tickled his nose. What would happen if he put his arm around her? He took the risk.

Sana didn't disappoint. She turned and wrapped her arm around his middle. Thanks to the tank top she wore, his fingers brushed the bare skin of her shoulder. She fit into the crook of his arm so well. He rested his head against the cushion. If he closed his eyes, he could easily imagine falling asleep like this day in and in and day out. Could it be that one day they'd get married?

Hah. It could never happen. Once she discovered the truth of who he was, what he'd done, she'd run as far away from him as possible. He'd take what he could get now. And that meant having one very lovely lady curled up beside him.

He'd deal with the fallout from his past later.

7

Fiona Mercedes slouched on a chaise lounge on the balcony of the third-floor walk-up apartment she shared with Skylar. Her evening had turned out way differently than she'd planned. When she'd dropped off her six elderly customers at the airport, she'd anticipated meeting Skylar at Regions, dining on a good supper of salmon, and romancing him in his office.

Victor Chavez had ruined it all for her. Well, Skylar helped, that traitor.

Now, a hot wind rolling off the nearby desert dried the sweat that had gathered on her brow. The lights from the hotels and casinos along The Strip shimmered as the desert floor continued releasing its heat. Traffic rumbled, punctuated by an occasional car horn.

It sounded like the couple below them—a stripper and her bartender boyfriend, if she remembered correctly—were still up. A television played through their open door. Glasses clinked, and the stripper giggled.

Geez, couldn't she and Skylar at least get better digs? Like maybe a house or something? No, that was impossible since she put aside every surplus dollar she had for opening her air cargo business. Eight months into it, that little pot of money hadn't grown much at all. A million, or at least what she could net from the job Victor offered, would go a long way toward her goal.

As she lit her third cigarette of the night, her gaze wandered to the bottle of Chardonnay in its ice bucket on the table between the two lounges. She'd brought it outside with the intent of being good and ripped by the time her beau showed up. Sure, she'd opened it, but she had yet to pour a glass. The goblets sat empty beside it, the frost on them long since dissipated in the arid night.

So the *Peacemaker* thing. Did Fiona really not care like she'd projected to Vic? No, she did care. She'd seen Somalia for herself, not once, but many times during her tenure as a CIA contractor pilot. She knew way too much about pirates, especially since she'd carried cargo to some of the dirty devils the CIA thought had needed supporting. If Vic hadn't been the one asking, maybe she would have said yes.

She'd rejected him out of principle. What that was now, she couldn't remember.

Through the open sliding glass door, she heard the deadbolt of the front door slide back. A shadow temporarily blocked the warm glow of the lamps in the living room. She shifted and stubbed out her unfinished cigarette in an ashtray.

"Hey, babe." Skylar joined her on the balcony.

She assessed him. He'd taken off his tie, most likely draping it across the back of the couch. He'd shucked his jacket too, meaning it most likely resided with the tie. And his hair? Only slightly disheveled. Nothing hinted at how tired he must be. Except for the sigh he emitted as he eased onto the other lounge.

She glared at him. "So the traitor finally arrives home."

He responded by leaning forward and kissing her. Oh, she lived for those. Big time. Except that it should have been while they lay together on his couch at his closed restaurant. Her mood nosedived again.

He nodded toward the wine bottle. "You going to drink that?"

"Have it."

He picked up the bottle and poured glasses for them both. "I missed you tonight."

"I don't dine with traitors."

"Enough of that, all right?"

"What do you want me to say?" Her nostrils flared as she flushed. "You sold out to Vic about the *Peacemaker* thing."

"I didn't sell out." He swung his legs onto the lounge and took a sip. "Man, oh, man. I love this label."

Did it matter? She wanted to take the wine and pour it on his head. "But you're going on the mission. Even after the way he treated you."

Skylar sighed. "Yeah, I am. It's one mil, babe. What do you want me to do? Turn it down?"

"Yes!" She threw her hands in the air.

"Fi."

"Look. I'm happy here. And Tori? Well, she should have known the risks. We know what can and does happen in that part of the world. I'm sorry she's on a ship that's been hijacked, but it happens. It's the cost of doing business over there." Okay. So maybe she overdid it a bit. But she had to convince him not to go before he convinced her to go.

Skylar, for one, remained unruffled by her theatrics. Figured that she'd fallen in love with the one guy who could put on the best poker face in the world. Rather than react, he sipped his wine. "Hey, I know that. Believe me, I know. But do you believe the whole thing that it's the 'cost of doing business'? She's on a hospital ship, for cryin' out loud, not some Carnival cruise liner. It's like the pirates bit the hand that could help them the most."

Fiona shrugged. The fingers of her right hand sought out her left forearm. Automatically, she located the bump where the broken bones from a fall off a horse in the spring of 2014 had healed. Curse the way they began rubbing the bump. She had to try a new tactic. "I think it's hopeless. I mean, once the press gets ahold of the crew manifest, it's over."

"No, it's not. We can help them."

"How? We haven't trained together in a year."

"So? We'll all make a mil per. With no strings attached, I might add."

"Aren't you worried?"

He shrugged. His nonchalance about the whole thing unnerved her. "Not really. We worked well together when we managed to set aside our personal differences."

She snorted.

"Seriously." He studied the skyline. By now, his glass was almost empty.

Fiona drew her knees up. Her neck stiffened, and she bit her lip.

He speared her with those blue eyes of his. "What are you afraid of?"

"Nothing." Her fingers rubbing the bump betrayed her. "I don't scare easily."

Liar. She did under certain circumstances, like those from May of the year before. Makmoud's face as he'd loomed over her after her fall flashed before her.

"Hey, I know that." He eased over until he sat on the edge of her lounge. He stroked her left forearm before clasping her rebellious fingers. "Are you thinking about last year?"

Fiona didn't reply because of the lump in her throat. She closed her eyes as her mind fought to avoid the moments of terror she'd faced when Makmoud had ambushed Skylar and her as they'd protected Deborah's daughter and sister. Somehow, she forced out her question. "What would have happened to us?"

"When?"

"Last year. When Makmoud held us hostage? I mean, if he'd gotten his way and shipped us to South America?"

Skylar picked up her left hand. For a moment, he massaged her palm with his thumbs. "Oh, Butch, Vic, Suleiman, and me? He would have killed us or broken us. Or probably just killed Suleiman. He seemed to have a grudge against him. You and the girls, including Deb's children? He might have broken DJ. Probably made you ladies concubines. I mean, you're hot. So's Diana. And Anna—"

"Stop." Her heart raced. She didn't want another visit from the nightmares that had plagued her for a month after the ambush.

"You're worried Tori might meet the same fate?"

"You and I both know how things work over there. Slavery isn't dead. No, it's thriving."

"Then all the more reason for us to go and get her out. Look." Skylar fell silent again, probably as he tried to figure out how to persuade her. "I think Vic's right. The South Africans think we have time we don't have, and it's clear the president isn't going to offer America's services. We go over there. We watch each other's backs. We get the girl and her pals. And we get a cool mil per. You know that by combining yours and my earnings, you could have enough capital to start your air cargo business."

This was news to her! "You'd...you'd do that?"

"For you, yes. The restaurant's making money. I'd rather help you out." Skylar brought her hand to his lips, and he kissed her palm. "So, what'll it be?"

"I..." This wasn't how things were supposed to turn out. No, she was supposed to have had it out with him before stating rather firmly that she'd not go on the mission. What was *wrong* with her?

"C'mon." Skylar leaned closer. The peppermint of the candy from his restaurant whispered across her cheek. "You and me? We're a team. Let's do this together. Then we can forget about the rest of Shadow Box. What do you say?"

"Skylar..."

"Seriously. I'll look after you. Please, Fi."

She closed her eyes. He was right. At the rate she was going, she'd be too old to fly by the time she got the money to start her business. Skylar's earnings could put her over the top. Not to mention, the flying she did now wasn't what she knew she could do. And she yearned to at least attempt to get Tori out of Somalia before it claimed her. Oh, and it didn't hurt at all that Skylar pulled her into a kiss at the precise moment when she made her decision

She was in. All the way in. She smiled as he pulled back. "I'm in."

"Glad to hear that." He rewarded her well.

8

"Did you see the news? Did you?" Norm Walters's voice blasted across the cell phone.

Victor held it away from his ear, and he could still hear the billionaire. Almost reluctantly, he brought it closer. "About Mercy Medical Missions being hounded to release the crew manifest? Yeah, I did."

"What's your status?"

"I've got everyone but my pilot and procurement officer."

"And where are they?"

"On their way." One could hope. Truth be told, they were late—if they were coming at all.

"Can't you do this without them?"

"Not when I need Skylar's contacts in Africa as well as Fiona. Sure, Butch has his pilot's license, but he doesn't have the hours Fi does in the kind of aircraft we need."

"You call me when they're onboard. Right now, I've got a C-130 en route to you."

"A what?" Had he heard Norm right?

"C-130, as in a kind of plane. And it's already decked out to sleep eight and with awesome avionics and comms systems. I've got my sources, all right?"

"I understand."

"And a sniper rifle. I'm a gun nut, so I can appreciate how nice it is. The rest you'll have to get out of the country." He murmured something. "I've got to go. You call me as soon as you know something."

"Wilco." Victor paced as he shoved his phone into the back pocket of his jeans. The Las Vegas sun had already begun pounding the pavement of the Hampton Inn where he'd stayed. Where were they? Maybe Skylar hadn't been able to work his magic. It wouldn't be the first time the ex-CIA agent had betrayed him. For good measure, he dialed his number.

No answer.

He clenched his jaw and checked his watch. Already half past eight. If Skylar and Fiona weren't there by nine? The mission would be a no-go.

A white Nissan Maxima with darkened windows pulled into the parking lot and slowed as it traversed the already sizzling asphalt. It pulled into an empty slot beside Victor's white Jeep Commander.

He let out a breath when both Skylar and Fiona climbed out. "I was wondering what happened to you."

"Traffic." Fiona shrugged. She lowered her glasses and and gazed over the rims at him. "I don't know why I'm doing this, but I am. So let's get going before I change my mind. Again."

Victor couldn't have agreed more. With him leading, they headed into the desert toward the cooler climes of Flagstaff and the surrounding mountains. As the urban clutter of Las Vegas quickly faded in his rear-view mirror, he began developing his to-do list. Get the plane retrofitted, if need be. Get a list of remaining needs to Norm that day. Be sure to call Norm and tell him they were all in. Like, now. When his client answered, all he said was, "We're on our way with a full team now. We'll keep to our plans and leave at first light day after tomorrow."

Operation Peacemaker

Thursday, June 25, 2015 1045 hours Pacific Daylight Time, between Phoenix and Flagstaff, AZ

The desert sped past them as Suleiman and Sana barreled up I-17 toward Flagstaff in Suleiman's ancient Honda Civic. Behind them, the headlights from Diana's white Acura RL shimmered in the heat along the interstate. Sana rode shotgun and smiled as she chatted on her cell phone with Victor. Finally, she hung up and dropped it into a cup holder. "Guess what? Hell froze over."

He grinned. "Oh?"

"Fiona said yes. We leave day after tomorrow."

"How did that happen?"

"Skylar worked his magic, whatever that means. Of course, that opens up a whole other challenge." She shifted in her seat so she faced him. "Do you think we can set aside our differences long enough to get this done? I mean, Fi almost took my cats away. And she absolutely hates Shelly's messiness. And I don't like the way she and Skylar sleep together in the Women's Building. Grrr!"

"I know you can do it."

She sighed, then giggled. "I'll be sure to keep my cats in my room."

"Or at least out of her closet."

She laughed. "Hey, I can't help it that my cats disliked her enough to pee on her boots. Anyway, when we get to the ranch, you and I are supposed to take the new sniper rifle and scope out to field test it. So no rest for the weary."

With that, she turned on the radio. Country music filled the car's interior as much as the AC did. She reached down and pulled out her Bible, study guide, and notebook. Once more, she chewed on the end of her highlighter as she read through the study guide. Occasionally, she scribbled something in her notebook.

Though he kept his eyes on the road, Suleiman focused on the night before. They'd dozed together until shortly after midnight. When he'd finally lifted his head from the couch's back cushion, her hair tickled his chin. He buried his nose in it and inhaled the clean scent of her shampoo.

At his motion, she came awake. Seeming to realize where she was, she whispered a hurried goodnight before practically bolting upstairs. He stayed where he was until her door softly shut.

How could he forget the way memories of his distant past had driven him out there? Maybe Sana had some answers, or maybe she didn't. There was only one way to find out. Ask.

"Sana?"

She cocked an eyebrow at him. "Yeah?"

"What do you say fear is?"

"Fear?"

"Yes."

She tapped her pen on her chin for a moment. "I'm not sure. There's lots of definitions. I guess you can break it down into respect, terror, or worry."

"I do not understand."

Sana reached for the radio and turned it down. "If you fear someone or something, say a lion, you respect the power they have over you. Terror might be like if you fear a nuclear war. Worry might be if you fear that the stock market won't do well."

"I'm confused."

She sighed. "I know. It's hard for me to describe without a dictionary, and I don't have any apps on my flip phone, remember?"

"What about in your own words?"

She drew in a sharp breath. "I think...I think sometimes, fear is a sin."

He stared at her for a brief moment before returning his gaze to the road. "A sin?"

"Yeah." Sana shifted in her seat so she faced him. "A sin. You know. Not trusting God."

"No, I do not know."

"Don't get me wrong. In a lot of ways, fear can be healthy and is a gift from God, like fearing a lion. At that point, fear can keep you alive. Or fear as respect like fearing a king. But when fear can be synonymous with worry, that's when, at least in my mind, it becomes a sin. I mean, we worry about stuff all of the time, especially the future." She lowered her gaze as she ran her finger down the page. "Have you heard of 'Fear not, for I am with you'?"

"No."

"That's from Isaiah. But there's stuff all over the Old and New Testaments about that kind of fear and why we shouldn't do so."

He rubbed his chin. "I truly do not understand. Why do you think fear as worry is a sin?"

Once more, she shifted so she faced him. "I think it takes going back to what a sin is. What does Islam say sin is?"

"Bad works." He only had to look at his own life over the past few weeks to name several.

"Like?"

"Oversleeping when I need to get up. Having a cross word with Nate at work. Not getting my wet clothes out of the washer so someone else could use it. And—" He stopped himself before he confessed his discovery in Victor's studio. Too many bad works had piled up for him already. "Anything that is considered bad works. So…what is sin to you?"

Sana hesitated. She stared at him, her dark eyes wide and doubtful. Did she think he'd judge her? Hardly!

"Please tell me. I won't be angry with you or judge you."

"My personal definition is that we sin when we put ourselves above God." Those words came out softly, almost like a burbling brook. "I think it manifests itself in not doing God's will."

"But aren't there laws? Moses provided the Ten Commandments, yes?"

"Yeah. God gave those to the ancient Israelites as signposts to show them where they'd gone wrong. And to point to Christ as the Messiah. Only they got it all wrong. They thought the law was the only means to an end, that sacrifices would solve it all. Break the law? Sacrifice an animal to be absolved. Maybe it did in their time, but they missed the whole point of that particular system."

"If not for absolution, what was the point?"

She laid her head against the headrest. "I'm sorry. Let me try again." Silence reigned for a few seconds. "Here's an example from my own life. I put myself above God's will all of the time. Anything from being late because I'm reading something I want to read to turning to a life of crime as a cat burglar. Back then, I was so full of myself." She shook her head. "I was in love with myself. I wanted to get back at Papa for never offering me love with no strings attached, and I wanted the wealth that thieving could bring."

A wince pinched her pretty features. "It took being in prison for two years for me to realize that the way I'd been living brought nothing but heartache." She fiddled with her highlighter for a second. "So if you want my definition, we sin when we're too scared to trust Christ and want to work out our own destinies."

Her voice quavered, the only revelation of the turmoil she must have been feeling at remembering her own fall.

I love you, he wanted to tell her. The words remained stuck in his throat.

She opened her study guide again and focused on it as if it were the most incredible thing in the world.

He reached to adjust the air conditioning vent at the same time as she moved to turn up the volume on the radio. Their hands brushed. Without hesitation, he took hers.

She mouthed, "Thank you."

He didn't let go for the rest of the trip.

9

The man had waited all day for his target. All day in this stupid, cold, stinky alley for one Chloe Martin, Mercy Medical Missions' HR rep for the *Peacemaker*, to stick her nose out the blank steel door across from him. He didn't care what it took. He'd get his hands on that crew manifest. And when—not if—he passed it to the gossip rag in London that had hired him, he'd be 5,000 Pounds richer.

Problem was, Chloe had been working longer hours than he had anticipated. Understandable. But the weekend was almost upon them. Surely her bosses would be kind enough to allow her to leave work a little earlier than she had these past couple of days.

The man shifted and lit a cigarette. At least the smell covered the aroma of rotting squid, leeks, and other exotic Oriental food coming from a dumpster at the mouth of the other end of the alley. After enduring the stench while staking out MMM's back door all day, he wasn't sure he could stomach Chinese anymore.

The door creaked open. A young woman stuck her head out. Even in the dim light emanating from the bulb above the door, he noted her pert nose and wide-set, expressive eyes. Chloe Martin. Just the person with whom he needed to talk.

The man withdrew further into the shadows.

She panned the area. Slowly, she stepped through and let the door slap shut behind her. Stress turned down her full lips. It also created furrows in her brow. She'd be a pretty lady if she weren't so worn out.

"Excuse me, miss," he called, his British accent running at full tilt.

She froze and gripped the straps of her bags to the point where her knuckles whitened.

The man tossed down his cigarette and ground it out with his toe. "I'm sorry. I didn't mean to scare you."

She took a step back. "My answer is no comment."

With that, she turned and hurried toward the mouth of the alley opposite where the rest of the press waited at MMM's main entrance. Even in three-inch heels, she moved like a striker down the football pitch. He almost had to run to keep up.

"Who said I was asking questions?" He hated the way he puffed at the slightest exertion. Time to cut back on the cigarettes.

She barely looked at him. "Why else would you wait for me?"

He smiled. She was spunky. And wary like a deer. No overplaying his hand allowed. "True. But notice I didn't tell any of my 'friends' at the other end of the alley that I knew about a back entrance."

She slowed and stopped next to the stinking dumpster. "What do you want?"

He held his hands out, both palms up. "Only to chat a little. I'm sure you have been very busy."

"Little do you know," she muttered. She grimaced and resumed her walk, this time at a slightly slower pace.

He followed. "Where are you headed?"

"To the pub near my flat where I can get a pint before falling into bed." Her steps quickened as if she anticipated a little relaxation.

"May I join you?"

"No, I'm fine on my own."

Patience. He had to try something else. A lie might prime her for more information later. "Perhaps you'd rather know my name first. It's Richard."

She cut her gaze toward him, pursed her lips, and then shook her head as if debating the impact of revealing even her name. Finally, she said, "I'm Chloe."

"So, Chloe, how long have you been doing this?"

Without slowing, she turned left onto a busy street.

At this pace, he might collapse. Time to lay off the beer, too. After this little assignment. "I know. Too personal."

"Too long. How's that for an answer?"

"As in…"

"Too long. University seems alike a long time ago."

Meaning, most likely, she was barely out of school. Now that he saw her in better light, he noted her pursed lips and jutting chin. MMM management must have imbued all of its employees with fear of the wrath of God if they leaked anything. Still, that didn't mask the innocence radiating from her eyes. "I'll bet you never expected this."

"No." A smile flickered and died. "I think I've perhaps slept six hours in almost forty-eight. You said you're a reporter?"

"Off duty."

She stopped at a heavy door leading to a pub. "Are reporters ever off duty?"

Not this one, he wanted to say. He offered a smile. "Sometimes we sleep."

This time, hers came easier. "Good to hear."

She pushed through the door.

Her rudeness wouldn't put him off. If someone handed out medals for persistence, he would have gotten one a long time ago.

Chloe shouldered her way through the crowd to the dark, scarred wood of the bar. She must have been a regular because the bartender poured her a mug of beer without even asking her what she wanted.

As she slapped down a few bills, Richard ordered a dark lager.

She guarded her drink like a mother hen her chicks.

His job had just grown in difficulty. He'd wait. Surely, she'd slip up somewhere. If she didn't? He'd be SOL, and some other enterprising reporter would snatch the manifest out of his clutches.

"So tell me, *Richard*," she emphasized his name as if she didn't believe him at all, "you said you were a reporter. Which one of the many newspapers or other media outlets do you work for? A newspaper? Social media site? A real news network? Or, heaven forbid, one of those despicable gossip rags?"

The game was up. She was on to him. The best he could hope for would be to slink out quietly and find someone else to trick into releasing the manifest.

Her phone rang. She frowned as she glanced at it. It kept ringing and fell silent. It rang again. This time when she looked at the caller ID, she muttered something under her breath, then glanced at him. "Excuse me a moment. Work. Yes, I just left. Okay…"

She briefly turned away.

Richard ran with it. He reached into his pocket and withdrew a glass vial. It contained a few small pills. Roofies. It'd helped him have his way with women when he was at University. Now, it'd help him have his way in another manner, that of obtaining information. He dumped one into her drink and watched as it dissolved on its way down.

She set her phone on the bar, frowned at the mug, and called, "Jim."

The bartender turned.

"I didn't want this ale."

"But that's what you always get," the bartender said.

"I changed my mind." Her phone chirped, and she glanced at it. "I'll have what he's having."

"Coming up. Sorry, Chloe." The bartender took her old brew and poured it down the drain.

Which was where Richard's chances of getting his hands on the manifest were going. He needed a new plan—and fast.

The bartender placed a new mug in front of her.

Just as she picked it up, her phone began ringing. Chloe heaved a sigh as she glanced at it. "Mum. Normally, I would ignore it, but she's already called five times today."

Time to take a chance. Richard palmed another pill. This time he dropped it into his own brew, which he had yet to touch.

"Mum, this isn't a good time." She sighed, glanced away, and swept a hand through her brown hair. "Honestly...No, I'm sorry I haven't called."

Richard moved his mug to be even with hers and lifted hers to his lips.

She finally set her phone on the wood. "So sorry. My mum. Sometimes, she doesn't take no for an answer. So where were we? Oh, something about your employer."

"I thought I was off duty."

"No, you said that sometimes you sleep." A smile crossed her face as she sampled the lager. "Hmmm. Nice. I've not had this one before."

Keep her talking. Keep her downing her pint. That would be all it took. He leaned against the bar. "I do try to get my eight. But seriously. I'm not all about work. Tell me what you do for fun around Cape Town."

She began chatting some more. As she did, she finished her beer. His questions kept her talking. The drug helped. At least until she set down the empty mug with a thump. She yawned. "I'm sorry. I must be exhausted. I think I need to head home."

She slid off the stool and stumbled. He caught her arm. "Let me help you there."

"I can make it." She shouldered her briefcase and purse and made it as far as the door before bumping into the doorframe. "Ouch! I don't know what's going on. I'm feeling...dizzy all of the sudden."

"Are you sure you don't need me to walk you home?"

"No." She swayed.

"I think I'd best do so. Where is your flat?"

"I'm..." She sagged into him. "You're right. It's a block that way."

He followed her increasingly slurred directions. By the time they reached the stairs leading to her flat above a pharmacy, he practically carried her to her door. "Where are your keys?"

"My purse. I think I need to go to bed."

He found them and undid the lock.

"Almost there." He lifted her bags from her shoulder and set them on the floor. Once in the bedroom, he laid her on her side on the mattress. He tucked her in before whispering, "'Night, 'night, Chloe."

Richard pulled back and watched. She remained still, her shoulders rising and falling in a steady, even rate. Good. She'd be out until morning, then wake up in a confused haze. He returned to the main room that was a living/dining room combination adjacent to a small kitchen. A thorough search of her bag revealed only her computer, a mouse, and a mouse pad. No jump drive. Not one to be deterred, he powered on the laptop. An access screen popped up. A fingerprint or password was required.

Then he shrugged. So what? The owner of the fingerprint slept in the next room.

He peered inside. "Chloe?"

He poked his head into the room.

She remained still.

"Chloe," he called louder.

Nothing.

Good.

She'd used her right hand to fiddle with her phone while they'd talked at the pub, so he assumed she'd use one of those five digits to gain entry into her computer. He placed his bets on her index finger. Carefully, he eased onto the mattress beside her. With her computer on his lap, he picked up her right hand. She was so deep in the grip of the drug that she didn't even stir when he slid her index finger across the pad.

The laptop chimed.

In the stillness of the room, it sounded like church bells ringing. Chloe moaned. His breath caught. Nothing else. He wasn't going to press his luck by sticking around in the bedroom.

Once seated on the old, worn couch, he familiarized himself with the file structure and began opening folders. Several related to general items associated with HR such as forms and standard operating procedures.

Then he found it.

A folder called Peacemaker. One level down was a file called Crew Manifest. It listed all three hundred crew members, from the captain to the chief medical officer to the lowliest cook.

Richard pulled a small thumb drive from his pocket. He inserted it into a USB port and copied the list before drilling down to another level. A chuckle started deep in his throat and built until he imagined himself laughing like an evil scientist. How perfect could it get? He stared at a folder titled Contact Information. It would take some time, too much time to spend at the apartment, for him to go through each of the three hundred names. So what? After he copied them, he had all night.

After doing so, the man shut the computer down and returned it to its case. He rose and opened the front door. Before leaving, he turned and whispered, "Parting is such sweet sorrow. Goodbye, Chloe. Thanks for your help."

This time, he did laugh.

It took him only a few minutes to hail a cab to the ratty hotel he'd called home for the past three days. With the drive in his hand, he bolted up the stairs. He tried to ignore the bickering behind one of the doors and the loud, blaring television coming from the other occupied room on his floor.

Once inside, he locked all three locks before lifting his mattress and removing his laptop. It powered up, and he lit a cigarette as he combed through all of the contact information files. As the cancer stick burned down, so did his patience. Nothing. Just a bunch of no-name, do-gooder missionary types who wanted to save the world one person at a time. Most likely, their families were all dirt poor and completely sold out to the Lord. Pah. What a waste.

Then he hit the Ws. When he opened the second file, his eyes widened. His mouth dropped open, and he caught the still smoldering cigarette in his hands. "Youch!"

He tossed it into an ashtray beside his bed. Trembling, he Googled the name of the person's emergency contact. Now his eyes bugged.

"I'm golden!" He jumped up and did a little victory dance as he lit another cigarette. This was more than a 5,000-Pound find. No, this was more like a 10,000-Pound find.

He grabbed his phone from beside the computer and punched in a number. "Answer. Answer. Answer!"

His boss finally did.

"Davie, there's a lot more to this *Peacemaker* thing." The man stared at the woman's face glowing on the screen. "A whole lot more. Like I want double what you offered. And if you don't like it? I can go somewhere else."

10

"Do you want me to set the targets up downrange?" Sana asked as she and Suleiman arrived at the rifle range tucked in a far corner of Last Chance Ranch and accessible only by horseback.

Suleiman slid from his mount. "Do that, and I will tie up the horses. Set the targets at 100, 250, and 500 yards."

She handed the reins of hers to him before approaching a wooden box under the portico at the firing line. She opened the lid and reached inside. With paper targets in hand, she stepped into the bright, hot day and strolled down the path toward the metal target stands.

For a moment, he followed her with his gaze. She was so beautiful, and holding her hand earlier that day had been…Well, words failed to describe the feelings that had rushed through him at the time. He'd finally connected with her. He had hope.

Maybe.

Still, he worried. She'd hate him if she discovered what he'd done. Not that she'd find out. He'd once more stuffed those concerns into the box of dark secrets in his soul. He envisioned himself sitting on that box. Except now, the lid threatened to pop off.

I'm not going to agonize over this, he reasoned as he tied the horses' reins to a rail in the shade. *I can handle this. It happened. It's over. End of story.*

That seemed to work.

He pulled out hearing protection and a couple of mats, laid the backpack he'd carried across his shoulders on the floor, and undid the Velcro straps. Once he unzipped it, he whistled softly through his teeth. Since when was the last time he'd fired an MK11 sniper rifle? Since never. He ran his fingers down the barrel. They skittered along the smooth metal. "Nice."

Once he lifted the components free of the backpack, he assembled it, attached the scope, and activated the bipod. Oh, he couldn't wait to do some test fires with this weapon. He set the stock down and angled it so it pointed away from the trail Sana had used.

He lifted another scope from the smaller pack Sana had carried and set it up on its tripod.

Gravel crunched, and a moment later, she plopped down beside him. "Done. Anything else?"

"Look at the scope."

"What kind of rifle is that?"

"An MK11 sniper rifle, the same used by the SEALs." Once more, he caressed the smooth metal as if it were Sana's face. "What I do not understand is why he has one."

She shrugged as she stretched out so she lay prone on a mat. "He's a billionaire. Need I say more?"

"Not at all." He smiled at her as he pulled out a box of 7.62 mm ammunition and loaded a magazine. "Going live." He inserted the magazine into the big gun. After turning his baseball cap backward and adding muffs over his ears, he lay prone on his mat. "Safety off."

With that, Suleiman pressed his eye to the scope and located the target at a hundred yards. He lined up the crosshairs on the bullseye. With the slightest pressure to the trigger, a loud report echoed off the nearby mountainside. To the left of the portico, a flock of crows cawed at them as they bolted from the underbrush.

Sana kept her eye to the spotter's scope. "Nailed it."

He fired another round.

"Either you missed the target and stand, or you drilled the exact same spot."

Suleiman smiled. "I did not miss the target."

She giggled, its sound like the tinkle of small bells. Could he perhaps garner another opportunity to hold her hand this day? He'd have to bide his time. Right now, work that was his passion called. He shifted to the target at 250 yards and fired two more shots. Oh, so absolutely beautiful. Beauty rested only in Sana and an MK11 sniper rifle.

"Five hundred yards now." Sana shifted her scope. She murmured to herself as she did the calculations for him and gave him directions.

He adjusted the scope. There. The target came into sharp focus.

He took a deep breath, held it, and released it over a period of seconds.

His heart rewarded him by slowing.

He reacquired the target.

His finger began tightening on the trigger.

A blonde stepped in front of the stand. Tall and svelte, she captured his attention. Honey-colored hair tumbled around her shoulders and tousled her cheeks. And her eyes? Even that that distance, he noted their vivid blue color. What? How could she have gotten down there? Recognition oozed over him like a cold slime.

Rachel Marina stood before him.

He sucked in a breath. "There's someone at the target."

"What?" Sana cocked her head. "There's no one there. Only scorpions and snakes. And I'm not seeing anyone."

"Are you sure?"

"Positive." She pressed her eye to her spotter's scope. "I'm looking at the target now."

He shook his head and resumed his work. Good. It was like Sana said. He must have been seeing things. He shifted his breathing pattern, but this time, his heart rate refused to drop.

He fired.

The bullet ripped the paper just outside the rings.

"You missed."

"I know." Oh, he knew all too well why. Seeing Rachel had shaken him. He peered through the scope. Good. Nothing.

Until Rachel stepped in front of the target. She still wore the black suit she'd had on in his earlier vision. This time, scarlet bloomed directly over her heart.

His eyes widened, and he gasped.

She gazed at him. Her mouth formed a word. "Traitor."

He could have sworn he felt her hair brush his cheek as she whispered the accusation into his ear.

He blinked.

She'd vanished.

He flinched just as he pulled the trigger. The bullet barely penetrated the paper. Sweat built on his brow.

"Suleiman?" Sana's question broke into his mind.

He refused to gaze at her out of fear that she'd see how rattled he'd become. "I am fine."

"Are you sure? I can see the way the muzzle's shaking."

"I'm *fine*."

"Whatever," she muttered.

He tried to ignore the hurt in her voice. Without waiting for his breath or pulse to settle, he fired. The bullet punctured the top right of the stand, meaning he'd completely missed the target.

"Argghhh!" He threw the rifle down. Jumping up, he stalked to the end of the portico as he clenched his teeth and grabbed his hair. He kicked the post at the end—hard. A jolt shot up his leg. He turned and slid downward against it. His T-shirt rode up, and splinters poked his back

"Traitor. Traitor. Traitor." Rachel's one word singsonged in his ears like a playground taunt.

He gripped his hair tighter to the point where his scalp burned. "Make it stop!"

"You're scaring me." Gentle hands touched his shins.

Suleiman cracked his eyes open.

Sana knelt in front of him. Her ball cap remained backwards over her black hair.

He leaned forward and rested his arms on his knees. *Calm down. Breathe. Breathe. You can tell her you're frustrated that you missed the target.*

Before he opened his mouth, she added, "Ever since we got the *Peacemaker* job, you've been so wound up, like if I say anything wrong, you'll explode. That's not like you."

What could he say? That she was wrong? He knew he was normally laid back. Mellow was what Butch had called him. And now? She was right. Like it or not, his past had emerged, kicking and screaming, out of the box where he'd tried to keep it. Sweat trickled down his temples. "What do you know of my past?"

Her shoulders rose and fell in a small shrug. "What you told me. That you were Hezbollah and at a compound in South America. That you walked away and never looked back."

"My brother was the leader of that."

"What? I'm not sure I understand."

"My given name is not Suleiman al-Ibrahim. It is Ibrahim Hidari." His hands began trembling, and he clenched them into fists.

Sana cocked her head. "As in, you're related to Makmoud Hidari?"

"He is my half-brother, twenty years my senior. His younger brother is Jibril." This was it. She'd leave him now, leave him to deal with his past on his own.

She drew in a sharp breath and shook her head slightly. "Oh, wow. But I don't understand why that upset you—"

"Did you know Victor was engaged?"

"Yeah, we talked about that. Remember?"

"I killed his fiancée." His shoulders heaved, and he hunched forward and buried his face in his arms.

Silence fell. She'd left him. He knew it.

"Suleiman, please. I'm not understanding." Her soft voice reassured him.

"I was with the kidnapping team that went after Maggie McCall that night. Jibril was with me high up in the sniper's nest." Pain shot through him as he confessed to shooting Rachel at Makmoud's order. By the time he finished, he shook from head to toe. His sides heaved as another panic attack threatened to overtake him.

Sana didn't hurl accusations at him, didn't threaten to call the cops, didn't run away. Instead, she shifted until she sat on her knees beside him. Her warm arms enfolded him, and her chin rested on his head. Suleiman gripped her forearm.

"Did you know who Victor was? Or Rachel?"

"No. I...I knew no names or even faces because Makmoud and Jibril kept the details of the mission to themselves. I killed her, Sana." His grip tightened. "I broke Victor's heart, and I destroyed his career."

Low cries emanated from his throat as he tried to reign in his agony. The panic attack exploded on him, and now, he could do nothing but hunker down and wait for it to pass. He leaned into Sana, who didn't loosen her hold on him. He tried to listen to the horses nickering softly to each other, the cry of a hawk as it soared overhead. He felt the warm breeze, smelled the subtle, sharp scent of the pinion pines.

Gradually, ever so gradually, he realized Sana wasn't going to leave him. He forced his eyes open.

"I've noticed one thing about you." Her soft voice added further reassurance. "You have a gentleness about you that is endearing. I would have never known you had killed Rachel. I can tell that you're a different person than the person you described a few minutes ago. What... what changed you?"

"How long do you have?"

"All afternoon and evening—if you let go of my arm."

He released his grip.

Her warmth disappeared.

He opened his eyes and found her once more on her knees in front of him.

This time, she rubbed her arm where his fingers had created red marks.

Regret hit him. "I'm sorry."

"It's okay."

He took a deep, shuddering breath before he recounted the way Makmoud had kidnapped him from Marseille and brought him to the compound deep in the Venezuelan jungle. "At first, I refused to bend, but then he broke me. He had a sensory deprivation chamber, something everyone called The Dark Room. I spent five days there, and it was enough. I was too scared to mess up again. Then I felt welcomed as part of their team."

"What happened to change that?"

Weariness hit him, and all of the sudden, all he wanted was a nap. He leaned his head against the post and closed his eyes. Snippets of memory flashed before him, including Jibril's arrival at the compound in February 2012 with a wan blonde. "Her name is Susanna," he'd told Suleiman. He included no last name. Thanks to Suleiman's bed being next to the wall adjoining her room, he heard her tears at night. He vowed to protect her, almost as if he were her little brother.

Then came the day, a few weeks after they'd returned to the compound after the failed kidnapping attempt. Suleiman slept during the day thanks to an illness. A feminine cry from next door awakened him. He tried to stop Makmoud as he dragged Susanna down the steps. After sending her into the Dark Room, Makmoud hurled him into the mud. His half-brother's threat still echoed in his ears. "You listen to me, and listen to me good because I'm only going to say this once. You stay out of my business, understand? And what I do with Susanna is *my* business." He popped Suleiman across the face. "You do it again, and I promise I will beat you senseless even if you are my brother."

Makmoud broke Susanna over a period of five days, then took her as his lover. When Suleiman made that discovery one dark night, anger boiled inside of him. He'd failed to protect her.

Suddenly, reality skewed back into place. Had he really told Sana the whole sordid story? "It is like broken…broken…"

"He broke the faith with you."

"That is it." He swallowed hard. "I could not abide by what he did. So I walked away. On the pretext of seeing my girl in San Rafael, I left alone. Only I went straight to Caracas and walked into your embassy."

"And that's how you wound up in the States under an assumed name."

"When Gary found me two years ago, he took away my choices. Either I join Shadow Box, or he would lead Makmoud to me."

She took his hands. "I think you made the right choice. You walked away from Hezbollah, and that speaks a lot to your character." She swiped at the tears that had trickled down her cheeks. "What you did to Rachel—and to Victor as a result—was terrible."

His heart dropped. She hated him.

"But I can tell you've changed. When we were meeting that first time a couple of years ago, I remember how adamant you were that we not kill unless it was necessary." She shifted so she sat beside him. "I think...I think your eyes are now wide open. You see what you've done and you need forgiveness. I'll pray for that."

"You don't hate me?" He tightened his grip.

A small smile crossed her features. "No. I can tell you've changed, and that means everything to me. Confession is good for the soul."

"But...I do not know if I can face Victor. Knowing what I do, and..." He shuddered at even the notion of confessing to his mentor his role in Rachel's death.

"You're right. But will you ever have peace in your soul if you don't?"

She had him there. "I do not know what to do."

"We'll pray." She released him and climbed to her feet. "Now, if we don't finish up here, Victor's going to wonder what happened to us."

A small smile crossed his face.

Sana hadn't judged. If anything, she'd drawn closer to him.

The tension drained from him, leaving him weary and strangely relaxed. As he once more resumed his position and picked up his rifle, he tried to set aside his worries.

Then the nerves returned. He doubted Victor would be so understanding of his confession.

11

Victor switched off the light to the master bathroom. On his dresser, which remained hidden by boxes, his phone chimed the sound for a text. He wove his way through the mess and studied the message.

Norm had written, "New intel arrived. Ransom demand is fifty million plus a safecracker."

Victor tapped out a reply before heading down two floors to the kitchen. Warmth filled it, as did the smell the chili he'd cooked for his family and crew earlier that evening. In the big eat-in kitchen, the team had gathered around the plans for the *Peacemaker* as well as satellite imagery for the harbor in La 'Amal, all of which which lay on the large pine table.

Assorted mugs and beer bottles held down corners. The team's voices rose and fell as they discussed the various options for rescuing Tori. And if the increase in volume indicated anything, they weren't getting anywhere.

He joined the crew.

"If only we could get into the pirates' minds," Fiona muttered.

Butch stood behind his seat and sipped some beer from a bottle. He lowered it as he stared at the sheets of paper. "That'd be a scary place to be."

She rolled her eyes. "Yeah, but at least we'd know how they thought."

Victor studied the the drawing. "Why don't we make some educated guesses? Look." He leaned over. Using his pen, he pointed to some of the ship's levels. "We know the bridge is on the third level above the deck. On the second level is the captain's quarters. The first mate's and second mate's quarters, kitchen, and dining hall are on the first level. Here." He tapped the paper. "It's where they take their meals, have movie night, chapel, etcetera. It's probably the only space large enough to house the entire crew. So if the pirates were going to do that, then this would be the place."

"Keep everyone together." Butch nodded and seated himself on the bench. "Logical."

"Except that if one or two hostages made it into the kitchen, they could get the upper hand." Diana leaned against the table and shook her head. "If I were them, I'd keep everyone in their cabins." She gestured to the lower levels. "What do we know about those?"

Butch rested his elbows the wood and studied the ship's drawings. "The first level belowdecks contains the operating rooms toward the stern. There's a central area." He used the other end of a fork to point that out. "That's where the elevators are. The forward portion of the hall is for the doctors. Nurses and other crew are all on the next lower level along with the library and workout facility. The lowest level is storage and the engine rooms."

She put her chin on her hand and tapped her fingers against her lips. Her brow furrowed as if she thought hard about it. "If I were them, I'd put two guys in the central area on each deck with orders to shoot anyone who poked their nose out. Then have two on the bridge and others patrolling."

"Manpower intensive," Skylar muttered.

She shrugged. "Or, he could do it with one on each level. I doubt there's any cover in the hallways."

"And how would we get in there?" Victor asked them.

With both knees on the bench, Sana planted her hands on the table. "Sometimes the best covert operation is overt."

"Huh?" Skylar squinted at her.

She switched her attention to the team's procurement officer. "What could he want from the safe?"

"The crew manifest," Victor said.

"Right. And probably any baubles that someone might have placed in there as well." Sana smiled. "So he'll be shopping for a safecracker, right?"

Victor began nodding. It seemed possible, especially with the news he'd just received, and maybe—

"Not going to happen, little lady." Skylar leaned back in his chair and laced his hands behind his head as he smirked.

Sana glared at him. She hopped onto the bench to add more height to her five-foot frame. "I resent that remark, you jerk."

"Easy, Sana. Down girl." Butch tapped her on the leg.

"Jerk," she muttered, but she resumed her seat.

"Right now, I'm not throwing anything out." Victor settled onto his chair at the other end of the table. "Sana, that might hold water."

Skylar frowned. "Why's that?"

"Norm texted me right before I came down. The pirates must have issued their demands. Fifty mil plus a safecracker."

"So we can safely assume that the captain is most likely dead." Sana nodded. "Why else would he need a safecracker?"

"She's a woman," Skylar said.

"So what?" Her cheeks reddened. Once more, she hopped to her feet, jabbed her fists onto her hips, and glared at him. "So what if I'm a girl?"

"He's got a point, Sana. You go there unprotected, and he'll have you for lunch, ninja or not. But," a slow smile spread across Victor's face, "you're right. He wants a safecracker, we'll give him a safecracker, complete with bodyguards and a business manager."

Butch began chuckling. "A rock star safecracker. I like it."

Skylar snorted. "Yeah, and she can play the diva really well. Ouch!" He glared at Sana, who must have kicked him when she resumed her seat. "Was that necessary?"

She scowled. "Yeah, it was."

"You know, I might as well have not come all this way if all you're doing to do is kick me."

She folded her arms across her chest. "Then don't call me a diva."

"Sana, if you can get in there, then I can drum up some gas that would knock them out." Diana grinned. "Get them crowded around the safe. Shove on some gas masks, get the gas going, and voila. Knocked out pirates."

"Then we can get the crew out, get the girl, and go home." Butch grinned. "Not bad. It needs some fine tuning, but it's definitely doable."

"Let's start working on that." Victor frowned as his phone began warbling at his waist. Norm. "Start talking, and I'll be with you in a moment." He rose and stepped to the rectangular archway separating the kitchen from the great room. "Victor Chavez."

"Vic, Norm here. We have a problem."

"What's that?"

"You haven't heard?" The billionaire's voice shot up an octave.

"Heard what? I haven't had a chance to listen to the news today."

"Turn on the television."

"Which station?"

"I don't care which." Impatience raged across the airwaves.

Victor bit back his sigh. He returned to the kitchen and picked up the remote from beside the television he'd installed the year before. He located CNN.

On the small screen, the anchorwoman talked animatedly about something. Then he noted the topic. *Crew Manifest Revealed. HR Representative Fired.*

"Oh, no," he muttered as he raised the volume enough to hear. Apparently, an unnamed source had revealed the crew manifest of the *Peacemaker*. All three hundred names' worth. And the biggest one? Tori Walters, plastic surgeon aboard the ship and daughter of Norman Walters, president and CEO of Walters Enterprises.

"You see what I mean?" Norm blustered.

"We're still on schedule to depart at first light day after tomorrow."

"You can't leave tonight?"

"You and I both know we're not ready." Victor turned his back on his team and retreated to the great room. "Look. We now have a solid plan.

Why don't you come over, and I can go over what we need? We're working as fast as we can, but the last thing I want to do is to send the team in half-cocked. You've got to trust me, okay?"

Huffing reached him as if Norm struggled against shouting orders. "All right. I'll be there. But I'm notifying the president."

"I'm sure he knows. See you soon." Victor said his good bye and returned to the kitchen.

Conversation had dwindled to nothing, and now, the seven other Shadow Box members crowded around the television.

"Not good." Skylar shook his head. "Not good at all."

Butch returned to the table first. His brow furrowed as he stared down the others. "Looks like we'd better get a move on. Before something else happens."

12

Sweat. How much of that could a body do? Tori had perspired a lot before, like after a long summer run or when she'd worked at a clinic in tropical Africa. But now, as she slumped on an operating table next to the one holding Klaus, she redefined that verb. All thanks to the pirates insisting on a complete engine shutdown. And since the idea of auxiliary power from shore was unheard of in Somalia, they subsisted on the remaining charge in the ship's batteries. In the OR, only essential lighting, medical equipment, and a whirring fan remained.

Lifting the fabric of her scrubs, she grimaced at the way its dampness sheened her fingers. She smelled her own body odor. Clean? Hah. Not anymore. How long could they last like this? Had a ransom demand gone out?

No more. If she entertained any more unanswered questions, she'd surely go insane.

Eyes half open, she turned her head. Her water bottle sat on a tray that served as a table. Almost empty. She'd not get another one until morning. Meaning she'd have to conserve it as long as possible. As if to taunt her, thirst invaded her awareness like a ninja team sneaking over a wall.

She sighed as she once more stared at the dark ceiling before closing her eyes.

An insistent beeping broke into her stupor.

Her eyelids fluttered open.

Her hearing sharpened.

High, loud, and insistent, the noise certainly got her attention.

She turned on her side.

A light on the monitor tracking Klaus's blood pressure had begun blinking in time with the alarm.

"Oh, no." She made the jump from the alarm to what it indicated. His blood pressure had begun falling. No, downright plummeting.

Tori jerked upright and bolted to her feet. Her head spun at the sudden change in orientation, and she stumbled to his side as her muddled brain tried to make sense of the signal. A hundred over fifty. Not good at all. She stared at his face.

He'd paled. His lips moved, and he rasped, "Wha…what is happening?"

"I think you're internally bleeding somewhere." Tori grabbed the portable x-ray machine and wheeled it over. She centered it over him. "I've got to get that bullet out, and to do that, I need to know where it is."

Forget proper procedure. She snapped an x-ray standing not ten feet from him. She shoved the machine into a corner. Time for the next step. Call up the image. When she turned toward the computer, she yelped and jumped back. Her heart hammered in her ears.

Stinky, her guard for that shift, stood a mere three feet from her. His smell, a cross between dried sweat, onions, and lack of hygiene, filled her nostrils. His narrowed, bloodshot, and watery eyes scared her the most. "What you do?"

His foul breath could have knocked out an elephant.

Her gaze slid to Klaus. "He needs an operation. Fast. Or he will die. I need my nurse. Nattie." She tried to slow her breathing. "She's in her cabin. Please."

"I check with leader." He raised his radio to his lips and jabbered away in Somali.

She didn't have time to wait, only to act. She called up the image and studied it. The bullet had penetrated his lower lung. It must have hit a rib, bounced off, and lodged in one of the liver's major blood vessels. Like a cork, it had prevented a major bleed-out. No more. It had to come out. Now.

Her shoulders tightened, and her breath came in short, sharp puffs. Not since her training in medical school had she been directly involved in anesthesia. The intricacies of putting someone under seemed locked away beneath layers of other knowledge. She stalled by focusing on Klaus as she reached over and took his hand. "I have to operate. That means I need to give you anesthesia. Do you understand?"

This time, his lips formed the word "Yes," but he was too weak to speak.

Get moving! She yanked on a pair of nitrile gloves, grabbed a clean tray from another table, and wheeled it over. She reached into a drawer and began pulling out the instruments she needed. *Lord, please let Nattie help me. Otherwise, I'm in deep, deep trouble.*

"What are you doing?" Abu Waheed shouted from the doorway.

Tori cried out and whipped around. Automatically, she placed herself between Klaus and the Somali pirate. "He's bleeding. If I don't operate, he'll die."

The man drew his gun. "I can help him do that."

"No!" Her nostrils flared. "No, no, no! Please. As a doctor, it's my priority to save him."

Abu Waheed glared at her. "Then you operate. But nothing more."

"I need my nurse. Nattie, the one who relieved me earlier. I can't do it without her."

He turned on his heel and left.

Behind her, Klaus groaned. Oh, no. His blood pressure had fallen even more. If she didn't act now, he'd die before her eyes.

Heart racing, knees trembling, she began washing his chest. An overwhelmed feeling, something she'd never experienced in her career, washed over her and threatened to pull her under. She didn't want to kill him with the anesthesia. But if she didn't put him under, he'd die anyway.

"Lord, please," she whispered. "I'm so scared. Please guide me."

"Tori!" Nattie's Australian accent sent a wave of relief through her.

"Thank God!" Tori's knees buckled. Had she not caught herself on the edge of the operating table, she might have collapsed.

Nattie didn't wait. She darted to the sink and washed her hands. "What do you want me to do?"

"Get him prepped while I put him under and wash up." Tori cast a disparaging glare toward Stinky. "He's contaminated the OR, but that doesn't mean Klaus has to be. When he's under, get him hooked up to the equipment and intubated. So what if we use up the rest of the ship's power on lights?"

"Will do." Nattie switched on the operating table light.

Her calmness soothed Tori, if only briefly. She placed a mask over Klaus's face. "Breathe deeply and count backward from ten."

His eyes drooped closed.

She stuffed her hair into a scrub hat and donned a surgical mask, then darted to a nearby sink and began scrubbing her forearms and hands with a brush and soap. She glanced over her shoulder as clippers buzzed. Nattie finished wiring Klaus to the various machines that would monitor his condition. She intubated him, and a machine took over his breathing as she adjusted the anesthetic drugs.

With hands held high to avoid any further contamination, Tori approached. Like the team they were, Nattie tied Tori's surgical gown for her as Tori slid on her sterile gloves and approached the table. "I'll start while you gown up."

With that, she turned on the recorder, noted the start of the surgery, and picked up her scalpel. An unnatural calm settled over her. Like a seasoned gladiator, she now resided in the arena where she normally worked. With a quick breath of prayer for comfort and guidance, she began.

Friday, June 26, 2015, 2300 hours local time, La 'Amal, Somalia

Thrones felt like this. Abu Waheed lounged on the massive captain's chair with a leg thrown over one of the arms and smoke streaming from a cigarette in his fingers. Onshore, fires on the beach winked at him. The only lights in town glowed from his compound, which also housed the on-ly quay. A warm breeze blew through the open doors of the bridge and whispered along his cheeks.

Nearby, Wasim, his lieutenant, lounged with another guard.

One ship. Three hundred hostages. A ransom demand of fifty million. He could agree to twenty million. Not that the South Africans needed to know that. Oh, they'd already tried to get smart with him by creeping close to the ship. He'd ended that by threatening to start killing a hostage a minute until they retreated to five kilometers away.

His threat and hunger had made him cranky. Relief came in the form of food delivered from the villa. None for the hostages, of course. They would have to subsist on what they had stored. And if any complained? He'd offer to take them ashore and sell them. That should shut them up. He had a new supply of *khat*, too.

So perfect.

He reached into the burlap bag resting on his lap and removed a few fresh, green leaves. He stuffed them into his mouth and began chewing them as if they were tobacco.

Hearing and sight sharpened.

Once more, his chest puffed out.

He perked up.

His eyes darted everywhere, from the windows to the open door where Wasim stood to the three monitors hanging from the ceiling in front of the captain's chair. In Somali, he softly called, "Wasim."

Wasim turned. "What is it?"

"Since you know about technologies, how would the captain use these televisions?" Abu Waheed gestured to them.

His second-in-command shrugged. "Probably for tracking the weather and such." Wasim joined him and studied the remote that rested in a small tray on the right-hand arm of the chair. He pressed a button, and an image appeared. "Ah. It appears as if they have satellite television. Press these buttons to change channels."

Abu Waheed took the controls and flipped around. He came upon a news channel. There, a brunette chatted with someone, an expert, perhaps.

Then the screen turned to a blonde who appeared to be reading the news. The night's top story? Of course. The *Peacemaker* Incident, as the media had taken to calling it.

Except something seemed different.

Abu Waheed fumbled with the remote. "The sound. I must have sound!"

Wasim took the control from him and hit a button. A woman's British accent filled the room. He raised the volume.

The blonde reported that someone had revealed the crew manifest.

Abu Waheed leaned forward and listened.

A picture of a woman in a doctor's coat with brown hair spilling over her shoulders flashed on the screen.

He stiffened.

His jaw fell open as his mind groped for the reason why.

The woman in the picture.

He'd seen her before.

The screen switched to a news conference. A stocky man with graying red hair stood behind a podium. He seemed familiar. "Wasim, who is that?"

Wasim scanned the caption. "A man named…Norman Walters. Chairman and CEO of Walters Enterprises. You recognize the name?"

What self-respecting, ambitious pirate wouldn't? The man was a pirate's dream catch. A billionaire. Wait. *Billionaire?* Forget dream catch. If he ever fell into his clutches, Abu Waheed could buy all of the women, mansions, and Mercedes cars he wanted.

What good fortune! The woman who operated on her friend one level belowdecks had a billionaire for a father. Like water filtering through sand, the realization of his discovery trickled down to him.

His cheeks flushed. The warmth spread throughout his body as if generated by the news and the *khat* streaming through his blood vessels. Then he realized his wealth of knowledge. New strength flooded him as his pulse skittered upward several beats. He jumped to his feet. "Wasim, come with me."

He checked his gun. Good. A bullet in the chamber. Perfect if needed. And his knife. He slid it from its sheath. Straight edge and serrated edge. She'd cower before him, especially when she saw the dried bloodstains on the blade.

Now he'd stake his new claim.

Friday, June 26, 2015, 2305 hours local time, La 'Amal, Somalia

"We're finished." Tori's hands trembled as she tied the final knot in the sutures. She stared at the closed incision, which ran from slightly below Klaus's ribcage to just above his belly button, and let a small sigh escape her.

"You did a good job." Nattie made notations of his vitals on a tablet where they had recorded information throughout the surgery. "Pressure has stabilized. Saline is helping that. If we keep him quiet, he should recover fully."

"Thanks." Tori's knees began shaking as her mind fought to make it all the way to the finish line of the operation. She rattled off medications and dosages of antibiotics and painkillers. "Can you fix the dressing? I...I feel like I need to sit down."

"Certainly. Are you all right?"

"I think I'm dehydrated." Tori clipped the thread.

Rough hands whipped her around!

The scissors flew from her paralyzed fingers and clattered into a corner. The hair rose on the back of her neck as adrenaline exploded through her.

Abu Waheed.

Watery, red, bloodshot eyes. Green teeth from those leaves she'd seen him chew.

Hot, foul breath.

Wild, vacant stare.

He was high.

Her stomach tightened.

"I know who you are!" His fingers gripped her tighter.

She squirmed against his grasp. "What? I—I—I don't understand."

He ripped off her mask and scrub hat. He shoved her, sending her staggering her across the room.

"Stop!" Nattie's voice barely penetrated.

Tori stumbled. She caught herself on the operating table where she'd lain and whipped around. "I don't understand."

He blasted a foul name toward her. "You are the daughter of a billionaire!"

Oh, no. Had Captain Jameson given up the combination? No, she'd heard he'd died. But then—

He slapped her hard across the face and shoved her again.

Off balance, Tori slammed into one of the storage cabinets. Its doors popped open. Bottles, vials, and boxes tumbled onto her head. She slumped to the floor. Nattie's cries and Stinky's harsh orders barely registered.

Abu Waheed grabbed her ponytail and yanked—hard. He got in her face. "You thought you could hide from Abu Waheed. You hide nothing from me!"

Hot breath full of onions, some sort of seafood, and that leaf filled her nose.

Her stomach leapt. No. No throwing up. Not now. She huffed out a breath and sucked in another. Big mistake. She tasted bile and forced it down. Gasping, she stammered, "I—I don't know wh—what you're—"

"Shut up!" He dragged her to her feet and practically threw her toward the hallway door. "You go with me!"

Tori caught herself on the door frame. She spun around in time to see Nattie yank free from Stinky.

Abu Waheed backhanded her best friend.

Nattie sagged to the ground and begged, "Leave her alone. Please. She has done you no—"

"Shut up, nurse." Abu Waheed drew his gun. "Or shall I shoot you?"

Stinky pulled her away as he babbled something that sounded like a warning.

Despite the heat, cold sweat drenched Tori. She started mewling as Abu Waheed thrust her into the hallway.

He grabbed her hair again and marched her in front of him.

She clawed at the walls. No purchase there.

When her fingers did grasp something, he only ripped them free.

They passed through the central core and by the shocked guard.

Abu Waheed shouted something at him before propelling her forward with such force that she fell to her knees.

Her stomach finally gave way, and she threw up. She began hyperventilating as her world spun before her.

"Get up!" He kicked her in the solar plexus.

Agony raged in her side.

He took her by the hair and began dragging her.

Her scalp burned. "Stop! I will if you'll—"

"Shut up!" At least he stopped.

Except that he hauled her to her feet. He slammed her into the bow-most wall. Her door banged open.

"Get in there!" The pirate hurled her into the room with such force that she careened into the far wall next to the porthole. Pain exploded in her nose, and blood began oozing down her face like slime.

She whipped around. Black spots danced in her vision. She whimpered when she noticed the wicked gleam in his eyes.

Abu Waheed advanced toward her. "Now it's just you and me, Tori Walters."

He grabbed the neckline of her top and ripped it.

Then terror piled upon terror until Tori faded into a numb grayness.

13

Friday, June 26, 2015, 2000 hours Pacific Daylight Time, Flagstaff, AZ

Victor stared at the large-scale, laminated aviation maps Fiona had spread across the kitchen's pine table. They needed to plot their route and finalize their cargo, but the list he'd given Fiona seemed hopeless, like trying to cram too much into a suitcase for a trip to paradise. Except that their mission was to hell, not paradise. And their suitcase? An airplane that wouldn't even make it off the tarmac if it were too heavy. And if they couldn't make it off the runway, then range wouldn't be an issue.

Problem was, each time she punched the weight of a piece of cargo into a program on her laptop, the range of the C-130 shrank, as did the amount of available weight until they teetered too close to zero for his comfort.

She sighed as she leaned her chin on her hand and tapped her fingers against her cheek. "Are you sure we need everything we're carrying? We're maxed out on weight, and it's impacting our range."

"I'm afraid we might need something we might not have. I'd rather go with more than less," he said.

"But all of this medical equipment?" Fiona blinked. "C'mon, Vic. We're rescuing people on a *hospital ship*."

Couldn't she trust his judgment? Experience had taught him to plan for everything. "Fi—"

"Really? I'm sure they have all of the gauze, needles, and x-ray machines we could ever want or need."

He clenched his fists. Maybe he should have told her to stay in Vegas because he'd forgotten how arguing her was like willingly sitting on a cactus. Painful. Not to mention, it would lead nowhere and waste time they didn't have.

From where he sat at the head of the table, Butch cleared his throat. "But what if Tori's separated from the ship?"

"All right, *fine*. I get it." Fiona rolled her eyes. "Still, we're taking everything but the kitchen sink."

Butch jumped up. "That's it!"

"What?" Victor cocked his head.

"The *Kitchen Sink*. That's what we name the airplane. Then we truly are taking everything."

Victor began chuckling. He stopped. "You're...serious."

"As serious as this mug of coffee." Butch held up his over-sized mug.

Skylar, who sat beside Fiona, guffawed. "Hey, I like it. Good one, Butch."

"One of my more stellar moments." The team's mechanic and escape-and-evasion specialist grinned.

Fiona opened her mouth, closed it, and sighed. "Whatever. Let me check my numbers one last time to make sure they're correct." Her fingers flew across her keypad as she ran through the list of cargo for the plane. "Two Humvees. Fuel. Fuel containers. Water. Water containers..."

This could take a while. Victor tuned her out. His attention wandered to the den where DJ and Anna watched television. Deborah, who'd left the kitchen after cleaning up a quick supper of hamburgers, said something. Anna replied. Which left his two youngest. They were too quiet for his tastes. His newly formed Dad radar began its scan. Giggling reached him. He tensed to rise and check on them.

"Hey, boss, question for you." That came from Butch.

"What is it?"

"I know this is small, but every pound counts. Hemp rope weights a lot. What about lighter-weight rope?"

"I'm concerned that if we have to use it to get Tori out of Abu Waheed's compound, that she'll be too weak to grip something thin. A wider rope and knots will help her descend. And we can leave that behind for the return trip."

Butch rubbed his goatee. "True."

Fiona shrugged and smiled a bit too brightly. "No biggie. No biggie at all."

Liar.

The lead of her mechanical pencil snapped. Grumbling, she pushed some more through before hitting a key and flipping the computer around. "Voila. Here's our range."

Victor stared at the black box where 2,300 glowed in green. A tall order to go anywhere outside of the western hemisphere. "So we have to find the shortest route across the Atlantic."

"Exactly." She chewed on the eraser of her pencil. Her gaze flicked to him. "Unless Norm has a refueling aircraft at his disposal."

He shook his head. "Nope."

Butch pulled the maps showing the northern Atlantic closer. "What about Greenland? We fly up the East Coast, through Canada, and jump via Greenland. Then we head down to Great Britain and continental Europe to Africa."

She nodded. "Makes sense to me."

"Not to me." Skylar said.

"Why not?"

He folded his arms across his chest. "We're not working for the feds, remember? Yeah, so what if we're Norm's lackeys? What's going to happen when we make our entrance into Canada, let alone Great Britain? Before we could even refuel, we'd wind up in jail for being a C-130 carrying military-grade stuff."

"We could bluff our way through the Canadians and Brits," Fiona replied.

"Okay, so what if we do?" He shrugged as he if were debating which featured dish to serve at his restaurant rather than the potential fate of the entire team. "What do we tell the Spaniards? They come across all of our cash, and they're going to ask exactly which African government we're planning to topple. Somehow, I don't think they'll buy our intent to rescue hostages. I mean, for all they know—"

"I got it, okay?" Fiona stiffened and glared at him.

"Babe, I'm just trying to help."

"And I'm just trying to get us there." She blew out a sigh and raised her gaze to the ceiling. "Okay, Einstein, what's your idea?"

"What about a southern route?" Skylar shuffled the maps. "Here." He stood up and leaned over as he traced the route with his pen. "We go down through Central America, across the northern coast of South America, and make the leap from Brazil into Senegal."

Victor studied the route. It could work. "What about refueling?"

"Once I get estimated times for landing, I'll make sure we'll have fuel waiting on us," Fiona replied. "Sometimes being a former contract pilot for the CIA does pay off. I think I know the fixed base operators in every backwater country there is."

"Good enough." Victor resumed his contemplation. At least until more giggling reached him. He peered between Fiona and Skylar. Behind them, both Marie and Gracie slithered almost in a combat crawl into the kitchen. They snaked their way toward the table. Marie had something tucked to her chest. Was that a pink—

"Vic, you're good with this?" Fiona asked.

He eyeballed the gap between South America and Africa. "We've got the range to do the crossing?"

"I think so, but let me check." She picked up a compass and adjusted the width.

"Wow. You still use a compass?" Butch grinned at her. "You're ancient."

She chuckled. "Sometimes old school is best."

She began measuring out the route.

Whispers and white fur once more distracted him.

Victor stood up just in time to see—

"Rats," he muttered.

"Huh?" Butch raised his eyebrows at him.

One of them skittered toward the pilot. It ran up her pants leg.

She shrieked!

Fiona jumped onto the narrow strip of pine bench. She flailed her leg, and her foot connected with Skylar's jaw. Her boyfriend tumbled from the bench.

Like a rodent gum ball machine, the rat came flying down and out the chute of her pants leg. It pinwheeled. When it landed, it scrambled toward Butch.

The other one bolted up her pants and onto her fleece before leaping onto the maps. It slid across the slick laminate on it its belly as if it were on a Slip 'N Slide.

Fiona screamed again. She hurled her compass at it and nearly speared Butch in the process.

He dove to the floor.

The tip buried itself in the wall.

"What the…" Victor whirled.

Where the kitchen led to the great room, Gracie and Marie sat on their knees and laughed.

He turned—just in time to see the first rat scramble onto Butch's mug, where it promptly fell into the dark liquid.

Butch scooped it out.

It bit him.

"Ow! Easy there, buddy."

The mug toppled over and spilled its contents across the maps.

Still moaning, Skylar began crawling toward the safety of the hallway leading to the mudroom.

Fiona's hollering reached new volumes when she saw the children. She leapt onto the table as she pointed at them. "Get. Them. Out. Of. Here!"

Butch started laughing, which dumped more fuel onto the fire of Victor's anger. "Gracie! Marie! Get in here. Now!"

His face flushed. They'd ruined the team's plans. Like a wide receiver darting through a wall of linebackers, he wove his way around the table, just in time to see Gracie and Marie dart away. Their laughter taunted him. When he got his hands on them—

A loud whistle stopped him cold.

Two fingers in her mouth, Deborah stood in the open french doors of the den. Her face had paled to a sickly yellow beneath her tan while her slate blue eyes had widened. "V—Vic, y—you need to see this."

Gracie and Marie would have to wait.

"What?" He stomped after her. "What happened?"

"It's Tori." She pointed to the television.

Tori's battered face filled the screen. Both eyes were blackened and downcast. A cut ran down her cheek. Strands of dark hair clung to tearstained skin. She spoke in a monotone as she read what seemed to be a ransom statement. "…billionaire. To free me, you must pay five hundred million American dollars. It will take time to liquidate your assets to meet such a demand. You have a week. You will be contacted about where to pay. In addition, you must send a safecracker to the *Peacemaker* within the next five days. We are also requesting fifty million from the South Africans for the remainder of the ship. That is all."

The screen went blank before the face of a newscaster reappeared and began discussing the video in the gravest of tones.

Things had slid out of control, not only at home but overseas.

Forget having precious little time.

Now they had none.

"Dang," Butch muttered.

Victor turned.

Butch, Fiona, and Skylar had followed.

Victor's phone began chiming. Norm. Double the "oh, no" part. He shoved his way past his three teammates and retreated to his study. "I saw."

"How—how could they?" Norm's voice shook. "This… this is going to sink me. There's no way I can do that." Panic melted the steel in his voice. "I'm going to call the president and tell him you can't scramble fast enough."

"Listen to me." Victor paced to the door. Deborah's demand for answers echoed off the high ceiling of the great room. Everyone spoke at once. From Fiona's furious tone, he worried that she'd up and leave that night.

Someone started crying, and he doubted it was his pilot.

He shut the door. "Please, listen closely. I can guarantee you the president is aware of this. Don't push the issue with him or the South African prime minister. They're handling it. Do you understand that if someone storms the ship without adequate planning, the pirates could kill all of the hostages and make Tori disappear?"

"But—"

"We're prepped to leave at first light in the morning. Everything is in place, and Fiona's going to file the flight plan within minutes."

If she could get past two rats running all over her.

"We'll be on-site Monday morning."

"Monday!" Norm blustered. "But that's—"

"Sunday night our time. It's a long ways over there, understand?"

"Is there anything I can do to help this along?"

"Praying would be a good start." He thought about how well the plan Sana had proposed fit with the pirates' demands. "And you can tell them you've dispatched a safecracker. You're staying in Flagstaff?"

"Yes. My wife and Tori's fiancé have joined me."

"I promise we'll be in touch throughout."

"Okay. But you call me each day, you hear?" With that, he hung up.

"I do," Victor replied to empty air. He sighed.

Worry knotted his stomach, and he hung his head. They'd done their best, but someone had surpassed them. Pain in his hand distracted him. He'd been gripping the door frame so tightly that the tendons in his hand bulged. He loosened them and rubbed the back of his neck, where tense muscles began aching.

He'd been so sure they were on the right track.

Until now.

In the end, their best might not be good enough.

Friday, June 26, 2015, 2230 hours Pacific Daylight Time, Flagstaff, AZ

Victor placed his coffee mug in the dishwasher, started it, and leaned against the counter as it hummed. It was something normal, routine. Suddenly, he craved the boring, predictable life. And the quiet that had fallen over the Big House—at least once Fiona had calmed down enough to retreat to her room and file the flight plans while Butch and Skylar headed to the airport to finish loading everything aboard the plane.

Anna and DJ slipped away to their rooms. For the next hour, Deborah scolded Gracie and Marie before sending them to bed. If he let his imagination roam, that was all that was happening. He couldn't. Within a few hours, he'd be airborne with a very uncertain future.

For now, he settled for his nightly visit with his children before finally falling into bed for some rest. Surprisingly, DJ and Anna had already turned out their lights. He headed to the room of his youngest two. The aquarium burbling on Gracie's dresser cast a pale blue glow into the room. It seemed like so much time had passed since Marie had excitedly talked about the fish they'd bought when in reality, it was only two days ago. He turned his attention to the rats. Her fur still sticking up in little white clumps from when Butch had washed her, Cupid slept in a tight ball. Valentine rubbed her paws across her face and ears as if none the worse for the wear. In the gerbil cage, Woody cleaned his whiskers while Buzz got in his daily workout on the wheel.

Gracie slept.

Marie, her back turned to the door, sniffled. Her small shoulders quivered.

A lump filled Victor's throat. His love for her throbbed deep within him. Forget the fact that he wasn't related to her by blood. She was his daughter. He wondered how Deborah would react if he proposed adopting them. Once he eased onto the edge of the bed, he put his hand on her hair.

"Daddy, I'm sorry."

Double the size of the lump at the sound of her tiny, tearful voice.

"Forgiven." And he meant it.

Marie turned onto her back. She clutched Lambkins, her stuffed lamb, to her. "Mommy said that because of what we did, we can't ride horses or let Cupid and Valentine outside of their cage until you get back. How long are you going to be gone?"

"Not long. I'll be back by the Fourth." He tucked a curl of her brown hair behind her ear. "And if you're good, I'll bring you something."

"Can I have a giraffe?" Leave it to Marie to brighten immediately at the thought of a gift.

A tender smile turned his lips upward. "Maybe."

"Cool. We could cut a hole in the roof of the barn."

Forget the Great Rat Caper. She'd re-won his heart. "Maybe. Did Mommy say prayers with you?"

She nodded.

He kissed her on the forehead before rising.

"Marie now wants us to put a hole in the barn's roof for the giraffe she thinks I'm going to bring her," Victor announced once he'd shut the door to the master suite.

Deborah scowled from where she sat on the bed with her Bible on her knees. "*Marie* is grounded until you get back."

"So she says."

She closed the book. "To be honest, I even thought about giving away Valentine and Cupid."

"Nah." Victor shucked his hiking boots and his shirt. "They were just pawns in the Great Rat Caper."

"At least the girls apologized to Fiona. Trust me when I say she was in her room throwing stuff into her suitcase. I admit I did my own groveling." She wrapped her arms around her knees and rested her chin on them. "I just feel so horrible after disciplining them, you know?" Finally, she turned her gaze toward him. "But then I realize that God feels the same way about disciplining us."

A small chuckle escaped him. "True." He remembered his earlier thought. "I have a proposal for you."

That earned a weary laugh. "At least it's not a proposition."

"Huh?"

"I'm too tired for a nightcap. And too stressed."

That got his attention. Forget his nightly routine and final packing. He cocked his head as he joined her. "About the *Peacemaker* thing?"

She swallowed hard and nodded. Her hand snaked to the cross she wore around her neck. "Yeah. It's, well, the whole thing tonight shook me up a little. I guess..." She blinked rapidly and stared toward some unknown point. When her gaze returned to his, it sparkled with unshed tears. "You haven't really trained together for this mission, and that's what worries me. And your unity... I'm worried."

So was he. During his Special Forces days, his team had been together day in and day out. They'd known each other's strengths and weaknesses and had sought to play to each individual's strengths and minimize their weaknesses. Tonight's escapade had enhanced how fractured the Shadow Box team remained in some ways.

Victor drew her close and stroked her hair.

They'd be fine.

They had to be.

"We'll do this."

Deborah's shoulders quaked only once. "I know. And I believe God has given you this mission. I'm... it's difficult to trust Him sometimes." She cocked her head. "I hear Marie."

He didn't, but he let her be.

She hopped to her feet and hurried from the room. In some ways, she had the raw end of the deal. She had four children, had relocated to a strange place, and barely a week after arriving, her groom was deserting her to travel halfway across the world on a mission where he might die.

No, they wouldn't. They'd double-down, and they would succeed.

One way or the other, by the Fourth of July, Tori would be free.

So he hoped.

14

Suleiman lay in his bed, but it was if he'd used Super Glue to paste his eyelids open. He simply couldn't rest. Each time he tried, adrenaline trickled into his system. His eyes popped open, and his breath quickened. If this kept happening, he'd not sleep at all. He sat up, and the blanket fell to his lap. He listened.

In the common area, Butch murmured something. Skylar replied. Their doors thumped shut, most likely as they turned in for the night.

Suleiman rose and pulled on a T-shirt, jeans, and a fleece. Once he'd laced on his hiking boots, he grabbed a flashlight. His gaze slid to the black, leather-bound book on his desk. Earlier that evening, Sana had left a Bible on his bed with a note. Her recommendation? Start with the Book of John. He'd do that.

The waxing moon lit his way, and with his sharp night vision, he arrived at the barn without a problem. He pushed the doors apart enough to slip into the gloomy interior. The homey smells of manure, hay, and horse hit him and conjured memories of those first days after Shadow Box had fallen apart before his eyes. Rather than face the fallout with Sana, he'd left her to fend for herself by retreating to the barn and finding solace in the supposed simplicity of ranch life. If only it were that easy now. He had a larger enemy, or two if he counted the upcoming mission.

He clicked on the flashlight. By its dim glow, he located a nearby bale of hay. He sat on it cross-legged and propped the Bible open on his knees. Where was the Book of John? After flipping through the various books, he came to the back, to something called Concordance. What was that? It seemed like an index.

Their conversation on the way to Flagstaff echoed in his mind. Fear. It preyed on him like a shapeless shadow. He thumbed through the delicate paper until he came across the word fear. The phrases were strange, especially since the letter "f" seemed to stand for fear.

The fear of the Lord is pure. Suleiman stared at that one for a moment. What? That didn't make sense. At least to him, it didn't. He sighed and stared at the next sentence. *Through the darkest valley, I will fear no evil.* He rested his chin on his hand. Why did he get the sinking feeling these verses would remain a mystery to him? *So do not fear, for I am with you.* Was God saying He was with those who loved Him no matter what? How could that be when God was someone far off, out of his reach? *Do not fear their threats.* Again, the message delivered in that verse didn't make sense to him. *The one who fears is not made perfect in love.*

He tossed the book onto the bale and rested his chin on his hand. *I give up.* One thing came clear. He needed to talk with Sana. And sooner rather than later. Maybe they could discuss this on the flight to Somalia.

A shadow moved, and his sniper alarm began blaring in his head. He froze.

A silhouette blocked out a part of the pale glow from the streetlight outside the barn.

He hit a button. Darkness enshrouded him. His breaths came out in short puffs. Had Victor come to check on the horses one last time? Suleiman remained still and watched.

A petite figure slipped inside. Sana. The tautness of his shoulders relaxed slightly as he drank in her silhouette. Almost immediately, the sensations that had percolated inside of him when he'd taken her hand the day before once more trickled through him.

Her beam blinded him. She yelped as she snapped it off. "What are you doing out here?"

He blinked to clear his vision. "I couldn't sleep. Like you, eh?"

"Yeah, like me." She dragged over another bale and crawled onto it. "It's a good thing we're leaving tomorrow."

"What do you mean?"

She sighed. "The pirates found out who Tori is. They beat her up really good, maybe more." A shudder ran through her slender frame. "They're ransoming her for five hundred million, plus a safecracker."

Any thought of talking her out of the plan they'd concocted the day before vanished like snow in the Sonoran desert on a hot day.

She leaned against him, and her shoulder brushed his. "What are you looking at?"

"Your Bible. I'm...confused."

"Let me see." Her black hair swung forward as she gazed at the pages. "Oh, that's a concordance. Kind of like an index. See?" Her finger found the verse she'd shared a couple of days before. "'So do not fear, for I am with you; do not be dismayed, for I am your God. I will strengthen you and help you; I will uphold you with my righteous right hand.' That's Isaiah chapter 41, verse 10."

"What about this one?" He pointed to the last verse he'd read.

"First John, chapter 4, verse 18." She turned to the appropriate book. "'There is no fear in love. But perfect love drives out fear, because fear has to do with punishment. The one who fears is not made perfect in love.'"

"What does that mean?" Truly, he didn't understand.

She continued, her voice growing stronger with each word. "'We love because he first loved us. Whoever claims to love God yet hates a brother or sister is a liar. For whoever does not love their brother and sister, whom they have seen, cannot love God, whom they have not seen. And he has given us this command: Anyone who loves God must also love their brother and sister.'" She closed the Bible and set it on the hay beside her. For a few moments, only the sounds of a lone coyote wailing and the night insects penetrated the stillness. Then she spoke slowly, almost as if she measured each word with great care. "I think what John, who wrote this book, was saying is that we fear punishment. That's what verse 18 says to me."

Could he argue with her? No. Not after his confession the day before.

She took his hand. "Do you fear Victor will hate you or kill you if you confess?"

Suleiman nodded. "How could I not? He has every right to kill me. Wouldn't you feel the same way?"

Her shoulders rose and fell in a shrug. "How would I know? I'm not standing in your shoes or his." She shifted so she faced him. Her voice shook as she said, "God's love does cast out fear, especially the fear of punishment. When He died on that cross, He took on our sins—mine, yours, all of those who trust Him for their salvation. It's a gift."

A gift? Impossible! He started shaking his head.

"It's true, Suleiman. I promise it is." She reached out and took his hands. "Look. To me, God is personal. He's known my name ever since before the beginning of time. And he loves me as His own daughter. He loved me so much that He sent His Son to die for me."

"How can He be personal?" He drew in a deep breath. "Allah doesn't care about His followers. He's up here." He held his hand high above his head, then moved it to his knee. "And we're here, far below Him."

"What happens when you pray?"

"What?" He cocked his head. "I don't pray. Not anymore, at least."

"When you did pray, what did you do?"

"I said my *salats*. Five times a day, like any good Muslim."

"But what did you do?"

Why was she so insistent? He blew out a sigh. "I would bow when required. And say my prayers. There are words for each that I would say each time. Why is this so important?"

Sana dropped his hand and picked at the hay on the bale. "Praying is different for me. It's like a conversation between God and me."

"And does He reply?" Almost immediately, guilt hit him. He'd tried to bait her. Add one more bad work on top of his pile that was higher than the largest junkyard.

A small smile crossed her face. "Maybe not audibly. But I know He does. Sometimes He speaks through His peace. Sometimes through a friend. And yes, a few times, I've heard His voice just like I hear yours.

What I'm trying to get at is that God is personal. That's why I said Jesus died for me. And He died for you, too." She pulled out a bit of hay and ran it between her fingers. "All of those bad works you have, He took those upon Himself."

"Christ was a prophet."

"No, He was a fulfillment of those prophecies. Don't you remember our discussion about the Law when we were coming back earlier today?"

He nodded.

"After Christ died on the cross and rose again, a path opened up between God and us. Now, when God looks at His children, He doesn't see them with all of those bad works. We all have them, and they're all equally bad in His eyes. Instead, God sees His Son interceding for us. Eternal salvation. That's a gift to us because we can do nothing to earn it."

Suleiman rested his elbows on his knees and put his head in his hands. No. Never would it be that easy, especially for him. As he started tallying up every bad thing he'd done in the week, he cringed as if expecting lightning to strike him at any moment. He quickly lost count. The worst? What he'd done to Victor. "It can't be that easy."

Sana expelled the smallest of sighs. She rested her hand on his knee. "It is. I promise."

And what would happen if he confessed to Victor? His mentor would arrest him. As a part-time sheriff's deputy, he had the legal power to do so. If he were really lucky, Victor wouldn't kill him. New fear piled on top of the old. "Perhaps when we return...I should leave here."

"Suleiman, no." She flinched as if he'd pinched her hard. "Why?"

"Victor will hate me if I stay. Want to kill me. And he would have good reason to do so."

"How could he hate you?"

"I don't—"

"How could he hate you?" She scrambled to her feet and began pacing. "Look. He's been a Christian for over a year now. I know he's read that verse because we talked about it in April when we all were in North Carolina for the wedding." She whipped around. "How can he hate you yet love Christ? He can't."

Slowly, she approached him. She took his hands again. "Why do you think running to someplace far, far away would make it better?"

He kept silent as he considered that. If he got right down to it, running away would do nothing, only isolate him from those who could help.

She released him and eased onto the bale so close to him that they would have looked like a dating couple to an outsider. "Look. I became a believer while in prison. My mentor, the woman who brought me to Christ, was serving a life sentence for murdering her philandering husband. When she talked about Christ, I was so skeptical because I thought I was beyond hope. But here was this woman who'd killed her husband with a knife now telling me that God had forgiven her because Christ had died for her sins. She said it was the most incredible gift she'd ever received. Believe me when I say she lived with great gratitude in her heart. If she could accept that gift of grace, why couldn't I? I had no more excuses."

As if she'd had too much coffee, she jumped up again and stepped to one of the stalls. An Appaloosa nuzzled her, and she stroked his nose. "She had this saying, something like fear enslaves us to secrets. What she meant is that when we fear a secret getting out and its consequences, our fear places us in bondage to it. Only when we let go of the secret and speak about it can we truly be at peace."

In front of him, she sank to the ground, almost as if she were a servant of his. She reached out and touched his denim-clad knees.

Suleiman almost jerked at the jolt of electricity that shot through him.

"Please consider what I said. Christ loves you. Victor serves Him. I do, too. We've both discovered that joy of accepting the gift of grace. Can you do that?"

He stared. "It's impossible. Truly."

"Then I guess I wasted my time." She stumbled to her feet and grabbed her flashlight. She almost ran toward the door.

"Sana, wait!" Suleiman bolted after her. He caught her arm before she had a chance to make her escape. He spun her around and gripped her shoulders. "Please, stop. You heard the desperate words of a desperate man, one who finds himself backed into a corner with no options."

"You know you have one."

Did he? No. The idea that God could forgive him of killing Rachel—and all of the other countless bad works he'd done—made him want to scream. And confessing to Victor wasn't an option either, especially with leaving for Somalia in hours. He reached up and ran some of her hair through his fingers. It was as silky as he remembered from a couple of nights before. "My only option is not to speak of it again. It's…over. Nothing can change what happened."

She tried to pull free. "Suleiman—"

He maintained his grip. "Those words a few minutes ago? You are right." He gathered her close. "To flee would solve nothing."

A small shudder ran through her. She tensed as if to flee.

His heart pounded at the idea of losing her. He couldn't. Not when he knew he'd gladly lay down his life for her. "I love you, Sana. Truly, I do, even if I'm not sure about what you say about grace being a gift."

Could he mess things up even further?

Trembling beneath his fingertips, she stared at him and pulled back. First one pace, then two.

He let her go.

Suleiman's heart hammered. He'd scared her away. She didn't love him. Did she?

The smallest of smiles crossed her face. It disappeared before she fled into the night without another word.

He'd overplayed his hand, confessed before he was ready. The words had popped out of his mouth.

And he meant every one of them.

Sana had his heart. No other. And if her smile meant anything, she wanted to reciprocate. From somewhere unknown, the tiniest bit of peace sifted across his soul. On its heels came a sobering thought.

If they didn't take care on the mission, forget about it being too late for Tori. It would be too late for them as well.

15

The murmur and crackle of radios and static filled the cockpit as Victor joined Fiona. Shadow Box's pilot had her headset around her neck as she ran her finger down her knee board and programmed in radio frequencies. Her Ray-Bans sat on the dashboard.

"How's it going?" he asked as he leaned against the copilot's chair.

"Like a breeze." Fiona, seeming none the worse for wear from the night before, raised her gaze to him. "I don't know what kind of sources Norm has, but this plane is awesome. I don't need a navigator or engineer, and I almost don't need a copilot. Speaking of copilots, could you send Butch in? I need him for startup checks. We leave in ten."

"Will do." His stomach did a quick flip as he located the team's mechanic checking the tension in the chains holding one of the two Humvees to the floor of the plane.

The sleeve of Butch's white T-shirt rode up to reveal the scaly tail of a dragon tattoo.

"Hey, Butch."

"What's up?"

"Fi's ready for startup."

"Wilco. We're in good shape here. I'll check again at the next stop."

Victor found the rest of his crew plus his family huddling under the left wing in the predawn chill. His heart jumped. Within a few minutes, they'd leave safety far behind. He cleared his throat. The subdued chatter faded. "Okay, everyone. Time to go and find a restroom before getting on the plane. Hop to it."

His team turned and headed toward the General Aviation building for one last pit stop at a civilized toilet for the next forty hours. Deborah and the children remained behind.

"Dad, are you sure I can't go in there?" DJ asked. "Uncle Butch said it was huge!"

"Big enough for a giraffe?" Marie asked.

"Not for a giraffe." He scowled at his little sister. He turned to Victor. "When are you coming back?"

"By the Fourth of July. Listen." Victor mussed his hair. "Help your mom out, okay? And don't let anyone, and I mean anyone, onto the property unless you know them."

DJ straightened as if he understood the importance of his duty. "Sheriff Rodriguez said he'd pop by. And I know how to use a shotgun. And a rifle."

"You get uneasy, you call Sheriff Rodriguez before you pull those out." Victor lightly chucked him under the chin.

His stepson threw his arms around his stepfather. "I love you, Dad."

"Love you too." Victor released him and turned to Anna. She stood there, a perfect replica of how Deborah must have looked at her age, all arms and legs and tall. Memories of the year before when Makmoud had kidnapped his oldest threatened his peace. He took a deep, shuddering breath. "Help your mom out, okay? Keep the peace. Hug your brother and sisters."

"I will."

Victor drew her close and kissed her hair.

Anna brushed some strands from her face and scooted away.

He knelt in front of Gracie and Marie. "Come here, you two."

They charged into his arms. He buried his face in their hair and deeply inhaled the little-girl scent of soap and flowers to imprint the aroma of innocence on his mind.

"Daddy, I'm so scared you won't come back." Marie's voice trembled.

"I will." He pulled back. "Look at me."

She turned her face away.

Victor drew in a deep breath. "Marie, Gracie, both of you, look at me."

Marie finally met his gaze. So did Gracie.

"Be good for your mama. Hug her when she gets lonely. Help out around the house. And if I get good reports, I'll bring you back something."

Briefly, ever so briefly, Marie's eyes brightened. "A giraffe?"

"Maybe." He ruffled her light brown curls. "I love you both." With that, he straightened. "Anna, please take the kids to the Suburban."

Victor turned to his bride. His chest tightened at the thought of leaving her. "Part of me doesn't want to go."

Instead of worry, peace now radiated from her like warmth from an electric blanket. "We'll be fine."

Once more, images from the year before assaulted him. Butch had told him of their frantic flight to escape Makmoud, the way Deborah had fallen and hurt her knee. Then came those of the ambush by Gary Walton, his best friend, that betrayal of trust, and the beating he'd taken at the hands of both Gary and Makmoud. "But if Makmoud—"

Deborah stopped him by placing a finger over his lips. Then she wound her fingers through his. "This isn't my first rodeo, cowboy. You forget I was a Delta wife for seventeen years. Deployments, even if you don't call this that, are nothing new to me."

His breath eased out.

She rested her forehead against his. "God has us—all of us—in the palm of His hand."

"But what if Makmoud—"

"I think Makmoud Hidari has more on his mind, like evading capture, than risking a trip back into hostile territory to even a personal score." She met his gaze with a strength in hers that surprised him. "I know God wants you to go on this mission. Otherwise, everything wouldn't have come to-gether like it did. Remember that we take each day by faith."

Slowly, he released a sigh. He smiled and closed his eyes as he savored the softness of her hands. "You're right." He couldn't bring himself to let go. "I promise I'll call each day if I can."

"You do that, mister. And I promise I'll keep Norm and Elizabeth in-formed for you. And hopefully his 'staying at an undisclosed location' will hold out these next few days. And most importantly, I'll be praying." She reached up and ran her hand down his face. "You go and bring Tori back."

"I will. And until then…" He kissed her slowly, lingeringly. With great reluctance, he broke it off. "That's something to keep you."

"I'll be waiting." She released him.

He could have sworn his heart ached as she did so.

"God go with all of you."

With that, she retreated to the Suburban.

Victor turned and found the tarmac empty. His team had already boarded. They were strapped into the webbed chairs along the sides of the plane closest to the bulkhead. "You guys ready?"

Skylar gave him a thumbs up. "Ready as we'll ever be."

Victor slipped into the cockpit and settled onto the navigator's chair. "Let's do it, Fi."

"Roger that." She opened her window and called, "Clear!"

She pressed a button. The inner starboard engine began spinning. She started the inner port engine, then the remaining two.

Victor glanced out the window.

Deborah stood with her hands on Marie's shoulders. Gracie clung to her leg, and DJ and Anna huddled next to her.

He swallowed hard. He didn't want this to be the last time he saw her. *God, if it's Your will, bring us back safely soon. Please.* He faced forward as his hands gripped the seat.

Fiona contacted the control tower. She released the brakes, and they rumbled onto the taxiway. Once at the edge of the runway, she held short and ran up the engines in one last test. The *Kitchen Sink* bucked as if it couldn't wait to jump into the sky.

The tower announced, *"Kitchen Sink, you are cleared for takeoff."*

"Roger that." Fiona taxied onto the runway. For a brief moment, they sat there. Then Butch placed his hand over hers, and they pushed the throttle full forward. The plane began the takeoff roll and gathered speed. Outside, the buildings of the small terminal flew by. Then, almost with a great leap, they soared into the sky and into an uncertain future.

Sunday, June 28, 2015, 0230 hours local time, somewhere between Aruba and Georgetown, Guyana

The noise of the engines throbbed through the hold of the *Kitchen Sink*. It flew through the tropical night as they skirted the northern coast of South America. Inside the plane, the darkness would have been complete except for the ghostly glow of blue lights next to the ladders leading to the top row of bunks, which resided aft of the seats on the walls of either side of the plane. Most of the team had already crawled into their racks for some sleep.

Not Suleiman. His body still thought it was before midnight. He sat on the lower, port-side bunk closest to the seats and leaned against the hull. Thankfully, the noise-canceling headphones created a quiet atmosphere where he could think. By the glow of the portable light he'd clipped to his borrowed Bible, he'd finished reading the Book of John and now read the Book of Matthew, the recommendation Sana had whispered to him earlier, right before everyone plunged into a marathon game of Uno during the first leg of the trip. She'd challenged him to look up in the Old Testament each of the prophetic references Matthew had made. He did so.

Suleiman stared at the scribbles he'd made on his notepad. So many verses prophesied about a coming king, all written hundreds of years before the birth of Christ and all by different people. He knew in his soul. Christ was the Messiah. He had too many references completely dissociated from one another to deny it. As he laid the Bible on the mattress, he considered the import of his discovery.

Sana said it meant grace was a gift.

No.

To him, it wasn't. It was too easy simply to state that he was a sinner and that Christ had died for his sins. And then there were the years of schooling where he'd learned how the Koran specifically stated that the way to paradise was through works and that no one was ever one hundred percent certain about their status until they drew their last breath. And maybe not even then.

But how could he deny the peace that radiated from Sana, Butch, Diana, and Shelly? He knew all of them had been Christians for a long time. Victor may have come to faith only the year before, but Suleiman remembered the way he and Butch met each Wednesday. Discipling was what Butch had called it one time when he'd asked.

He needed to let his mind and body rest. His gaze flicked through the hold. Curtains covered the starboard bunks where Diana, Fiona, and Skylar slept. Butch's, which was across from him, was empty since he flew the plane. And Victor, Diana, and Sana? Same result.

Or maybe not.

On the starboard-side bulkhead sat the toilet. The ladies had strung up three shower curtains to provide some privacy and enough room for changing. One of the curtains twitched, and Sana emerged. The LED lights of the communications panel above the seats next to it gleamed against her shiny, dark hair. She wore a long-sleeved T-shirt and leggings, her usual sleeping outfit when it was chilly.

She scurried to his bunk and settled beside him. With her fingers, she signaled him to turn his headphones to channel one-two-four. When he did, her melodious voice filled his ears. "I noticed that no one was on this frequency. I have to say these headphones are the bomb."

"More slang?" He grinned and nudged her.

"They're the best." She giggled before touching the page where he read. "Matthew?"

"Yes." He nodded. "It is interesting. I cannot believe the number of prophecies about the Messiah that are in there."

"What are your thoughts?"

He considered her question. "I do see how you believe that Christ is the Messiah. We know He was a great prophet, but I now know that it goes far beyond that."

"But do you believe He died for your sins?"

Part of him wanted to say that he did. But a larger part, the one steeped in years of Islam, remained in disbelief. After all, what she asked meant that he turn his back on a lifetime of learning. "This... grace. To see my salvation as grace, or a gift, as you put it, is still too easy in my mind."

She didn't scold him for his thoughts, didn't try to argue with him. Instead, she gestured toward the Bible. "May I?"

"Sure." He handed it over.

She flipped a few pages. "Have you read through the Beatitudes?"

"The what?"

"Here. It starts in chapter 5. They're some of my favorite verses in this book." She ran her finger down the page. "Here's one for you. 'Blessed are the peacemakers, for they shall be called children of God.' Verse 9."

A peacemaker. Something akin to anxiety crawled into his soul. She intended to bring up what he most wanted to forget. He couldn't undo the past. And he'd already faced it and admitted it to Sana. He knew that when Makmoud had broken Susana and threatened him, something inside of him had changed. Now, he wanted to move on with the rest of his life. "Sana—"

"I think you need to make peace with Victor. And with yourself." Leave it to her to be direct.

"I told you I wanted to let it go. I did a terrible thing. I learned from what happened, and I've changed. You know that."

Oh, why didn't she simply nod and agree with him? She didn't move. Didn't smile. Didn't say anything. Her dark eyes bored into his.

Suleiman gripped the mattress.

"I think you need to address this with Victor."

"Why? It's over. It happened."

"I know, but I can tell you're not at peace. And you won't be until you talk with him."

"I will be—"

"No you won't." Her sharp tone stunned him.

He clenched his teeth. "Why are you suddenly so insistent?"

"I've never not been that way. It's too important. Look." She reread the verse. "I've read up on this. When I was in prison, the library had a great commentary on the Book of Matthew. One of them said that the peacemaker is an active person, not a passive person. To me, that means two things, making peace with yourself and with those who you might have impacted. If you're a true son of God, you'll be desirous of doing that."

He folded his arms across his chest. "He'll hate me."

Sana closed the Bible and laid it on the mattress. She lowered her head. When she lifted her chin, the determination in her eyes startled him. "I think you underestimate him. You can deny it all you want, pretend like things are fine. But, I can guarantee it will poison you." She raised her hand to his cheek. "And us."

"What?"

She dropped her hand. "Don't think I missed what you said last night. Truth be told, I can't deny it, even though we're of different faiths." She reached down and laced her fingers through his. "I love you, Suleiman al-Ibrahim. That means that like it or not, my future is interweaving with yours." Her grip tightened, and in the dim blue light, her eyes glimmered with unshed tears. "This is tearing me up, and it has the potential to wreck something that might not ever have a chance to start. That's what's killing me."

With that, she scrambled off his bunk and scurried up the ladder. The one above him shook as she lay down.

Suleiman stared after her, both excited and terrified. Excited because he now knew how she felt. Terrified because he knew she was right. They could never be together because of their differing faiths. And that secret he'd shared? He'd indeed shackled her to him. She now walked with that burden, and he saw no way to relieve her of it.

As he shut off his light and stretched out, one thought kept running through his mind as if it were on a Wall Street ticker.

What have I done?

16

Sunday, June 28, 2015, 1530 hours local time, Dakar, Senegal

Ocean crossing, check. Finally. Though the propellers had spun down, Victor's ears hummed as if they still throbbed. The team now resided on the westernmost part of Africa. Part of him wanted to relax, but he couldn't. Not when he'd pick up the money they'd need for their upcoming arms deal.

Butch undid his harness. "Hey, I'm gonna go and pop the ramp. And check the chains."

"Roger that." Victor leaned back as Butch squeezed his bulk past him and into the hold. In the pilot's chair, Fiona continued her conversation in French. Finally, she lowered the sat phone and handed it to her commander. "Fuel's on the way. Should be here at 1545 hours. I want to leave at 1630 hours. When's Baxter supposed to arrive?"

"1600 hours."

"This had better not take too long. I'm serious about our departure." She scrubbed a hand across her face as she muttered, "And we have hours and hours ahead of us. I can't believe I signed on to this."

So she was tired and cranky. Everyone was.

He totally got that. "You knew what you were getting into, all right? Get some fresh air. And keep that fuel truck away from the tail. No need for us to reveal our cargo if we don't have to."

123

He rose. At the back of the hold, motors whirred as the ramp lowered. Thanks to the heat and humidity, sweat beaded on his arms. A breeze sought entry and then exited with him through the side door as he joined his crew on the tarmac under the wing. Like a spirit, an odor invaded his nose, something like body odor and manure all mixed together. He grimaced.

Shelly summed it up for him. "Ew! What is that smell?"

"It's Africa, baby." Butch mussed her hair, and she ducked away. "What? You've never been to Africa or Asia?"

"Uh, no. Only to Europe"

"You'll get used to it."

"Boy, I hope so." She shook her head.

Victor raised the sat phone to his ear and called Deborah. It was approaching mid-morning in Flagstaff, and she reported all to be calm. Norm, Elizabeth, and Jake remained in anonymous seclusion, so no reporters harassed them. He doubted it would stay that way. The kids were unpacking and lounging by the pool.

Butch called, "Hey, boss, we've got something to our twelve."

He glanced at his deputy. Butch stood in the shadow of the plane's nose and held a pair of binoculars to his eyes. Victor followed his gaze. Two white specks grew larger as they raced toward them from the hangars. Oh, no. Someone had discovered their destination. He muttered under his breath and said, "Deb, can I call you back?"

She asked, "Vic?"

"I think Baxter's here." At least he hoped one of the vehicles contained his contact with Walters Enterprises. After a hasty goodbye, he lowered the phone. His mind darted in all directions. They had no guns except for the sniper rifle. Fighting back would be like trying to break into Fort Knox with a toothpick.

"Got a fuel truck and a Land Rover. One occupant in each," Butch reported.

Victor's breath eased out as the truck parked near the wing. The Land Rover pulled to the other side.

Fiona, who'd joined them, strode to the fuel truck and began talking with the driver. She gestured toward the tanks hanging from the wings and guided him away from the tail. Good. At least she'd listened to him.

A man in a khaki linen suit hopped down from the Land Rover and scurried toward Victor. "I know I'm a bit early, but I also know you have a schedule to keep. I'm Baxter Winstead, Chief of African Operations for Mr. Walters. You must be Victor Chavez."

"I am." Victor shook the man's hand. He took his arm and led him toward the Land Rover. In a low voice, he asked, "You have what I need?"

"Right here." Baxter pulled a duffel bag from the backseat. "All one hundred thousand American dollars, as requested. Please sign here, if you would." He offered a clipboard. "So I can prove I handed over the money, you see."

Victor scribbled his signature. "Thank you. I appreciate your willingness to meet us here."

"Not a problem at all. And this." He reached inside and extracted another briefcase, this one of plain leather with locks and with enough scuffs to give it a good sense of patina. Victor wondered if someone had thrown it into the street and kicked it around several times. "After you called, Mr. James contacted me and asked that I add this to the order. Fifty thousand, all in American dollars. Unmarked twenties, just as ordered."

"Do I need to sign for this?"

"Oh, no, no. Not for this one. To be used as needed." He nudged Victor and winked.

"Huh?" He frowned as his mind raced.

"That's what Mr. James said." Baxter chuckled as if the joke were on Victor. "Well, cheerio. I'll see you in Mombasa." With a wave, he climbed behind the wheel of the Land Rover and sped toward the hangar.

Skylar, what have you done this time? Victor's eyes narrowed. From the second he'd met Skylar James, he knew he worked with a natural-born liar and one who didn't hesitate to bend the rules or downright break them, even if he went too far. Why else would the CIA burn him and dump him in his hometown? Of course, that had been because he'd not shared the profits from the little arms-dealing side business he'd had in Pakistan with his employer. Men like him were a necessary evil in times like this. In Victor's mind, chances were good that the briefcase and its contents might disappear. He'd hold his procurement officer accountable for this.

And where was he? Just follow the stink of the cigar. He found him lounging on the lowered ramp in the shade created by the hold. Ray-Bans similar to Fiona's covered his eyes, and the sun gleamed off his blond hair. He wore a button-down shirt with the tails out over a pair of cargo pants. Suave meets tropical Africa. Victor scowled and dropped the duffel on the hot metal. "There's our arms money."

"Excellent." Skylar blew some smoke rings.

Victor tapped his foot and set down the briefcase. He folded his arms across his chest. "Why didn't you tell me about the fifty grand?"

Skylar finally pushed himself upright and rested his wrists on his knees. "'Cause I knew you'd make a fuss over it."

"That's why you went behind my back?"

Skylar shrugged. "Hey, it's bribe money. Pure and simple."

"I realize that. Why didn't you request me to order that?"

"Because I wasn't sure you'd approve it."

"And why didn't I have to sign for it?"

"Gag, you're sounding like a dang parrot." The team's procurement officer rolled his eyes. "Because it's *bribe money*. It's not like you could itemize it on an expense report."

Victor got it. After all, he'd worked in Africa and Asia where sneaking money into the hand of a greedy person in power was common. Still, at that tone of voice, as if Victor were a babe in the woods, his cheeks heated, and a headache sprang up at the base of his skull. He nudged the briefcase with his foot. "Open it."

"What?"

"Open it. I want you to count every bill in front of me."

Skylar cocked his head. "You really think I'd steal some? Take my cut or something?"

"Isn't that why the CIA burned you?"

Skylar muttered something, but he counted out every single bill. As he did so, the only sounds filling the air were those of planes landing and taking off and fuel whooshing into the tanks. Once he returned the packs to the briefcase and closed it, he shoved it forward. "Satisfied?"

"I am. And when we're done, you're going to account for every dollar. What we don't use will go back to Norm. Understand?"

Skylar snorted. "Yes, sir, Mr. Man-in-White-Hat."

Victor ignored him. Regardless of what happened, he'd refuse to compromise his morals on this one if at all possible. He turned away and retreated beneath the shadow of the other wing where he had some privacy. He dialed Deborah's number. When she answered, he said, "Deb, I need some prayer. Pray I won't 'accidentally' leave our procurement officer in Somalia when we head home."

Sunday, June 28, 2015, 2330 local time, approaching Yaounde, Cameroon

Suleiman gripped the frame of his webbed seat as the descent on their final approach into Yaounde, Cameroon, steepened. The plane creaked as it passed through bumps in the air created by leftover thunderstorms.

The door to the cockpit opened. Victor joined them and sat on the step leading downward. "Listen up, everyone. We're now ten minutes out from Yaounde's airport. This is where things have the potential to head south if we're not careful. We're going to taxi to a far part of the airport and do the arms deal. Upon completion, our contact with Walters Enterprises has arranged for a fuel truck to meet us. We'll refuel and be on our way to Mombasa for the last leg."

"Hallelujah," Skylar muttered.

"For this deal, Skylar, Butch, and I will handle it. Sana will take care of any snipers, and she'll provide backup to Suleiman. Shelly, Diana, and Fiona, I want you three to stay out of sight, okay?"

"No problem there," Fiona, who was on the same frequency as the rest of the crew, replied.

Suleiman cast a glance at Sana, who sat to his left. She wore a black jumpsuit. And how could he miss the dagger strapped to her right arm?

Straps on her left arm held two shurikens. No gun for this ninja. At least not now.

"Stand by, then." Victor retreated to the cockpit.

In his mind, Suleiman swung through the plan. Release Sana as the plane taxied toward the rendezvous. Secure any snipers. Set him up as primary sniper on top of the plane. Take care of business. Then get into the air before the Cameroonians got too suspicious as to what went down at their airport. Simple in theory. Not so in reality.

The plane bumped as it touched down. He released his grip on the seat. The cockpit door banged open, and Butch, his wireless headphones still in place, joined them. "Sana, get ready. We're going to drop you as soon as we get off the taxiway. Suleiman, I need your help over here."

He knelt and popped a belly hatch. When he lifted it, the asphalt seemed to fly by.

She wasn't going through that, was she? Suleiman's gaze shot to Butch. "Are you sure this is safe?"

Butch grinned. "So long as she doesn't dart to the left or right until we're clear, she'll be fine."

She approached them. Now she wore her hair in a stubby ponytail. "So stop, drop, and roll?"

"Easy as that. Just don't get to your feet until the plane's gone." Butch nodded. "Fi will slow a little. Let us know you're okay. We'll be on this frequency."

"And Sana." Fiona's voice crackled in his ear. "There should be a fuel truck in front of Hangar 4. Keys will be in the ignition according to my contact. When you're done, bring it on over."

"Got it." Sana lifted her headphones and handed them to Suleiman, who set them on her seat. She smiled at him and mouthed, "I'll be fine."

He wasn't so sure. Not that he could tell her otherwise.

The plane slowed.

Not enough for Suleiman's comfort.

"Now, Butch," Fiona said.

Butch patted the gymnast on her back and pointed to the hatch.

She thrust herself through the opening. Long seconds passed as they waited for confirmation that she'd exited safely. Finally, she said, "Three is safe. Heading toward the hangars."

Good. Her comms device, which had longer range than the head-phones on the airplane, worked. Suleiman thought through the plan. If anyone was on the roofs, they'd be more distracted by the plane than someone running away from it in the dark.

They slowed and groaned to a stop. Gradually, the engines wound down, and blessed silence fell. Victor and Fiona joined them. "Suleiman, crawl into the cockpit, take this, and see if you see anyone along the top of the building. They probably posted a sniper there to take out the pilot and any sniper we have on the call of the dealers."

Suleiman took the offered night vision periscope and snaked his way into the cockpit. Using the copilot's chair as cover, he began scanning, first the terminal and then the hangars located in the General Aviation side of the airport. Nothing moved on the glowing green screen. He was about to call all clear when a shift of pixels from light to dark caught his eye. He focused on the area. His brain translated a blob on the screen to a human. A man was setting up something, most likely a sniper rifle. "We have some-one on the roof to our eleven o'clock position."

Seated on the floor of the cockpit behind the pilot's chair, Victor nod-ded. "Exactly the way Skylar figured. Three, you know what to do."

"Roger that." Sana's reply came as a breathy whisper.

A tense few minutes passed. Suleiman followed the action from afar. The man had begun peering through the rifle's scope. If she didn't succeed, they were stuck. He suddenly disappeared. Then came Sana's report. "Threat neutralized. I have control of the gun."

Suleiman expelled a quiet sigh.

"Do you see anyone else?" Victor asked.

"Negative. Just me now. My guy's out cold with cable ties around his ankles and wrists and tape over his mouth."

Victor snaked his way into the cargo hold and gestured for Suleiman to follow. "Your turn."

Butch rose from where he'd crouched with the others. He climbed onto the hood of the nearer Humvee. With his height, he easily popped an upper hatch before he turned to Suleiman. "Come on over. I'll give you a leg up."

"You have so much slang."

The hulking former Special Forces soldier grinned. "That means in redneck that I'll boost you onto the top of the fuselage. Just be careful 'cause it'll be slick up there."

He formed his hands into a stirrup. Almost reluctantly, Suleiman put his foot in his hands. His friend pushed him upward until he gained purchase on the lip of the opening. He crawled onto the top of the plane—and almost instantly began sliding. Not good. He'd splat onto the tarmac, which would seriously hurt. He flinched and grabbed the edge. "You are right. It is very slick."

"You stable?" Butch asked.

"I think so." Suleiman hugged the plane in the desperate hope that friction would keep him on top. With one hand, he carefully adjusted the boom mike of his wireless headphones.

"Here's the rifle." From beneath, Butch lifted the rifle through.

"Remember to chamber a round," Victor advised through the comms system. "Keep the safety on unless you hear me say 911. Got it?"

"I do." He'd emerged ahead of the tail. Inching his way toward the rear, he stopped just in front of the tail. Oh, so carefully, he brought the rifle to the ready position and activated the bipod. He shifted to get as comfortable as he could and adjusted his aim so he focused on where the truck of the arms dealer would arrive. "I'm in position."

"Three?"

"Ready up here," Sana reported.

"Butch, lower that ramp."

As the whine of the ramp lowering trembled through the fuselage, Suleiman pressed his eye to the scope.

The waiting game began.

Operation Peacemaker

"Skylar, it's your show." Victor scowled at the black T-shirt and khaki cargo pants along with combat boots he and Butch wore. At the moment, knives in their boots served as their only weapons. Huh. Some bodyguards they made. Not that their visitors would know that. "Do you think we're intimidating enough?"

Skylar, who now wore a white tropical-weight business suit with a black shirt, grinned. "You'd better be. Of course, they don't know about our little surprises." He stepped to the front bumper of the first Humvee. "You ladies comfortable in there?"

"Just get it over with." Fiona's voice floated to them from the bulkhead. "And I don't even have a frying pan I can throw at them if things go bad."

Victor nearly laughed at her gallows humor. If things went bad, a frying pan would be one hundred percent useless. Maybe she should dig out the combat knife he'd seen her pack.

Skylar scanned the surrounding area with a pair of night-vision binoculars. His panning stopped and focused on the far end of the airport. As he lowered them, he turned his head. "Here they come. Looks like a Jeep and a truck. Y'all stay sharp now, you hear?"

Uh, no. *Skylar* would have to be the one who was sharp. Their survival depended on his ability to discern twists and turns—or betrayals. If things went bad, they'd not stand a chance. *Stop thinking that way,* he ordered himself. As if sensing his worry, Butch grinned and shrugged. Leave it to the team's mechanic to remain nonchalant. Even years ago when they'd served in Special Forces together, Butch had been calm under the most withering of gunfire.

Victor's gaze slid to the duffel sitting on the plane's deck between them. All one hundred thousand remained tucked inside the nylon. That's what the dealer had wanted, and Skylar had reported that he always agreed to a fixed, non-negotiable price.

The rumble of the two vehicles grew louder until they eased to a stop twenty or so feet away. The truck's air brakes wheezed, and a Caucasian man climbed from the passenger side of the four-door Jeep. He straightened the lapels on his suit and thrust out his chest.

Like he knew he had an ace up his sleeve.

Not good.

Skylar led the way down the ramp until they stood on the tarmac at the base with Victor and Butch slightly behind Skylar and off his shoulders.

Victor's hackles raised. He glanced at Butch, who cocked an eyebrow.

When the dealer spoke, his German accent assaulted Victor's already frayed nerves. "Mr. James, so good to see you again."

"Helmut, my friend." The two men briefly embraced and slapped each other on the back.

"Pakistan has not been the same since you left."

"What can I say?" Skylar shrugged. "My bosses didn't like my little side business, so I left before things got bad. But that didn't mean I cut all ties, right?" He nudged him as if they were old fraternity brothers.

Helmut cocked his head. "When my contacts received your call, I was curious. Why could you possibly need my services?"

Skylar reached into his jacket pocket and pulled out a cigar. He took his time unwrapping it. "Oh, just a job I've got going on." He extracted a cigarette lighter in the shape of a bowling ball pin. After touching flame to tobacco, he returned the lighter to his pocket. "You see, I needed a little firepower. And when I need it and need it quickly, I know who to call. That's you. Rifles. Ammunition. RPG. Semtex. One-stop shopping is what I like. So, we have an agreed-upon price of one hundred thousand dollars, American."

Helmut said nothing. A sneer curled his lips.

A double-cross. Skylar had scored on this one, which was why they'd put contingencies in place. What was that cliché? No honor among thieves? Or arms dealers, for that matter. No surprise there.

Victor reached for the pistol he didn't have.

For some bizarre reason, an image of hurling a frying pan at Helmut filled his mind. He wanted to laugh.

He couldn't.

Not now.

Especially when the driver and two more Africans joined the dealer with rifles raised.

Skylar took a puff, and the offending odor enveloped Victor in a cloud of stink. He nearly gagged as the procurement officer said, "You want to tell me why you're violating our agreed-upon price?"

Helmut shrugged and spread his hands wide. "What can I say? We never agreed in writing."

"We've *never* had anything in writing." Skylar took a menacing step forward. Butch and Victor closed ranks as if emphasizing his angst. "What was it you told me oh, so long ago?" He rubbed his chin as if trying to remember. "Oh, that's right. 'An honest man only needs a handshake, nothing else.' In other words, a verbal agreement. And you, my *friend*," he nearly spat the word, "you have always been one to negotiate, then go with a firm price at the *time of the deal*. Why the change?"

Helmut didn't reply. He shouted something in German that Victor didn't understand.

Skylar, who knew ten languages and spoke German passably, shook his head. "Tsk, tsk, tsk, Helmut." He sighed as if dealing with a disobedient puppy. "You should have known better than to try and take out my sniper. You know I always come prepared. Two, paint him."

A red dot appeared on Helmut's forehead, a dot brought about by Suleiman activating the laser on his scope.

Victor smirked.

Skylar inhaled and blew smoke in Helmut's face. "Now, I'm going to try this again. I'm offering hundred grand in American dollars as we agreed."

Three more of his cronies joined the standoff.

"Will you never learn? Three, your turn."

This time, from her high perch, Sana activated the laser on the scope of the sniper rifle she now possessed. This red dot came to rest on the chest of one of the henchmen. The intended target's eyes widened, and he began jabbering in the local dialect.

Skylar turned his back and walked a few paces away as if to signal his trust in the laser web in which he now had his adversary. He whipped around. "My second sniper has that pretty rifle your boy had. Since you seem so intent on doing something stupid, I want all but two of your boys to drop their weapons, get down on their knees with ankles crossed, and put their hands on their heads. Do it."

Helmut hesitated.

"You, too. Now!"

Helmut issued his orders. Slowly, four of the six Africans got down on their knees. He joined them.

"Butch, take everyone's guns. We'll keep those as our service fee for the troubles you caused."

A snarl on his face, Butch jerked the rifles away from the six lackeys. He handed one to Victor, who slung it over his shoulder. After keeping one for himself, Butch laid the others on the ramp.

"Vic, bring me the cash." Skylar snapped his fingers.

What a— No, Victor wouldn't think that thought because he might go through with his desperate plan to leave Skylar in Somalia. He had to play the part of the obedient bodyguard. Victor brought the duffel over and placed it at Skylar's feet. After unzipping it, he handed Skylar a pack.

He brandished it and fanned the bills. "It's all there. All you requested. And since I'm honest—unlike you—you've got to trust me on that."

Victor nearly barked out sarcastic laughter. Honesty and Skylar couldn't reside in the same room together.

"Now the two of your boys who are still standing will go and get the crates, open them, step back, and assume the position of their buddies. Move, gentlemen."

Helmut glared at him. A bead of sweat trickled from his hairline down his cheek. At least he didn't have the audacity to try and wipe it away. "This is too much, Mr. James."

"Not after you broke the faith."

The men placed five crates in a rough semicircle in front of them.

"Open the tops." Skylar paced in front of them and took another puff.

Using a crowbar, they undid them before stepping back and sinking to their knees with their hands on their heads.

"Vic, Butch, check everything. Make sure the firing pins aren't filed and that we have everything we asked for."

Victor stepped forward and began inspecting the rifles and pistols. He paid careful attention to the firing pins.

Overhead, Helmut and Skylar began trading insults in a mix of German and English. Or at least, they argued. Victor could have cared less as he focused on the list he'd made. The quantity matched what they'd ordered. Thankfully, the firing pins were in perfect condition. He glanced at Butch and murmured, "Everything's there?"

Butch nodded. "And in good order."

Victor loaded a pistol and handed it to Skylar, then did the same for his and Butch's sidearms. "We're good."

"Excellent. Three, we need the fuel truck." Skylar returned his focus to Helmut. "Get those tops nailed down, and my boys will load them."

A few minutes later, the fuel truck rumbled to a stop behind the trio.

Hammer blows echoed through the night, and once the crates were re-sealed, Victor and Butch carried them aboard while Skylar and Suleiman kept the men immobile with the threat of impending death.

Minutes of tense silence passed until finally, Butch checked on the fuel. He returned. "We're done, Mr. James."

"Excellent." Skylar nodded toward the duffel. "If you would be so kind as to hand over our payment."

Butch placed the duffel at Helmut's feet.

Their procurement officer tossed his cigar to the pavement and ground it out with the toe of his Italian leather loafer. "I want you and your boys to get up and leave sans your weapons. Don't look back, 'cause if you do, I'll kick your butt from here to Lahore, and it won't be pretty. *Capiche?*"

Helmut struggled to his feet. He winced as if his knees hurt. "You are a hard man, Skylar James."

"I'm hard because boys like you make me that way. You try and double-cross me, and I get cranky."

Helmut nodded to the bag, and one of his men hauled it to the Jeep. "Fair enough."

"Now get out of here. Vic, Butch, make sure they keep their word." Skylar stalked up the ramp.

Victor held his rifle at ready and trained it on the motley group until they left.

"What about the fuel truck?" Sana asked from where she'd been leaning against the rear wheels.

"I'll drive it a bit away, and we'll get going." Butch wasted no time in hopping into the cab. The engine groaned to life.

Victor joined Skylar, who'd looped a nylon strap around the five crates. Victor added a second strap and began tightening it. "Good job."

Skylar refused to meet his gaze as he ratcheted the strap until it had no give. "I can be honest when necessary."

Victor refused to answer as he checked the nylon. Good. No give at all.

"We've got a mission to rescue someone," Skylar added. He tossed the ratchet so it landed on a coil of rope. His gaze hard, he glared at his commander. "In no way am I going to screw that up for personal gain. I don't do that when lives are on the line."

With that, he climbed to his feet and headed forward, most likely to change into the clothing he'd worn earlier that evening.

Victor shook his head. Had he been too hard on the procurement officer? Maybe. Then he shrugged as he followed. "Fi, let's get going."

"What was that about?" Sana asked as she undid her jumpsuit to reveal a tank top and shorts.

He followed her gaze to where the shower curtains around the toilet swayed at Skylar's entrance.

"Don't ask." He shut the side door.

The ramp began closing, and Butch passed them on the way to the cockpit. The propellers spun up as the engines whirred to life. A few minutes later, the plane rolled forward. It turned onto the runway. With barely a hesitation, it gathered speed. A few seconds later, they soared into the inky sky.

Destination: Mombasa.

17

Victor peered out the windscreen as a tug trundled *The Kitchen Sink* into a hangar for Walters Enterprises where Norm stored his private jet when visiting his holdings in Africa. The interior yawned before them like the mouth of a giant sea dragon.

Thanks to the bright, late morning light, he couldn't discern what lay in the shadows at the edges. That worried him. As did not seeing Baxter waiting with two trucks. He gripped the armrests of his seat.

Fiona pulled off her headphones. "Your pal's late."

Could she not state the obvious?

"Is there any way to get back into the air?" he asked.

"What?" She stared at him as if he'd asked her to flap her arms and fly. "We can't do that. I mean, we've shut down. And we're too low on fuel. Short range because of all of that stuff you said you needed. Got it?"

"Fi—"

"Besides, I'm tired. It's been a long trip." With that, she tossed the headphones onto the dash, rose, and pushed past him into the hold.

Victor tensed to follow.

"Hey, boss, you got a sec?" Butch caught him up short.

With a sigh, he resumed his seat. "What is it?"

Butch set his sunglasses beside Fiona's headphones and shifted his bulk in the copilot's seat so he looked his friend in the eye. "Fi's tired and cranky. You are, too. Heck, we all need to rest. So give a little grace right now. We're where we need to be."

It certainly didn't feel like it. A hum filled the hangar as the doors began closing. Like it or not, they were committed. "You're right. But let's wait a bit to pull out our gear. I want Baxter here before we do that."

"Agreed."

A yawn fought its way loose as Victor stepped from the side door. He noticed Fiona chocking one of the wheels. "Hey, Fi, do you have a remote for the door?"

She straightened. "No. Maybe the tug guy hit the button as he left."

Or maybe he'd read his instincts right. He turned as he peered around the hangar, made all the more difficult with his eyes adjusting to the gloom. Was that really a shadow? Or a man shifting into position? Every sense jumped to alert. "Ambush!"

A squad of soldiers burst from hiding with rifles raised.

Their shouts for the team to get on their knees reverberated off the concrete floor and walls and corrugated metal roofing.

He knew better than to argue. He sank to his knees and clasped his hands on his head. His captor roughly patted him down and removed the Beretta from its holster at the small of his back. Victor glanced at his comrades. They'd all made the mistake of deplaning right after him and now sat on their knees in the same position.

His heart sank. End of the road. Done before they even really started. If the soldiers found the crates in the back, they could kiss seeing freedom again goodbye.

A door creaked open, and heavy footsteps echoed off the concrete floor. The soldiers' voices fell from a murmur into silence. He followed their gazes. Double the doomed part. The new arrival was massive, probably taller than Butch and just as muscular. Not a drop of fat on him. Had Victor put them in a mixed martial arts ring, Butch would have probably lost.

The red on the man's epaulets and the seal of his black beret indicated one thing. He was the commander. In a bass voice, he demanded, "Who is in charge here?"

"Uh, you are." Victor swallowed hard. This new arrival was going to pound him to a pulp.

No change in expression as the man stopped before him. "Your name?"

"Victor Chavez." Did his voice squeak like he was in junior high?

"You're coming with me, Mr. Chavez. Cuff him." The man turned away.

"No!" Sana's cry rocketed through the air. She scrambled to her feet.

"Sana, stay down!" Suleiman shouted.

Too late. She rushed toward them.

A soldier caught her.

She slapped him across the face.

He pushed her away and drew his pistol.

Another guard grabbed her.

"Sana, it's okay," Victor said as his guard yanked his hands behind him and manacled them.

The guard hauled him to his feet.

"Don't take him!" She struggled before being wrestled to the ground.

"Sana, stand down. I'll be fine."

Yeah, right.

Victor forced his guard to stop. "Butch, you're in command."

If they were freed.

His captors shoved him through the hangar's pedestrian door. A white Land Rover with darkened windows waited for them.

The commander opened the left front passenger door. "Put him in back."

Victor found himself crammed between two soldiers. The cuffs bit into his wrists, and within seconds, he lost all feeling in his hands. His heart hammered. Hopefully, they were taking him for questioning and nothing more. He didn't want to visualize what more could be. His chest tightened. "What about my crew?"

"They will be safe." The man said something to his driver.

Why didn't he believe him? Victor curled his fingers. Or tried to. His mind raced. He had to keep alert and look for a way out. Problem was, with guards on either side, he had no opportunity.

The man's cell phone rang. He chattered away in a muddled mixture of English and Swahili. Victor thought he heard the words guns and explosives. As they wound through the busy city, he tried to focus on their route. They seemed to stay on a coastal road headed south.

After several minutes, they arrived at a gate. It opened, and they pulled through and stopped under a portico. The man snapped an order at his comrades.

His guards dragged Victor from the backseat. He stumbled between them until they reached a conference room on the second floor. That was strange. Why weren't they taking him to an interrogation cell in the basement? Not that he'd argue. A conference room was fine in his mind.

They pushed him inside, spun him around, and slammed him into a wall. His hands came free.

He whipped around as a door shut. If the Kenyan flag, mahogany table seating twenty, and wood paneling meant anything, he stood in a room where meetings of the leadership occurred. How strange.

On the other side of the door, a silhouette stood in front of the smoked glass. A guard. Not that he'd insult the hospitality of his captors and try to escape. Victor wanted nothing more than to avoid the inside of an African prison. He paced as he rubbed his wrists. The feeling began returning to his hands.

He stopped and peered through a bank of windows running the length of the room. The blue of the Indian Ocean glinted at him as if taunting him. They should be preparing to leave, not remaining stuck in a hangar—and some sort of military headquarters.

The door opened, and the commander of the squad stepped into the room. All of the sudden, what had seemed so big shrank. "Mr. Chavez, have a seat."

Victor sat in a chair on one side near the end of the table. He'd dare not break protocol by seating himself at the head.

The man folded his arms across his massive chest. "I'm Colonel Josef Bakari, chief of intelligence and commander of our Special Forces. When you entered Kenyan airspace, air traffic control notified me. After all, a C-130 that does not belong to a country's air force strikes us as suspicious. Tell me why you came and why my men discovered Semtex, rifles, and other ammunition in the hold of your aircraft."

The game was up. Where was Baxter in all of this?

Victor opted for the truth because it was all he had. "Norman Walters of Walters Enterprises hired us to rescue his daughter from Abu Waheed, who has hijacked the *Peacemaker* and is holding it hostage in Somalia. Baxter Winstead, his chief of African operations, was supposed to discuss this with you. I don't know what happened."

"Neither do I." Josef remained unmoved, both figuratively and literally. The door opened, and one of his aides approached. He whispered something into his superior's ear. Josef chuckled and gave him an order in English too low to hear. A quick smile creased his face. "Ah, Baxter Winstead. My Jack Russell Terrier."

Victor cocked his head. "I'm not sure I understand."

He did a second later. The door banged open, and two soldiers marched into the room with Baxter caught between them.

The Brit squirmed against their hold. "I tried to call you, Colonel Bakari. I truly did. But I got in late from Dakar. Then when I was put on hold *by your office*, I was cut off, and I had to get the trucks and petrol and—"

"Enough, Baxter." Josef shook his head. "Is what Victor Chavez says true?"

He yanked himself loose and straightened his suit. "It is. They are going to rescue Tori Walters and the rest of the crew."

Josef switched his gaze to Victor. His lips twitched between a smirk, sincerity, and a sneer. Victor imagined what he thought. *This team* was going into Somali pirate territory? Fools, all of them. "Why do I doubt this?"

"I promise they are, sir." Baxter almost danced around the colonel.

Yep, check the Jack Russell box.

Josef scratched his chin. "I do remember your e-mail now. Yet you never followed up."

"I tried, sir." Baxter drooped, and if he'd had a tail, it would have been between his legs.

"It is of no matter." The colonel glanced up and took several file folders and a shipping tube from an aide, who remained nearby. He seated himself at the head of the table, and the chair groaned under his bulk. "Victor Chavez, what do you know about the situation?"

Victor straightened. "The ship's location. Its layout. An estimated number of tangos."

"Yet what happens if they take Tori ashore?"

"We won't let them."

This time, Josef chuckled, and he got the sinking feeling that his knowledge of Abu Waheed far surpassed his own. "You must understand one thing about Abu Waheed. You must not underestimate him. You see, since Kenya borders Somalia to the south, we have concerns about events, especially those related to piracy. Abu Waheed's real name is Musa Waheed. We estimate him to be in his thirties, though his day and year of birth are uncertain. Until about ten years ago, he was a *khat* dealer in Mogadishu, a quite successful dealer."

"What would cause him to change careers?"

"We are uncertain. We think a deal with someone went bad. We know nothing else because the man is so paranoid that if he even senses, for right or wrong, that a person is disloyal to his operations, he kills them."

Not good. Vicious and paranoid made for a deadly combination.

"He's been a pirate for about ten years now. His targets have mainly been small vessels such as yachts and sailboats." Josef laid several photos on the table. "His victims."

Victor stared. He couldn't help it. What lay before him were Before and After photos. Mostly western men and women. The After versions showed them beaten up, many dead. "He ransoms them?"

"Sometimes." Josef's broad shoulders rose and fell in a shrug. "He takes them ashore. The men, he'll usually beat up and kill. He'll keep the women for his own pleasure until he tires of them or the ransoms are paid. Those are the lucky ones."

He placed another stack of photos in front of Victor. "These are the less fortunate."

More women, again western, and this time mostly younger and beautiful. Victor met his gaze. "Less fortunate, as in?"

"They have been sold on the slave market. From pictures I have seen, Tori Walters fits into this category. We have already heard rumblings through our sources that Abu Waheed is interested in selling her if her father does not pay the ransom. And beware if your ladies fall into his clutches."

Sana's wide eyes right before he'd been dragged from the warehouse flashed before him. Then came the image of Anna's tear-streaked face when Makmoud had held them hostage.

Gradually, he became aware of Baxter and Josef in a quiet conversation. The Brit slipped from the room, and the colonel returned his full attention to his guest. When he spoke, his voice rumbled low and gentle, like thunder from a distant storm. "Your intent is noble, and it seems as if you are as prepared as you can be. Though we cannot officially assist you, I can unofficially do so and will." He tapped the other folders and the tube. "This information will help. It is more about Abu Waheed. The mapping is of the town. Strike once if you can."

Victor nodded. That was his intent.

"But do not underestimate him. His men are loyal and ferocious. If they get off the ship, it will be even more dangerous to rescue her." The colonel slid a card to him. "My contact information. Put that number into your phone. It goes straight to my phone, so no worries with having to go through someone else. Anything you need, we will do our best to support. My men will take you to the hangar and escort your team to here. Baxter is moving the yacht so you can load it here with the least amount of suspicion. Now my aide will return you to the hangar."

Stunned, Victor rose and shook his hand. He followed the colonel's aide into the hallway. What had just happened? It had to be a God thing. Whatever it was, he wasn't going to argue.

When he rejoined the team at the hangar, Butch asked, "Did we fall down a rabbit hole or something?"

Victor barely registered the way Suleiman and Skylar had begun loading the weapons crates into a Kenyan army truck. Or the way that Diana and Shelly carried their own equipment.

"Or something." He shook the captain's hand and watched as he joined the small squad of soldiers who would be their escorts. Stranger things had happened, but right then, he knew they had a badly needed ally.

18

The *Waverunner* rode easily over the waves in a gentle rhythm that soothed Suleiman's weary nerves as he entered the spacious lounge behind the bridge of the yacht. China and crystal dishes. Chairs made out of mahogany. Soft beds. What luxury! And perfect for Sana's persona as a high-dollar safecracker. If he closed his eyes for too long, he might fall asleep, especially after the tasty meal of seafood that Victor had prepared for his crew.

Or if he sat on the couch of soft leather. He settled for the floor.

The rest of the team filtered into the lounge. Skylar almost fell onto a love seat. He popped open a can of Coke. Fiona joined him and leaned against him to the point where, if he hadn't been there, she would have oozed onto the floor. Diana took one end of the sofa with a mug of coffee. And Shelly? Nothing but hot chocolate for her. Sana and her cup of tea immediately caught his attention as she curled up on the couch to the right of Shelly. She yawned and rested her head against her best friend's shoulder. Butch leaned against the open doorway separating the bridge from the lounge. He held an over-sized mug of coffee.

Victor eased to the floor beside Suleiman and set a steaming mug of hot chocolate on the corner of the coffee table. "How's everyone doing?"

"What time is it?" Sana raised her head. "Matter of fact, what day is it? I'm so mixed up, I don't even know anymore."

Victor smiled. "You're jet-lagged. It's Monday evening."

Butch added, "And if you stay up until your normal bedtime, you'll get over it a lot quicker."

"He's right." Victor set some folders on the floor underneath the table. "We're not going to get into final preparations until tomorrow morning, so stay up until ten, okay?"

Sana asked, "So what did Josef Stalin tell us? Did he apologize for kicking us around? Literally?"

Her eyes narrowed.

"His name is Josef Bakari, chief of Kenyan army intelligence and their Special Forces." He laid a map tube beside him. "Seems that he's well-versed in the likes of Somali pirates."

Skylar nodded. "Seeing that he's got to have Kenya's best interests at heart, he would be."

"Exactly." Victor rose to his knees and pulled something from the tube. When he spread it out, Suleiman saw it was an aerial map of a harbor. Victor secured the corners using his and Suleiman's mugs as well as a couple of paperweights. "I want to show you this. La 'Amal. As you can see, it's a natural harbor with a river running into it on the northern side of town."

"No Hope," Suleiman muttered.

Diana frowned at him. "Huh?"

"It means no hope in Arabic."

Shelly asked, "What kind of town names itself No Hope?"

"Hey, it's Somalia," Butch supplied. "'Nough said."

Victor cast him a glance. "And that's what we're going to have if we don't get this right. Abu Waheed's quarters are here."

With his finger, he tapped what appeared to be a compound with a dock running into the murky harbor. The river passed on the far side of the villa from the town.

Fiona stared at him. "And does this Colonel Bakari have eyes on Abu Waheed?"

Victor lifted a folder and set it on the table. "He does but not on the inside. Seems that our pirate friend is incredibly paranoid to the point that if he senses the faintest disloyalty—real or imagined—he kills the person. His real name is Musa Waheed, but he's been going by Abu Waheed ever since he began dealing *khat* in Mogadishu." Victor held up a picture. "This is what he looks like. Memorize his face."

Suleiman studied it. Dark, dark skin. Aquiline features that hinted of a heritage from the mix of African and Middle Eastern trade routes of that part of the world. Maybe the ladies would have called him handsome. He called him dangerous. Even on paper, Abu Waheed's dark eyes bored into his. And they were going to allow Sana to get close to him? No. They couldn't. His gut tightened.

Victor laid a few photos on the table. "This is what happens if ransom isn't paid."

Shelly and Diana gasped at the pictures of women beaten to death or with throats slit. Fiona remained unmoved, and Sana stared at her boss. "If you're trying to scare me from doing this, it's not working."

"No, I wanted to show you why we need to strike once and only once." Victor shifted to a more comfortable position. "Chances are good that if we fail, he'll take Tori and the others ashore, which will make our job a lot harder. And word has it that he's already seeking a buyer for Tori."

Skylar frowned. "Meaning he doesn't intend to accept the ransom."

Victor shrugged. "We can't be sure."

They began debating Abu Waheed's intentions. Suleiman stared at the pictures of the women. His mentor hadn't said as much, but he knew what had happened to those unfortunate souls. Most likely rape. He'd watched Tori's ransom video as they'd traveled to Kenya. The same thing had probably befallen her.

His gaze swung to Sana. He drank in every detail, from the way her dark eyes flashed as they talked to the gentle swing of her hair as she leaned forward and gestured at the map. He loved her so much. So very much. How could he let her go right into the jaws of danger? He couldn't. No, he wouldn't. He jumped to his feet. "We can't do this."

"What?" Victor cocked his head. "I'm not sure I follow."

"We can't send Sana in there. He'll—"

"Excuse me, but that's the plan. Our only plan." Sana shot upright and glared at him.

"But if he gets his hands on you—"

"What? I can take care—"

"It's too dangerous." His heart hammered like an out-of-control kick drum.

"You don't think I can handle it?" She threw visual daggers at him as the color drained from her face.

"I—"

"Gee, thanks for the vote of confidence." She stumbled back a step. "I was chosen for a reason, and I can handle him."

"Sana, please. Don't go." Who cared if he begged?

She reeled as if he'd struck her. Her mouth opened, but no sound came out. With a small cry, she spun away and slammed through the door leading to the stern deck. Awkward silence filled the room.

Skylar smirked.

Shock rippled across Shelly's, Diana's, and Fiona's faces.

Butch withdrew onto the bridge.

Victor lowered his head and began gathering the photographs. "Okay, everyone. It's obvious we're not going to get any further. Stay up until ten. We'll reconvene at nine tomorrow morning."

Suleiman barely noticed the way everyone drifted from the room, save for Butch and Victor.

They conversed in the doorway leading to the bridge.

He bowed his head and closed his eyes. Thanks to his exhaustion, dizziness assailed him. Or was it something else? He shoved his hands into the pockets of his cargo pants as he thought about that one. He'd hurt her, might as well have slapped her.

"You love her, don't you?"

His eyes snapped open.

Only Victor remained. He'd shut the door between the bridge and the lounge.

Suleiman's cheeks reddened as he met his mentor's gaze.

It was too much. Suleiman resumed examining the floor. How had he missed the fact that it was polished teak with Oriental rugs scattered over it? "I do."

Victor seated himself on the couch, rolled up the map, and shoved it into the tube. "She's a special lady. I'll give you that."

"And if she goes in there, he'll kill her."

"That's why you, Butch, and Skylar are going with her. Look." Victor set the tube aside. "She's right. This is our only way in. Abu Waheed wanted a safecracker, and Sana fills that bill perfectly. What he won't assume is all of her other skills, like ninjitsu."

Nausea from the coffee, exhaustion, and worry roiled Suleiman's stomach. "Even that won't save her if he takes her as his hostage."

Victor nodded. "Agreed. But think about something. Why did Gary recruit all of us for Shadow Box?"

Suleiman thought back to two years before when Victor's friend had visited him with an offer he couldn't refuse—work with Shadow Box or look over his shoulder for the rest of his life. "Our specialties."

"I'll grant you that. But what else? What did we learn during our training?"

What had Victor stressed during those initial days of training? "How to work together as a team."

"Yes, but there's more. Think about it."

"We can think on our feet."

"Exactly." Victor leaned forward and rested his elbows on his knees as he focused on his protégé. "And Sana, more than anyone else I know, is very adept at that. If she hadn't been able to do so, I'd not be standing here right now. Also, she's gutsy. She wouldn't have competed at the Olympic level in gymnastics if she wasn't. So trust in her and her abilities. And remember that you three will be right there with her, all right?"

He had no choice but to do what Victor asked.

Victor clapped him on the shoulder. "I think you've got some fences to mend. See you later?"

Suleiman gave up trying to understand his slang. He nodded. He needed to apologize to Sana. And keep in mind Victor's wisdom. Because if he broke character once they were aboard the *Peacemaker*, Tori might not be the only one who would need rescuing.

Monday June 29, 2015, 2030 hours local time, off the coast of Kenya

A smoke. Suleiman needed one before approaching Sana. Nicotine always soothed his nerves. More than that, he needed advice on what to do when he hurt someone he loved, especially since for the past hour, he hadn't been able to come up with any ideas. Maybe Butch would have some.

When he opened the door between the lounge and bridge, darkness enveloped him. Perfect for his mood. He stepped inside and gazed out the window. To the east, lightning flickered. The radio crackled with a warning from the Kenyan coast guard about storms a few miles off the coast. A soft glow emanated from the controls and reflected off Shelly's glasses as she chatted with Butch.

Great. He'd wanted to talk with Butch alone.

"Hey, Suleiman." The big man smiled at him. "Come to catch the view?"

"Something like that." Automatically, his gaze slid forward to the prow. A small form sat hunched close to it.

Sana.

His heart caught.

"Looks like you need to give her a bit of grace and trust her." Butch pulled out a cigarette, cupped his hands around it, and lit it.

Shelly said something too low for Suleiman to hear, and Butch chuckled.

Was she talking about him? Suleiman folded his arms across his chest as he considered his friend's statement. "Grace. What do you say it is? Either of you?"

Shelly slid onto the captain's chair. "Are you talking in terms of a believer?"

"That's what you are, aren't you?" Oh, he hated the way he'd adapted a combative tone!

She fell silent, then spoke so softly that he barely heard her above the hum of the engines. "Grace is knowing that Christ died for my sins, that no matter how badly I mess up, I'm forgiven. When He looks at me, God sees Christ instead of me. Christ is there interceding before God on my behalf."

"How long have you been…a believer?" That sounded strange to him.

"Since as long as I remember."

How could she even conceive of the depths to which he'd fallen? "So you don't know what it's like to need grace."

"I think we all do, Suleiman," Butch moved closer to Shelly as if protecting her. "Being a child of God doesn't mean we're sinless. It just means that we know how badly we need a savior. We're messed up, and we know it. Sounds like we need a man-to-man talk."

"That's my cue." Shelly hopped off the chair. "I'll be reading belowdecks."

With that, she brushed by him without another word.

Suleiman hunched his shoulders as he stared at the floor. He'd hurt Sana. Now he could add Shelly to that list. Who was next? Fiona? No, she'd beat him up before she'd let him hurt her. He fumbled in his shirt pocket for a cigarette and pulled one from his pack.

"You need a light?"

Suleiman nodded. A flame sprang forth from a silver lighter with a skull engraved in black on the side. He inhaled, then blew out a stream. "Thank you."

"Anytime." Butch resumed his position at the controls. "So. Grace. We all need it. Vic. Shelly. Sana. You. Me. All of us, even Deb, though I consider her to be a saint at times.'"

"What is your story?"

"Mine? Who says I have one?"

"Butch!"

"Sorry. Just pulling your leg."

"Stop with the slang, will you?" Immediately, shame slammed into Suleiman as one more bad work piled onto his dung heap. "I—I'm sorry."

"No offense taken. Long story short, I know what heavenly grace is, and I know what earthly grace is. Earthly grace is when a judge takes pity on a poor, teen-aged boy who beat the snot out of someone and expressed sincere enough regret that the judge offered to wipe his slate clean so long as he went into the Army and learned discipline. Heavenly grace comes from the way the victim came forward and forgave the teen-aged boy when, by all rights and purposes, he could have hated him for the rest of his life. You know why he did? Because he knew Christ had forgiven him for his own sins."

Suleiman stared at him. "Is that... what happened to you?"

For a moment, Butch didn't say anything as he took a long drag from his cigarette. He blew a stream of smoke through his nose. "She's quite a lady."

Suleiman got the hint. And playing dumb might work. "Who?"

He chuckled. "Oh, I think you know. I've been watching her for the past hour or so."

Suleiman peered through the windows. On the bow, almost on the prow, Sana remained hunched. A lump filled his throat. He gripped the cigarette tighter, took another breath, and began coughing. Curse smoking.

"Ashtray's there." Butch nodded to a small glass dish next to the controls.

Suleiman jabbed his out.

"She's got you tied up in knots. Now I ain't the brightest person out there, but even I can tell you're crazy for her."

"Have you ever been in love?"

"A long time ago."

"What happened?"

Butch took another long drag. He let the cigarette hang to his side. "Guess you could say I let her slip through my fingers."

Again, his reticence told Suleiman not to press him any further.

"So if you love her like I think you do, go and clear the air."

Forget a smoke. Butch was right. They needed to talk. With a deep breath, Suleiman stepped onto the walkway outside the bridge and descended to the deck. He slipped around the hot tub and the chaises beside it.

Sana uncurled from her tuck and leaned back on her hands. As if sensing his presence, she turned her head.

"Before I scare you, I'm here," Suleiman softly called.

She faced forward. "What? Have you come out here to chastise me more?"

Uh, huh. Lots of work remained to earn her forgiveness. He crept forward and settled beside her. "No. I...I wanted to apologize to you. I doubted you where I should not have. Forgive me."

She remained silent.

He began thinking about what groveling might entail.

Then, almost too quietly to be heard above the waves slapping against the prow of the yacht, she murmured, "I forgive you."

At her almost instantaneous reaction, relief filled him. He released the breath he hadn't realized he'd been holding.

For several minutes, they remained shoulder to shoulder in comfortable silence.

"When I was in gymnastics, I did some pretty dangerous stuff." Sana drew her knees to her chest and wrapped her arms around them. "I mean, it may not seem like vaulting off a horse or doing aerials on the uneven bars is dangerous, but if I screwed up, I could have killed myself. And even then, I broke my ankle on the vault. It took guts. So did some of the stuff I did when I was a cat burglar." She turned her face toward him. In the gloom, her eyes were like deep, dark pools where he could drown. "But I never felt fear. Just as I don't now."

"This is not a game."

She fell silent at his rebuttal.

His stomach clenched. Had he overstepped?

Then she sighed. "Neither were those two things I did. I don't call rappelling down a fifty story building to the forty-fifth floor to break into a condo an easy thing, but I did it. Or doing a triple flip, double twist a good fifteen to twenty feet in the air during a gymnastics competition. Back then, I thought it was my talents and training that got me through. Now, I understand that God gave me those abilities and that He protected me, even in my foolishness when I was so far from Him. I know He gave me those abilities for a reason, and our mission is one way to utilize those abilities. I have to do this, Suleiman."

She ran her fingers along the deck's wood. He couldn't take her hand. Not yet. Once more, he considered groveling.

"Last year." She clasped her hands and rested her cheek on her knees. "When Makmoud had me in a death grip. I had to take the chance. I had to jab that throwing star into his shoulder. If I didn't, I knew Victor and I would die."

He closed his eyes as that final battle the year before replayed itself. His shout at Makmoud echoed in his ears. And how could he forget that protective anger had overwhelmed him? Finally, he put a name to that anger. Undefined love for Sana. Why else would he have been willing to kill his half-brother?

Suleiman took a chance. Oh, so carefully, he wrapped his arm around her shoulders.

Beneath his fingers, her taut muscles relaxed slightly. She leaned into him. "I'm not saying I wasn't scared. All I'm saying is that I knew that God had given me the abilities I had, and one of those was to adapt quickly. I knew I was where I needed to be."

"And I'm thankful for that. It's one of the traits that drew me to you." He kissed her hair.

She rested her head on his shoulder. "There's one thing that keeps me going in times like this. Peace isn't the absence of danger. It's being in the presence and will of God. If I'm walking in His will, then I know He will protect me as He deems fit."

A lump filled his throat as he considered the implication of her words. "And if He let's you get hurt?"

She turned her head, and he wanted to drown in the peace he found in the dark depths of her eyes. "Then so be it. All I know is that He will be with me. Always."

19

Scuba diving. Not Victor's favorite, even when in clear water like the Caribbean. And at night in the murky, polluted waters of La 'Amal's harbor? Gross, even with the full moon. Oh, joy of his heart. The sooner they got underway, the sooner they'd be out of the water.

He sat on the couch of the darkened lounge of the *Waverunner* and began pulling on his black dive skin. Sana and Skylar remained belowdecks while the rest of the team except for Diana, who stood at the controls, gathered on the stern. He glanced toward the bridge, where only a crack remained between the two rooms. "Are we facing them?"

"We are," Diana confirmed.

He zipped up the front of the skin and headed onto the stern deck. Victor glanced over his shoulder. The *Peacemaker* stayed at anchor approximately five hundred yards off the bow of the yacht. Even from that distance, the blue stripe running the length of the hull and red cross on the bow stood out in stark relief against the white paint, as did its name.

"Hey, boss, we're over here," Butch softly called.

After zipping up his booties, he joined Fiona, Butch, and Suleiman on the low pool deck. "Time to rumble."

Shelly, who sat on her knees nearby, asked, "If he's so intent on the five hundred million, why does he even want to get into the safe?"

Butch chuckled. "Once pirate, always a pirate. Safes for pirates are like catnip to cats. He's gotta know, so we gotta go."

He crouched in a black pair of cargo pants and T-shirt of the same color. A checkered shemagh hung around his neck, reminding Victor of one of the missions they'd run together.

Butch had stolen into the camp. Using his disguise, which had included a shemagh, he'd infiltrated the insurgents' hideout and secured it without a shot being fired. Now, his friend grinned as he nudged Shelly.

"Arrggh." She rolled her eyes.

Victor cringed as he gazed at the black water.

"I could do this," Butch said.

"Nah. They'd beat me up and take my lunch money. You? You look like a bodyguard. Not so sure about Suleiman, though." Victor mock-punched his sniper.

A quick smile flitted across Suleiman's features. "I can stand tall when needed."

Victor chuckled. Gallows humor always helped. "Fi, you ready to go?"

She maintained her game face. "Let's get it over with so I can get back here and take a bath in disinfectant."

"Your tank, m'lady." Butch helped her into the buoyancy control device that would double as a tactical vest. He turned the knob on the tank. "Check your air."

She did so. "Good to go."

Victor did the same. He swiveled and gained another visual on the *Peacemaker's* anchor chain. Perfect. The heading remained true to the one he'd taken earlier.

Suleiman verified that air flowed from Victor's tank. Then the two divers did one last inspection. Victor pulled down his mask and hung his feet into the water. "Let's do it."

The two of them slid into its warm murkiness with barely a splash.

Butch handed a waterproof bag containing some of their weapons to Fiona. The MP5 submachine gun would remain strapped to their chests by a retractable line. "Diana's watching for you. As soon as you give the all clear, we'll head over in the Zodiac."

"Will do. See you onboard." With that, Victor stuffed the regulator into his mouth and gave the thumbs down, an indication for them to descend, to Fiona.

The water closed over his head and filled his ears as he began sinking. He equalized pressure until they were forty feet down, a perfect depth to cruise to their location. Water transmits sound easily, and he picked up every creak and groan coming from the *Peacemaker's* anchor chain. The whoosh of his respiration into the rebreather filled his head as the darkness surrounded and disoriented him. He turned his head and cringed. Where was Fiona? There! He noted the faint glow of the chem sticks attached to her tank. A tiny bit of relief filled him.

Time to focus. He turned until he picked up the heading that would take them to the *Peacemaker*. He began kicking. When they'd rehearsed in the pool at the ranch, he'd figured out the distance one cycle took him. Five hundred kicks would take them to the chain. He glanced to his left. Fiona kept the bag close to her and matched him almost stroke for stroke as he counted down using a clicker.

At last, he paused and hung motionless in the water. No chain. Not good. Not good at all. Had he taken them in the wrong direction? He couldn't have because navigation worked the same underwater as it did on land. If he couldn't find the chain, he'd have to surface. That could lead to disaster. His respiration shallowed. *Chill down.* Anna's teasing advice echoed in his ears. Doing so would head off an oxygen deficit. He turned his head from side to side, then looked upward.

Illuminated by the full moon, the chain stretched above him like a thin snake on a pale green background. They'd overshot by ten or so feet. Big deal. They'd arrived, which was all that counted. At least he had. Where was Fiona?

She bumped him and pointed to the chain.

No problem there. He couldn't wait to get out of the water.

Creeping hand over hand up rusty links longer than his forearm, they made their way toward the surface, all the while making sure they let out enough air from their vests to avoid popping up prematurely.

Victor eased his head above the water. Only a small breeze stirred up tiny waves and a smell he tried to place. Rotting seaweed. Yuck. It floated all around him in slimy strands along with strands of something else. Jellyfish. He cringed as the clear, cup-like creatures floated near him and intermingled with the seaweed. The sooner they got out of the water, the better.

The hull of the *Peacemaker* loomed over them. No one stood at the railing as a hostile greeting party. He spat out his regulator, and Fiona released his tank. He did the same with hers and secured both with a Velcro strap to the chain for Diana to pick up later.

She handed him a tranquilizer gun, which he attached alongside his MP5 to a retractable line on his chest. His Beretta went into a thigh holster. After one last check, he began the long climb up the chain. *Careful. One step at a time. Don't rush, or you could fall off. And wouldn't that be nice?* No, not nice at all. A splash would be like knocking over a fire ant nest and stomping on it.

Fiona kept close behind.

Each link brought him closer to safety and danger at the same time. Safety because they'd be off the chain. Danger because the next part of the rescue would begin. If someone did show up, he'd be in a precarious situation to shoot. *Lord, it's You and me. Make us invisible to the pirates.*

They reached the opening where the chain passed into its housing on the prow. A huge winch took up most of the room. Undoubtedly, when the ship was sailing, the chain took up almost all of the space. Now, they had barely enough space to maneuver.

He clicked on his red light penlight. There it was. A ladder with a horizontal hatch leading to the deck. Mercy Medical Missions had indicated that the door could be opened either from the inside or the outside. A point in their favor.

Fiona joined him.

"You ready?" he whispered.

"Ready as I'll ever be." Her grip tightened on her tranquilizer gun.

Victor nodded. He put on his headset and adjusted the small boom so it hung in front of his lips. "One and Seven are in. Send in Three."

20

Tuesday, June 30, 2015, 1900 hours local time, La 'Amal, Somalia

Abu Waheed paced along the width of the bridge. He peered through the windows toward a sunset that sent purple hues into a sky rapidly fading to black. Off their port side, a yacht bobbed on the waves. One owned by Norman Walters? Or this safecracker? In his transmission, the billionaire had hinted that the safecracker was the best in the business. Maybe he was if the yacht were any indication.

He turned to Wasim. "When did he say he would arrive? Where is he?"

Using a pair of binoculars, his lieutenant peered through the windows. "They are approaching in a raft."

Abu Waheed joined him. He tingled all over. Suddenly jittery, he wished for some *khat* to wipe out his sudden burst of nerves. He'd get some—after he saw what was in the safe. "Bring him to the bridge."

Without a word, Wasim handed him the binoculars and headed downward.

Abu Waheed's heart pounded. He tried to focus on something—anything—but his mind jumped from the safe, to the hostages, to the doctor, and back to the safe. He wiped suddenly sweaty palms on his pants.

The elevator whirred. A moment later, the door opened, revealing Wasim, two of his guards, and four people. Wait. Four? What? He tried to approach. A hulking bald man with a checkered shemagh around his neck glared at him. He bulled him away. "You stay back."

Abu Waheed clenched his fists. "Who are you?"

The man, easily half a meter taller than he, replied by forcing him back a few more steps.

A man in a business suit followed.

Then he saw her. A small woman in a black jumpsuit. A *hijab* of sheer black and adorned with diamonds covered her hair.

Warmth rushed through him. His mouth moistened, and he licked his lips. Who was she?

The last person, another bodyguard, it seemed, joined them. Something burned in the dark depths of his eyes. A warning. Do not touch this woman. Abu Waheed sneered. Who held the upper hand here?

He turned to the businessman. "Are you my safecracker?"

The man, his blond hair perhaps signaling he was German, smiled and shook his head. "No, sir," he drawled in English with a strange accent he'd never heard before. "Just the business manager. The name's Skylar James. I represent her."

He nodded in the direction of the woman.

A woman doing such a job? Impossible! "You lie."

"No, sir. I never lie."

Abu Waheed stared at her. "You? *You* are a safecracker?"

Her gaze stayed on his face. She even lifted her chin as if challenging him to doubt her. Normally, he would have slapped her for such a gesture. He couldn't, not with her bodyguards standing next to her.

The shorter one stepped to her side.

All too easily, he read the controlled fury in the young man's eyes. Anger battled with sudden lust.

"Mr. Walters said you needed my expert services. My name is Sana." An almost musical lilt. Indian, perhaps?

"How do I know you are a safecracker?"

"I thought you might wonder. Skylar, show him my work."

"Yes, ma'am." The manager opened a slim portfolio and pulled out a sheet of paper. He handed it to him.

160

Abu Waheed stared at it. It had pictures and type that was meaningless since he'd never learned to read. "Wasim, tell me what this says."

His lieutenant recited a list of her accomplishments. Impressive. Especially the last one, a diamond heist in 2014.

He lifted his chin. "You have not worked in over a year."

She shrugged. "One must go to ground on occasion, yes?"

"How do I know this is true?"

"I have no reason to lie to you."

"I have doubt."

The woman's eyes narrowed. She took a step forward. Even though she was a few centimeters shorter than he, her presence filled the bridge. "Why?"

"You, a woman—"

"Who is very good at her job." She came even closer. "Mr. Waheed, you must understand one thing. I took a great risk exposing myself. I could have stayed where I was, hidden away in my own little paradise. Instead, when Mr. Walters spread word that he would pay handsomely for this venture, I decided to risk my own life—"

He snorted.

"You think I do not?" She jabbed a finger into his shoulder. "Those ships out there." She jerked her head toward the starboard window. A South African frigate and several American ships were clearly visible just beyond the mouth of the harbor. "They know I am here and let me pass. Why? They know they can capture me, so I leave at my own peril. Only a sincere person would come to your aid. It is your decision. Utilize my services, or I leave. You have three seconds to decide."

"I—"

"Three... two..."

"Come with me. The safe is one level below." He gestured for her to precede him to the spiral staircase.

"Not without my guards."

Her nerve! "You try my patience."

She got into his face once more and forced him to take a step back. "And you, mine. They come with me, or I do no work. The same with my business manager."

Greed overcame caution. "This way."

He led her downstairs and pointed to the safe that had remained exposed. "It is there. My men will stay here with you."

Sana stepped forward and began examining the safe. Jasmine and peppermint filled his nose. He devoured her with his gaze as a plan formed in his mind. "Wasim."

"Yes?" Wasim stepped to his side.

"Let them get into the safe," Abu Waheed murmured in Somali. "Then kill her manager and the bodyguards. I will have her. She will not leave the *Peacemaker* alive without me."

Wasim nodded. "As you wish."

Abu Waheed returned to the bridge and settled in the captain's chair to wait. He inhaled. Even now, he smelled that tantalizing scent of the woman. His palms moistened.

He'd have her.

One way or the other.

Her and the doctor.

The jitters returned. He rose and headed down the outside stairs until he reached the main deck. Then he stepped inside and took the stairs down one level. Getting his fill of the doctor would suffice for now.

Tuesday, June 30, 2015, 1910 hours local time, La 'Amal, Somalia

Suleiman fought a smile as Sana rolled her eyes at Abu Waheed's retreating back. Her lip curled in the smallest of sneers. She tapped the man Abu Waheed had called Wasim on the shoulder. "This safe will take no time. You may leave now."

"We stay here."

"Then step back. I must have quiet to work."

Wasim didn't budge an inch.

Butch took care of that. He put a hand on the man's shoulder. "The lady says she needs room to work."

No movement.

Suleiman joined Butch. This time, the pirate shifted, as did the other two guards who remained.

"That's all she needs. Give her room to work." Butch retreated slightly as if to show no hard feelings. Suleiman did the same and glanced at Sana, who knelt in front of the safe.

She said, "I need my bag, Skylar."

"What?" Skylar edged closer.

"My *bag*." She snapped her fingers. "Now."

"Yes, ma'am." Skylar placed a duffel at her feet.

Suleiman muffled his smirk. Inside lay the tools of her trade with canisters of the knockout gas that Diana had prepared at the ranch on the bottom. Sana caught his eye. A slow smile played about her lips. So this must have been what she looked like when preparing for a routine on the balance beam. Cagey. Confident. Like she knew she was in total control.

Out of sight of the pirates, Suleiman reached into his pocket and felt the reassuring shape of the nose clip Diana had given each of them.

"Just one moment." Sana fiddled with a cannister.

Suleiman cast a long look at Skylar, then Butch.

"Ma'am, do you have everything you need?" Skylar asked as if he were the attentive business manager rather than a comrade confirming they were ready for the next step.

"I do." She fiddled with the can. Hissing erupted from it.

Suleiman took a deep breath and held it.

As if surprised, Sana dropped it onto the floor.

Within seconds, the colorless, odorless gas filled the room. All three pirates collapsed. She tossed small pony bottles of air to Butch, Skylar, and Suleiman. Once he slid the clip over his nose, Suleiman inserted it. She handed him the other cannister, and he crept up the spiral staircase. With a quick flick of his wrist, he opened the valve, pushed upward, and rolled it along the floor before ducking down.

Thuds told him all he needed to know. Success. He rejoined the group. The windows hung open to dissipate the gas. Butch knelt beside Wasim and secured his hands and feet with cable ties. He slapped a piece of duct tape over his mouth. Good. Everything was secure below. But up top?

Suleiman drew his pistol. Gun held at ready, he crept up the stairs and swept around him. Two men lay unconscious on the floor. Perfect. He came all the way up and looped cable ties around their wrists and ankles before turning on a fan at the open starboard door to increase the breeze through the bridge. Butch gagged them and got the fan going on the other side. Almost immediately, the cross breeze picked up.

Stepping partially through the open door, Suleiman removed his pony bottle and took a deep breath of fresh air.

"Good job, man," Butch called from where he stood. "Problem is, no Abu Waheed."

Skylar joined him. "Right before we headed down, I saw him leaving, probably to go belowdecks."

Suleiman nodded. "Where's Sana?"

"She's coming up." Butch grinned. "And there she is. The diva."

Sana did a mock bow but didn't move toward the doors. She reached up to remove her pony bottle.

Skylar shouted, "Sana, no!"

She took a breath and smiled. "I try to…"

Her words dribbled away, and she fainted to the deck.

Shoving his pony bottle back into his mouth, Suleiman rushed forward and dragged her toward the port door where the others stood. He dumped it. "Sana! Sana! Wake up!"

He shook her shoulder.

Nothing.

He fumbled for a pulse, then hung his head in relief. Out cold.

Butch crouched beside her. "It must still be a little thick in the middle. Man, we needed her. She's going to be out for the duration." He stared down Suleiman. "Get going."

Suleiman shook his head. "I can't leave her. We're still in danger, and—"

"And so are Vic and Fi. Get going 'cause they need you on overwatch." Butch jerked his head in the direction of the ladder that ran upward along the side toward a modern-day version of a crow's nest. "I've got her."

Could he trust anyone else with her? He had to. "You'll protect her?"

"Like she's my sister, because she is in a way. Go now." Into the boom mike in front of his lips, he murmured, "Three is down for the count."

Victor's reply blurred in Suleiman's head. He swallowed hard. Fiona and Victor counted on his protection. Butch would take care of Sana because the team had each other's backs. But still… He shouldered his backpack. With one last, long look at her still form, he began the climb upward. Once up top, he assembled the rifle. "Two is ready."

"Copy that," Victor said over the comms. "One and Seven are making their move."

Tuesday, June 30, 2015, 1915 hours local time, La 'Amal, Somalia

Sweat dribbled from Victor's hairline and down his neck. It trickled down his face and his body, which added to that overheated feeling that came from staying in a sauna for too long. Any more waiting, and they would have been in serious trouble. Now he lowered his night-vision goggles. "Two, are we good?"

Suleiman's reply crackled slightly. "Good to move."

He crept up the ladder and carefully worked the lever for the door. Hinges that must not have been oiled in years groaned as if a monster had been wounded. He winced and raised the top enough to slip into the blessed coolness of a ninety-degree night. Crouching behind one of the air intake structures, he recalled the deck's layout in his mind. Three air intake structures aligned in a row. Two horizontal hatches for emergency escapes sat off those structures by about three feet.

"Chatter's on the radio," Butch reported. "Someone heard you."

Uh, oh. Company so soon? Victor chambered a tranquilizer dart and double-checked his MP5. Beside him, Fiona did the same. At a crouch, he shifted and peered around the corner.

On the green haze of his screen, an apparition of a guard with rifle raised approached. Victor leveled the tranq gun and fired. His quarry collapsed. As he slumped to the deck, his finger squeezed the trigger. A shot blasted through the air.

Victor flinched and ducked. The bullet cracked overhead.

Great. That one shot would surely bring out the rest of the pirates. Another pirate shouted a warning and charged toward him.

Victor bolted forward and slammed against the next air intake housing. "Two, I need an assist."

Suleiman answered with his own shot. Its report echoed through the night air.

Victor's adversary collapsed.

Fiona joined him at the housing, and he raced to the first horizontal hatch. No give. Someone must have locked it from the inside.

More bullets flew toward them. Victor fired a brief burst from his MP5 and dove against the third housing. They were split up since Fiona remained pinned against the other one ten feet away. "Two, some help here."

"No dice." Butch swore over the radio. "They got him pinned down. He pokes his head up, he's toast."

Victor's mind scrambled for a solution. "Fi, we toss our flash bangs on my count. Three... two... one!" He raised his NVGs and tossed the grenade toward the sound of footsteps. Brilliant light and a boom echoed across the harbor. Using the temporary distraction, he bolted to the second hatch and yanked. Success. "Fi!"

Bullets pinged against the metal.

"Got it. Go on!" She unleashed her own fusillade and dashed toward him.

Victor crept downward. The hatch clanked shut, and she joined him.

He listened. Like agitated crows, two pirates chattered away in high-pitched Somali. Tori had to be nearby. Otherwise, they could have used one guard per hall. Victor slid a mirror from his vest and extended it into the hallway. Two toward the bow. He shifted the other direction. A third stood at midships and ignored his comrades. His mind whirled. He needed to come up with a plan. Fast.

The hatch rattled.

Fiona nudged him.

He nodded as it began opening.

Like it or not, someone else was joining the party.

She shoved a dart between her teeth for quick reloading and raised her tranq gun.

Victor did the same with his to back her up.

One pirate stepped into the gloom. He lowered the hatch.

She fired.

The pirate tumbled down the stairs.

He slammed into her.

She stumbled against Victor, and his tranq gun fired uselessly into the wall.

The voices in the hallway ceased. Someone called out a question in Somali.

Uh, oh.

Heart pounding, Victor remained still. His hand shot to where a couple of more flash bangs hung from his waist. Except now, his foes were too close. Toss one, and he and Fiona would wind up moaning on the floor as well.

Footsteps approached. His attacker said something in a singsong taunt.

Victor pressed his body against the wall. *Closer. Come closer.* He caught Fiona's eye, and she pointed to the dart still between her teeth. Instantly, he knew what she wanted. He'd have only one shot at this.

A boot appeared.

Like a snake, he struck by grabbing his foe and dragging him into the alcove. Fiona jabbed the dart she held into the man's chest. The fast-acting tranquilizer did its job, but not before the he bellowed a warning.

Using the wall opposite the opening as leverage, Victor shot into the hall, delivered a short burst from his MP5 toward midships, and propelled himself into the alcove. "I got enough to make the midships guy get his head down. I think the other one ducked into Tori's cabin."

"So we're still stuck." Fiona muttered something. "Maybe we both come out at once."

"We'd be too exposed."

"Yeah, but—"

"Eight has cleared level two, and I'm coming your way," Skylar murmured. "Where are you?"

"Bow emergency staircase closer to midships," Victor replied. "One tango at midships."

"Roger that. Just hang on."

A moment later, the rat-a-tat of an submachine gun on short burst and thump told Victor what he needed to know. The remaining pirate in the hall was down. He peeked outside. Deserted save for Skylar now in the central area. His procurement officer gave a thumbs up.

"Let's go, Fi." Victor brought up his MP5. Keeping the gun at ready, he began the final advance toward Tori's cabin.

21

Tori cowered on her bed in a set of scrubs and faced the wall. Behind her, Abu Waheed argued with one of his men. She didn't care. Not when her insides ached from his latest assault. Her heart too.

A week had passed since the hijacking. Five days since he'd dragged her into the little chamber of horrors that once had been her sanctuary. Would her father pay the ransom? Or would she remain as a hostage forever? She tried not to think about the latter. Having done so already, she realized how it would make the tears come with depression not far behind it.

She had to be strong, be brave.

Then there was the matter of her captor's buddy joining them. The two bickered in low, urgent tones.

A pop resounded above her. She raised her head from the pillow. Running footsteps and another noise that sounded like gunfire lifted her faltering spirits.

Rescue had to be imminent.

She pulled the thin sheet tighter around her.

"Get up."

Abu Waheed. Again.

She ignored him.

"Get up, woman!" He seized her arm and yanked her so hard that she fell from the narrow bed onto the floor.

She pushed herself upright and stared at him.

He towered above her in a tactical vest with bandoleers of bullets draping across his shoulders and grenades hanging from his belt. He hauled her to her feet. "I say now, I mean now!"

He shoved her toward his pal, a man so tall and thin that she called him Stick. He caught her and slammed her into the wall. "No move!"

"No!" Tori screamed. If rescue were near, she wanted them to know exactly where she was.

Abu Waheed grabbed her and spun her around. He drew back his hand and slapped her—hard. Pain burned across her jaw and momentarily stole her vision. She moaned as her knees gave way.

Stick's firm hands steadied her.

She forced her eyes open.

Watery red eyes blazing with anger, Abu Waheed grabbed her wrists. "No defying me!"

"I will!" She kicked. Thrashed. Pulled against Stick. All to no avail.

Her tormentor lashed her wrists with cord. Her fingers curled into claws.

She could still fight him.

He yanked one of the orbs from his belt. Before she could utter a word, he shoved it into her hands, pulled the pin, and tossed it away.

She gasped. No. Not… "A grenade?"

Abu Waheed smirked. "You hold handle down, you live. You let go, boom!"

He laughed as if he didn't care that he'd die as well.

Rescue is so close! I don't want to die. I don't. She tightened her fingers around it like she cradled an egg made of the finest porcelain.

Abu Waheed grabbed her so his right arm pinned her arms to her sides. With his left hand, he brandished a long knife before her eyes.

Oh, no. She gawked at the serrated edge on one side and smooth edge on the other. She allowed herself only one guess as to the origins of the dark stains in the dull steel. Her head spun.

"You struggle, you die, too," he hissed as he brought it to her throat. He snapped something in Somali.

Stick opened the door.

They stepped into the hall.

Tori's heart leapt as she stared at the man and woman in front of the second emergency staircase. Dressed all in black, both brandished guns. Surely Abu Waheed couldn't break through that. Within a few minutes, she'd be a free woman.

If she kept the grenade's handle down.

She tightened her grip even further around it.

"Stay back," Abu Waheed hissed.

Tori swallowed hard. Surely they could take care of the pirate. She cried, "Shoot him!"

As punishment, a burning line etched its way along her throat.

"Do not come any closer," Abu Waheed leaned into her and forced her forward a few steps. "If you do, I will cut her throat, and we will all die because of the grenade in her hands."

Not if she could help it. Her hands began aching.

"Let her go, Abu Waheed." Rivulets of sweat ran down the man's face. Anger sparked in his dark eyes. "It's over. We have control of the ship now."

"You step back." Abu Waheed shoved her forward another couple of steps.

The man and woman remained still. The woman raised her gun and squinted as if taking aim.

"Drop him. Please drop him," Tori begged again. She wheezed when his arm tightened around her chest. He rewarded her by jerking the knife. The burning increased.

"Lower your gun, woman." Abu Waheed took another step forward.

Stickiness trickled down Tori's neck.

"You give her to us," the man said.

"Save me. Save me," Tori tried to shout. Parched lips and fear reduced her cry to a faint whisper.

The man held his ground. "You let her go, and we'll let you walk."

Abu Waheed shoved her forward again so they came even with the nearest emergency staircase.

The burning widened, and Tori flinched. Her grip on the grenade lessened slightly.

He snatched it out of her hands.

"No!" she cried. This wasn't supposed to happen. She was supposed to be rescued.

He tossed it toward her rescuers before bodily lifting her off her feet and into the alcove.

"Grenade!" the man shouted.

Stick charged ahead of them and released the hatch.

Abu Waheed bounded up the stairs. Pain added on pain as her feet banged against each tread.

A massive explosion shattered the air and deafened her. The walls trembled. She couldn't breathe.

He threw her onto the deck.

Moaning, Tori lay there. She tried to move. Her limbs only twitched. It was as if the explosion had disconnected her brain from her body.

She stared at Stick—or two Sticks.

As if in a time-delayed exposure, he raised his radio to his lips. His words, surely shouts, remained garbled.

Her rescuers had most likely died in the explosion. Numbness filled her. She rolled onto her back and closed her eyes.

Hands grabbed her under her arms and hauled her upward.

Abu Waheed.

Wouldn't he leave her be?

He shoved her toward the railing on the starboard side. She slammed into the metal, which knocked the wind from her. Gasping for breath, she stared at the unfolding scene before her.

A small speedboat had pulled up to the side. Its engine rumbled as it pressed close to the *Peacemaker's* hull.

No. This couldn't be. She was supposed to be rescued. Tori sagged against the railing as her head spun.

Abu Waheed shouted something at her.

She couldn't understand him, not with her hearing damaged.

He struck her across the cheek.

She cried out. "I don't understand!"

"Jump down. Now!"

Had she heard him right? "Wh—what?"

Another vicious slap answered her question. "Go!"

"I—I can't!"

Abu Waheed grabbed her and heaved her over the railing. Before she realized what had happened, she plummeted through the air. Her legs pinwheeled, and she somehow landed upright.

She tumbled forward from her momentum.

A bench rushed at her.

Pain exploded in her head as she collided with it.

Tori dropped into blackness.

Tuesday, June 30, 2015, 1925 hours local time, La 'Amal, Somalia

"Grenade!" Victor shouted.

The deadly orb rolled toward them.

Victor didn't have time to think.

Only act.

He grabbed Fiona and shoved her into the alcove.

Like some sort of evil Weeble, the grenade wobbled into view.

Still holding firmly to her, Victor threw them toward the stairs. They tripped over the unconscious pirates.

As if in slow motion, they dropped into empty space.

An explosion ripped the air.

Victor twisted to protect Fiona.

Stair treads bit into his back.

Sparks popped in his vision as his head rapped against one of them.

He slammed into a wall with Fiona against him.

Stunned, he moaned and sagged to the side.

Someone shook him.

He opened his eyes to find Fiona on her knees in front of him. Disoriented, he blinked.

"Vic!" she shouted as she touched his face. "Are you okay?"

Through the ringing in his ears, her words came across as horribly garbled.

"I'm—I'm fine." He groaned as he pushed himself to a sitting position. Alarms began blaring.

Fiona grunted as she hauled him upright. "We still have a chance. C'mon!"

Victor staggered upward with her. Somehow, they made it past the mangled alcove and pushed up the stairs. He found his comms unit around his neck and returned it to its proper place. He couldn't hear anything. Had his tumble damaged it? Even with the volume dialed all the way up, Butch's frantic calls remained a whisper.

"We're fine, Five," Victor reported to Butch.

"You're shouting."

"What?"

"You're shouting!"

"Hearing issues."

"We've got fires on level one near you. Wait! Good news. The crew's spilling out of their cabins to take care of it."

Victor charged through the hatch.

A bullet zinged by his head.

On the starboard side, Abu Waheed tossed Tori over the railing.

A tall, skinny pirate fired at them again.

With Fiona beside him, Victor dove for cover behind an air intake housing. He popped up and released a burst from his MP5 before it clicked. Empty.

The skinny pirate hung over the railing with blood pooling beneath him. But no Abu Waheed.

Victor rushed to the railing just in time to see the speedboat pull away. "Two, I need you!"

"I cannot, One," Suleiman reported from up top. "They are bouncing too much. I miss, and I could kill her or blow up the boat or sink it."

"No!" Victor shouted in frustration. He staggered to the air intake and kicked the wall. "Five, I need a sit rep."

"You saw the speedboat," Butch reported. "Two and I tried to stop them, but no go. They pinned him down in the crow's nest and me on the bridge."

Silence fell.

"Five?" Victor braced his hands on his knees. "You good up there? Talk to me."

"Down, boss. Sorry. Forgot you can't hear well right now. We've got the helmsman and first officer, a Commander Ching."

"Get us out of here. Now. When we get clear, Four and Six, I'll need you to join us. Some of the *Peacemaker* crew can take the *Waverunner*."

"Roger that," Diana replied.

"And, Five, get one of the crew to contact the Navy. Tell them the *Peacemaker* is secure."

Butch's calm reply reassured him. "Wilco. See you in a jiff."

"Why, God?" Victor sagged to his knees, put his elbows on the housing, and rested his face in his hands. His head pounded, and nausea nipped at his stomach. They'd rescued all of the hostages unharmed. All except for the one who mattered the most to his client—Tori. A great, long sigh escaped him as he tried to imagine Norm's reaction.

A bell clattered. Beneath him, the deck shuddered as the engines started. The chain for the anchor began clanking. Even before the winch finished its job, the ship surged forward in a wide, slow turn to port.

At the feel of a hand on his arm, he opened his eyes.

Fiona sat on the housing next to him. In the dim glow now coming from the dining room and the bridge, her eyes glimmered. Unshed tears, maybe? "Vic, I'm sorry. If I'd had time..."

She swiped a hand across her face.

He pushed himself upright and eased down beside her. "No. If we'd stayed on that landing, we'd have been shredded. We did what we had to do."

"But it wasn't enough." She muttered something and lowered her gaze.

"I'm not stopping." The turn had brought the starboard side parallel with the shoreline. Victor stared at La 'Amal, more precisely at the structure he knew to be Abu Waheed's villa. He snatched a small pair of binoculars off his vest and focused.

The speedboat pulled up to a dock. Two people carried the inert form of a woman ashore. Had they already killed her? No. Tori was worthless to the pirate dead. But alive?

He lowered the binocs and set his jaw. "This isn't over. Not by a long shot. Not until the last hostage is safe." He fixed Fiona in his gaze. When she nodded, he continued, "We'll go back. Regroup. Then we'll strike with so much force that they won't know what hit them."

With that, he rose and trudged toward the stairs leading to the bridge.

Tuesday, June 30, 2015, 2030 hours local time, La 'Amal, Somalia

Suleiman remained in his position until they passed into open water. The ship picked up speed, then slowed as the *Waverunner* drew close.

Sana.

Where was she? Certainly not on the radio. She must have revived by now.

Fearful for her condition, he packed his gun in the backpack, slung it over his shoulders, and scurried down the ladder as fast as he safely could.

He burst onto the bridge. Only three of the *Peacemaker's* crew and Butch occupied it.

"Where's Sana?" he demanded.

"Downstairs. Hey, the boss wants us on deck at the bow," Butch added when he made to bolt toward the spiral staircase leading to the captain's quarters.

Suleiman hesitated.

In a surprisingly graceful move for a big man, Butch slid across the floor and blocked his way. "Would it help if I said she's fine and wants to be alone as she cracks that safe?"

"But she is well?"

"More embarrassed than anything. So leave her be. Can you do that?"

What could he say?

Sana wanted to be alone.

He'd cede to her wishes. With a sigh, he nodded. "Is everyone else there?"

"Everyone but you and me. I was waiting on you, so let's go." Butch led the way onto the outside walkway and down three levels to the deck.

Someone must have supplied camp chairs because everyone sagged on them or the nearest air intake structure in various stages of battered exhaustion. Only Skylar and Shelly seemed none the worse for the adventure. Diana's brow wrinkled as she tapped something on her Panasonic Tough Book. Butch yawned and eased onto a chair, which groaned under his bulk. Fiona had some swelling and a small cut on her forehead. Victor slouched on the air intake housing and winced as he pressed an ice pack to the back of his head.

Though banged up, they'd survived.

Suleiman settled on the deck with his back to the housing.

"Sir, excuse me." A woman and her colleague, both dressed in scrubs, approached with bottled water in their hands. Behind them, Commander Ching, the acting captain of the ship, carried two duffels.

Victor offered a polite, weary smile. "Yes?"

"Mr. Addison said you all could use some water," the blonde added in an Australian accent as they handed over the bottles.

Suleiman popped the lid on his and savored its chilliness.

With a small bow, Commander Ching set the duffels on the deck next to Butch. "These are Tori's belongings, at least her clothing and some books, for her to use. The rest we will send to her parents' house when we reach Cape Town."

Would it make a difference? Suleiman blinked. He hadn't missed the way the commander had referred to Tori as if he fully expected her to return. He held onto hope that she'd be rescued. Shouldn't the team?

Commander Ching added, "And I want to thank you for rescuing us." He swallowed hard. "And…"

Emotion choked his voice. He lowered his head.

"Bring her back," the blonde urged.

"We will." Victor rose and extended his hand to the commander. As they shook, he added, "We will. I'll join you in a few minutes, Commander Ching."

The trio turned and retreated.

Where was Sana? Should it have taken as long as it had? Suleiman tensed to rise when she practically materialized from the darkness. Her downcast expression summarized the collective feelings of the group.

"I'm sorry." Her voice barely carried above the noise of the ship cutting through the water.

Suleiman asked, "What did you find?"

"Maybe ten thousand max in valuables. I left those with the commander. Her passport." She extended that to Victor, who took it and slid it into the front pocket of a fresh shirt. "It also had all of their emergency contact info."

Skylar muttered, "Which was really the most valuable."

Sana slid downward so she huddled next to Suleiman. She rested her head against the housing. "What's going to happen? Colonel Bakari said we had to get it right the first time."

Victor remained silent for a moment. Slowly, he drew a breath. "Sana, when you were training for Team USA and you took a tumble, what did you do?"

"Get up and do it again until I got it right."

"Exactly. You didn't let it stop you. You kept at it until you succeeded." He fixed each person in his gaze. The determination flashing from those dark depths startled Suleiman. "And that's what we're going to do here. Sure, Abu Waheed and his goons got the best of us, but we freed almost three hundred people, right?"

She nodded. "So then why do I feel like we failed?"

"Because one is still out there. The one who matters the most to our client. And we're going to get her back. But right now, we need to return to Mombasa and regroup."

Shelly asked, "What if they take her away?"

"I talked with Colonel Bakari a few minutes ago and let him know we have the *Peacemaker* but not Tori. He has ears on the ground in La 'Amal. He promised to let me know anything he hears. In the meantime, we need to get some rest, see what new information we have, and formulate a plan. Not to mention, we got five pirates alive, including Abu Waheed's second-in-command. Which means we can get some great intelligence and possibly a hostage trade."

"If we stay on this ship, it'll take overnight to get there," Shelly said.

Victor rose and stretched. "The Kenyans have sent two speedboats toward us, one to pick up the captured pirates and one to take us to Mombasa. They'll be here in twenty minutes. So take a few minutes to rest. We'll meet up downstairs at 2100 hours. I'm going to talk with Commander Ching."

With that, Victor trudged toward the bridge.

Everyone nodded, but no one else moved.

Sana shifted so her shoulder touched Suleiman's. On the deck, out of sight of the rest of their comrades, her fingers sought out his.

Suleiman took her hand. *I love you,* he told her in his heart. He didn't dare voice those thoughts aloud, not in front of everyone else. Right then, it was enough to know that Sana was safe.

Finally, Butch stirred. "Let's move out, gang."

Slowly, Suleiman climbed to his feet. He didn't want to let go of Sana's hand, but he didn't want to reveal his relationship to the others. As he released her, a sad smile rippled across her face.

Despite the success of rescuing the other hostages, he chalked the night up to a failure. With his own silent vow to rescue Tori, he followed the others toward midships.

22

Wednesday, July 1, 2015, 0100 hours local time, Mombasa, Kenya

"Sir, I promise we're doing everything that we can to get to Tori," Victor said as he stood in front of a web cam above a huge monitor hanging from one wall. They now resided in the same room where Josef had brought him upon their arrival in Mombasa. His jaw ached from clenching it, and his head pounded from his ride down the stairs during the rescue.

Now this.

How many times had they been over the same ground in twenty minutes?

Norm's face had reddened, and he glared at them through the monitor that linked them back to his secure location in Flagstaff. "You let them escape! How could you? And you know what happened? The pirates say I broke faith with them by ordering the rescue. So now all deals are off."

Let them? Really? *Calm. Keep calm. Don't escalate.* He took a deep breath. "Sir, with all due respect, he had a knife to her throat and had put a grenade in her hands. Which he grabbed and tossed toward us." Victor shook his head. Even that simple motion sent a wave of pain through his skull. "We were lucky we weren't killed. I confirmed that they took her ashore to his villa, and Colonel Bakari has eyes on it as we speak. We're retooling as we get new information."

Norm slammed his fist onto the desk where he sat. "I don't care! You lost her. That's all that matters. And now, I'm never going to see her again." He muttered something unintelligible. "That's it. I'm done with this. I'm asking President Badin to deploy the SEALs."

Double the staying calm part. Victor put his hands on his hips and began pacing . "Sir, with all due respect, the SEALs do not have a working relationship with Kenyan intelligence. We do. I don't consider our mission complete, and I'm going to—"

"You'll stand down."

"You'll lose too much critical time if you rely only on the SEALs. It'll take time to get them activated even if they're in the area. And they don't have the intelligence we do." He left out the fact that the team's intelligence actually consisted of members of Abu Waheed's crew. The SEALs could figure that out later. "Let us continue."

"I'm coming over—" Norm stopped in mid-sentence. He turned away and conversed in hushed tones with a woman. His wife, Elizabeth, most likely, if the faint strains of a southern drawl wafting across the speakers meant anything. Finally, he faced them again. The stormy clouds had calmed to a steely gray. "All right, then. You win. You stay on the job. But I'm still calling President Badin and asking him to deploy the SEALs since this is now *strictly an American matter.*"

He emphasized those words as if it was all their fault that Abu Waheed had held a knife to Tori's throat.

"I understand."

Without another word, the big screen went blank. Victor took a deep breath. He turned away from the monitor and faced his team. Butch and Skylar stared at each other. A small smile curled Butch's lips, and he wondered if they already collaborated. Suleiman seemed deep in thought as if he too had ideas on how to proceed. Fiona put her head in her arms. Diana gazed at him with concerned eyes. Most likely, she worried that his very mild concussion had worsened. So what? He couldn't stop now. Shelly fiddled with something on her laptop. And Sana?

Anger blazed from those dark depths. She punched to her feet. "He doesn't understand that we almost lost our lives. And what about the other hostages? Don't they mean anything? I mean, seriously! I'm ready to go back in now and—"

"Sana, have a seat."

"Vic—"

He lowered his voice into an order. "Sit down."

Though she opened her mouth to object, she obeyed.

"I want to discuss this rationally." He bowed his head and rubbed the back. Ouch. The lump was the size of a small egg and tender. He needed to stop touching it. "I have some ideas, but the first thing we need to do is interrogate Wasim. Colonel Bakari reported that he's Abu Waheed's second-in-command. Guys, stick around for a bit. Ladies, go ahead and get some rest."

"I'm staying," Sana said.

"You need to rest."

She rolled her eyes. "Why? Because I'm a girl? No, I don't. I'm staying."

What had gotten into her? Victor stared at her for a long moment. "All right, then. You stay. The rest of you, grab some shuteye."

Fiona muttered, "You won't get any argument from me." She rose. "C'mon, Diana. I need my beauty sleep."

Once the other three had filed from the room, Butch asked, "What's the plan, boss?"

"We have two tasks. Skylar, find Colonel Bakari and see if he can provide us with some good, solid mapping of the southern part of Somalia as well as other info that could help us infiltrate. The rest of us will have a chat with Wasim." He focused on Suleiman. "I want you to take the lead on this."

"Me?" Suleiman gaped at him. "What do you say, Butch? I don't have any super powers?"

"You're probably the only one who speaks Arabic," Butch said.

"You both do." Suleiman's gaze darted between his leader and deputy.

Victor nodded. "Passably."

"I speak it, but my accent's horrible," Butch said in Arabic.

"Ugh." Suleiman grimaced. "What was that accent? It sounded like cats being murdered."

Butch chuckled. "That would be Arabic with a Cajun accent. So, you see, you're the one who speaks it both fluently and beautifully."

"I did not know beautiful was a requirement." The sniper sighed. "What do I say?"

"You'll figure it out." Butch winked. "Right, boss?"

"The most obvious would be what Abu Waheed has planned for Tori," Victor said. "Then run with it from there." He clapped his comrade on the shoulder. "I know you can do this." He shifted his gaze to the safecracker. "And Sana, you stay here. Got it?"

"I—"

"You're staying here." He narrowed his eyes in anticipation of a challenge from her.

"Whatever," she muttered. She folded her arms and pouted.

"And Suleiman, don't worry. We'll be right there with you. Let's go." Victor led the way into the hallway. Hopefully, within an hour they'd have the answers they needed so badly.

Wednesday, July 1, 2015, 0130 hours local time, Mombasa, Kenya

Suleiman's mind spun as he pondered his options. If he didn't ask the right questions, he'd not find out enough for them to formulate a plan. And no plan meant no rescue. Maybe Victor was right. Ask a couple of questions and go from there.

They slowed at a metal doorway guarded by two Kenyan Special Forces soldiers. One of them nodded, unlocked it, and opened it for them.

The darkened room with a single bulb over a table reminded Suleiman of a crime drama. At first he nearly gagged from the smell, the iron tang of blood mixed with feces and something else. That wasn't something the crime dramas portrayed. And even though it had to be close to ninety degrees outside, a distinct clamminess clung to him. Before he realized it, he shivered. The door clanged shut behind them. He cast a glance at Victor, who gestured for him to proceed to the table.

Wasim slouched on one side with his hands manacled to a bar on top. As if challenging them to get the information they craved, he stared at the new arrivals through deadened eyes. If the cut above his right eye that oozed blood meant anything, Colonel Bakari had failed in that task. This would not be easy. Not at all.

Time to act. Suleiman studied him as he made his final approach. Channeling his inner television detective, he pulled out a chair from the opposite side, turned it around, and straddled it. Almost in slow motion, he withdrew his cigarette pack from his shirt pocket. He shook one out with studied precision. Faint boredom meets interrogator.

Wasim's sullen gaze vanished. He focused on the white stick.

In Arabic, Suleiman asked, "You smoke?"

"Who doesn't?" Wasim replied. "Who are you with your Arabic?"

"Someone who has a vested interest in Tori Walters." Where had that come from? He extended his pack to Wasim. "You want one?"

Wasim eagerly snatched his own. He rested his elbows on the table. "I do not understand. Abu Waheed wanted a safecracker."

"Which we were able to supply." Suleiman flicked his lighter and lit the prisoner's cigarette. He puffed on his own as he let him ponder his latest statement.

Wasim took a drag. His brow furrowed, and his dark eyes narrowed as if he tried to figure out Suleiman's true identity.

Some bluffing would probably help. "You do realize that all of your comrades we captured have confessed. They sang like birds."

"They would." Wasim sneered. "They had nothing to lose."

And by his statement, he did. A smirk curled Suleiman's lips. "I imagine the opposite is true for you."

The pirate had begun lifting the cigarette to his lips for another puff. His hand shook as he took one. "H—how did you know?"

"Your comrades told us. In exchange for leniency, of course. Perhaps they won't look down the barrel of a gun now."

Like an abused dog, Wasim jerked back so hard that his manacles slammed to their fullest length. "Wait! I—I know you."

Suleiman's heart raced. How would he? He'd never seen the man before in his life. "You know me?"

"Eleven years ago, when Abu Waheed was in Mogadishu. I was with him then. He sold *khat*, you know."

He remembered that Victor had included that tidbit in his briefing on the pirate. Perhaps it could be of use later. "Continue."

"You were there when we kidnapped two of your men." Wasim eagerly puffed away.

Behind Suleiman, Victor shifted. Maybe this could be something that would lead them to a way to rescue Tori. How could Suleiman string it out of their prisoner? He'd carry this act on as long as needed. He leaned against the chair. Mind spinning, he took a lazy drag and blew a stream of smoke toward the light. It dispersed over his prisoner, who hacked. "You act surprised."

"Why would Hezbollah work with a government?"

What? *Hezbollah?* As in the group in which his half-brothers were embedded? How had Abu Waheed come into contact with them?

"Who says we are? It was an act for the Kenyans." A slow smile spread across Suleiman's face. "Think about it. What better way to get someone to trust you than to act like saviors, yes? Now refresh my memory. Eleven years was a long time ago."

"You were there to recruit men for your cell. Except that one of Abu Waheed's men left to join you. He murdered two of your guards. Then you exacted retribution on Abu Waheed. You kidnapped one of his dealers and a lieutenant in broad daylight. You eviscerated them and left them at the gates of his compound as a warning to leave town and the *khat* business."

"I see." Time. He needed time to process this. Again, the question as to how Wasim assumed they were Hezbollah crossed his mind. Then it hit him.

Members of that group came from all backgrounds, even those who'd been recruited from inside Iran. It wasn't difficult to assume that Victor, with his Japanese, Filipino, and Navajo heritage, could be mistaken for a member. Or Butch with his African American, Native American, and Caucasian background. Oh, how he wished he could turn to Victor for guidance! He couldn't, not without blowing his cover—or revealing his true relationship with Makmoud. He focused on his cigarette. "You see this, Wasim?"

"The cigarette, yes."

Suleiman rose. He walked toward their prisoner. With a grand gesture, he tossed it onto the concrete, stomped on it, and ground it into the floor until it joined the other ravages of interrogation. "That is what we do to liars. If you do not tell me the truth, you will die like your comrades so long ago. Understand?"

Wasim's eyes had widened until they gleamed under the dim light. "I promise I will help you so long as you don't harm me or let me be with the Kenyans."

Victor stepped forward and handed Suleiman a digital recorder.

He placed it on the table before him and hit Record. "Then talk. Now."

Wasim did. As Suleiman guided him with questions, he told them all about Abu Waheed's compound, the number of men there, where Abu Waheed's quarters were and where he would most likely keep Tori. And yes, he planned to sell Tori to the highest bidder since all ransom deals were off the table, which would pretty much ensure she'd disappear forever.

Suleiman's mind churned. Did that get them closer to a plan? Perhaps. Victor would know better than he about how to utilize the information they'd collected. He reached to cut off the recorder.

"There's something else," Wasim said.

"Oh?" Suleiman cocked an eyebrow. "What?"

"Abu Waheed has one major weakness."

"You would further betray your leader?"

"He will kill me anyway once he discovers I confessed." Wasim rested his head against his fists. He met his gaze. "But I want a deal."

"A deal." Suleiman tapped his chin as if pondering such a proposal.

"You let me join your Hezbollah cell. And I will tell you his primary weakness."

"I will consider it."

"Then no deal."

"Perhaps you could join us." Suleiman's eyes narrowed. So the man had a backbone. Not that it mattered. Right then, obtaining as much information as possible was what mattered. "Then tell me."

"You will let me join?"

"If it is in my power." How was that for a non-answer?

Wasim grinned, revealing teeth badly in need of a dentist. "He is terrified of Hezbollah, especially you. For weeks after you kidnapped and killed his men, he had nightmares."

"I see." Suleiman rose.

"Please! I helped you. Now help me," Wasim begged. "Let me join you."

Suleiman stepped to the door and turned. "Not such a good idea. But we will put in a good word with the Kenyans. Perhaps they will let you go."

Wasim's shout barely reached him as the guards shut and locked the door. His mind spun with ideas. Dangerous ones, but it might be the only way in.

Victor summed it up for him. "Hezbollah, eh? We need to think on this one."

"Boss, are you thinking what I'm thinking?" Giddiness almost overtook Butch's recently somber countenance.

"Maybe." Victor cast him a glance. "C'mon. Sounds like we've got a bit of planning to do."

Wednesday, July 1, 2015, 0300 hours local time, Mombasa, Kenya

The men plus Sana huddled around the conference table with an aerial map of the compound between them. They'd listened to the recording of the interrogation enough to glean the information they needed. In an hour and a half, that information gave birth to what would be the final push to save Tori.

Hope rose in Suleiman. It was risky and would call upon all of the skills of each team member, but it would work. Most likely. He tried not to think of the consequences if it didn't.

Victor winced and rubbed his temples. "I think that does it."

Sana straightened from her spot beside Butch. "Not quite."

"What is it?" Victor asked.

She lifted her chin. "Abu Waheed needs to die."

Victor stared at her. He blinked as if he had a hard time processing what she'd said. "No, he doesn't. That's not the objective of the mission. The objective is—"

"I know. I know. To get Tori back. I get that." She scowled. "But after what he did to her? I'm no dummy. You don't have to dance around the fact that he's raped her, probably repeatedly."

Victor swiped his hands through his hair. It stood up in spikes. "I know what you're saying. I'm angry too. But our stated objective does not include assassination. You know that. I know that."

She folded her arms across her chest. "It's not fair."

Butch sat back and laced his hands behind his head. His biceps bulged against the sleeves of his T-shirt, which rode up to reveal part of his dragon tattoo. "You ever hear of poetic justice?" He scratched his goatee. "Sometimes, you let nature take its course. You'd be surprised at the way God works. He deals out justice in His own time. Not our time."

"I don't need a Sunday School lesson." Sana pushed to her feet and backed away from the table.

"Sugar, I'm not offering that. Just some unsolicited wisdom."

"Which I also don't need." She shoved her chair under the table so hard that wood met wood with a loud crack. "Since my opinions obviously don't matter, I'm headed to bed. Good night."

"What's gotten into that girl?" Skylar asked. At least he hadn't inflamed the situation by calling her little lady.

"I don't know." Victor grimaced and resumed rubbing his temples. "Hey, could one of you scare us up some water? And maybe a cup of coffee for me? I need to pop some more ibuprofen. And also see if Colonel Bakari has any last words of wisdom. Then we'll go over this plan one last time before catching some rack time."

"Sure, boss." Butch hopped up. "I'll find the vittles. Skylar, you find the colonel."

Both men made their escape.

Victor fell silent for a few seconds before asking, "Do you know what's gotten into Sana?"

Seeing the ransom video. Being gassed. Abu Waheed's escape. Suleiman had watched the anger building slowly in the woman he loved. Now, it threatened to boil over. "I think knowing what happened to Tori upset her. Sana is a very just person, and it galls her that Abu Waheed is getting away with it, at least in her eyes."

"Finishing the mission means getting Tori out. No more."

"I agree. But she does not see it that way." A yawn forced its way loose as they fell into a companionable silence. Maybe it was his exhaustion or the most recent topic of their conversation, but his mind wandered straight to Sana. And then to Rachel before finally resting on what he'd done. Why?

"May I ask you a question?" The words popped out of his mouth before he realized it.

"Certainly." Victor leaned back in his chair.

"What…what does grace mean to you?"

As if taken aback, Victor cocked his head. "That's an interesting question. Why do you want to know?"

Suleiman's cheeks flushed as he realized his potential blunder. His weary brain scrambled for an answer. "I…I have been talking with Sana." Oh, no. He'd dug his hole even deeper. "She brought it up, and we started talking about it."

"I guess you could say that I started understanding it in 2014. I still remember that spring. It was that trip I took right before Makmoud ambushed us." The corners of his mouth turned downward as if he'd conjured up bad memories. "I'd been so focused on finding out the truth about Rachel that it was like I'd made her an idol in my mind. Deb called me on it, but I was so bull-headed that I ignored her."

"But how did grace work in that?"

"Grace came into play when, that night as I realized that I'd probably never know the truth, I had to ask God's forgiveness for clinging to that quest for so long." He sighed and ran his fingers along the grain of the table. "That led to a long list of sins throughout my life. All I know is that when I asked for forgiveness and let Christ be Lord of my life, I felt a peace I totally didn't understand, like I'd been absolved of all of the sins I'd committed."

"Absolved?"

"Forgiven. Made free from guilt."

Suleiman thought about that one. He opened his mouth to ask Victor about what he'd learned regarding Rachel—at least until he noticed a deep sadness in his eyes. His mind darted in all directions, and he blurted, "How fiercely did you love Rachel?"

Chills washed over him, and he wanted to rescind his question. Not that he could without raising his mentor's suspicions.

Victor bowed his head and winced. When he met his gaze, those dark depths spoke of the tragedy that had befallen him three years before. "At the time, she was my life. When she died, I thought I'd lost my reason for living. Somehow, I stumbled through each day. But when Gary recruited me to lead Shadow Box," he paused, "it gave me new purpose. Even now, there are still days when I fiercely miss Rachel. We'd been looking forward to a life together, maybe even one that had children." He lowered his gaze to his left hand, where he twisted a platinum band on his finger. "Deb says that God takes those griefs in our lives and uses them for good, to glorify Himself. I have to agree. I miss Rach, but God gave me Deborah—and salvation."

Nausea once more stirred in Suleiman's gut. He tried to tell himself it was from his weariness rather than the confirmation he'd received. And why had he asked him? Was he going to confess? He was crazy. Not in the middle of the mission! How foolish could he be?

"Is this about you and Sana?" Victor asked.

Grabbing his out, Suleiman replied, "I love her. Love her so much. I just... wanted to know..."

His courage waned.

The door banged open, admitting Butch, Skylar, and the colonel.

Butch held three mugs of coffee, Skylar three bottles of water.

The colonel followed. Exhaustion and worry added more depth to his weary face.

"This can't be good," Victor said as they settled at the table.

"It is not." Josef tossed a folder onto the table in front of Victor. "We just received some intelligence you may want to consider. From where and from whom, I'm not at liberty to say."

Victor flipped open the folder. He drew in a sharp breath. "Makmoud Hidari is en route for Tori?"

Suleiman's heart sank, then pounded with new fear. His half-brother was coming for her. "But…why?"

Colonel Bakari shrugged. "My source did not know. Perhaps he is buying for someone? Who remains a mystery. Or perhaps for himself. Regardless, my source saw him in Nairobi. He slipped away before we could get enough of a lock on his location to take him into custody. But my source got close enough to learn the purpose of his visit."

"This is not good," Victor muttered.

Butch grinned. "Maybe it is, boss."

Suleiman scowled at him. "You mystify me at times."

"You don't remember?" Butch leaned forward. "Because our buddy Wasim obviously thought for some reason Hezbollah was coming back, why not capitalize on that? We've probably got what, a day's start, on Makmoud and his pals?"

Colonel Bakari nodded. "If you move quickly, yes."

"Then let's make the most of it."

Suddenly, it all clicked into place for Suleiman. He had to draw them away from questions about his relationship to Makmoud. "Wasim mistook me for Makmoud? Impossible!"

"Nope. Not impossible." Butch shook his head. "You do look somewhat similar, and you're right."

Too right. Suleiman cringed. "But I was fourteen then."

"So? You still look like a youngin' to me." Butch chuckled. "I say we run with it. Go in like a Hezbollah cell. Make the announcement that we're here for the girl. And get Tori out before the real Makmoud carries out the deal and she disappears for good."

"Agreed." Victor refocused on the aerial and pulled over another map, this one satellite imagery of the southern part of the country. "Let's adjust and move out in the morning."

Wednesday, July 1, 2015, 0400 hours local time, Mombasa, Kenya

Suleiman's insides quivered when he realized how close he'd come to confessing to Victor about his role in Rachel's death—and his relationship with Makmoud. What was he? A fool? Mama's advice from when he'd been a boy popped into his head.

"We have two ears and one mouth for a reason. Listen twice as much as you talk, and you'll avoid foolishness."

Like he'd done that tonight. Hah!

Sana. Since she was the only one who knew his secrets, he had to confess. Where was she? He made his way to the top story of Special Forces Headquarters where the colonel had shown them several rooms and a bathroom for their use. Sana had drawn the short straw of sleeping in a room that was so small it was almost a hot and stuffy closet. Nope. No Sana.

A staircase at the end of the hall led upward. Most likely, she'd slipped up there. He tiptoed upwards and found her lying on top of her sleeping bag. Dressed in a tank top and leggings, she lay on her back with her hands laced behind her head as she gazed at the stars.

She shifted her gaze to him. "If you're coming to ask me why I've lost my mind, I haven't. I'm perfectly sane."

"That is not why I came."

"You couldn't sleep?"

"No."

"Me neither. Too much adrenaline or something." She sighed and sat up. "What about you?"

"We just finished planning the mission. We head out at nine for the airport." He settled beside her as he considered his next words. "I…I almost confessed to Victor."

"What?" She blinked.

"I almost told him what I did three years ago. It was like…like I had this spirit on my shoulder, urging me on. Perhaps an evil spirit?"

"Try the Holy Spirit," she murmured. She snuggled next to him so their shoulders touched.

He reveled in her nearness. "But now is not the time. Not when we're going to La 'Amal."

"I know." She fell silent. "What were your thoughts?"

"About my near confession?"

"Not that, but now that you mention it—"

"He would kill me." Suleiman shuddered. "When she died, he lost his purpose for living." He scooted past everything else Victor had said. "I can't now, not when we need everyone to be at—how do you say it—the top of their game."

"You're right." She sighed. "Now isn't the time or the place. But what I originally meant was what your thoughts were on the mission."

"Victor is right. We must hold to our objective."

She pulled back and stared at him. In the moonlight, her dark eyes glimmered like polished onyxes. "How can you say that after what he did to Tori?"

"I know what he did." He hesitated and considered his words with care, lest his send her into the stratosphere "And yes, it angers me just as it angers Victor and everyone else. But if we diverge, are we any better than he?"

She pouted a little. "The man is vile. I don't know how else to describe him."

"I agree. But we need to respect the mission's objective."

They fell silent.

Sana ran her fingers up and down his bare arm.

Warmth shot through him, and the hair raised on his arms and neck.

She turned and faced him head on. As she leaned forward, she said, "I have another question."

"Much less complicated, I hope?" His head spun as she reached out and placed her hand on his arm.

"Maybe." Never breaking her gaze, she lay back and arched her back ever so slightly. With her free hand, she reached up and brushed his cheek. "You haven't shaved."

He stretched out beside her. "Th—that's your question?"

"No, silly." She lifted her chin. "That was an observation."

He propped himself up on his elbow. "Then what was your question?"

She turned her gaze to the sky. "Would you help me take Abu Waheed out?"

Had he heard her right? "Sana, no." He touched her cheek and turned her face toward his. "You heard Victor—"

"I know what he said." Her eyes sparkled with something. As she shifted to close the distance between them, she smiled, almost inviting him to come nearer. "I'm not saying deliberately going out of our way to do so."

"I don't see how—"

"I'm saying that if the opportunity presented itself, would you help me?" Her fingers brushed her throat.

He shivered as every nerve ending stood on edge. His hands moistened. "Sana—"

"Please?"

He swallowed. "I shouldn't—"

"Would you do it for me?" She parted her lips.

His pulse thudded in his ears like a galloping horse. "I…"

She drew him close and kissed him.

Oh… Something akin to electricity arced through his soul.

She put her hand on his chest and pushed him back slightly. They broke contact.

Suleiman trembled. He reached out and ran his hand down her cheek.

She raised her chin, and his fingers drifted to her throat where her pulse beat as quickly as his.

"Please, it would mean the world to me." She licked her lips.

Suddenly, Suleiman would do anything for her, even kill if that was what she wished. He covered her mouth with his, this time with a little more familiarity. When they broke off, his world spun, and he was helpless. "I will. For you, Sana, I will."

23

Time to do it. Now or never. Get Tori back or die trying. Victor put his hands on his hips and faced his team. They sat on folding chairs in a ragged semicircle in the *Kitchen Sink's* hangar. Sleep, though short, had revived them, as did the Kenyan coffee most sipped from stout mugs supplied by Josef Bakari. Like race horses straining to run, they focused on him for the words that would send them into battle.

Behind them stood the twelve Special Forces soldiers, all dressed in plainclothes and shemaghs, who were hand-picked by Josef. Locked on. That's what Victor noted about them as he reached for his clipboard.

"Okay, gang. I'm going to brief you on what we concocted a few hours ago. It's hasty and probably has several holes, but it's the best we could come up with. And this time, we have no second chances because we have knowledge of at least one buyer coming for her." He hesitated as he considered their old foe. "Makmoud Hidari has been confirmed to be heading toward Somalia."

"What?" Fiona gasped. "But...but why?"

Similar questions exploded through the hangar. He raised his hands. "I don't know why. But what I do know is that we now have an in."

Diana frowned. "How?"

"This is how." For the next half hour, he explained the plan they'd fine-tuned until Victor had finally shambled to bed at four. The team asked only a few questions. Everyone knew their roles, all of which would be vital. Finally, he set the clipboard on a chair. "One more thing. I know some of you don't care, but I do want to pray because without God's protection, we're not going to make it through alive."

Surprisingly, no one scoffed at the idea.

Victor took a knee and bowed his head. "Lord, we pray for our work today. We pray for protection. Protect Tori. Encourage her. Protect us during the flight up, the drive in, and while we're on the ground both coming and going. Guard us with Your angels. Amen."

With that, he lifted his head. "Let's move out."

Everyone rose. Chairs scraped along concrete. The team filed up the ramp and squeezed by the Humvees, which now displayed scratches, dings, and scores in the paint, courtesy of the Kenyans, as a disguise for being older. Patina was what Butch had said when he'd first seen them.

Led by the captain who was Josef's aide and commander for this mission, the Kenyans came aboard last and settled as best they could on the remaining seats.

Butch hit a button and the ramp hummed upward, sealing them in almost darkness.

Victor's heart echoed in his ears as Butch settled into the copilot's seat.

Once a tug had pulled them into the open, Fiona started the engines. The *Kitchen Sink* eased from the shadow of the hangar into the bright morning light.

He glanced at Shelly, who'd joined them in the flight engineer's seat. Her eyes were wide but calm as if the Holy Spirit flowed through her. He wondered how the remaining four team members and the Kenyans fared.

Fiona murmured something into her headset. "We're cleared to taxi and take off. I don't know what kind of man Colonel Bakari is, but he seems to have a radical kind of pull."

"Agreed on that," Victor gripped the arms of the navigator's chair.

She guided them onto the runway, and without hesitation, she and Butch pushed the throttles all the way forward. As they had in Arizona, they leaped into the sky.

With almost clipped words, she notified the tower of their departure before turning toward Victor. "It's going to be a really fast trip. A little over an hour."

He stared down at the city rapidly falling behind them. Before them, Somalia yawned with the vast tans and browns of the desert. Butch and Fiona exchanged few words as if they'd worked together long enough to know what to do without speaking.

"Border up ahead," she reported. She hit a switch. The noise of the flaps lowering vibrated through the cockpit. She activated the intercom. "Everyone, we're starting our descent. It's going to get real steep real quick, so buckle up and hold on."

She nodded toward the windshield. "Butch, find me that road we picked out."

"Roger that." Butch peered ahead.

"Crossing the border. Tactical descent starting now." Fiona increased the plane's pitch so they seemed to point almost directly down.

Victor's stomach did a flip as the C-130 imitated the first descent of a roller coaster. He squeezed his eyes closed and gripped his seat. Several prayers for a safe landing bounced around in his head like marbles in a jar.

In front of him, Fiona muttered orders to Butch, and together, they brought the plane in an almost controlled fall toward earth. It flared, and their wheels smacked onto the ground hard enough to keep them from zinging into the air again. Both pilot and copilot stood on the brakes until they groaned to a halt.

"I'm turning us around to face into the headwinds, so tell everyone to hold on." Fiona began hitting switches as they swung around in a tight turn and taxied down the road in an abandoned national park to where they'd landed. "Butch, eyes out for any unfriendlies." She reoriented them for a takeoff and shut down the engines. "Welcome to Somalia."

Without humor, Butch muttered, "Prime tourist destination of Africa. Complete with a pirate town. Yo, ho, ho, and a bottle of rum."

He undid his harness, rose, and squeezed past them into the cargo area.

Victor followed. His legs still quivered from their entrance into Somalia. He eased onto the top step. "How is everyone?"

"Freaked out," Sana reported.

Skylar gave him a thumbs up. "We're good."

The ramp began humming downward, and Victor rose. "Let's get going."

The Kenyan captain snapped orders, and they climbed to their feet as they shouldered their weapons. They exited first and secured the perimeter they would hold until the team returned later that night. Now, their fates truly depended on how the next twelve hours went.

Butch and Skylar released the chains holding the Humvees. With a rattle, they pulled the links free and climbed into the driver's seats. The engines cranked to life, and the Humvees backed down the ramps.

Suleiman joined them, helped secure the guns to their mounts, and added the remaining gear. He began handing out the rifles, bandoleers, and pistols to each team member.

"Butch, take the second Humvee. I'll take the first. Suleiman, you've got shotgun with me. Fi, you're on the gun. Skylar, take the gun on the second. Shelly and Diana, ride with Butch. Sana, with us. Keep your faces covered."

Victor checked everyone over. Each now wore cargo pants, light-weight jackets for sun protection, and T-shirts with shemaghs around their necks. They wound them over their faces, not only as a disguise but to keep the sun and dust out.

"Let's do it."

They climbed aboard. With a roar, they headed toward a destination that would be either their success or their death.

24

Wednesday, July 1, 2015, 1200 hours local time, La 'Amal, Somalia

Suleiman had forgotten how much he hated dust. Despite his wraparound sunglasses and the shemagh around his face, it coated his mouth with a grimy film. He sneezed, then hacked, which drew a look from Victor.

And the heat. The midday sun burned so hot that he'd already sweat through his T-shirt. His jacket too. His thirst raged, but he had to be careful and not drink too much water. Otherwise, he'd run out long before they finished the mission.

Regular lines of the roofs of buildings came into view. It reminded him of the planet Tattooine from the *Star Wars* movie so long ago.

Victor, who drove, slowed.

The buildings grew large enough for him to discern distinct units. Only one had three stories. The others contained no more than two. According to the colonel, Abu Waheed had razed any building greater than two stories so nothing was as tall as his.

The arrogant bastard.

Victor stopped the Humvee.

Swagger. That word shot through Suleiman's mind. As if surveying his impending challenger, he rose, put his hands on the edge of the windshield, and stared at the town. He resumed his seat and nodded to Victor.

At a leisurely pace, they continued. As they reached the edge of town, Victor gunned the engine. They spurted forward. Colonel Bakari had estimated the town to hold a couple of thousand souls. Several seemed to be away, most likely fishing or scraping a menial living from the hard soil. Those who milled around in the heat screeched and scurried from the vehicles like frightened squirrels.

As planned, Victor did a circuit of the town to confirm the layout. It was simple. Three main streets, the one closest to the beach being a sad commercial area consisting of a food market and stalls selling other assorted wares. Five streets plus several alleys ran perpendicular to them. At the northern end of town was Abu Waheed's villa, all three stories of it with a hefty wall for protection.

Victor wheeled to the left to do the backstretch of their trek around town. They passed another villa, this one only two stories and reported to be deserted. It would be their hideout until time to grab Tori and run. In a quiet voice but loud enough to be heard over the engine noise, Victor asked, "Thoughts on our hideout?"

"Steel door. Walls, most likely topped with broken glass. Stairs across the street leading to the top of another building." Suleiman frowned. "But why is it empty?"

"Who knows? Our contact confirmed it was, though. We'll have to take him at his word." Victor whipped them into another turn.

People gave them a wide berth, and they slowed to a stop in front of the villa.

"Your turn, *Makmoud*," Victor said with a wink.

If only you knew, Suleiman almost replied. He choked that back. Now he had to learn to swagger. Quickly. He tried to imagine Skylar working a crowd at his restaurant. The procurement officer may have been many things, but he knew how to do so with the best of them.

With chest thrust out, Suleiman strutted to the door.

He knocked with his fist.

Wimpy, even to his ears. His confidence waned, and he touched the butt of his pistol for comfort.

A small hatch slid open, and a pair of eyes glared at him. "What do you want?"

"I'm here to inquire about the girl," he said in Arabic. He could have sworn his voice squeaked. Some arrogance that was.

"Oh?" The guard laughed. "She is not for sale."

He slammed the hatch shut.

Suleiman needed to try again—and fast. This time, he summoned up images of the time when Makmoud had kidnapped him off the streets of Marseille. When he'd been with Makmoud in that cold cabin of the cargo ship on his way to Venezuela, helpless rage had filled him. Now, anger swooshed through him as he remembered his humiliation.

He yanked out his knife. Flipping it around, he banged on the metal with the hilt end. The clang echoed through that end of town.

No answer.

He did it again and kept at it until the hatch slid open.

The eyes stared at him again. "I told you, the girl is not for sale."

The hatch started sliding closed.

Not this time.

Suleiman jabbed the blade into the slit.

The guard yelped and barely avoided getting his eye poked out.

"That is not what we heard," Suleiman growled. He shifted enough to give him a good look at the comrades he'd brought.

Victor even saluted.

Suleiman narrowed his eyes as channeling his inner Makmoud came easier. "You go tell Abu Waheed, that lying sorry excuse of a human being, that Hezbollah has come to make an offer on the girl. And if he refuses to see us? Then he should start counting his last hours on earth because we will raze this place to the ground and kill all of you—slowly. Now you go and tell him that. I will wait. You have five minutes."

The guard's eyes had widened. He stared at him as if doubting his words.

Suleiman withdrew his knife. "Your five minutes have started."

The hatch screeched shut. Feet scurried away. The guard had fled to find his boss.

Wednesday, July 1, 2015, 1205 hours local time, La 'Amal, Somalia

Abu Waheed hated having his sleep disturbed. Especially by a persistent tapping at his door. He lay sprawled on his stomach on the old mattress of his room. Every part of his body hurt, especially his head. What had he done? Run out of *khat*. He needed more—and fast. He opened his eyes.

"Owwww!" The midday sun nearly blinded him. With a groan, he snapped them closed.

Here came that knocking again. Who dared disturb him? "Go away!"

"Sir, I must speak with you."

Faoud, that annoying pest.

"I said go away," he growled. He rolled onto his back. The ceiling fan whirled above him. Had he turned it on? He couldn't remember. No, it was the whole stinking room that spun. Not good. He needed *khat*. Now. With one elbow, he pushed himself to a sitting position. His head began pounding. He moaned and clamped it between his hands.

"Sir! I must speak—"

"Shut *up!*" Abu Waheed rose. He opened the closet door. On the floor sat the burlap bag of *khat* his dealer had brought earlier that morning when he'd been enjoying his time with the doctor. With shaking hands, he undid the string holding it closed and dug out a handful of green leaves. He stuffed them into his mouth. He began chewing. A drugged calm oozed over him. He spat some green juice onto the floor as a sigh of relief escaped him. So good.

At least until the tapping resumed.

Almost snarling, he flung open the door. Faoud, his new lieutenant, stood there with hand raised. His eyes widened.

Abu Waheed shouted, "What is it that could not wait?"

Faoud cowered. What a fool. "Someone is here about the girl."

Abu Waheed swiped his hand across his nose. He wiped it on his pants. "I am not ready."

"But you did put out the—"

"I know what I did. She is not for sale."

"Ali tried to tell him, but—"

"Not. For. Sale." Abu Waheed ground out those words. His head still hurt. More *khat*. That was what he needed. That and for his drip of a lieutenant to leave him alone. Why had Wasim had the poor grace to get captured? He turned away and pulled on a dirty undershirt.

Shuffling feet told him one thing. Faoud hadn't left.

"Did I not tell you to leave? Go!"

"He is Hezbollah."

That one statement stopped Abu Waheed. Hot anger fled, to be replaced by fear, the kind that threatened to loosen his bowels. "He is what?"

"Hezbollah." Faoud straightened. "He wants to buy the girl and said that if you do not agree to set up a meeting time within…" he checked his watch, "three minutes, they will destroy this villa and kill all of us. Slowly."

Abu Waheed swore under his breath. The stark image from eleven years before of his dealer's entrails hanging out while he delivered that fateful message rushed back at him. His words before the man and his lieutenant died echoed in his ears.

"You must…leave…Mogadishu."

He flinched.

Eleven years before, his own foolishness had nearly gotten the lot of them killed. Only when the Hezbollah man had shown pity on him had they escaped by the thinnest of hairs. Abu Waheed wouldn't make the same mistake again. Not this time. He'd deal with the Hezbollah man on his own terms. Stimulated by the *khat*, his mind began spinning. Planning. Plotting.

"Sir?" Faoud shifted nervously from foot to foot.

"Tell him ten tonight. We will see what he says. Go now."

Faoud almost ran downstairs to escape his leader.

Abu Waheed turned and stared out the french doors. What he really saw were the two men slowly dying before him years before in Mogadishu. He'd been foolish then. He'd not be so now. This time, he'd plan better and not let his temper get the best of him.

Still, his fear remained. He needed to dominate, to chase away that fear of inadequacy. If he listened carefully enough, he thought he heard the doctor's tears. His face flushed as his chest tightened. He'd get his fill. And if the price were right, he'd sell her that night.

With a lift of his chin, he strutted toward the door adjoining the two rooms.

Wednesday, July 1, 2015, 1210 hours local time, La 'Amal, Somalia

Suleiman waited by the door. A scene from *Return of the Jedi* came to mind, one of when Princess Leia, in disguise, had demanded to see Jabba the Hutt. It was almost the same thing. Could have been, all the way from the desert town to the rusty door in front of him. Except for the salty tang of the air.

The hatch screeched open, and a pair of eyes glared at him.

Suleiman asked in Arabic, "You have word for me?"

"Be here at ten tonight. And if you are late? All deals are off." With that, it banged shut.

Suleiman returned to the Humvee and nodded to Victor. "Success on all counts. He agreed to the time of ten o'clock tonight."

"Perfect." Victor nodded. He put the vehicle into gear, and they rumbled away from the coast toward the inland-most street. "Now we set up shop and wait."

They pulled up to the gate of their hideout.

Victor peered at it. "Check to see if it's unlocked."

As he climbed down, Suleiman surveyed the street. When he heard giggling, he paused and turned.

Several young children peered at him from behind adjacent buildings and garbage heaps. Their eyes were wide. From what? Fear? Curiosity?

He pushed on the gate. It shifted slightly, and he leaned into it. With a groan upon hinges that probably hadn't been oiled in years, it opened. The two vehicles pulled inside.

Suleiman peered up and down the street one last time.

The children had run away, their conversation bouncing from wall to wall and rapidly fading.

"Suleiman," Butch softly called. "Get in here so we can button up."

He joined his team.

Butch now had his shemagh around his neck and placed several duffels on the ground. "What did you see?"

"Several children."

"Did you see any adults?" Victor asked. He pulled out a tarp and began securing it in the gap between the two Humvees to provide a modicum of shade.

Suleiman shook his head. "None. It makes me a little suspicious."

"Um, guys, come here," Skylar softly called.

"What is it?" Victor asked as the team joined the procurement officer.

The sun glinting off his blond hair, Skylar led them toward one of the main rooms of the villa. Suddenly, Suleiman realized they'd pulled into the courtyard of what had once been an elegant villa. Now, time and most likely Abu Waheed's dominance had destroyed any semblance of luxurious days of the past.

They approached a living area that opened onto the courtyard. Dust coated the walls, Oriental carpets, and furniture. The gold paint on the crown molding had begun chipping off in the harsh climate.

Suleiman stopped short and gasped. Six bodies littered the area carpets, bodies so decomposed that the only things remaining were tattered clothing over sets of bones. The eye sockets of a skull stared at him as if taunting him for even considering staying there.

Had Abu Waheed murdered them?

He shivered. A hot breeze puffed. Sure, the vultures and worms had finished their work, but the stink of the owners' passing lingered. Death lurked nearby. The shiver turned to a stomach flip.

Skylar summed it up nicely. "If I were superstitious, I'd call it bad juju. I think this is why the place is deserted and why we've seen no adults around. Abu Waheed must have murdered these folks and left them for the vultures."

Butch asked, "Do you think this might have been the lair of a rival group?"

"Maybe." Victor visibly cringed as if he felt the evil emanating from the town. "I hate this place."

"You aren't the only one," Fiona muttered. "Thank goodness we're out of here tonight."

"But hopefully there's enough local lore for people to assume it's haunted." Victor shook himself. "Let's get a move on it."

The team sprang into action. Skylar took a bundle and stepped toward one of the other rooms that hopefully didn't have bodies in it. Butch began laying out mines that would serve as protection at the gates. Shelly began pulling out the communications equipment. Sana also slipped away.

For a few seconds, Suleiman traced her movements with his gaze. But he had his own task. He headed toward one of the staircases leading upward. A second set led toward the roof. At the top, he paused and peered toward Abu Waheed's villa. Not good at all. If the pirate were smart, he would have stationed a sniper of his own on the roof of his third story, which would have offered a perfect tactical position. Using a pair of binoculars, he scanned the villa's roofline.

Nothing. No one had a rifle aimed at him.

Still, he wasn't going to take a chance. And he wasn't going to bake in the sun, either. Butch could help him harden his position.

Just as he reached the bottom of the stairs, Sana stepped into view from between the vehicles. She wore a black jumpsuit that fit her closely like a dive skin. A belt hung from her waist with a thigh holster attached. A pouch on the other side held throwing stars. On both of her biceps and across her chest were knives of various lengths. A black shemagh hung around her neck. Gymnast morphs into ninja in full warrior gear.

Shelly dug into her duffel and extracted several small units with microphones and ear pieces. She approached the small group. "Throat mikes for all."

Suleiman took his.

"What do we have up top?" Victor asked.

Suleiman sighed. "A poor tactical position. Abu Waheed's villa overlooks this one, but he has no sniper posted. Camouflage is our best solution. And I need protection from the sun."

Victor nodded. "Butch can help you with that."

An old man in ragged robes and a turban hobbled into view. His eyes were dark, and his skin was so wrinkled that he could have herded goats all his life in the strong desert sun. He grinned, revealing missing teeth. But when he spoke, the southern drawl betrayed him. "Dang, Sana. You look like the Black Widow."

"And you look like an old man," she retorted. "Staying out in the sun is bad for you, you know."

Skylar laughed as he took his comms unit from Shelly.

Victor gestured for the group to gather around. "Okay, gang. Skylar, you, Diana, Shelly, and Sana have surveillance until sunset. Then Sana infiltrates while the rest of you return. Report back on what you see, especially if anyone else shows up who might be a buyer. Sana then gets inside and sets up our escape route. In the meantime, Suleiman has overwatch with one of us relieving him. Fi, Suleiman, Butch, and I leave here at five 'til ten. Questions?"

No one had any.

"Ladies, get changed. Butch, see if we can't get something together to offer a little shade up top."

Sana stared at the *abaya* Diana extended to her. She heaved such a deep sigh that everyone chuckled. "Do I have to?"

"Sorry, but yes." Victor grinned.

She sighed again.

The women headed toward one of the villa's rooms. When they returned, the only thing differentiating them was their height. What with the pack that Sana wore, she looked like an old, hunch-backed lady. Skylar grinned. In his best redneck accent, he announced, "Well, looky here! I got me three old wives!"

"Shut up!" all three women chorused.

Sana kicked him in the shins.

"Ow!" He grimaced and hopped on one foot.

"Serves you right," Fiona told him. She snickered.

They did a final comms check. Everything worked, and Skylar faced the women. "Okay, ladies, I'm an old, married man. Sana's my first wife, but you all have to act old." He pulled out a cane. "Sana, use this. Just don't hit me with it. And all of you, pull on those gloves that came with the *abayas*. Otherwise, your hands will give away that fact that you're not old."

"I hate this," Sana muttered.

Skylar faced her. "Be glad you don't live here, then."

Images of Sana being compromised in town flew through Suleiman's mind. If that happened, he'd be helpless to provide an assist. Never mind the fact that under everyone's robe, they were well-armed with her topping the list. Their talk from early that morning on the roof in Mombasa came roaring back to him. "Sana, a word."

She stopped. "What? I'm starting to roast in this thing."

What he wanted to say suddenly vanished. What could he say? Stay safe? He nearly laughed. If anyone could handle herself, it was her. Then he sobered. He drew her away from the rest of the group.

Victor raised an eyebrow.

"Please, don't even consider what we talked about on the roof."

"If I see the opportunity—"

"No!" He threw a glance toward the rest of the group. Only Victor continued to gaze at them. Suleiman turned so they faced away from him. In a quiet voice, he continued, "Don't. It is not worth running the risk of capture. I—I've seen enough to know what would happen. So please, don't."

Through the slit in the cloak, she stared at him. Her eyes remained expressionless. Then she nodded. "I'll cede to your wishes."

Would she? He doubted it.

"I need to go."

He caught her hand and squeezed it. "I love you."

This time, her eyes crinkled at the corners. "I love you too."

She joined the rest of the group.

"Suleiman, get going," Victor said.

Without a word, he grabbed the sniper rifle and headed toward the roof with Butch hot on his heels. It took some doing, but they were able to arrange crates, pottery, and other flotsam so they concealed him from Abu Waheed's villa. A camouflage net broke up the sun enough to provide cover. Butch left him with the assurance that Victor would relieve him at dusk.

He completed a scan of the streets. The sun, which was now high in the sky, had chased most people into the shade. In the heat, the town fell quiet. No children played. No noises emanated from the marketplace. Siesta had come. He reported, "It's clear."

Victor's voice filled his ear. "Excellent. Okay, everyone. Let's do it. All, save for Three, be back by sunset. Three, let us know when you make it inside."

The gate creaked open, and three figures in black and one in ragged robes stepped through. For a moment, Suleiman stared in shock. Skylar, the master of disguise, had done it again, this time transforming the four of them into an old man with three old wives. They shuffled down the road. Sana had even gotten the gait of an old, hunch-backed woman down pat. They limped around the corner and out of sight.

He pulled away and took a deep, shaking breath. During his background research on Somalia, he'd seen pictures of the horrid deeds done in Mogadishu nearly twenty-two years before when US Special Operations troops had run afoul of an angry populace. He shuddered and tried not to envision the foursome being discovered by a mob of townspeople. It was too horrible to contemplate, and it stole any semblance of peace from him.

Sana's lilting voice echoed in his ears. "Peace isn't the absence of danger but the presence of God."

Such a statement wouldn't save her if she got into trouble. His hands began trembling. Not good if he needed to take a shot. He lowered his head. "God, please take care of Sana. Please!"

25

Sana hated the *abaya*. Absolutely hated it. How on earth did women in this part of the world tolerate it? She was suffocating. Sweat drenched her jumpsuit, and she wondered if she was getting dehydrated. Even furtive sips from her Camelbak hadn't totally slaked her thirst. At least they'd seen no new activity. Skylar had reported back to base every fifteen minutes as they'd wandered around town and acted like an old, married foursome, all the way down to the bickering between Skylar and Diana in Arabic. Shelly and Sana played the silent, compliant wives.

The sunset call to prayers began. It wailed over the town and reminded her of the times when she'd visited her grandparents in northern India. It'd sounded like a dirge then. It did now. As if triggered by a hypnotic suggestion, people began wandering toward their dwellings.

Skylar murmured to them, "Okay, ladies, time to make like a shadow at dusk and get out of here,"

He took Sana's hand and led her into an alley.

The stench of sewage filled her nose. She gagged.

"Easy there," he whispered. He squeezed her hand.

For once, she was grateful for his comfort.

213

"There's our deserted dwelling." He tugged her toward a rundown building that might have been a shop at some point, at least until the town grew and it became an out-of-the-way place. They slipped inside.

In the gloom, Diana turned to her friend. "Give me your *abaya*."

No problem there. Sana lifted it and ripped it from her head. She shucked her gloves, wadded the whole thing up, and handed it to the team's doctor. She began shivering as her body, so used to what had to be hundred-plus degree heat underneath, adjusted to somewhat milder temperatures in the nineties. She took a long swig of water before wrapping her shemagh around her face.

She peered into the alley. Still not dark enough for her to make her move.

"We're headed out," Skylar murmured into her ear. "You be careful, you hear?"

"No worries on that end. You be careful, too."

With that, the three Shadow Box members passed into the growing gloom.

Finally, she could barely discern the buildings across from her. Time to go. After one last look around, she flitted through the deepening shadows. To the west, the sun gave one last gasp of red before ceding to the rapidly approaching darkness.

She checked around her. Nothing moved in what they'd discovered was the commercial district. Everyone must have already buttoned up for the night. Not that she blamed them when a despicable person like Abu Waheed ruled with an iron fist. They'd overheard enough around town to know that anyone out and about at night would be beaten.

She approached the beach road and crouched behind some benches of a man who sold pottery. Now those benches were empty with the pottery securely locked away, but they provided cover for her. Across the road lay the beach. To her left, five buildings down, Abu Waheed's villa loomed. She'd have plenty of time to get up and over and lay out their escape route.

Sana began rising.

The growl of large motors startled her. Headlights reflected off the tan stone of the villa's walls. She dropped to her knees and peered between the benches. As they stopped in front of her, she didn't move.

Lord, cover me. Her breath came in shallow, silent gasps. Their faces were hidden behind shemaghs, but if she had three guesses, her first would have been that Makmoud had arrived. She pegged the figure standing in the middle four-door Jeep as Suleiman's half-brother. Mind racing, she counted off their numbers. Nine. Not good if they had a close encounter with her. Not good at all.

The leader said something, and they rumbled toward the villa. She poked her head out enough to see that they didn't stop and instead made a turn to run the same route the Shadow Box team had completed earlier that day.

Into her throat mike, she murmured, "Our friends have arrived. Nine of them. Two, get your head down because they're doing a pretty intense look-see."

They must have found nothing because within minutes, they turned onto the beach road again. This time, they pulled onto the strand and formed a rough triangle.

Her mind raced. Did Shadow Box need to know their plans? Maybe Makmoud and company had called ahead and had an appointment at the same time. That would spell disaster on so many levels. She had to get closer, had to overhear anything that would provide a hint of their plans. She flipped up the cover on her watch. Half past seven. She had time.

Sana pulled a small set of binoculars from a pouch at her waist. She focused on the group. Three four-door Jeeps with the tops off. Two with gun mounts. Nine men who now seemed to be preparing for the night. Two pulled guard duty. The others tossed packs onto the sand or created a fire pit. Everyone lowered their shemaghs. Confirm Makmoud. And his brother, Jibril. She shuddered. Even from where she stood, she heard their voices, though no distinct words. She had to get closer since she had no directional listening device with her.

But how? It wasn't like she could run up and hide on the other side of one of the Jeeps. She surveyed the beach. There! A fishing boat with a hole in its hull sat overturned about ten feet from one of the points of the triangle. If she could get to it, she'd have the perfect position to eavesdrop. And the boat was practically across from her. Perfect. She only needed the right time.

A fire began glowing. Someone laughed, and dishes clanked. She waited. She had to until an opportunity presented itself. The new arrivals talked in low voices. Not loud enough for her at thirty feet away to discern words but enough to catch their mood. It sounded like one of them told a story as they got supper going over the fire. What with the way they all smiled and chuckled, it must have been a funny one. Then came the punchline. Everyone, including Makmoud, guffawed. The guards turned toward the fire as well.

Sana wasted no time. She bolted across the road and flattened herself behind the boat.

The story turned to idle chitchat. Now that she was closer, she was able overhear the conversation in Arabic. She had Suleiman to thank for keeping her well-versed in that language.

"I don't understand why we have to do such…stupid errands," Jibril said in his bass rumble.

Makmoud replied in his baritone, "We do it because we were ordered to do so. But only for a bit."

"When do we go?" someone else asked.

Sana peeked around the prow of the boat. Her pulse hammered in her ears. Those not on guard duty slouched on sleeping bags around the fire. Makmoud, a mug of something steaming in his hands, leaned against the wheel of one of the Jeeps and faced her hiding place. He was going to see her. She remained as still as a gazelle sensing a lion.

"Tomorrow morning is plenty sufficient. We go in and demand to see her. And if my client likes what he sees when I send him the pictures, then we shall get her by noon."

"I still don't like this," Jibril muttered.

"Oh, I don't either, my brother. But orders are orders, and we fulfill them to get back into the leadership's good graces, do we not?" Makmoud suddenly looked up.

It was as if he met her gaze. Her heart pounded. She almost dared not breathe. Crud. Had he seen her? She couldn't tell. And she couldn't move, not when he'd pick up on any motion.

After what seemed like the longest time, he turned his head and focused on his brother. A slow smile spread across his face. "Then, when we do that, we will even the score where appropriate."

Yep, he'd seen her.

Expecting to be busted at any moment, Sana cringed. *God, cover me.* She waited. Her hand tightened around the knife on her left bicep as her breath came out in short, silent pants. Nothing came. The murmurs decreased. Makmoud told the guards to switch up.

While they were distracted, she eased away from the boat. Rather than opting to dart back into the shadows of the shop's stalls, she escaped down the strand before crossing the street. Once safely in the stalls of the market nearest the villa, she glanced at her watch. Nine. No room for error any more. She had to get moving.

She peered at the main road as it looped in front of the villa and turned toward the back stretch. Nothing glowed from any of the closest houses. And thanks to no streetlights, darkness ruled the area. She crossed the road and pressed against the back wall of the compound. From where her hands touched, it was far from the smooth wall it had appeared to be at a distance. Maybe not good for the average person to free climb, but for her, it was a piece of cake.

Sana pulled on thick leather gloves and scaled it in record time. She perched on top. The gloves and the thick soles of her climbing shoes protected her from the shards of broken glass topping the wall. She peered around. A generator rumbled and belched smoke into the bare back part of the courtyard. Thanks to that and the darkness, no one skulked around. And also maybe because Wasim had told them the truth when he said that Abu Waheed had lost half of his total crew in the failed hijacking. The other half kept mainly to the villa, which had allowed her entrance into the compound undetected.

Sana leapt from the wall and into a forward roll that dissipated the energy from her jump. Once on her feet, she raced toward the back of the villa and pressed herself against the wall.

No one shouted a warning or called out a question.

She made her way toward the front. A weak glow emanated from the side facing the sea.

Sana ducked behind piles of discarded fishing gear, motors, and other junk littering the ground. Using those as a cover, she shifted seaward.

Three or four pirates lounged on the porch under the bare glow coming from a lone bulb overhead. They laughed and rolled dice that tinkled on concrete. All lifted cigarettes to their lips. The smoke from them rose on the hot, salty breeze and wafted toward her. Yuck. Plain and simple.

She glanced upward. According to Wasim, Abu Waheed had his private quarters on the seaward side. Thing was, it was on the third level. Her gaze shifted to a large palm tree next to the terrace. Perfect for scaling and keeping out of sight of the porch.

Sana crept to the base of the trunk. With one eye on the dice game, she began climbing. They seemed none the wiser, most likely because they thought they were safe in their compound. Her lips curled. If they only knew what was coming.

Near where the fronds clacked together in the breeze, the palm bent toward the terrace. She hopped onto the railing and whispered, "Three is in."

"Excellent." Victor's voice comforted her. "We're leaving in five minutes, so hang tight."

Was it already so late? She checked her watch. Sure enough. She'd wasted too much time trying to garner information from Makmoud. Now she had to act fast. She hid behind a pile of pottery, wood, and canvas. Two sets of french doors faced her. Which belonged to the pirate? She didn't want to contemplate what lay behind the others. She was about to creep toward the ones on the left when the interior light flashed on.

Sana scurried back to her hiding place. She'd have to wait and bide her time.

26

Tori wanted to die. How could she think of living now? Especially after more abuse heaped upon her during the day? With each thump of her heart, pain strobed through her skull. With each breath, her soul bled afresh. She tried to tell herself that when He'd hung on the cross, Jesus had suffered more than she. It worked for a few minutes—until she shifted slightly and fresh agony shot through her. *God, where are you? Where?* Maybe He'd deserted her.

Weakness surged over her. She couldn't move from the soiled mattress, not even to raise her head. No tears came, not any more. It was like her body had given up its will to resist, to fight. She shifted her head. Even at that small movement, her world spun. Maybe if she stayed absolutely still, she could open her eyes.

Oh, so slowly, she tried a peek at the room that had become her prison. No furnishings whatsoever except for her bed, a stool, a chair, and a crate that was a sorry excuse for a nightstand. She didn't see any way to kill herself to leave her awful reality. Sure, she could have thrown herself off the terrace—if she could have gotten beyond the stout padlock and chain on the french doors.

Tori shuddered and pulled a threadbare sheet tighter around her. It was all she had left now in terms of modesty.

The lock on the door at the head of her bed began rattling. It banged open, admitting Abu Waheed, one man carrying what seemed to be a watering trough, and three others with smaller buckets full of something that steamed. The first man slammed the larger basin onto the floor, and the others poured their loads into it.

Its fresh smell hit her nostrils. Water. Steaming, clean water.

Despite her circumstances, her spirits lifted.

At least until Abu Waheed dropped two bundles onto the crate. He yanked the sheet off her. Tori curled into a ball.

"Bathe, perfume yourself, and put these on. Thirty minutes. You do not finish? I do myself."

Tori cringed at the thought. Once the door shut behind her, she uncurled from her tuck and shoved herself upright. Thankfully, the dizziness remained at bay. She staggered to the crate and held up the outfit of fine cobalt blue silk. Her chest tightened as she realized it rivaled something from *I Dream of Jeannie*.

The realization hit her so hard that she gasped and dropped the outfit onto the crate.

Someone had come to buy her.

Nausea swelled in her gut. A small sob escaped her. She had no options. None. "No. Oh, God, please, no!"

Tears trickled down her cheeks as she climbed into the hot water. Not that she could drown herself. There wasn't enough room to go all the way under. She took a deep breath. What could she do? As the hot water relaxed muscles injured from her misfortune, her mind loosened as well. Maybe she could convince her buyer that she wasn't worth anything, to go ahead and kill her rather than let her suffer any longer. Would the man be that humane? Hah! She doubted it. She had no choice. She'd have to get used to the reality of never drawing another free breath again.

With almost robotic motions, she finished bathing and dried with a threadbare towel that had been with the second bundle. Using a comb, she worked through all of the tangles in her damp hair until it fell her almost to her waist in a stream of rich chocolate. Her eyes filled once more as a memory struck her. George, her brother, had always called her Chocolate Head.

I cannot cry anymore. No, I won't. She took a deep breath and squared her shoulders. Then she applied the makeup that had been part of the bundle.

Once finished, she settled on the edge of the chair, clenched her hands on her lap, and faced the door to await her fate.

Wednesday, July 1, 2015, 2200 hours local time, La 'Amal, Somalia

Sana ground her teeth as she surveyed the third floor from her protected position on the terrace.

In the room on her right, Tori's shoulders drooped as she applied makeup. The hostage put her head in her hands. She shook with emotion.

Though Sana knew Tori's "buyer," she hated the way Abu Waheed had forced her to dress. Like she was some sort of slave to the man of the house. Of course, if they didn't succeed, she could very well become that.

From the street, Suleiman banged on the door.

A smile curled Sana's lips. Tori's redemption had begun, even if she didn't recognize it yet.

In a raised voice, Suleiman demanded in Arabic, "I am here to buy the girl. Let me in. Immediately."

Sana returned her attention to Tori.

She sat on the edge of the one chair in the room with her back to Sana, who had to give her credit. Tori's chin had come up. Whatever happened, she'd go down with dignity.

The pirate barged into the room with two guards hot on his heels. He yanked her to her feet.

Tori struggled.

He raised his hand to strike her, and she cowered. He grabbed her wrists. Her guards manacled them.

Sana's nostrils flared. She bared her teeth. Ways to make the pirate pay began filtering into her mind. *This is going to stop. Tonight.*

The light switched off.

Sana sprang into action. She darted to the left-hand set of french doors. They popped open at her touch. Once inside, she paused. She had two tasks to complete—to lay a trap that would delay Abu Waheed if he chased the team onto the terrace. And to ensure they could escape from Tori's room. That wouldn't take long. She had time to do some snooping, right? Maybe she could find something useful.

Clicking on her red penlight, she focused on the dresser across from the french doors. Only shards of a mirror remained. Time and use had scarred the wood beyond belief. Stained it, too. From what, she had no idea. She began opening drawers. Nothing there except for some wadded up clothing. What about the closet? Only empty hangars. Not that Abu Waheed would own a suit. She nearly laughed at the thought. No, the pirate's choice of fashion seemed to be guns. He certainly had enough rifles inside to arm a small militia. And what was that bit of burlap she saw?

Sana knelt and drew the bag closer. She loosened the drawstring. What on earth? In the red glow of her penlight, the leaves were black, meaning they were green in normal light. She straightened as she considered her choices. Her conversation with Suleiman earlier that morning played low in her mind. She reached for one of the knives across her chest. Her hand tightened on the hilt.

No. Not now. She'd have time later.

Ever so slightly, Sana opened one of the french doors. From the pouch at her waist, she removed the three small containers of cayenne pepper she'd brought from Arizona and emptied them into a small basket Skylar had bought at the marketplace earlier that afternoon. Stretching to her full height, she balanced it on the door. The last thing she needed was for it to fall and blind her. That honor would go to Abu Waheed. There. It stayed.

She stared at the two interior doors. The one to the right most likely led to Tori's room. It opened at her touch and revealed the bed, crate, stool, and chair she'd seen from the terrace. She panned the room with her light. As she took in the soiled mattress, tattered remains of clothing, and sheet on the floor, heat flooded her. Her pulse pounded. Deep, dark anger, something she'd thought she'd eradicated from her spirit, uncurled and wound its way through her soul.

Abu Waheed had hurt Tori and countless other women. And no one seemed to care or had the will to stop him.

Except her. This *would* end tonight. Permanently.

Even if it was at her own hand.

Wednesday, July 1, 2015, 2210 hours local time, La 'Amal, Somalia

Suleiman followed Victor as they marched up the steps to the second level of Abu Waheed's villa. He kept his eyes on the backpack his commander wore. It held his sniper rifle, hopefully something they wouldn't need but he'd insisted that they have. Just in case, he'd said.

They emerged into a large room, most likely a gathering spot for the pirates. He took a swift count. Twelve total. All smoking. Many chewing *khat*. A stink permeated the room as if they hadn't bathed or brushed their teeth in days. Body odor and bad breath. Nasty. Everyone had guns. Twelve against four. He hated those odds. All the more reason to negotiate at this point and not try to fight their way out.

Their escort motioned for him to have a seat on a stout wooden chair. After making sure no trap awaited him, Suleiman slouched. Victor took up a position to his right. Fiona, her face covered like Victor's, stood to his left.

Butch set the briefcase full of *baksheesh* on the floor beside the chair. Into his ear, he murmured, "Here's your dough. I've got your back. Now remember you're Makmoud."

Right. How could he forget that? Suleiman bit back his nerves and schooled his face into an expression of boredom. He pulled out a cigarette and took his time in lighting it.

A pirate who was his height, with a narrow, rodent-like face down to the large, protruding front teeth, approached. "Mr. Hidari, Abu Waheed will be here in a bit with the merchandise."

Suleiman's eyes narrowed. He blew a stream of smoke in his direction. "You tell him I am tired of waiting. He has kept me waiting all day. And now he expects to do the same all night? Foolishness on his part. Go before I decide that you are not worth the bullet I have in my gun."

"Y—yes, sir." The deputy scrambled from the room.

Suleiman spat on the floor.

Silence fell as if his very action had offended his hosts. Murmuring began in Somali, and he wondered if he'd gone too far.

A chain clinked from the hall. Catcalls and what had to be lewd comments followed. The pirates leered, and some even licked their lips as if they'd get a chance at Tori.

Abu Waheed led her into the room and made her step onto a small platform just to the right of an empty chair facing Suleiman. The pirate had bound her wrists with chains as if he expected her to escape. Her outfit might have been someone's fantasy, but here, in this place—

Suleiman stopped the thought. They would end this tonight. With her next sunrise, Tori would see freedom.

With a grand gesture as if he were some sort of ringmaster, Abu Waheed bowed and in Arabic said, "Your merchandise, Mr. Hidari."

He nodded at Faoud, who took Tori's arm and rotated her.

She lowered her head.

Abu Waheed sprawled on the chair across from his foe. He smiled. "I open the bidding at ten million."

The smile turned to a sneer as if he dared Suleiman to defy him.

Remember you're Makmoud. What would he do? Of course he'd counter offer. His gaze wandered up and down Tori as if assessing her as a specimen. "Ten? I say two."

Abu Waheed straightened. "What? Are you crazy, man? She is worth much more than two."

"Why do you say that?"

"She is the daughter of a billionaire."

"My client doesn't care." Suleiman ground out his cigarette on the right arm of the chair. "Mr. Waheed, you must understand something about my client. He has high standards." He hated himself for the lies he had to tell. "And interesting…habits, shall we say. And one of those is that he be assured that he will like the merchandise."

Abu Waheed frowned. "I do not understand."

Now was not the time to show weakness. Suleiman leaned forward and focused on the pirate. He hardened his gaze. "I must 'test' the merchandise for him."

Abu Waheed laughed as if he didn't believe him. "She is not a car."

Though she obviously didn't understand a word of their conversation, a tear slid down Tori's cheek and left a streak of kohl in its wake.

"Oh, I agree. Not at all." A wolfish smile curled Suleiman's lips.

Tori dared to look at him.

The despair in those eyes nearly broke his heart. It also stiffened his resolve to free her. "Consider my offer."

The pirate fell silent. He rubbed his chin and narrowed his eyes as if he assessed his next move. His gaze darted to the briefcase beside Suleiman. "Four would be too low."

"Is it?" Suleiman raised his chin and allowed a smirk to cross his lips. "You would have to be living under a rock not to hear of your misfortunes as of late. It seems to me that you need the cash, no?"

Abu Waheed's eyes widened.

Had he pressed too hard? Of course, that was the nature of haggling, to aim low, give a little, and let the seller think he walked away with a fortune. Suleiman straightened. "I test the merchandise, and if she is satisfactory, six million. That is my final offer."

Abu Waheed rose. He ran his hand down Tori's face, then her neck, then lower.

She started crying.

Suleiman tried to encourage her with his gaze. *Tori, stay strong. You are almost free.* Hah. She probably thought he was sizing her up as if to eat her.

Almost as if in a trance, the pirate murmured, "Six, then, and whatever you have in that briefcase. I will allow you a half hour to test out the merchandise for your client."

Suleiman rose. "Then let us go."

"Faoud will take you to her room." Abu Waheed rose. He said something to his lackey, who approached Suleiman.

The weasel offered an insincere bow. "If you would, Mr. Hidari, this way."

Suleiman rose. As he turned to follow Victor, his gaze flicked to Abu Waheed.

The pirate resumed his seat. With narrowed eyes, he stared at him and pressed his lips together. Most likely, he plotted something that wouldn't be good for the collective health of the team. That much, Suleiman knew.

Faoud nearly yanked Tori from the platform. Her tears became more audible now. Victor led the way. Butch followed Suleiman, and Fiona brought up the rear. Butch muttered, "Good job."

They weren't finished yet. Faoud took them to the third story. He opened a door to a room. "You have thirty minutes. Or that would be seven and a half minutes each."

He cackled and slammed the door. A lock rattled. They were trapped with only one escape route available. Suleiman stared at the padlock and chain on the door. If Sana wasn't able to pick that, they could be in some serious trouble.

In front of him, Tori collapsed to her knees. She buried her face in her hands and sobbed. "P—please. Just…kill me. I've been dishonored and am not—"

"Tori, you're safe." Victor handed the backpack to Suleiman and knelt in front of her.

Her sobs stopped. She stared at him through reddened eyes now smeared with black all the way around. "You…you know my name?"

"I do." Victor lowered his shemagh, as did Butch and Fiona. "I'm Victor Chavez. Your father sent us to rescue you."

"W—what? I—I don't understand."

"We're getting you out of here. You've got to trust me on that. Can you do that?" he asked in a low voice.

Tori studied each of them. Her brow remained pinched, but seeing Fiona seemed to reassure her. She nodded.

At the sound of scraping and scratching, Suleiman turned his attention to the bed. Sana rolled from underneath. She scowled as she dusted herself off.

"We've got to get out of here, boss," Butch said.

"Agreed. Shove that chair under the knob, and let's do just that." Victor drew his pistol. "Sana, do we have the rope set up?"

"Ready and waiting. This way." Within seconds, Sana picked the lock on the french doors and led the way onto the terrace. From beneath some potsherds she pulled out a coil of hemp rope with knots located at set intervals. She lowered it over the edge. In a whisper, she said, "There we go. Head on down but stay away from the front because there's three guards playing a dice game. I'll take up the rear."

Victor nodded. "I'll go first."

Tori began shaking her head. "I—I don't think I can do that."

Butch asked, "Can you ride on my back, Tori?"

She nodded.

"Then hop on."

Suleiman focused his pistol on the french doors as first Victor, then Butch and Tori, went over the edge. Fiona followed, and he turned to Sana. "Go ahead."

"I've got it. You go down." Her face remained expressionless. Sana, the woman who wore her emotions plainly, now hid them behind her poker face.

Why? He didn't have time to debate the question. He slithered downward. Ahead of him, Victor and Fiona took aim with their tranq guns.

Tori leaned against the villa's wall as if she were too weak to stand.

Three clicks of their guns later, Victor hissed, "Let's go."

They scurried to the edge. Fiona and Victor took out the guards at the corner.

Suleiman kept his tranq gun up.

Almost without breaking pace, Fiona fired at the gate guard. He collapsed off his stool, and Victor caught him and lowered him to the ground without a word.

Almost there.

Butch removed some Semtex from a pouch at his waist. Within seconds, he rolled out the charge and placed it along the edge of the door. He attached a small detonator and pressed a button. A red glow emanated from the device. "Ready, boss."

"Go for it." Victor covered Tori's face and turned his own away.

Suleiman did the same thing.

Pops split the calm night air, followed by a loud clang when the metal door fell to the road outside.

Someone from the second level called out a question. When no one answered, he shouted.

"Let's go." Victor took Tori's hand and urged her through the rubble.

Suleiman kept close to Butch's back as they passed into the street. Five minutes, and they'd be at the compound. Tori stumbled and fell to her knees. Butch didn't hesitate. He swept her onto his broad shoulders in a fireman's carry.

"Sana, keep up with us." Suleiman reached back to take her hand.

Nothing.

She'd been right behind him as they'd passed through the gate. He was sure of it. So where was she? He paused and turned. Nothing but dark shadows thanks to the light from earlier compromising his night vision.

A silhouette scurried toward the back wall of the villa.

Sana.

It had to be by the way it scaled it in record time. She did exactly what he'd warned her against—going back to exact her own form of retribution.

Suleiman swore under his breath and tightened the straps of the backpack. He needed to get to the building closest to the compound—and to Makmoud and his crew. Most likely, the noise of the explosion had caught the attention of his half-brother. Using the closest alley, he darted seaward. There! A rickety staircase led to the second floor and then to the roof. As he reached the second story, the babbling of a worried family wafted through the open windows. He thought he heard Abu Waheed's name as if they feared retribution.

Using the darkness as a cover, he crept upward and onto the roof. On his belly, he wormed his way to the edge where he had a view both of Abu Waheed's villa and Makmoud's squad. Using the rifle's scope, he peered at the Hezbollah men. They stood or took a knee as they stared toward the villa. A couple of them held rifles in a relaxed ready position. Makmoud stood in front of the faintly glowing fire and surveyed the villa with a pair of binoculars. He lowered them, and a cunning smile played about his lips.

It's like he knows we're here. Or that Abu Waheed's going to do something really dumb like he did eleven years ago. Suleiman fervently hoped it was the latter. With skilled precision so that he barely made a sound, he began assembling the sniper rifle.

Makmoud wouldn't be the only one watching. No, Suleiman would be watching and waiting for Sana. And praying that she'd come to her senses before she got herself into trouble.

27

Abu Waheed slouched on his chair and nodded at Faoud, who had come downstairs. "You locked the door?"

His deputy grinned, revealing his two large front teeth. "I did. Their only way out now is to throw themselves off the terrace."

Everyone chortled at that. From the left-hand chair arm, Abu Waheed lifted his knife, the very knife he'd held to the doctor's throat when they'd made their escape from the ship. He ran his finger along the smooth edge. Sharp. Just like he liked it. Perfect for killing.

The serrated edge was just as sharp. Perfect for making his victims scream before they died. And that was exactly what would happen. Twelve against four. Horrible odds. Makmoud would pay dearly. He'd make him beg for mercy, then eviscerate him just as his foe had done to his comrades years before. He'd die slowly, and it would be a pleasure to watch. Then the doctor would go to the man who'd made an appointment for the next day. His offer was already in. A good offer. Better than the measly six million Makmoud had made. It didn't matter that the buyer scheduled for the next day hadn't revealed his name. Cash was cash.

Abu Waheed chuckled at the thought.

A muffled explosion echoed through the still night, followed by a massive whump. He jumped. "What was that?"

Faoud ran to the door that opened onto the porch. He called out a question.

Abu Waheed rose. Just as he reached the door, his lieutenant nearly collided with him. "What happened?"

Faoud's eyes had widened. "Someone…someone blew the gate!"

Was he under assault? What about the doctor? Without a word, he turned on his heel and dashed up the stairs. He rattled the knob to her room. Locked. His room was exactly the opposite. He cursed and burst inside. One of his french doors was ajar as if they'd indeed escaped onto the terrace. He shoved it open.

Powder cascaded onto his head, and burning erupted in his eyes. "Ar-ggghhh! My eyes! I need water! Now!"

He stumbled backward and turned. Blinded, he slammed into the foot of the bed and fell. His hand landed in something slimy. He grimaced and shouted, "Where is my water?"

"Here, sir!" Faoud must have knelt beside him.

He flailed about and knocked a bottle from his hands. "Get it to me."

Forget it. Unable to see, he staggered around the bed and toppled to the right. The flimsy door collapsed beneath his weight. Oh, the pain of landing on his side. His face flushed, and tears streamed down his cheeks as he climbed to his feet. He tripped over the chair and plowed into the trough that held the doctor's bath water. He forced his eyes open, and it washed the burning from them. Sweet relief.

Blinking several times cleared his vision. And what did he see? The stout padlock he'd used to secure the chain on the floor. Same thing with the chain. His adversaries were gone. Rage filled him. He pushed himself to his feet and returned to his room. Faoud had retreated. The fool had better be figuring out what happened.

Abu Waheed dashed down the steps. "What do you know?"

Faoud stood nearby with another man. "All four of our guards are un-conscious. They destroyed the gate and escaped."

Makmoud had gotten the best of him—again.

This wasn't over. Not by a long shot. He still had twelve men and tons of rifles in his closet. And *khat* would help fuel everyone's bravado. "Gather the men and get to the vehicles. We're going to pay a visit to Hezbollah. And guess who won't walk away this time?"

With that, he whirled and dashed up the stairs.

Wednesday, July 1, 2015, 2225 hours local time, La 'Amal, Somalia

Victor's lungs burned. His quads ached. But his spirits ran high. They'd gotten Tori out and now ran free with no one following—yet. That could change in a hurry. Into his throat mike, he said, "Eight, get that gate open. We're coming through."

In his reassuring, honeyed drawl, Skylar replied, "Roger that."

Ahead, the auto gate groaned on rusty hinges. His rifle at ready, he stepped into the street. "Welcome back."

"Thanks." Victor brushed by, followed by Fiona, who panted and braced her hands against her knees.

Chest heaving from the half-mile dash, she wheezed. "I—I'm out of shape. And I guess I need to stop smoking."

Butch barely panted as if he ran a half mile with over a hundred pounds across his shoulders every day. He eased Tori to the ground. "Here you are, my lady. Almost there."

Victor crouched beside her. "How are you feeling?"

A trembling smile crossed her lips. "Like I fell down a rabbit hole. Am I…am I really free?"

"Almost." He straightened. "Let's get packing so we can get out of here. What's left?"

"Just your guns." Skylar laid his on the hood of his Humvee and pulled out the cases for the tranquilizer guns.

"Those are the bomb," Butch said. "Diana, you think you could work on some stuff we could use in a sniper rifle?"

Diana, who'd knelt beside Tori, nodded. "Sure, if you and Suleiman could modify a sniper rifle."

Butch grinned. "We could do that. Right, Suleiman?"

No answer.

"Suleiman?"

Victor peered around. "Has anyone seen Suleiman?"

"I thought he was right behind me. Sana, too." Butch scratched his goatee. "Skylar, you didn't see them, did you?"

"Nope." The procurement officer shrugged. "Any reason why they'd stay behind?"

An image flew into Victor's mind, one of Suleiman locked into a tense, whispered debate with Sana. He'd turned them so his back was to Victor. He hadn't caught the words, but all too well, he remembered the former cat burglar's intense anger from the night before. "They wouldn't."

Butch approached. "Wouldn't, what?"

"Stay behind." Victor paced and muttered under his breath. Why had he bought into Sana's insistence that she go last? Had she talked Suleiman into going with her?

"Uh, oh. Not good at all. What do we do?"

"Contact them." Victor keyed his throat mike. "Two, come in. Three, come in. Where are you?"

Nothing from Sana. Then Suleiman spoke. "Two is on the roof near the villa."

"Why did you—"

"Three went back inside. I am covering for her, both the villa and the Hezbollah camp."

"She gets out, and you both get your butts back here."

"Will do," Suleiman replied.

"That's not like Sana," Shelly said from where she stood at the back door to one of the Humvees.

"Oh, I don't know about that," Victor muttered. His mind flew to the villa. Surely by now, the Hezbollah group knew someone had attempted to purchase Tori. And the pirates, high as they were on *khat*, would be in a frenzy.

Butch muttered something under his breath, then said, "Man, if they get their paws on her, she's toast."

Victor shuddered upon imagining what would happen if they caught Sana and Suleiman. What would they do then? He didn't want to contemplate that.

Fiona joined Victor at the front of the first Humvee. "Um, I hate to be the bearer of bad news, but if that Hezbollah team finds us here, we're sitting ducks. We need to get out of here."

"I know." Just as he knew their primary objective. Get Tori out. And get out of town—fast.

If that meant leaving Sana and Suleiman behind, so be it.

Really?

He didn't want to make that choice.

"Do we go after them?" Skylar asked from beside him.

Victor tamped down his anger and placed his tranq gun into its case. He snatched up his MP5. "No, we wait."

Wednesday, July 1, 2015, 2235 hours local time, La 'Amal, Somalia

So perfect. Sana smirked as she watched Abu Waheed bumble into the wash basin. She snickered when he fell into it with a resounding splash. Even through the closed french doors, she heard him shouting. He tore from the room as if his pants were on fire.

Time to move. From the palm tree, she hopped onto the railing. It'd been so easy to re-infiltrate, just climb the wall and dash to the palm. Now she'd get her own bit of vengeance by killing him. Then he'd never torment women again. It didn't matter what anyone else thought.

She darted into the room and opened the closet door. With a sharp intake of breath, she noted the briefcase that held the *baksheesh*. First things first. She focused on stuffing packs of money into every available crevice she could find in her pack. Once she'd slung it over her back, she stepped into the closet, closed the door, and drew one of the knives from one of the sheaths across her chest.

"Two, come in. Three, come in. Where are you?" Victor's urgent request filtered into her earpiece.

She dialed down the volume and silenced him.

Someone shouted. Feet pounded on the steps in the hall.

She'd jump Abu Waheed the second he opened the door to get his precious *khat*. Her hand tightened around the hilt.

"Don't do it, Sana."

The voice held a gravitas that froze her in her tracks.

She touched her earpiece, then removed it so it dangled around her neck.

Abu Waheed slammed open the door to his room.

She tensed.

"Don't do it, Sana Jain. You know better." That same voice. Suddenly, she recognized it.

Holy Spirit.

She wilted. *I must. He hurt Tori. And who knows how many others?*

Butch's words about poetic justice rang in her mind like a bell. Was he right? Could she trust God to mete out justice in His own time? Suddenly, she knew. This battle wasn't hers. Not at all.

Sana sheathed her knife.

The door to the closet flew open!

She didn't have time to think—only react. With a screech akin to that of a cat, she jumped onto Abu Waheed. With her on top of him, he tumbled backward.

She scrambled toward the french doors.

He caught her around the ankle and dragged her backward.

Her fingers clawed the tile. She winced as her face came into contact with something slimy. She flipped over and reared up with a punch.

It caught him across the face.

What would have stunned a mere mortal only antagonized him. She leapt to her feet. He slammed into her, and they stumbled backward.

She pushed him, then whipped around in a roundhouse kick.

He ducked. Like a football lineman, he charged her before she returned to a karate stance.

Off balance, Sana staggered backward. She crashed through the french doors and onto the terrace. Her head bounced on concrete. She groaned.

Abu Waheed sucker-punched her in the solar plexus.

Sana cried out. Her vision dimmed as pain surged through her.

He dragged her into the room.

Glass cut lines of pain into her back.

With a guttural cry, he lifted her.

Sana flew through the air.

Her back slammed into the remains of the mirror. She fell onto the top. It collapsed under her weight. Before she could move, he pounced again.

Abu Waheed ripped away her shemagh. "You!"

He drove his fist into her face.

Stars danced before her. *Gun! Get your gun! Your knives! Anything!*

Her limbs refused to respond.

He yanked her pistol from its holster and threw it across the room before relieving her of her knives. Each clink of the blades as they hit the far wall sealed her fate. She still had her shurikens—if she could get into her pouch fast enough.

He pulled the backpack off before calling her a foul name and shoving her face first onto the bed.

The smell of dried sweat and dirt filled her nostrils. Sana gagged.

With his free hand, he grabbed her hair so that her scalp burned. His Arabic blasted toward her. "So, my little safecracker, you were working for Hezbollah, were you not?"

"I—"

He yanked on her hair.

"Stop!" she cried.

He tightened his grip on her arm. Did she hear a pop? Pain bloomed in her shoulder.

"You thought you could get away with it, didn't you?" His breath, full of cigarettes, onions, and something she couldn't place, assaulted her nose. Her stomach churned as his fingers twisted in her hair. "You thought you could double-cross Abu Waheed, you and your minions. You're wrong! Where are you hidden?"

Terror replaced arrogance. Through the burning in her skull and shoulder, she couldn't think of the right Arabic words. She clamped her jaw shut.

He jerked harder on her arm. "Answer me."

Agony roared through her shoulder joint as something—a ligament?—gave way. She moaned. Finally, the Arabic words came. "On…the beach. Leave me…alone."

At least her diversion would give the others time to escape.

"Oh, no. You're coming with me. You'll pay for double-crossing me." Her backpack landed in front of her face, and three packs of twenties spilled onto the sheets. "And for stealing from me."

Abu Waheed snatched up her pack, hauled her to her feet, and shouted something in Somali. Two of his comrades charged into the room.

Heart pounding, Sana barely kept her feet under her as they almost flew down two flights of stairs and outside. An old car retrofitted with a gun mount and a pickup with the same waited for them with engines rumbling. Guns bristled from the four pirates in back of the pickup. The other two tossed more to their pals before hopping into the back of the car.

It would be a bloodbath.

"Get in there." Abu Waheed shoved her toward the pickup truck.

She slammed into the metal side and caught herself with her left arm. "How can I?"

With super-human strength, he lifted her and tossed her into the bed. She landed hard on her back. The pack wound up on her chest.

Above, her captors glared. One of them spat on her. Another kicked her.

She curled onto her uninjured side and grasped the pack. More pain blazed from a kick to the base of her spine.

Abu Waheed jumped up beside her and smacked her across the face. He grabbed her, this time by the shemagh, which suddenly felt like a noose.

She gasped for air.

They bolted forward and bumped as they rolled over the ruined gate. The engines roared. To her left, the strand passed in a blur. He'd bought into her lie.

Which meant one thing.

Their game was up. Makmoud would now have confirmation that the Shadow Box team had impersonated Hezbollah.

When it was all over with, she knew most likely where she would be. A hostage of Makmoud's, who would demand the life of his half-brother in exchange for hers.

What had she done?

The pickup bumped off the road and lurched to a halt. More yammering in Somali followed. Suddenly, Abu Waheed shouted in Arabic, "Where is Makmoud Hidari?"

Silence.

Then a man chuckled. "I am Makmoud."

"You're wrong! You are not the man who visited me and took the girl! Where is he?"

Sana remained as still as a newborn fawn. Maybe in his rage, the pirate would forget about her.

"You think I would be so foolish as to come myself? You spoke with my half-brother." Oh, she had to give Makmoud credit for fast thinking. He'd shifted into a cover story as quickly as a cheetah turning while chasing a gazelle. "Now why do you want a word with me? Why should I be so honored?"

"Where is the doctor?"

"What doctor?"

"You know who I'm talking about. You try to double-cross me." Green spittle rained down on Sana as his rage filled each word. "You try to take what is rightfully mine. Then you have the audacity to steal the money you gave me?"

"I still do not understand—"

Abu Waheed reached down and hauled her to her feet by her hair.

With one quick glance, she took in the scene. The loose triangular formation of Jeeps sat to her right. To her left was the overturned boat with

239

the hole in its hull. Makmoud stood in front of them with Jibril just off his right shoulder and the other Hezbollah men off his left. All save for Makmoud and Jibril held their rifles at ready.

Would this ever stop? She clawed at Abu Waheed with her left hand.

He drove his fist into her kidney and shoved her forward to the edge of the pickup's bed.

Sana cried out as her legs gave way. Had she not been a gymnast for years, she would have easily fallen on her face and possibly broken her neck. She ducked into a roll and flopped onto her stomach with a face full of sand as her only reward. Her backpack landed beside her. Another pack of bills spilled onto the sand. Cradling her injured arm, she pushed herself to her knees to stumble toward Makmoud.

Abu Waheed hopped down from the pickup and dragged her forward until they came even with the stern of the overturned boat. He caught her hair again and twisted, forcing her to raise her chin. Pain burned a line along her throat. He was going to kill her. "I caught her trying to steal from me. I know you have the doctor. Now where is she?"

Sana stared at Makmoud as she sucked in precious air.

His gaze boring into her, he approached them until he was a few yards away.

Jibril slipped into the shadows behind the boat.

A ghost of a smile rippled across Makmoud's face as he rubbed his bearded chin. "You think I would go to the pain and difficulty of gathering an army and raiding your compound? When I could take it on my own if I needed?" He laughed as he focused on her. "You are more foolish than I thought."

The knife quivered at her neck. This was going to hurt before she saw Jesus.

Abu Waheed's demand came out like a hiss. "You will return the doctor!"

"Even if I had her, I would not do that. Tsk, tsk, tsk." Makmoud shook his head as the smile melted from his face. His gaze flicked upward. The corner of his mouth quirked. "You are just as foolish as you were eleven years ago. You think you can march over here and make demands on me. Not this time. And not ever again."

He shouted something in Farsi.

Gunfire crackled around her like small firecrackers. Sana jerked and fell forward onto her good arm.

Abu Waheed shrieked.

She curled into a ball and gaped.

The pirate, his throat slit nearly ear to ear, stared sightlessly at her. He gurgled. Slowly, as if he were a building falling, he crumpled forward and landed beside her. Her hand shot to her mouth to block the scream that threatened to burst forth.

With a long-bladed knife stained in blood in his hand, Jibril towered over her. Behind him, bodies either hung from the vehicles or lay in front of them as the remaining Hezbollah squad approached.

She shivered. Nausea swelled, and she squeezed her eyes closed.

"Remove them," Makmoud ordered.

She risked a peep. Only the two Hidari brothers remained because the other men dragged the carcasses toward the sea.

Cradling her injured arm, she crawled to her knees.

Jibril pulled a rag from his pocket and wiped his blade clean. She focused on the bloody cloth as he sheathed the knife. The whole time, he kept her pinned in his gaze.

With his arms folded across his chest, Makmoud loomed before her. A smirk played about his lips. He had her right where he wanted her. As a hostage.

She'd messed up. Big time. Panic began pushing at the edges of what little calm she had left. "You...you should have killed me as well."

Makmoud knelt and lifted her chin. "No, no. You are worth much more to me alive. Where is the rest of your team?"

"I—"

"I will not hurt you. But, if you do not cede to my wishes, I will take you back to Venezuela with me and break you. Jibril has asked be in charge of that."

Jibril joined them. "I have. I'll take good care of you, my pretty girl."

Liar.

Panic drove her breath in a ragged gasp. She knew exactly what would happen, and none of her ninja skills or anything else would save her in the end. Sana bit back her whimper. She'd stay strong until she broke.

The smile melted from Makmoud's face. "Where is your team?"

"Take your hands off her!" Suleiman's shout echoed across the black night.

She nearly sagged to the ground. Help had finally arrived. Or had it?

Wednesday, July 1, 2015, 2235 hours local time, La 'Amal, Somalia

"Take your hands off her!" In his position on the roof overlooking the Hezbollah camp, Suleiman almost quivered from rage as he switched on the laser and painted Makmoud's forehead with a glowing red dot. "Sana, get out of there."

She grabbed her backpack and scrambled into the shadows.

Makmoud stilled. Then he smiled and said in Farsi, "Ah, Ibrahim! So glad you could join us. I should have known you were her guardian angel."

"You will not take her," he replied in the same language.

"It seems as if Jibril has that honor, not I." Makmoud raised his face and peered directly at his half-brother. He started chuckling. "I know what you really want. You see, I remember three years ago and the way taking Rachel Marina's life disturbed you. I didn't miss those undercurrents of disloyalty that bubbled through you after you killed her."

Suleiman drew in a breath. He'd forgotten how Makmoud could mess with his mind and make him question his own motives. *He's trying to rattle you. Do not let him.*

Too late.

Sweat sprang up on his brow, and he expelled a noisy breath. His muscles tensed. Not good at all.

He could even the score for Victor by killing the man who'd ordered the death of the woman his mentor had loved. Where would that leave him? He'd never have to fear his half-brother again.

The dot remained steady on Makmoud's forehead.

"Take your shot. I know where that laser rests because I can see its glow." Makmoud opened his arms wide as if offering himself as a sacrifice and challenging him at the same time. "You want to kill me so badly. I can feel it."

Suleiman closed his eyes. *I cannot. I must not!*

He saw Rachel crumpling to the ground and dying from his shot three years before. That image shifted to Victor when they'd talked only hours earlier about the impact of Rachel's death on him. His mentor's words hit deep in his soul. "Deb says that God takes those griefs in our lives and uses them for good, to glorify Himself. I have to agree. I miss Rach, but God gave me Deborah—and salvation."

His statement rang true. He couldn't deny it. But still—

"I'm waiting, brother." Makmoud's words taunted him.

Oh, to wipe that smirk from his half-brother's face! It would be so easy to take the man's life. Just a slight movement of his trigger finger.

He slowed his breathing as he worked to lower his heart rate for the shot.

Except that another image, this one from his time on *The Kitchen Sink*, filtered across his mind. He almost felt Sana's shoulder brush his as she said in her sweet voice, "Here's one for you. 'Blessed are the peacemakers, for they shall be called children of God.' Verse 9."

His breath slowed even further. His pulse dropped accordingly as his finger tightened on the trigger.

It would be a perfect shot.

But would it bring peace?

No.

He lowered his head.

I cannot. I will not. I want to be a peacemaker.

He switched off the laser. "No."

Makmoud laughed. "Then you are a fool, Ibrahim Hidari."

Coldness washed over Suleiman. He climbed to his knees. He needed to get out of there, to find Sana, and—

A strong hand grabbed his collar and hurled him backward. His rifle flew out of his hands as he landed on his back. He wheezed.

Jibril loomed over him. "You fool. What did I teach you? Situational awareness. Now it is to my advantage!"

Suleiman reached for his pistol.

Before he could react, Jibril knocked the gun away.

He yelped as his half-brother dragged him to his feet. "You're coming with me."

Suleiman squirmed. "I want nothing to do with you."

"Oh, but Makmoud wants everything to do with you. You see, he has allowed no one but he to have the honor of killing you for your betrayal of us three years ago. So you will—"

Suleiman drove his elbow into his gut.

"Oof!" Jibril staggered backward. He jumped him, and they crashed onto the roof.

Suleiman stroked downward.

Jibril caught his fist. He planted his foot in his middle and shoved hard.

Suleiman flew backward, and his head slammed into the parapet wall. He saw stars as he sagged downward.

"You will come with me." Jibril grabbed his feet and began dragging him toward the edge. He shrieked!

Suleiman stared at the shuriken now impaled in his half-brother's shoulder. He thrashed and broke free just as Sana rushed forward.

In her weakened state, she was no match for Jibril.

He slammed his fist into her injured shoulder.

With a cry, she collapsed.

Jibril yanked the shuriken out and tossed it out of play. He nudged her with his foot. "And you will come, too!"

No, they wouldn't. Not if Suleiman could help it. He snatched his knife from its sheath at his waist and drove hard at Jibril.

No dice.

He blocked him and knocked him backward.

Suleiman held hard to the blade. In one, last-ditch effort, he lunged forward and thrust it into Jibril's calf.

He barely heard his half-brother's cry. Scrambling to his feet, he grabbed Sana with one hand and the sniper rifle with the other. "Come on!"

She snatched up the pistol he'd dropped and stumbled after him. They raced toward the edge of the roof. "Go!"

Without hesitation, she leaped the narrow gap. When she hit the roof of the opposite building, she rolled and stayed in a heap.

Suleiman hesitated. Just as he jumped, pain exploded in his right glute. As he fell short, he hurled the rifle away and clawed the building. His fingers caught the parapet, and his body slammed into the dried mud wall. Oh, no. He scrabbled upward.

Across the way, Jibril laughed.

Get up. Now! Suleiman searched for something—anything—to use as a foothold. His fingers burned from the strain. They weakened. His arm muscles shook as he tried to hold on.

He would make it. He had to. A small bit of support timber poking through the mud wall caught his attention. He'd push off of that. If not, he'd fall within seconds. *Think about The Mushroom.* Memories of that climb surfaced. He swung his uninjured leg upward and pushed against the support with all of his might. He heaved himself onto the parapet and risked a glance toward the other side.

Jibril approached. He aimed his gun.

Sana grabbed him and dragged him on his front until he crumpled off the ledge. Mud chips flew into the air.

"He got you in the butt." She yanked out the knife and threw it toward their attacker. "Can you run?"

"I—I think so. Give me your gun and go."

She pressed the pistol into his hand.

He whipped around and fired off a shot. It wasn't accurate, but it forced Jibril to get his head down. With the rifle and pistol in his hands, he limped after her, and they raced toward the other side.

"Stairs!" she called.

Behind them, Jibril grunted as he crossed the chasm almost like he were leaping a narrow creek.

"Go down." Suleiman turned. He lined up a shot and fired.

Jibril ducked, and the bullet flew over him.

Suleiman charged down the stairs he'd noted when they'd arrived at their hideout. They already shook from her steps. Would it hold him?

Another bullet whistled past his head.

No time to wait.

He dashed downward and tried to ignore the creaking from the old wood.

As he hit the lowest run, the rotted tread beneath his foot cracked into splinters. Dropping the guns, he caught the one below and dropped the remaining few feet. He collapsed with a grunt.

In front of him, the gate opened. The first Humvee poked through with Skylar behind the wheel and Victor in the passenger's seat.

"Victor!" Suleiman hauled himself to his feet. "Rooftop."

"Got it." Victor aimed his rifle and fired just as Jibril poked his head over.

Another miss, but he jerked back.

Suleiman picked up Sana and bodily threw her into the back. He took a flying leap and followed.

The engine roared, and they raced toward safety.

28

Thursday, July 2, 2015, 0030 hours local time, Mombasa, Kenya

Butch carried Sana toward one of the empty offices in the warehouse where they'd stowed the *Kitchen Sink*. Suleiman limped after him and found he almost had to run to catch up. The simple motion of walking pained him, and as she'd stitched up his rear on the plane, Diana had told him to take it easy. With sitting on a cushion to alleviate his discomfort and no exercise for a month, most likely he'd have complete healing. He'd gotten off easy.

Not Sana. With each step Butch took, she whimpered as the motion jolted her injured shoulder, which now bulged with a cold pack underneath her jumpsuit.

Butch asked, "Hey, Suleiman, you got the stuff Diana told you to bring?"

"Right here." He held it up a small cooler and a nylon bag.

Butch stopped and stood back. "How about get that sleeping bag spread out so she's not resting on concrete?"

Sana huddled against his bulk with her good arm wrapped around his neck. Like a small child, she tucked her head beneath his chin. But no tears, even though her mouth twisted in a grimace of pain.

Suleiman reached to touch her cheek.

"Go on," Butch urged. "She ain't getting any lighter."

He unzipped the bag and settled it across the floor.

The team's mechanic knelt and eased her on the soft material.

Suleiman fell to his knees on the other side of her. He brushed some errant strands of ebony hair from her cheek. "Take my hand."

She did. A weak smile crossed her face and disappeared. "Butch, are you mad at us?"

Butch, who reached into the small cooler Suleiman had dropped, paused. "Scared spitless was more like it. Don't do that again, girl. I don't need any gray hairs in my goatee. I'm too young for that."

His response earned a weak chuckle from Suleiman.

"Now the boss? I'm not so sure about him. Here." He extended a water bottle to her. "You want some more?"

She shook her head.

"Suleiman, take it and make sure she drinks. You too 'cause I know we're all still a little dehydrated." He set out another bottle. "I told Diana I'd take down her exam table. See you guys on the plane, okay?"

Suleiman nodded. Once the big man shambled from the room, he pulled a cold pack from the cooler to replace the one Diana had applied earlier. "Should I even ask how your shoulder is?"

"N—no." Sana shifted and winced. "I—I'm sure Abu Waheed dislocated it. Or at least damaged a ligament."

He twisted the pack, which caused two chemicals to mix. In the reverse of a fire, their combination produced a ready-made cold pack. He flushed when he thought about what else he had to do. "I, um, well, I need to place this directly against your skin like Diana did with the other."

"That's okay." She gritted her teeth.

He took her good hand again and kissed her fingers. "Not much longer. I promise."

With that, he drew the jumpsuit's zipper down far enough to push the material out of the way and remove the other pack. As he caught a glimpse of her olive skin, heat rocketed to his cheeks. He tried not to envision what it would be like to marry her one day.

What? Where did that come from?

Such a thought rendered him motionless.

"It's okay." Thankfully, a bit of humor danced in those dark eyes of hers. "It's not like either of us is in a romantic mood."

He pressed the pack over her shoulder, took her good hand, and added it. "Keep it there."

A weak laugh escaped her. "There's nothing like pleasantly numb."

Suleiman draped a blanket over her. Mindful of the injury to his rump, he took the small cushion Diana had given him and eased onto it so he leaned against the wall. He closed his eyes. No, he couldn't do that lest he fall asleep. He turned his attention to her, and she offered a small smile.

Footsteps approached. Not Butch's lumbering ones or Skylar's strut. Or any of the women's. These were masculine and full of purpose. Uh, oh. Victor. Trouble any way he sliced it. They slowed.

Their leader stepped inside and closed the door behind him. As he stopped and planted his feet wide, he tossed Sana's pack on the floor. It landed on its side, and bundles of cash spilled out.

They were in trouble.

Suleiman rubbed the back of his neck. His insides quivered as he noted the flinty look in his mentor's dark eyes.

Victor folded his arms across his chest. "You want to tell me what the hell you were thinking, Sana? Do you realize you could have died? Or been captured?"

"I—"

"And that if it hadn't been for Suleiman's quick thinking, you'd be re-siding with Makmoud right now?"

"I—"

"We were lucky we didn't get caught up in it. Your actions could have gotten us all killed!"

"I'm sorry, all right?" Her nostrils flared. She struggled to sit up, moaned, and sank onto the sleeping bag.

"Why did you do it?"

"He. Hurt. Tori." She ground those words out.

Suleiman reached out and stabilized the pack on her shoulder with one hand. "Sana—"

"I'm talking to her, not you." Victor sent a white-hot glare his way.

Suleiman got the point. Stay out of it.

Victor kept his focus on Sana. "I don't disagree with you, but we have mission objectives for a reason. You understand why, right?"

She rolled her eyes. "To keep everyone safe."

"No, not to take any unnecessary risks. Because deviating from that objective can get people hurt or killed." He nudged the backpack, and more packs spilled onto the floor. "Going after him to kill him and get our money was plain suicidal." He scrubbed his hands through his hair, and it stood up in black spikes. After muttering something in Spanish about stubborn women, he said, "I thought I taught you better than that."

"You did. And I'm sorry. At least I got everything back. All but eight thousand."

This time, Victor growled something in Spanish that Suleiman didn't understand.

Victor crouched in front of her. "I want you to remember something, Sana. I appreciate your willingness to think independently. I truly do. It's one of the biggest strengths you bring to our team. But I want you to think on one thing. If Makmoud had gotten his hooks into you, it would have been your life for Suleiman's." His gaze flicked to him. "For some reason, he's got a thing for you."

Let me count the reasons why, Suleiman thought. He clamped his jaw shut.

"And because I know about how much Suleiman cares for you, he would have gladly traded his life for yours." Victor sighed as if all of the energy from his anger drained away. He straightened and leaned against the wall next to the door. "So next time what will you do when we go on a mission?"

Suleiman didn't miss the when rather than if.

"I'll stay within the parameters of the objective." Once more, Sana's poker face had slid into place.

"I'm glad we have that understanding." Victor pushed away from the wall. "Okay, you two. Diana's going to be here in a minute. Then if you want to get clean, showers are down the hall. And I highly suggest that you sleep on the plane because if you oversleep and aren't aboard by six, we're leaving you behind."

With that, he strode from the room.

Suleiman let out on uneasy breath.

Another smile crossed Sana's face. "I'll stay within the mission's parameters." Then she slid out her good hand to show how she'd crossed her fingers. "Maybe."

He couldn't help it. He chuckled as he leaned over. Gently, he kissed her on the lips before pulling back. "I love you, thief of my heart."

With that, he took her hand to await Diana's arrival.

Thursday, July 2, 2015, 0100 hours local time, Mombasa, Kenya

Finally, Tori understood the meaning of clean.

Completely clean.

At least in body.

She drew great comfort from the soft feel of cotton leggings and a long T-shirt against her skin. And from the team doctor's report. Antibiotics would take care of all of the garbage Abu Waheed had given her. Thankfully, the rapid assay Diana had done for HIV had turned up negative. They'd do checks at one, three, and six months for extra reassurance. Her concussion, though severe, seemed to be under control even if her headache hadn't gone away yet. Diana had promised it would, especially with lots of rest. Both of them would be on the lookout for any symptoms of complications.

But emotionally? The hurricane of her captivity had left her spirit in shambles. In her one call to Dad after her exam, he'd pressured her to fly home on the private jet heading her way. He wanted her immediately to hold a press conference and assimilate into life. She'd cowered, at least until Victor had taken the phone from her and explained that Tori was an adult who had a choice. It was her decision, and if she needed her space, so be it. Bless him for standing up to her father.

Why hadn't she done that? The answer came quickly. Her stint as a hostage had impacted her own sense of freedom. Even though Abu Waheed had held her only for a little over a week, he'd dictated everything regarding her basic needs, from when she slept to when she used the restroom to when she ate. She'd been rendered helpless to take a stand on anything.

With that revelation, her thoughts, which seemed to flit this way and that thanks to the concussion, alighted on her fiancé. Waves of unworthiness washed over her. What would he think now? Would he call off the wedding? Break up with her? And where was God in all of this mix? Tears welled in her eyes. The headache, which had begun receding, flared. She hung her head and rubbed her temples.

"Hey, what's going on?"

Diana.

Tori only shrugged. She tucked her knees to her chest and buried her face in them.

The doctor dropped a backpack onto the concrete floor and took a seat on the bench beside her. "You know that if you want to head back to Charleston on your dad's plane, I'll go with you to monitor you. You don't have to ride back with us."

"No, no. I want to go with you. I don't want to…" The lump in her throat choked off her voice. She sucked in a breath with a ragged gasp as she shivered. "I'm not ready for all Dad wants me to do. And to see Jake…I'm so scared. I'm scared he's going to take one look at me and call off our marriage."

"Why would he do that?"

"Because of everything that's happened! I mean, I'm not worthy—"

"Stop right there." The doctor held up her hand. Her sea green eyes flashed. "Don't ever think that because of events out of your control, you're worthless. You are God's child, Tori Walters. He loves you fiercely and always will. And one of His embodiments of that love is your Jake. Sure, this experience has changed your view of the world, of your life. That's a given, but I sincerely doubt it's changed Jake's love for you."

"But—"

"Take one day at a time. That's all that God asks of you, right?" Diana took her hands, and the team doctor's grip was surprisingly strong.

Too choked up to speak, Tori nodded.

"Don't…" Diana looked away. She blinked fast as if holding back tears. "Don't throw something away because you're too scared to trust God. You might not get it back."

Stunned, Tori stared at her. "You…you sound like you speak from experience."

Her new friend sighed. "That's because I do." She rose. "Head to the plane. Fi said you could use her bunk. We've got some noise-canceling headphones that I want you to wear. You know what to do. Minimal sensory stimulation. That should be easy since we'll be spending forty hours flying home." She picked up her pack. "Well, let me get a shower."

With that, Diana almost fled into the deserted shower area.

Tori stared after her. She leaned back against the wall and closed her eyes. Through the headache, she thought she heard Jake whisper, "I love you."

How could he now? Or was Diana right in her wisdom? Right then, it hurt too much to think. With a sigh, Tori picked up her toiletries kit and trudged toward the plane.

Thursday, July 2, 2015, 0630 hours local time, Mombasa, Kenya

Through the door leading to the cockpit, Victor noted Fiona and Butch as they worked their way through the startup list. Steaming mugs of a hot drink sat in the center console between them. His nose twitched. Hmmm, coffee, something he could use himself since he hadn't slept in over twenty-four hours. "Smells good."

Fiona turned. "We found some in the warehouse's break room. Colonel Bakari's men have been keeping us stocked with a steady supply. Speaking of which, if you want to say goodbye to your new friend, now's the time to do it. We're wheels up at seven sharp."

"Huh?" Victor frowned.

She nodded to her left. "He's standing with his groupies at the hallway leading to the offices."

"Promise I'll be back. You guys need a refill?"

"We're good, boss." Butch nodded before murmuring something to Fiona.

Victor noted the rest of his crew. The bottom bunk to his left had its curtains pulled. Tori rested there as per Diana's instructions. Sana, her arm now in a sling until a specialist could assess her injuries, sat on one of the seats and chatted with Suleiman and Shelly. Skylar bobbed his head to something on his MP3 player. When he noticed Victor, he grinned and gave him a thumbs up. Diana had a book in her hands. Her brow furrowed, and she stared at the page as if she didn't really see it. At least everyone had boarded so he didn't have to hunt through the offices.

He stepped through the passenger door and joined the colonel and his retinue of bodyguards. He held out his hand. "Colonel, thank you for your assistance. You've been invaluable in getting Tori back."

Josef's earnest countenance didn't change. With a small bow, he stepped aside and gestured for Victor to precede him. "Come to the break room for a moment. I know you are leaving shortly, so I will not keep you. But I did want to talk with you for a few minutes."

Victor followed him into a small room that held a counter, sink, and a coffeemaker. He instantly picked up the rich aroma he'd smelled in the cockpit. His mouth actually began watering at the anticipation of stocking up. First, he knew they had a final bit of business together.

Josef shut the door and leaned against the edge of a table. "Mr. Walters called. I assured him that the arms you all used will remain in safe storage until Baxter can obtain the proper clearances to ship them to your company."

Huh? This was news to him. Still, it was something that could keep until they were in the States. "Thank you. I appreciate it."

A cunning smile crossed Josef's face. "And I understand that Abu Waheed met a most unfortunate end at the hands of the real Hezbollah."

A flush started low in Victor's cheeks. He hadn't had a chance to talk with the colonel, and in no way did he want to leave on a sour note. "He did." On the ride to Kenya, his jaw had dropped as Suleiman had described blow by blow the events surrounding the pirate's demise. "He did. I apologize for not briefing you earlier, but—"

"No need to apologize." Josef waved him away. "The bigger matter is that he is dead. His network has collapsed. His cronies are gone as well, and it seems as if the Hezbollah cell has established itself at the villa. Perhaps we have changed one problem for another one."

Suddenly, Victor realized how true his words were. "Maybe we should have done something differently."

"No, no. It was probably the only way to free Dr. Walters. And what this has done is to create an opportunity for me to request additional manpower to have intelligence on the ground beyond our borders. It's something I have badly needed, so a win-win, if you would. And do not forget the way your team freed three hundred hostages." A smile finally broke through his somber countenance. "Now I understand you have four children, correct?"

"Three daughters and a son. They came with the wife I married two months ago." Suddenly, Deborah's face floated before him, and Marie's giggles echoed in his ears. His heart ached. He badly wanted to hold Deborah close, but he'd have to wait another forty hours, it seemed.

Josef opened the door and called for someone. "You cannot return without gifts. You see, I spoke with your wife when I heard you were safely in the air back to Mombasa. She told me your youngest daughter wanted a giraffe."

A soldier slipped into the room, his arms laden with packages. One of them was a giant, stuffed giraffe.

With a small bow, the colonel presented them to Victor. "For your Marie. And for your other children." He handed him smaller packages. "Take these as a sign of our thanks."

Victor's heart filled as he held out his hand that wasn't occupied with the gifts. "If I can ever repay the favors you provided us, you call me."

Josef's smile now reached his eyes. "Will do, my friend."

Victor returned to the plane at a minute before the hour.

"'Bout time you showed up." Fiona chuckled as Victor settled into the navigator's chair. She shouted, "Clear!" through the open window and began starting the engines. Within minutes, they taxied through the brightening Kenyan morning for the last time. After only a brief pause, they soared into the sky on their way home.

29

Tori sensed the excitement onboard *The Kitchen Sink*. It floated through the air like a delicious scent, a cinnamon roll warming in the oven. Delicious. Long anticipated. As she watched Shelly and Sana giggle at something, it hit her. The team, the very ones who'd rescued her and her friends from hell, had traveled essentially around the world to save them and had almost lost two of their own in the process.

God had protected them. And what about her? Fortunately, the headache, which had gradually subsided during her rest, didn't flare at the thought. Had He protected her? She didn't know. That's what scared her.

Fiona's voice crackled over her headset. "We have begun our final descent into the Flagstaff airport. Please ensure that all tray tables and seat backs are in an upright position. Once we have landed, please remain seated until the plane is safely at the gate. Be aware as you open the overhead bins that items may have shifted. We thank you for flying Kitchen Sink Airways. We know you have a choice in air travel, and we appreciate your business and hope you will consider flying with us again."

Skylar called, "Not on your life if you take us to Somalia."

Everyone laughed.

Except for Tori. The best she could muster at that point was a smile.

Once the plane had touched down and taxied to a stop, Victor clambered into the cargo area. After weaving his way around the mess of rucks held down by a net, he knelt in front of her and took her hands. "Tori, your family's here."

Her stomach twisted on her last snack of hot chocolate and an energy bar.

"I—I don't know what to do."

"They'll want to see you. What happens next is up to you, okay? I know we've talked about you staying with us, and if that's your wish, we have plenty of room. But we'll also understand if you want to return to Charleston. That's your decision."

Swallowing hard, she nodded.

He smiled and squeezed her hands before rising.

Tori barely heard him instruct the team to wait on the plane until she'd disembarked.

He popped the side door.

Light flooded the interior of the plane.

She squinted, and her eyes watered as they made the adjustment.

Then she saw them. Dad stood with Elizabeth next to a white Lexus SUV. A tall man with sandy blond hair leaned against the left rear fender.

Jake.

Her heart caught.

Victor hopped onto the concrete and helped her down.

Tori's heart pounded.

Then Jake opened his arms wide.

With a low cry, she rushed into them and held on as tightly as she dared as all of the longing and worry culminated in that one embrace.

"I love you," he whispered over and over.

She wanted to stay in his arms forever.

"Tori." Her name came from Dad in a low voice, almost like a command.

She pulled back.

Dad, his graying blond hair tousled by the wind, stood there with Elizabeth, her stepmother, by his side.

Tori rushed into their arms and held on. A week ago, such a gesture had seemed so alien, like a dream that always faded when she opened her eyes to her nightmare of a reality. She pulled back and swiped at the tears trickling down her cheeks.

Elizabeth reached out and held onto her.

Tori rested her head on her shoulder.

"I prayed so hard for this day," her stepmother whispered. "Welcome home, sweetie."

"Not quite yet." Dad released her completely and gestured toward the General Aviation building. "Our pilots are waiting to start preflight, and I told them we'd be leaving in a couple of hours to return to Charleston. I promised Congressman Carlson that Lizzie and I would be at his cookout tomorrow night. Then Monday morning, I want you to…"

Tori's mind raged and blocked out his chatter. So nothing had changed. Maybe not in his world. But hers? Her ordeal had turned everything onto its head. Why couldn't he see that she needed time to readjust? She began shaking her head as she wrung her hands. "I'm staying here."

Dad stared at her. "Excuse me?"

Movement over her shoulder distracted her as Victor and Butch joined her

"I—I need some time to decompress, to…think about what happened."

"But I need you to—"

"You don't need me to do anything." Her face burned while chills washed over the rest of her.

Dad folded his arms. "There's no need to be difficult about this."

"I'm not being difficult about it." Her heart began pounding, and her palms moistened. Her headache, which had all but completely disappeared, began a comeback like a football team forcing its way toward the end zone. "Things are different now. Please try to understand."

"And why can't you—"

"May I?" A blonde joined the group. Where had she come from?

Then Tori noticed the way she took Victor's hand. Deborah, his wife, his bride of only two months, if she remembered correctly from what Victor had said when he'd shown her pictures of his family.

Deborah continued, "Norm, it's very normal for a former hostage not to feel like re-integrating into their previous life immediately after their return. Tori's right. She needs time to process and…"

Butch put a hand on Tori's shoulder and steered her toward the plane. "Let them duke it out, okay?"

Choking back the tears, she nodded and huddled on the concrete next to the passenger door, where the rest of the team silently deplaned.

From the way Dad's face reddened and his gestures in wide, swooping arcs, he wasn't happy with Victor. No, he was furious. She had to admire the man who'd led the rescue effort. And his wife, too. Neither flinched as if dealing with billionaires who didn't get there way and acted like two-year-olds happened every day with them.

And Jake? He kept his arms folded across his chest and his mouth shut. What a wise man not to become a target of Dad's wrath.

Finally, Norm yanked open the door of the Lexus. He slammed it. Tires chirped as he sped toward the General Aviation building.

Tori stared at the pavement in front of her and ran her fingers along the little ridges. How did they put those in it?

As Deborah rejoined her children near a silver Chevy Suburban, Victor, Elizabeth, and Jake approached Tori.

Without breaking eye contact with the pavement, she said, "I'm sorry."

Victor crouched in front of her. "For what?"

She shrugged.

He straightened. "You can stay as long as you like. Well, let me say an official hello to Deb and the kids. Butch, can you get me those gifts? And can you guys unload the plane? Norm wants to meet at 6:30 to go over the invoice before he leaves."

Elizabeth settled beside her. "We'll be staying, too, okay? I told Norm you were far more important than any cookout."

Why couldn't Dad see that?

"Hold on, boss." Butch boarded and returned with several packages.

Victor, his arms laden with the gifts, strode toward his family.

Two little girls sprinted across the concrete and ran into his arms.

Tori's eyes filled.

Victor hugged them tightly. Then he embraced the two older children, a boy and a girl, before stepping to Deborah. For a moment, they gazed at each other.

Victor kissed his wife. Even from that distance, their intimacy radiated from them.

Would she ever feel that from Jake? Tori's heart ached.

Once more, those waves of unworthiness washed over her. How could she have such a relationship with Jake now? A lump built in her throat. She put her head in her arms and squeezed her eyes shut.

"Tori."

She lifted her face.

Jake sat on his knees in front of her. He lifted her chin with his finger. "I love you."

Tears began trickling down her cheeks. "I—I'm not ready."

"I know." His eyes glimmered. "I know you need time. But I want you to know one thing."

You want to break our engagement. Her breath hitched.

With his thumb, he brushed her cheek. "Nothing that happened over there changes my love for you. You may not see it that way, but it doesn't. I'll wait for you."

"Even...even if it's forever?" There. She'd voiced what had preyed upon her mind during all of those endless hours on the flight home.

His Adam's apple bobbed. "Even if it's forever."

With that, he leaned forward and gently kissed her. He rose and joined Elizabeth, who now stood a few yards away with her back turned.

Tori's heart physically ached. Is this what a broken heart felt like?

"It'll be all right," Butch murmured as he extended a hand and helped her to her feet.

It certainly didn't feel that way. "I...hope so."

"God's got this in His hands. And now, we're gonna unload this bird before heading home."

"May I help?"

"Nah. You can supervise. That's what my grandpa would always say." Butch picked up a camp chair, unfurled it under the wing, and plopped it down by the port-side wheel. "So stay there. Chill out. We'll grab you in a few."

Tori did what he asked. She watched as the team members sans Victor unloaded their gear and the Humvees. The late afternoon air blew across her face. Above the smell of jet fuel, she sampled ponderosa pine. And once the racket of a departing jet faded, she relished the silence. Oh, it was good to be on this side of things. She closed her eyes and soaked in the new sensations.

She must have dozed because the next thing she knew, the team piled their rucks into the bed of a silver Ford F-250. When had that arrived? She must have really been out of it! The remaining gear and Diana, Skylar, Shelly, and Fiona crowded into a white Acura RL. Butch opened the back doors to the pickup. "Suleiman, Sana, climb on up. Sana, you need a hand?"

"I'm good." Even with her sling, she swung into the backseat.

Suleiman did the same beside her.

Butch opened the front passenger door and bowed. "Madam, your chariot awaits."

Tori couldn't help it. She giggled and allowed him to help her up.

The ride took a total of twenty minutes. As they approached the ranch, a surreal feeling overcame her. She was free. And home. Okay, not quite home since she planned to reside in Charleston, but home enough. A long-overdue feeling of peace draped itself over her. She barely listened as Butch chatted on his phone with Victor.

They bumped over a cattle guard. Butch said, "Here we are. Last Chance Ranch. Home of these hooligans."

"Thanks, Butch," Sana called from the back. She chuckled.

"Truth hurts sometimes." Butch grinned as he pulled to a stop at the back of the house. "We'll unload here before I put my baby up for the night. Tori, the boss said your daddy's headed out after they do their business. Supper will be at seven, so you've got a chance to clean up and take a nap. Lord knows we're all pooped."

"Where am I staying?"

"In the Big House."

Her eyes narrowed. "What? A prison?"

Butch laughed and gestured to the house of glass, wood, and stone. "Nope. We call Vic and Deb's house the Big House. The boss said there's a room ready for you. C'mon." Hefting her duffels on his shoulders like they were grocery bags, he led the way onto a terrace and into a mudroom. A wide hall bordered a kitchen to the right before opening to a great room. They crossed over hardwoods and headed up a flight of stairs close to the front of the house. He nodded toward an open door. "There you are. You're gonna have to share a bathroom with Gracie and Marie, so watch out for tub toys."

He placed her bags on the floor next to a dresser.

"No worries there." Tori smiled at him. "Butch, thanks."

"No problem." He tipped an imaginary hat and, whistling, shambled down the stairs.

With a sigh, Tori eased onto the edge of the bed. She understood the whole cleaning up part. After forty hours on a plane, she redefined grimy. Unpacking would come later. Right now, a shower took precedence. She reached for one of the identical bags and undid the zipper.

She'd opened the one that held miscellaneous items like books, music, and photos. And her Bible. She picked it up and settled onto the bed as she ran her hand over the leather cover. She didn't miss the small bump.

It hit her. When her ordeal had begun, she'd hidden her engagement ring inside. She flipped it open to the page where she'd taped it. Could she get it off without ripping the paper? With her fingernail, she picked at the edges of the clear tape. By the time she worked the ring loose, she'd torn a hole in the delicate paper.

She swallowed hard and turned to the duffel. A picture of Jake sat on top. She picked it up and ran her finger down the glass. "Oh, Jake. I'm so sorry this happened." She closed her eyes against the hot tears suddenly flooding them. "I'm so sorry. Can you forgive me?"

Forget taking a shower. With his picture in her arms, Tori curled up. Loneliness surged over her. It was like she slid back into the pit of her despair. The look on Jake's face when he'd vowed to wait for her flashed before her. Deep sadness. She had no other way to define it. She'd hurt him so deeply that she had no hope. And maybe it would never return.

Friday, July 3, 2015, 1830 hours Pacific Daylight Time, Flagstaff, AZ

As it began its descent toward the horizon, the sun cast a warm glow into the studio. The breeze caressed Victor's cheeks in soft touches, almost like Deborah had done only a couple of hours earlier.

He really wanted to be in the Big House with his family. But no, business called. All because Norm's pride had been hurt by Tori's refusal to plunge back into a normal life right away. It'd been the billionaire's petty way to punish the man who'd risked life and limb and those of his team to rescue his daughter.

He sighed, his fingers poised over the keyboard. He really needed to finish the invoice for the job they'd just completed, especially since Norm was due any minute. Problem was, he couldn't take his eyes off the terrace of the Big House. On his lab chair, he swiveled to the right.

Anna unfurled a tablecloth that settled across the wrought iron in a curtain of red and white.

Butch turned on the grill, and when Deborah joined him with a massive plate of steaks, he laughed and pointed at the grill.

DJ, who slouched in a chair with his feet swung onto the edge of the fire pit, flipped pages in a magazine, most likely something related to cars. He gestured to Butch and said something. His deputy nodded.

Yep, check the car thing. His stepson was already making plans to buy a fixer upper.

Grrr. Victor hated being hard at work only two hours after arriving home. What could he do? When he'd protested, Norm had threatened to delay payment. Probably as another way to make him pay for keeping him away from Tori. It didn't matter that she was an adult who could make up her own mind.

Victor tried to focus. If only Gracie's and Marie's chatter from the swing set didn't distract him, he'd be able to finish.

Okay. Back to work. He returned his attention to the screen and surveyed the itemized invoice. Good to go. With one click of the mouse, the printer whirred and began printing the document.

Footsteps pattered up the path. Her hair sticking out in wisps from her ponytail, Gracie stood on the other side of the screened door. Norm followed. His second youngest threw open the screened door. "Daddy, Mr. Walters is here to see you."

"Thanks, Gracie. I'll be at the house in a bit. Norm, come on in." Victor offered a warm smile to show no hard feelings from that afternoon.

Only a faint one came in return from the billionaire.

"Tea? Coffee? Goodness knows caffeine's the only thing keeping me going right now."

"Coffee would be great." Forced politeness radiated from his client. Norm seemed beaten, almost meek in some ways.

Victor paused. Had Elizabeth dressed him down for what had happened?

Finally, Norm sighed and ran a hand through his graying hair. "I owe you an apology."

Victor set a mug on a coffee table and gestured for him to sit on one of the two chairs that formed a conversation group with the couch. "For?"

"For earlier today. Lizzie, well, she'd warned me not to pressure Tori. I did and left in a huff, as you know. When she got back to the resort, Lizzie got all in my face and rightfully so." He picked up his mug and cradled it in his hands.

Victor took a seat on the other chair.

"I guess I so badly want to work on my relationship with Tori, but after I talked with a friend of mine who's a psychologist, I realize how pushing things with her is just plain wrong. Can you accept my apology?"

"Of course." Victor smiled and stuck out his hand to show no hard feelings. "Friends?"

This time, Norm shook. "Friends." He cleared his throat. "What do you have for me?"

"I've got the invoice here." Victor handed him the papers. "We agreed upon a flat fee, but here's our hours for the team. The second page shows our expenses. Fuel, provisions, etcetera." Using the pen he'd carried with him, he pointed out those lines. "As soon as we get *The Kitchen Sink* and vehicles clean, your pilots can come and pick them up. The rest of the gear too."

He placed the keys beside their mugs.

Norm frowned. "The what?"

"*The Kitchen Sink*. That's the nickname Butch gave the plane."

A small smile flickered across the billionaire's face. "You might as well go ahead and stencil that on there."

"What?" Had he heard him right?

Norm cleared his throat. "Deb told me about your dream to open a security company, and if you're going to be running missions like the one you just did, you're going to need some wheels, er, wings. And keep the Humvees too. And all of the other equipment."

Victor's eyes widened as his heart raced. "Norm, this is—"

"Consider it something like seed money." Norm shoved the keys in his direction. He reached inside his blazer and withdrew a folded sheet of paper. After smoothing it, he handed it over. "Here's a letter of intent that I'll make good on my word."

"I'm speechless."

Norm chuckled. "You did a good job. Seriously. And I'm sure word's going to get out. Look for the papers via FedEx next week."

Victor didn't know what else to do but accept it. He glanced toward the briefcase that had carried their *baksheesh*. "Did Baxter tell you about the bribe money?"

"He did."

"We were able to get all back but eight thousand dollars."

"Keep it as a bonus."

"You're...sure?'

Norm nodded. "Absolutely. You earned it."

"I'm—I'm dumbfounded."

"You got Tori back, and that's all that matters." He paused as if considering something else to say. With a sigh, he rose. "Well, I'll leave you to it. I'm going to head out so I can make that cookout. After what happened today, I'd like to stay, but I guess you can say there's business to be had there. Jake is working from here, and Lizzie will be staying here as well. Tell Tori that when she's ready, she can call me."

"I will." Victor saw him outside. He leaned against the door frame and watched as Norm strolled toward the small lot where the Shadow Box team parked their cars. Already, he had his phone to his ear as if he'd slipped into business mode. How hard would it be for him to realize that life wasn't all business? *Lord, reconcile this family.*

Victor returned to the worktable. He logged into the Internet and checked the news websites. Yep, word had spread like a virus that Norm had hired a private security firm that had staged the rescue of three hundred hostages, followed by the dramatic rescue of Tori. No names yet, but he knew that would change, especially when the South Africans as well as members of his own government started asking questions, like right then. Already, an e-mail from the South African embassy and one from the Department of Defense rested in his in-box. He began tapping out a reply the South Africans.

The screen door banged open, and Marie, her arms full of her giant stuffed giraffe, rushed into the studio. She almost bowled him over as she tried to hug him, giraffe and all.

"Easy there!" Victor laughed and slid off the chair, lest he fall over backwards. "Isn't Stretch an indoor giraffe?"

"I wanted to take him on a walk." She set him on the table and sent his mug wobbling. "Mommy wanted me to tell you that it's time to stop working."

He snagged the mug just in time. As he did so, his noticed the e-mail glowing on the screen. It could wait. Matter of fact, it all could wait until Monday. He closed the window without sending the message. Then, with her little hand in his and Stretch in his other hand, he led the way from the studio toward his family.

★ ★ ★

Friday, July 3, 2015, 2100 hours Pacific Daylight Time, Flagstaff, AZ

"Deborah, thank you for feeding us." Suleiman smiled at Victor's wife. With his belly full of steak and vegetables, even the coffee he'd drunk couldn't keep him awake. He wanted to stay there, in his chair, until he oozed to the ground in a blob of contentment as the flames from the fire pit kept him warm. Except then, his rump started bothering him. *Thanks, Jibril, for making my life a pain in the butt, literally.*

From where he sat across from him, Butch chuckled. "Hey, Suleiman, you might want to consider going to bed."

"I think we all need to go that way." Victor rose and stretched. "Gang, thanks. We'll reconvene tomorrow at ten to debrief, okay?"

"Roger that." Butch lifted his beer bottle in salute. "Anyone else staying up?"

"Not me." Sana shifted and winced. "I'm pooped out. Suleiman, walk me back?"

"Of course." He bowed. "After you."

Once away from the terrace, she took his hand. "Do you mind staying for a bit? I'm still kind of wired, but I wanted some time with you."

He smiled. "Of course."

They reached the Women's Building and collapsed onto the couch. Ah. He found the softness of its leather much better on his rear than the hardness of the wrought iron chair that even his cushion hadn't disguised. And they had the place to themselves, at least for a little while since the other ladies were still on the terrace.

Sana snuggled into the crook of his arm, and he scrolled through the shows they'd saved on the DVR. "What do you wish to watch?"

"Something relaxing," she replied through a yawn.

"HGTV it is, then." He heaved a mock sigh. "Only if I have to."

She giggled.

They turned to a program about taking an old house, gutting it, and turning it into something new. While Sana soon became enthralled, his thoughts wandered in his own version of a debrief of their time in Somalia. He'd thought that he'd view everything almost like he was a detached third party.

Wrong.

Once more, Makmoud's taunting echoed in his ears. His half-brother had dared him to shoot, to take his revenge against him for his mistreatment and to assuage his guilt over killing Rachel. His own replies echoed in his ears. Now, tension riddled his shoulders as he clenched his fists. He drew in a sharp breath through his teeth.

"Suleiman?" Her voice returned him to the reality of sitting in the Women's Building beside one very beautiful woman.

"I—I'm sorry."

"You were huffing and puffing and had your jaw clenched. I know this isn't your favorite show, so if you want me to—"

"I wanted to kill him." There. He'd said it.

"What?" Sana paused the program and shifted so she faced him. "Who?"

"Makmoud." Suleiman swallowed hard. "I had painted his forehead with the laser. All I had to do was squeeze the trigger. That is how deep my anger was."

"But you didn't."

"No, I did not." He leaned forward, rested his elbows on his knees, and raked his hands through his hair. "My anger shocked me. It was like…like I wanted revenge for Rachel's death, as if that would take away Victor's pain. And for everything that Makmoud did to me in Venezuela when he broke me. What sort of twisted human being am I?"

"A sinful one living in a fallen world, just like me. Just like Victor. Or Diana. Or Butch. That's why we all need a savior. It's like we snapped off our compass needle that pointed us toward God and have ever since then been spinning around as we try to seek direction. Christ is our True North."

He gazed at her. "In the end, I couldn't do it. And it almost cost both of us."

"No, my own actions nearly cost us." She fell silent and ran her fingers up and down his arm. Finally, she continued, "If you'd taken that shot, Jibril would have surely killed you because he was right there on that roof. After I got away, I saw him climb the staircase. I don't know how I did it, but I bolted over there and followed as fast as I could." She laced her fingers through his. "What do you think held you back?"

"I—I don't know."

"I think you do."

He puffed out a frustrated breath. "This is not the time for games."

"I'm not playing games. You know what I'm talking about. You told me yourself about a week or so ago. You're done with killing."

A week? He nearly laughed. So much had happened that he felt like he'd aged years instead of days. "But I killed two pirates."

"To save Victor's and Fiona's skins, you did. Saving Tori was part of the mission, and you were defending our comrades."

"Then why didn't I kill Makmoud?"

"Like Victor said, it would have been outside the parameters of the mission. Remember that only because of your distraction did I get away. I think Holy Spirit was holding you back." She fell silent. A muscle twitched in her jaw as she stroked his hand. "At heart, you're now a peacemaker. You do realize that, right?"

What could he say? No? She was right. He knew he had a talent, a dangerous one at that, one he preferred not to deploy to its extreme unless he had no choice. It was an awesome, burdensome responsibility. "Personally, right now, I wish to live a quiet life. Like the life I've had since last summer. I am finished with killing unless there is no other choice."

She snuggled close to him and unmuted the program. Something else seemed to stir in her heart because she kept shifting.

"Is your shoulder hurting?"

"I'm fine. Just thinking."

"You were right. I am a peacemaker—"

"Who still needs to make his peace with Victor. You said you almost confessed when we were in Mombasa. Please consider that."

"I'm fine now." Then why did he feel like he lied through his teeth?

"Are you?" She pulled away and faced him. "Are you really?"

The guilt and shame he'd felt days before uncurled within his gut, almost like they were monsters who'd slumbered during their trip to Somalia. Mentally, he shoved them away with his foot. "Why are you baiting me?"

"I'm not. I was serious about what I said on the plane. I know you're not at peace. How can you be when the man whose life you nearly destroyed sits not a hundred yards from here?"

She might as well have taken a baseball bat and hit him over the head. His throat tightened. Dizziness assailed him. He jumped to his feet. "How could you say something like that?"

He raced toward the door.

"I'm sorry!" Thanks to having one arm in a sling, she squirmed upright and almost fell off the couch. After catching herself, she staggered toward him and grabbed his arm. "Suleiman, please. I'm truly sorry. I guess I'm exhausted and—"

"Leave me alone," he growled, shook loose, and darted into the night. On the terrace, Butch seemed to be telling a story. Fiona, Diana, and Skylar laughed. Shelly snorted and giggled. How could they be happy?

Of course, they didn't have the burden of killing his mentor's fiancée on their hearts. He turned and fled in the opposite direction. Under the light of the waning moon, he picked his way along the trail toward the back of the box canyon. Victor's studio was dark, meaning he'd not returned to work after supper. No, he had a family now, one that had come at great cost. Once past the studio, the ponderosa pines remained thin. The barn came into view. One of the horses nickered as it smelled him. He ignored it and continued on as if he could seek solace in the furthest reaches of the canyon.

Though no change occurred visually, the ground's contours smoothed as he crossed the grate the team had repaired the year before after their frantic escape with Deborah and her children from Makmoud. At last, the box canyon narrowed as he reached the end until it was only about ten feet wide. Now he was out of options with nowhere else to run in more ways than one.

He pulled out his cigarette pack. Thanks to his trembling fingers, it fell to the ground. He snatched it up, yanked one out, and lit it. Not that the nicotine did any good. He turned around and studied the walls soaring above him.

Here, just over a year before, he'd faced one of the greatest tests of his life. His chest heaved. Almost if by magic, the sky seemed to lighten to that fateful afternoon. The pop of gunfire, which sounded almost like tiny fire-crackers, fueled the training Victor had ground into them. Calm prevailed where panic should have ruled. Sana shouted at him to open the storage bin where they kept the climbing gear. He tossed her a harness. She jumped into it, looped the fifty-foot climbing rope over her shoulders, and practically shot up the hand- and footholds they'd created. The rope snaked downward. As he helped their charges into harnesses, the battle intensified. But they'd made it. They'd achieved their objective of keeping Deborah and her three remaining children safe, then rescuing Skylar, Fiona, Victor, Liza, and Anna.

But only after he'd nearly killed his brother. Except that Makmoud had dived out of the way. That was so different than what had happened only days before. Why?

Was Sana right? Would he never find peace? Would his knowledge and secret come between Sana and him? She seemed to think so. What about between him and the man who'd become his mentor? Why hadn't he pulled the trigger on Makmoud this time when he'd so readily done so the year before? What could take away the stain of guilt from killing Victor's Rachel?

"God, no! No more questions!" He sank to a crouch and sucked in a smoke-filled breath. He began coughing. Sana's honesty from a few nights before—was it really just over a week?—echoed in his mind. The burden of his heart nearly crushed him.

She was right.

With his elbows resting on his knees and the cigarette still dangling from his fingers, he hung his head. His chest spasmed almost as if he were having another panic attack, except that this time, he wanted to break free of the bondage that had caused those. "God, is that all I have to do? Is all I have to do is ask for Your forgiveness and see what Christ has done?"

The wind whispered through the pines between the barn and house and on the mesa above.

"Is that truly all?"

Trust Me. That still, quiet voice spoke within him.

Suddenly, he knew.

Carefully, he stubbed out the cigarette and fell onto his knees, almost as if he were going to pray one of the *salats* in Islam. In Farsi, he whispered, "I know You are God. And now, like Sana said, I know full well who I am and what I have done. I am guilty of so many crimes, too many to even count. I know I cannot approach You except through Jesus. Forgive me, and let Jesus be Lord over my life."

He drew in a deep, cleansing breath.

He didn't see a light, didn't hear angels singing, but deep in his soul, something stilled as if all of the burdens of the past three years fell away.

He truly understood.

Sana was right.

Grace was a gift, not something earned.

No panic any more. Instead, pure, raw peace flowed through him. He had to tell Sana. Once he hopped to his feet, he raced to the Women's Building and stepped inside.

Her door was already closed, and he didn't see any light showing underneath. He cracked it and whispered, "Sana?"

No answer.

He slipped all the way inside and shut it behind him.

She lay sound asleep, her shoulders rising and falling in an easy rhythm beneath her comforter with its Indian elephants on it. An occasional sniffle escaped her.

Oh, Sana. He eased onto an easy chair he'd helped her buy from a local thrift store. It'd become her prayer chair, she liked to say. *I want to tell you so badly, but I also know you need to sleep.* He stayed where he was for a few more minutes until he felt drowsiness pulling him toward its cozy depths. If he didn't get moving, he'd fall asleep right then and there.

He rose. Ever so gently, he kissed her on the forehead. The touch of his lips on her smooth skin reminded him of the potential future they now had together. He whispered, "I will see you in the morning."

He slipped from the room—and nearly jumped out of his skin when Diana and Fiona clambered onto the porch and through the front door.

Diana started laughing. "You look like you just got caught with your hand in the cookie jar."

Huh? What did that mean? "I—um—well—I—uh—We were spending time together."

Fiona's eyes narrowed. "What kind of time?"

Both women started giggling.

"Uh, quality time." Oh, no. Their giggles turned to laughter as Fiona crossed to the wine holder on the kitchenette's counter and pulled out a bottle.

He flushed so deeply that he worried his skin would burn off from the heat. "Um, perhaps that was the wrong term."

"Maybe." A sly grin crossed Diana's face.

"I'll, uh, be leaving. See you in the morning." With that, he fled into the night. As his steps slowed to a walk, he took a deep, refreshing breath of air. Then he started chuckling to himself. Yes, any time with Sana was quality time. Wearing his newfound peace like a blanket, he strolled toward the Men's Building.

30

A rooster that lived near the barn crowed. Suleiman groaned and opened his eyes a crack. He lay flat on his stomach, his head on the mattress, his pillow tucked under his arm. With a groan, he squinted at the clock. What? Only six in the morning? Of course, he'd fallen into bed before ten the night before. Still. He closed his eyes.

The rooster welcomed the morning again. It sounded like he was closer, maybe near the studio. Why did he have to wander? Now Suleiman lay on his back. Somehow, he propped open an eyelid. Okay, so half an hour had passed. He clamped his pillow over his head and drifted again.

"Cockadoodledoo!" It came from beneath his open window.

"All right! That's it!" Suleiman bolted upright. Scrambling from bed, he shoved his feet into a pair of flip flops and stomped outside. Sure enough, the rooster was winding up for another call.

"Get. Out. Of. Here!" He ran at the bird, which cackled as if enjoying its early morning game. It scurried away in a mess of feathers and chortling.

He was already up, so he might as well make the best of it. When he returned inside, neither Skylar nor Butch had stirred. Matter of fact, snoring emanated from Butch's room. How could he, a veteran of Special Forces who claimed to be the world's lightest sleeper, remain comatose? Grumbling, Suleiman started the coffee before dressing for the day.

With mug in hand, he wandered outside. The air held a crisp touch to it that would dissipate as the sun rose higher into the sky. He peered toward the Big House. Someone stirred there, as the doors leading onto the terrace were already open.

This time, he desired no company. He wanted to contemplate his new status on his own. The pool house. Perfect since no one would be there. He also loved hanging out near the pool.

When preparing the property to house the Shadow Box team, Victor had renovated one of the old buildings that had housed ranch equipment. Now, it held a twenty-five-yard pool. In the winter, lowered garage doors kept the area warm. In the summer, they were raised to allow for air circulation. A patio outside held lounge chairs.

He sank onto one and sipped his brew. Besides the rooster getting him up, he deemed it a perfect morning. It was good to be home, to be where he belonged.

"Suleiman."

He raised his gaze and smiled.

Sana stood there, a mug of her own in her good hand, her eyes still half-closed in sleep.

He slid over. "Have a seat. But first…"

He kissed her long and slow.

"Gee, how can I refuse after that?"

He laughed. "You couldn't sleep?"

"Not with that stupid rooster deciding to visit close up."

He scowled. "How about try under my window."

She giggled, and its bell-like sound filled him with warmth, as did the way she leaned into him. "I want to apologize for last night. I was tired and not thinking clearly."

"Forgiven." He buried his nose in the silkiness of her hair. As he closed his eyes and inhaled the clean scent of her shampoo, the memories from the night before—after he'd left—surfaced. "I have something to tell you."

"What's that?"

"I…" The sudden rush of emotion stunned him. He took a deep breath to steady himself. "I—how do you say it—realize you were right. I need Jesus as my Savior, and I asked him to forgive me and be Lord of my life."

She pulled back. Her eyes pooled with tears.

His heart filled. At first, though her mouth worked, her voice didn't. Finally, she blurted, "Oh, Suleiman!"

"I wanted to tell you last night, but you were already asleep. It is…it is the only way to peace." He held her close. "I love you so much. I truly do. Thank you for being patient with me, for being faithful."

"You don't know how many people have been praying for you. Butch. Diana. Shelly, me. Victor. Others at church." Her gaze shifted to the studio, which was visible along the path cutting through the pines. Her brow knitted. "You need to reconcile fully with him."

She had to state the obvious. Why couldn't she leave it alone? If he could, why couldn't she?

"How can I?"

"What?"

"How can I do that? It would be like…like driving a knife straight through his heart."

"You know you must. To have peace fully, you must."

"Did you do so with your own crimes?" Talk about pulling out knives! He'd yanked out a big one with that. Why couldn't he keep his mouth shut for once?

For a moment, she didn't say anything. She lifted her mug of tea to her lips. The liquid trembled slightly, the only indication that he'd rattled her. With a sigh, she lowered it and rested it on her knee. "I did. When I was in prison and converted, I got all of the addresses of those I'd stolen from, everyone from my father to the director of the museum where I committed my last crime. I wrote every single person I'd hurt, a total of twenty letters. Also, I told the detective where I'd hidden everything. I think…I think that's what helped with the leniency for me to get out after two years. They understood my repentance was sincere."

"And what was the result of those letters?"

"Most were gracious. Some wrote back and said they forgave me. The director of the museum must have been a believer because she started writing me back, and we've been corresponding ever since and even got together for lunch a few times before I moved."

"But not all."

"Not my father." Sana sighed and turned her gaze away. "He...I shamed our family so much that we're barely on speaking terms." She set her mug aside and took his hand. "I guess what I'm trying to say is that there can be reconciliation if both parties are willing."

Could he trust that Victor believed those words she had read to him from First John? It took faith, he knew. Did he have that faith? "But what if Victor isn't—"

"That's a chance you must take."

Just contemplating the idea of facing his mentor soured his stomach. "I just...I'm not sure I'm ready."

"I know." She shifted and and ran her hand down his jaw. A sad smile crossed her face. "Forgot to shave again?"

"Lazy," he replied. His cheeks heated.

She rested her forehead against his. "Remember, I too share your secret. And it's a burden. Think of it like a stone attached by a chain to my leg. To yours as well. I feel, when I look at Victor now, like I'm living a lie."

His chest tightened, and he thought his heart would break. He couldn't deny it anymore. She was right. With his conversion, he didn't have to think hard to realize they would probably marry sooner rather than later. When he'd shared with Sana a couple of weeks ago, he'd bound her to his secret as well.

"I could go with you when you talk with him, you know. Think about it." With mug in hand, she rose.

He did too.

She stood on tiptoe and kissed him. "I love you, and I want you to be free."

With that and another sad smile over her shoulder, she wandered toward the Big House and left him to contemplate the consequences of his choices.

Saturday, July 4, 2015, 1000 hours Pacific Daylight Time, Flagstaff, AZ

"How's everyone doing?" Victor asked as the team arrived at his studio for a debrief.

Butch grinned and held up his coffee mug. "None the worse for wear, 'cept for that dang rooster that kept crowing this morning." He laughed when Suleiman, who'd arrived with Sana shortly before him, scowled. "Yeah, don't think I didn't hear you go after that guy. Better you than me. Otherwise, we'd be having fried chicken tonight." He settled onto one of the chairs in front of the dormant fireplace. "And, boss, thanks for the stiff brew. Can I say I'm ready for a normal life?"

Diana chuckled and took one end of the couch. "Normal? What's that? My life isn't going to be normal for a bit since I'll be spending the next few weeks moving."

"Oh, that's right," Shelly said as she curled up in the other chair with a tea mug. She took a sip and sighed. "I can't wait to get back up here."

Diana grinned. "Not too much longer."

Skylar and Fiona arrived just as everyone settled down. They joined Diana on the couch. Sana and Suleiman took a seat on the hearth. Something must have happened recently because they sat as close together as they could, and Suleiman held tightly to her hand.

Victor muffled his smile as he pulled over a lab chair and reviewed in his mind what he wanted to say. "Gang, good work. We're all here. We're all safe and relatively uninjured." He tossed a tennis ball from one hand to the other. "We're going to debrief like we did last year after training. Remember that whoever has the ball is the one to talk. Overall, I thought things went well. Very well. We operated under the best circumstances we had."

Butch nodded, and Victor tossed him the ball. He caught it with an easy swipe of his big hand. "It didn't hurt that Colonel Bakari gave us a wealth of information."

Skylar held up his hand, and his buddy tossed him the ball. "That's one thing we were terribly skimpy on. Intelligence. If it hadn't been for the colonel, we probably would have suffered a casualty or at least sustained more injuries."

Sana nudged him on the leg, and he handed it to her. "I still think we should have taken out Abu Waheed when we had the chance."

Victor wanted to run screaming from the studio. Hadn't they discussed that before they'd left Mombasa? "Sana, we've reviewed that."

"Yeah, yeah. I know. It wasn't in the mission objective." She waved her hand as if to dismiss his statement. "I mean, he hurt Tori. Big time. And the countless other women he kidnapped? And those who have disappeared and probably still suffer? I'm just saying, we should have done more."

This was going nowhere fast. "That wasn't what Norm paid us to do."

"It galls me, Vic. How many women have been sold into slavery because of him? Or men like him?"

Uh, uh. He wasn't going to get pulled into a philosophical battle. At least not today. "We've discussed and seen what happens when we deviate. All I can say is that quick, independent thinking saved your bacon."

She squeezed Suleiman's hand. "You'll get no argument from me."

With that, she tossed him the ball as if to state that she'd said her piece.

For the next hour, they talked through the mission step by step. Victor took notes until finally, he set the clipboard he held aside. Something he could only describe as joy filled him as he gazed at his complete team, one he'd worked so hard to build the year before, only to have it fall apart after Gary's betrayal.

During the mission, one thing had come clear to him. He wanted to lead all of them again. Now how did he convince them of that? "Okay, gang. Norm said he's cutting a check. As soon as I get it and it clears, I'll cut you each a check for a million. So you're free of any other obligations. But…" He took a deep breath. "I do have something for you to consider."

Skylar, the cool one of the group, raised an eyebrow.

"As you know, when Shadow Box fell apart, I started a company called Sentry Securities. My dream has been to develop it into a company that is a combination of what we just did and investigative services. Most jobs I could handle with a small staff, but" —he took a deep breath— "I'd like to utilize all of your talents when needed. With that in mind, I'm offering to bring you all onboard on a contractual basis. In other words, say, if I needed Suleiman for surveillance work, I could contract with him. Rates would be fair because I would negotiate that with our client." Here it came. Do or die time. "The thing is, everyone would have to be here in Flagstaff so we could train together as a team and to maintain our unity."

"Wow, boss." Butch rubbed his goatee. "So we wouldn't have to give up our day jobs?"

"Nope."

"I'm in." The mechanic grinned. "That's why I bought the shop. Flexibility."

"Count me in, too," Shelly said. "I mean, Diana and I are moving here and all, so that would be so totally awesome."

"And me." Diana nodded. "I can negotiate that with my new partners."

Victor chuckled to cover his surprise. "You don't have to tell me today."

"No thinking needed. Count me in too," Sana said. "It may fit well with my own plans."

"Which are?" Shelly asked.

"Not to be revealed until they're more solidified."

"I agree with Sana. A student and waiter is most flexible." Suleiman positively grinned. "Skylar? No pressure."

"Aw, shucks," Skylar drawled. "Last night, I saw this building for sale downtown. It might make a good second restaurant for Regions."

Throughout all of this, Fiona remained silent. Her face didn't reveal anything, but her eyes did. Conflict. Finally, she bit her lip and looked away as if she didn't want to object in public. Her knee jiggled up and down.

She needed more time, and Victor was more than willing to grant it. "Think about it, and you can give me your firm answers before you head out. In the meantime, you're free to hang out here for the Fourth. Anna's fifteenth birthday is today, and she's requested driving lessons followed by a barbecue."

"You have your last will and testament written?" Butch asked. He snickered. "I'll stay off the roads in Flagstaff."

Everyone laughed.

Fiona made for the door as if her hair had caught fire. Victor grabbed her arm. "Fi, could you hold short?"

"I—I need to get going and pack. You know. Vegas calls, and…" She sighed and stared at the ground. The rest of the crew cast curious glances their way as they filed into the rapidly warming day.

"I wanted to talk with you for a few minutes."

She gazed at the Women's Building, then plopped onto the couch again. She wouldn't look at him, which was so uncharacteristic of her. "Look, if you're mad at me for the way I acted in Vegas, I'm sorry."

"No, no. It's not that." He shifted the lab chair to the worktable and settled across from her. "It's more about how things actually are for you in Vegas."

"They're fine. I mean, I love the flying, and very gradually, I'm saving up."

Then why did she have liar written all over her face?

"Fi."

"It's true."

He tried another tack. "What's your dream, though?"

"I want to have my own air cargo business." Her face fell. "It's just that I don't get paid a lot, and I've still got bills to pay. Even with the payment from this job and Skylar offering to pool his resources, I'm a far cry from the cash I need to buy even one plane."

What? This was news to him. Maybe Skylar had truly turned over a new leaf. And maybe his own offer would dovetail with her plans. He hoped so. "Let me tell you a story."

She rolled her eyes.

"C'mon. Work with me. Okay?"

She shrugged.

"When Norm and I talked about the contract yesterday, he offered me a gift."

"That would be?"

"*The Kitchen Sink*. He's signing that plus the other equipment over to Sentry Securities at no charge."

"What?" Fiona's jaw dropped. Her sherry eyes widened.

"That's right. The plane plus the other equipment. Consider *The Kitchen Sink* as a starter plane. I'd be willing to let Sentry Securities lease it to your company for a very low rate, provided you would keep up the routine maintenance. I don't know what it costs to run a business like what you're considering, but I'm sure you do. Hopefully, that would free up some cash for you to get it off the ground."

Fiona started giggling, something totally unlike her.

He cocked his head. "What?"

"Off the ground. A perfect pun." With that, she calmed down and wiped the corners of her eyes.

"We've missed you and Skylar. For all that happened, you make this team complete in more ways than one. Would you consider a move to Flagstaff? Your old room will be available, and I'll even take out the bed I got as a replacement."

"I…Vic, this is incredible." Her eyes glittered with unshed tears. "You promise Sana's cats won't get into my room and pee in my boots?"

"I can't promise that, but I can promise that you will most likely find a place to operate out of Flagstaff."

"I'm…I'm still floored. But I accept your offer so long as you accept my apologies for a few days ago."

"Absolutely." Victor grinned. He tossed his clipboard onto the desk. "Now it's time for Anna's first driving lesson."

He saw Fiona to the door. Skylar must have been waiting for her because as she strolled to the Woman's Building, he caught her arm. They chatted for a few seconds, and he swept her up in a hug and twirled her around. When her back was to Victor, the team's procurement officer gave him a thumbs up.

Victor smiled and turned away. As he turned off his computer, the tension vanished from his body like a morning mist. God had provided. Before he headed to the door, he briefly closed his eyes and whispered, "Lord, thank You."

31

Over the past two weeks since their arrival home, Suleiman had learned one painful thing. Secrets are like gangrene. If not exposed to the light of God and properly aired, they would rot one's soul. As he approached the porch of the Women's Building, he realized how true that was.

How could he sit in the Bible study that Victor, Deborah, Butch, and Sana held without feeling like a fraud, especially when he gazed at his mentor? He couldn't. It had gotten so bad that Butch had pulled him aside and asked him what was the matter. And what had he done? Lied. He was tired. Distracted by work. One lie piled on top of another. Butch had seen through his excuses, which made it worse, but for some reason, he hadn't called him on it.

And then there was the matter of Sana. She'd been right. His secret chained her. Though she hadn't said anything more to him, its burden reflected in her eyes. After her outpatient surgery on her shoulder the week before, she'd spent most of her time in her bedroom, so at least Victor hadn't questioned why she avoided him.

Who else would he infect?

No one.

Today, he'd finally start obeying that inner voice. Today, he'd confess. Just the thought of it induced the fast breathing and hand sweats indicative of a panic attack. *I can do this. You promised to be with me, right, God?* He tried to recall those words Sana had read to him over the past week. He quelled at the notion of what would happen. *Oh, God, I don't want to do this! I will be driving a spike through Victor's heart.*

He settled onto the wood of the porch and leaned against one of the posts. What would it be like to unburden himself? He couldn't imagine right now.

"Hey." Sana, dressed in a pair of khaki shorts and a white golf shirt, her uniform for her work at the local Starbucks, stood over him. Her arm remained in its sling, but at least now, she was headed out of the woods, as she put it.

"You're going to work today?"

She eased to a sitting position beside him. "Corey asked if I could do eight hours."

"And you're up for it?"

She nodded. "I need the routine as much as you need the routine of your own job." She ran her thumb across the peel of an orange she held. "You're up early."

"I couldn't sleep."

"Hah. I wish I could sleep in." She snuggled up to him and whispered into his ear, "I want to enjoy my last night here with you before Shelly and Diana get here tomorrow and definitely before Fiona gets back in two weeks."

They both chuckled, and he flushed. "I think we could arrange that."

She giggled and handed him the orange. "Could you peel that for me?"

"Sure." It took him a few moments to strip away the peel and split the wedges, which he handed to her in the paper towel.

She offered him one.

He shook his head as his stomach twisted on itself.

"You don't want one?"

"No. Not this morning."

"What's wrong? You've never turned down orange slices before."

"I know." Suleiman swallowed hard and gazed at the Big House.

Victor came out onto the terrace. He waved and called a friendly hello as he strolled toward the studio.

Suleiman winced. "I—I'm going to confess to Victor today."

She drew in a sharp breath. "Uh, oh."

"I'm terrified," he confessed before he lost his nerve.

"I know." She reached out, took his hand, and held on tightly. "Do you want me to come with you? I can always call in and say I'll be a little late."

Oh, her support meant so much! He squeezed her hand. "I—I need to do this on my own. Please understand."

"I do." She leaned over and kissed him. "I love you, and I'll be praying for you."

His smile trembled with fear. "Thanks."

"Call me when you're done?"

He nodded.

She snuggled next to him and laid her head on his shoulder.

He remained with her. Maybe if he stayed there, he wouldn't have to do it.

Not that it lasted. She brushed her lips across his before rising. "I wish I didn't have to go to work, but I do. I'll be back at six, okay?"

He struggled to his feet. "I love you."

"I love you too." She wound her left arm around his neck and hugged him. "I'll be praying."

He nodded because the lump in his throat choked away all words. The screen door banged a moment later as she came outside with her green apron draped over her arm. With one last kiss, his support drove away.

God, I'm terrified. Truly, I am. Suleiman rose. He found it easier to procrastinate by puttering around the Men's Building. He straightened the common area. Then his room. Then he washed all of the breakfast dishes by hand rather than use the dishwasher. He even cleaned the bathroom he shared with Skylar. Butch's too. Something, anything, to keep from facing Victor. Maybe he'd clean Sana's bathroom. His watched beeped, signaling that it was nine.

He couldn't delay any longer. With one last, deep breath, he stepped onto the back porch. Two horses snorted. Pine needles muffled their steps as Tori and Deborah rode along the trail from the barn to the house.

Deborah paused. "Hi, Suleiman. I thought you had to work."

"Uh, tomorrow." He offered a weak smile. "Where are you headed?"

"Out on the trail to ride fence. And have some girl time." Deborah glanced at Tori before turning her attention to him again. Her eyes clouded. "Are you sure you're okay? You seem stressed out."

"I'm fine." Another lie. Built on top of the others. He thought he'd go crazy.

"Okay. Well, if you're headed in Vic's direction, tell him we'll be back in a couple of hours.

He offered a sick smile.

They rode on and disappeared around the side of the house. Where was Victor? One look revealed the answer. In the studio.

It felt like someone had dumped lead into his shoes as he trudged toward the small building of glass and stone. Chin in hand, Victor sat at the worktable, which was against the glass wall opposite the fireplace, and gazed at something on his computer's monitor. He hit a few keys on the keyboard, then chuckled.

Suleiman took a deep breath and knocked on the door frame. "Victor?"

He glanced up and grinned. "Suleiman, hey."

His smile felt fake, brittle. "May I come in?"

"Of course. Check it out. Shelly's been working on websites for both Sentry Securities and Fiona's company. I like Fi's the best."

"Kitchen Sink Air Cargo. We transport everything plus the kitchen sink. I love it." Suleiman clung to that bit of humor like a drowning man to a life ring.

"She's offered to be our webmaster for free, but I want to pay her something. Maybe I'll put her on retainer. And more good news. I think I've found office space. Deb and I are going to share offices, but we've got to figure out how to make that work in terms of layout." Victor hit a button and swiveled on his lab chair. "Sorry. I know you didn't come here to talk about my work. What's up?"

Suddenly, everything that he'd considered saying fled. His mind remained a blank canvas, one he had to fill, lest he run screaming from the room. He took a deep breath. "Do you remember when we first met about the *Peacemaker* mission a few weeks ago?"

"Yeah. It was just the four of us."

"Right. I noticed the picture of your Rachel."

Slowly, Victor nodded. "I remember."

He hated himself for what he had to do! Slowly, he asked, "What do you remember about that night? The night when she died?"

Victor frowned. He rubbed his chin as if assessing the young man standing before him for the reasons why he asked that question. His brow knitted. "Honestly? The only thing I remember is escorting Maggie McCall from the ballroom after she finished speaking. The docs told me that a lot of times, the brain has ways of suppressing traumatic memories. My next coherent memory after that was when I woke up in total pain in ICU."

"When you recovered, did you learn what happened?"

"Yeah. The lead investigator read me in on everything."

"I—I was there."

"No, you weren't. You couldn't have been."

"I was there that night. I saw the way Rachel let the door close behind you. She touched your back as you fled. Right before Makmoud shot you, you pushed Maggie McCall into the shadows of the tunnel so she wouldn't be visible." Trembling began deep within Suleiman. He turned away and shoved his hands into the back pockets of his jeans. "I was on the roof of the convention center with Jibril. Makmoud was on the ground with the kidnap squad."

"You couldn't have been."

He whipped around. "I was." Tears suddenly burned in his eyes. "I—I fired the shot that killed your Rachel."

Victor tilted his head and pursed his lips. "No, Suleiman, no. You weren't there. You weren't. How could you have been?"

His heart nearly pounded its way out of his chest. He drew in a breath. "My given name is Ibrahim Hidari. I am Makmoud's half-brother, twenty years his junior. I ran away from home when I was fifteen." As if in a waterfall, his words almost tumbled over themselves. "Five years ago, Makmoud found me in Marseille and kidnapped me. They took me to the

Hezbollah compound in Venezuela. Once there, he and Jibril broke me. They noticed I had a gift and trained me to be a sniper."

Victor huffed out a noisy breath as he cracked his knuckles. He advanced on him. "You...you *trained* for that?"

Suleiman stumbled backward and came into contact with one of the chairs. His knees began trembling alongside his heart, so much so that he sank to his knees. "I didn't know your name. Or who your were. Or Rachel's name. Victor, please! Please forgive me. I did not know what I was doing, did not—"

"You've lied to me all these years!"

"I did not know!" Suleiman couldn't look at him, especially now. "Honestly, I did not. Only Makmoud and Jibril knew your identities. Rachel had no name to me at the time."

"You killed her!" Victor yelled.

"I did," Suleiman whispered. He hung his head. "Please, I—I ask...I ask for your forgiveness. Had I known..."

Had he known what? Who Victor was at the time? Who Rachel was? How he would meet his mentor? His foolishness rendered him speechless.

"Get out." Calm, too calm for Victor after his outburst.

"What?" Suleiman raised his head.

Victor had his back to him with his arms folded across his chest. His words came across low, almost gravelly. "Get out. Get out of my sight. Matter of fact, I want you off this property."

"Victor—"

Victor whipped around. Now his eyes were as cold and flinty as the surrounding rock walls of the box canyon in winter. "Now! You have two hours to vacate before I use my power as a sheriff's deputy to arrest you."

Panic surged to the surface of Suleiman's calm. However, it was like his legs refused to work. He found that he couldn't climb to his feet.

Victor grabbed his arm in a viselike grip. He hauled him upright and shoved him to the door. With a guttural roar, he pushed him outside. "Go!"

Suleiman fell to the ground. Pain burned in his elbow as it made contact with a rock. He whipped around and stared.

Victor's eyes had widened to the point where he could see the whites, even from that distance. His former mentor jabbed his finger in the direction of the Man's Building. "Go!"

Suleiman fled. Stumbling over a root, he collapsed to his knees. Pain burned beneath his hands. He staggered upright and to the Men's Building. Fortunately, Butch was in town at his auto shop. And Skylar had headed to Las Vegas to close up shop. At least no one was around to witness his humiliation.

Where would he go?

Vegas. He could work in Skylar's restaurant.

The altercation tore at his heart. He'd done it. Seared new anguish into Victor's heart. Sure, he'd confessed, but did he feel free? No, not then. "Oh, God, why?"

He stripped the bed and threw all of his possessions into his suitcases. So what if everything was wrinkled? He'd have to leave his furniture. Suleiman collapsed onto the bare mattress. His mind spun as he considered his idea. He'd need a place to stay. Maybe he could take over Skylar's lease. He could start over. He'd done it before, after all. Several times. He was resourceful. He could survive.

Except for one thing.

Sana.

He reached into his backpack and pulled out the picture of her he'd taken from their climb on The Mushroom.

She'd struck a cute pose in her black climbing shorts and hot pink top. Even on paper, her eyes sparkled.

He lowered his head. His chest heaved. "God, I can't leave her. I can't!"

He had no choice.

New agony surged over him.

His phone began ringing. He glanced at the caller ID.

Sana.

Suleiman cut the phone off. "I'm sorry, Sana. I'm so sorry," he whispered. "I—I love you."

He gazed around the room. He couldn't leave, not without trying to explain himself to her. Suleiman extracted a notepad and pen from his backpack. Slowly, but with gathering speed, he wrote. Finally, after two pages, he ripped the sheets off the tablet and dropped them on the empty dresser.

His eyes filled as he stared at the Women's Building. "Sana, I'm sorry. I'm so sorry. Please join me in Vegas. I love you."

With that, he dragged his bags to his old Honda Civic. He climbed inside. With one twist of the key, he started the engine and fled.

Friday, July 17, 2015, 1000 hours Pacific Daylight Time, Flagstaff, AZ

On the far northern edges of the Chavez ranch land, metal clanged against metal. Victor grunted an accompaniment with each down stroke of the sledgehammer. Right then, only the hard work of repairing a break in the fence kept the demons of his past at bay.

Barely.

Like a pack of angry wolves, the memories burst from hiding. His first kiss with Rachel. His proposal to her. The agony that had surged over him in the hospital when he'd learned of her death. Gary's betrayal, not only of the team but of their fifteen years of close friendship. And now this.

He imagined pounding Suleiman to a pulp rather than the fence post. He raised the sledgehammer high above his head. With one last rush of strength, he slammed it onto the metal, driving it so far into the ground that he couldn't string any barbed wire to it.

Victor tossed the sledgehammer aside, gripped it, and pulled. Hard. It didn't budge. "Arrggghh!"

He tried again. It wiggled maybe half an inch. But no upward give. He'd messed up on this one.

Big time.

Had he done the same with Suleiman?

When he'd first met him as part of Shadow Box, the young man had been firm in his desire. No killing unless absolutely necessary. He'd been a quiet, calming influence, especially with Sana after the team had fallen apart the year before. If he hadn't been around, she might have sunk into a depression. Instead, they'd become best friends. And two Sundays ago. He'd practically radiated with joy when he'd told everyone about his conversion. Man, Victor had missed the mark on him completely, had so totally misjudged his character.

His heart ached. Sinking into a crouch, he covered his face with his hands. "I thought this was over. Thought I'd moved past it. Why, God? Why?"

"I'm sorry."

Deborah.

He lowered his hands and stared at red dirt. How much had she seen? "I thought you were riding with Tori."

"I was until Anna called. She saw you throw Suleiman out of the studio."

He moaned and hung his head. What kind of a father was he to think no one was watching? He couldn't face her. "How'd you find me?"

Leather creaked as she dismounted. Her hand on his back helped, if only a little. "You men can be creatures of habit. I knew you'd said something this morning about repairing the fence out here, so I knew exactly where to come."

Heedless of how sweaty he must have been, he drew her close and held her tightly. They fell into a sitting position that would have been comical had anyone been watching.

"Ummph. I, um, can't breathe," she muttered. "And you've got some serious man stink going on."

"Sorry." He loosened his grip.

"You want some tea? I have some."

"Sure."

She rose and opened one of the flaps of the saddlebag. In one hand, she carried a thermos, in the other, two plastic cups. "Sorry about not having any ice. We'll have to drink it European style."

For a few minutes, they sat in silence and gazed over the rangeland beneath the mesa. If he stared hard enough, he thought he saw the Grand Canyon. Numbness settled across him. "Suleiman came to me today."

"Why?"

"He told me he was the one who killed Rachel."

She frowned. "Come again?"

"The night of the attempted kidnapping, he said he was the one who shot her." He picked up some pine straw. "Honestly, I have no memory of it."

"I—I—I don't know what to say. How do you know?"

"He told me enough. He wasn't lying."

Her eyes filled, and one trickled down her cheek. She put her face in her hands and shook her head as if she couldn't process what he'd said.

This time, Victor put his hand on her back and rubbed it. "I'm...I don't know."

"I'm devastated. I ache. For him. For Sana." She raised her face. Tears streaked the dust on it in glistening, wet paths. She wiped at them. "For you as well."

She pulled the band from her hair. As it tumbled around her face, she swept her hands through it. She bowed her head and clenched her fingers at the back of her neck. Finally, she gazed at him. Her hand shot to the cross around her neck. "It's almost too much to take in."

Heat rushed through him, and sweat broke out across his forehead again. "He murdered my fiancée in cold blood."

She stared at the sweeping vista before them. "Did he?"

He cocked his head. "I—I don't understand."

Her gaze returned to him. "Was it in cold blood?"

"How couldn't it be?"

She shrugged. "Maybe he was under orders. Not from you but from Makmoud. Have you ever thought of that?"

He blew out an impatient breath. "Does it matter?"

"Maybe."

"How can it?"

"From what you and TL Jones told me and from what I learned about Makmoud, the man is a very gifted and charismatic leader. I could see how it would be easy to follow him blindly."

Victor jumped to his feet. "He killed three people! I have every right to arrest him and haul his butt to jail. He can rot there for all I care before he fries for his crimes."

"Vic!" She matched him in posture. "I can't believe you."

"Why? He killed people. He should pay!" As if to emphasize his point, he kicked the hammer. Pain shot through his foot, and he groaned as he hopped around.

"Have you thought about what you just said?"

"He's a murderer!"

"Who has repented." Seemingly unfazed, Deborah stood there, holding Daisy's reins. She stroked the horse's neck as if the motion calmed both human and equine alike.

For a moment, Victor tried to speak, but it was almost as if something had stolen his voice. Finally, he blurted, "How can you say that?"

"Because I know Suleiman al-Ibrahim."

"Who, by the way, is Ibrahim Hidari. He told me himself."

Deborah sighed. For a few moments, only the sound of his heavy breathing filled the air. Finally, she looped the reins over a tree branch, took his hands, and held on tightly. "I think Suleiman is more appropriate. Tell me something. Has he acted like an unrepentant killer?"

"He's a liar. He lied about his name after all. And goodness knows what else."

"Vic." The first signs of exasperation appeared. She released him and once more faced the vista before them. "What he did was horrible. In doing so, he destroyed the life you had. Your future with Rachel. Your career. Life as you knew it." She sniffled and stared at her hands. "But have you paid attention at all lately? Has he acted like an unrepentant killer?"

Victor thought through everything that he'd noticed about Suleiman. Words he'd used months ago when describing him to the young man's future employer came to mind.

Earnest.

Dependable.

Good-natured.

Calm.

Then came a statement from Butch the Christmas before when he, Sana, and Suleiman had visited North Carolina for Christmas. "He's a good guy, boss. He cares about people, and he's been really good to keep Sana's spirits up." And then what about when on the job? The year before, his shot at Makmoud had missed. And he'd had ample opportunity to kill his half-brother when they were in Somalia. He hadn't. Why? On the plane ride out of Somalia, the young man had briefly stopped speaking before he confessed, "I want to be a peacemaker."

Victor reached out, drew his wife close, and ran his hands down her arms. "No. He hasn't."

"Look. I'm not trying to defend his actions three years ago. I'm not. But he's changed. You know he has because of what happened two weeks ago when he converted. Sana later told me that it came after a lot of running from the Holy Spirit. He's a new man in Christ."

"But he killed her!"

"Didn't Paul oversee the killing of many?" Deborah pulled away. "Haven't we all murdered people in our hearts? Jesus spoke very sternly about those silent kills we can and do make every day. We all need a savior."

"He's beyond help."

"Why?"

He clamped his jaw shut.

A sigh escaped her. "You know Derek spent over twenty years with Delta Force, which included in his later years a war and three tours of duty in high-hazard areas. He didn't talk a lot about his time over there—mainly because it was classified—but he told me enough to know that on more than one occasion, he shot either members of the insurgency or the Taliban. Sure, he was under orders, but each kill took something of his soul. He knew he needed Christ as his Savior so badly." She cut her eyes toward him. "What about you? You were in SF. Surely you had the same situation."

Victor joined her in her observations of the landscape and thought about the man she'd loved until death had taken him almost six years before. He shoved his hands into the back pockets of his jeans, much the way Suleiman had. He didn't want to hear what she had to say. No, he wanted to wallow in his grief and anger. He didn't want to forgive, either. That was for sure. But she was right. During his time in Special Forces, they'd had missions where they'd come under fire and had fought back. "I did. We were under orders."

"So was Derek. So was Suleiman. But that doesn't change what happened." She paused, and the breeze sweeping up from the mesa blew her hair back in wheat-colored waves. "When we become a child of God, we recognize our own need for forgiveness. And we are forgiven. Think about it."

New agony filled him again. "I can't forgive him." He eased into a sitting position. "How can I?"

She snuggled next to him. "Do you remember how we've been studying the parables at church?"

He nodded.

"And how we got to the parable of the guy who owed a ton of money to the king? He owed so much he could literally never repay the king."

"Yeah." With a sinking feeling, he knew where this was leading.

"Well, the king forgave him. Wiped the slate clean. No more debt at all. Imagine the relief the man must have felt. Yet then he went to someone who owed him very little, demanded repayment, and sold the man's family into slavery when he couldn't cough up the cash. When the king found out about it, he threw the man into prison where he'd have no chance of paying off the massive debt he owed. Christ told that parable because, as we are forgiven, so we are expected to forgive."

Victor winced.

His wife was right.

A lump filled his throat, and he swallowed hard before rasping, "It's so hard."

"I know." She rubbed his back. "I'm not saying it's easy. I've seen how hard it is. How hard it is for a wife to forgive her husband who strayed while he was deployed. How hard it is for an adult child to forgive his father who had impossible expectations for his son to live up to. I can tell you, though, that when forgiveness happens, and if you get the privilege to witness it, you see God's grace in motion. And it's a beautiful thing."

Still, justice had to be served, right? "But he killed Rachel—"

"I know. I know it's difficult to contemplate. We live in such a fallen world. Truly, we do. Somehow, God takes those awful things that happened to us, like your losing Rachel and your career and my losing Derek, and He weaves a beautiful story out of it. That of your salvation. Of the way you and I met and married. And of the way Suleiman has come to know Christ as his Lord and Savior."

Ouch. The truth stung. But like it was an antiseptic on the gash in his soul, healing began. She was right. On all counts. "His confession brought back all kinds of grief."

"Oh, I'm sure. Maybe this is an opportunity to put all of that behind you once and for all."

Could she be right? Victor struggled to believe her.

"And think about one more thing."

"What?"

Deborah wrapped her arms around his middle and laid her head against his shoulder. "What about Sana? She loves him so dearly. Even before they were open about it, and even before he got a clue, I noticed the way she gazed at him. She's a good judge of character. Would she fall in love with someone who wasn't repentant about his actions?"

He wanted to shout that she was a former criminal herself. Those words remained locked in his throat as if the Holy Spirit had frozen them.

"She wouldn't. You know it. I know it. She can tell someone who's truly experienced grace because she knows she's so in need of it as well. We all are."

Still, it was so hard. "It makes me so angry. And the way...the way that Gary betrayed me." Victor raked his hands through his hair. The agony welled within. His shoulders shook. "I've been so angry at Gary. Now so angry at Suleiman."

"Maybe it's time to let justice flow to mercy on all counts." She held onto him.

Tears burned into his eyes. *God, please. Take these past hurts from me. Heal me. Heal me! I beg of You.* His chest heaved. His grip tightened, but Deborah didn't wince or pull away. "Do you...do you think it is possible?"

Her lips moved against his hair. "Yes. With Holy Spirit's help, you can forgive. That, I can promise."

It took a few minutes, but he finally steadied. Weariness surged over him even though it was barely past eleven. "I...I ordered him off the property. I—I gave him two hours to vacate."

"What? Vic?" Deborah pulled back. "Never mind." She glanced at her watch. "There's time. C'mon. You two need to talk, to clear the air."

He gazed at the fence.

"Silly, mending relationships is much more important than mending a fence. If the cows can't stay off the cliff, then they're not worth having. C'mon." Deborah swung into her saddle with the ease of a woman who'd ridden for years.

Almost reluctantly, he mounted Mack.

At a fast trot that moved to a canter, they bolted toward the Big House. As soon as they rode up the driveway, he scanned the cars. No Honda Civic. Suleiman had already left. "He's gone."

"Maybe not."

Victor swung from the saddle. He rushed into the Men's Building. "Oh, no."

Nothing remained in Suleiman's room except for a stripped mattress and empty dresser. He ripped open the closet door. Nothing. Behind him, paper rattled.

"Vic." Deborah drew in a sharp breath. She handed him two pages.

He whipped through them and closed his eyes. What had he done? Sana would never forgive him. "Where would he go?"

"I don't know. Wait!" Deborah set the sheets on the dresser. "Skylar. He said something in his note about going to Vegas."

"Maybe I can stop him." Victor raced toward the Big House. It took him mere seconds to charge upward three floors to the master suite. By the time he stumbled to his dresser, he sucked wind. After jumping into cargo pants and yanking on a clean T-shirt, he charged downward and ignored Anna's call to him. He found Deborah on the terrace. "I'll be back."

"And I'll be praying," she murmured.

He kissed her hard and ran to his white Jeep Commander. As he rumbled down the driveway toward the gate, he dialed the dispatcher. "Francine? Deputy Chavez here. I need a BOLO for a blue Honda Civic." He recited the license plate. "He's not armed or dangerous, just someone I need to talk to. If you could broadcast that and have people call me if they see him, I'd appreciate it. Thanks."

Friday, July 17, 2015, 1300 hours Pacific Daylight Time, west of Flagstaff, AZ

"Of all things!" Suleiman muttered when his car's engine began bumping and coughing. The Check Engine light came on. More than that, it began flashing. Not good. Suleiman shifted to the right-hand lane of I-40 heading west. A bang sounded, and he rapidly lost power. Once he'd limped to the edge of the highway, he twisted the key in the ignition. Only a gurgle.

Oh, great. Barely past Seligman, and his attempt to run away had failed. For a moment, he rested his head against the seat. Once he'd popped the hood, he climbed out and opened it. He gagged on the stinky smoke rising from the engine. At a crouch, he surveyed the underside. Oil, the lifeblood of any engine, leaked onto the pavement. No, it poured from the underside in a dirty brown stream.

For a moment, he eased onto his haunches and tried to figure out what had happened. He'd never been mechanically inclined. No, Jibril would have been able to diagnose the problem with ease. Or, had he been at Last Chance Ranch, Butch.

His freshly healed wound began burning from the hot pavement. He needed to stand, not roast in the sun as he contemplated this twist in fate. He scratched his head. What should he do? Seligman was too far east for him to walk, especially in this heat. And he didn't have Skylar's phone number. Not that Shadow Box's procurement officer would know anything more than he about fixing his problem.

Butch. His friend's words echoed in his ears. "Suleiman, you gotta get a new car. Sure, Hondas are great, but any car with 275k is going to go. It's like waiting for the big earthquake."

Despite all of his efforts to run away, he'd wind up right back where he started—at Last Chance Ranch—and too close to the man who now rightfully hated him. Still, he had no other alternative. He pulled his cell phone from the car and turned it on. Three more calls from Sana, and he was sure there were just as many messages behind the icon he saw.

At the sound of a motor rumbling, he glanced up. A lump rose to his throat at the flashing blue light on the dash of the white Jeep Commander and the man behind the wheel.

Victor.

Suleiman forced his attention back to his phone. "Why are you here?"

Gravel crunched, and Victor replied, "To ask you to come home."

Suleiman snorted. "Why? So you can arrest me? We are in Mojave County, my friend. Out of your jurisdiction, I believe."

"I erred."

"In what? Not arresting me when you had the opportunity?" Couldn't he just let it go? Not when the scrapes on his palms and elbow still smarted as much as his wounded spirit.

"I erred in my anger."

Suleiman cringed when a truck blew by too close for comfort. He shook his head. "You had every right to be angry with me. I killed your Rachel, after all."

Victor sighed, then asked, "Can we debate this a little bit further from the road?"

Without a word, Suleiman stepped down the shoulder until they stood next to the right-of-way fence that kept any wandering cattle off the highway.

"You said I had a right to my anger," Victor stated after a moment. He folded his arms across his chest. "You're right. We all have a right to anger. Thing is, where that anger crosses from just to unjust is a very short distance. I blew way past that this morning. I want to set things right with you once and for all. Will you give me that opportunity?"

Did he have a choice? Not when his well-being in the near future depended upon being in Victor's good graces. He nodded.

Victor lightly kicked a fence post. "It all started with one of these."

"I am not sure I follow."

"After I threw you out, I had to get out of there. I'd planned on doing some fence mending. Hah." Victor shook his head. "I think God has a somewhat bizarre sense of humor. Suffice it to say that I sent the post way too far into the ground."

"How does that have to do with your anger going too far?"

"Deb showed up. I guess Anna saw what happened between us and called." Slowly, halting at times, most likely to reign in his thoughts, Victor explained the concept of true forgiveness.

Stunned, Suleiman listened. A lump formed in his throat. He didn't want to believe what he'd heard. It couldn't be true. Of course, Victor forgave because he had to. Nothing more. Suleiman felt faint, but he didn't know if it was from his story or the sun blasting down on his head.

"There's one more thing," his mentor said.

"What?" Suleiman cleared his throat and pretended like the lump in it was from his thirst.

"As I raced out here to try and find you, I realized that forgiveness can be grudgingly or freely given. And with you, for us to live at Last Chance Ranch together, it needs to be freely given. That made me think some more. I've known you for almost two years now." Thanks to the dark glasses Victor wore, he remained expressionless. "And nothing I've seen indicates an unrepentant killer. If anything, you've been the most vocal about avoiding killing whenever possible. I know what happened last year and this year. Last year, when you came within a hair's breadth of killing Makmoud, you tried and missed. But this time?" He lowered his head before raising it. "This time, when Makmoud actually gave you ample opportunity, you backed down."

"It scared me how much I wanted to kill him," Suleiman confessed.

"I know. It's…it's in our nature to want to take justice into our own hands. I think we all learned that with the *Peacemaker* incident." Victor sighed. "You took the life of my fiancée and in the process destroyed my future."

Suleiman hung his head.

"Those months after Rach died were some of the worst I've had. But some way, somehow, God took those horrible circumstances and used them to glorify Himself. Which means that now, we're standing here having a somewhat strange kind of conversation at the side of the interstate. I guess you could say through great pain comes great joy, eh?"

Suleiman couldn't speak. Not at all. From the shock radiating through him as Victor's freely given forgiveness sank in or emotion, he didn't know. He stood there like a stone as he tried to process the news.

Victor cleared his throat. "So, with that being said, I want you to come home. Come back to Last Chance Ranch. We want you there. We need you there."

More than ever, he wanted to do so. Suleiman finally lifted his gaze and met Victor's. "You…you have forgiven me?"

Victor took off his shades. Now, instead of the storminess of anger in those dark depths, sadness radiated from them as a reflection of the way Suleiman's actions years before had impacted him. But there was something else. Peace. Blessed peace. "I have."

"Thank you," Suleiman whispered. Suddenly, he wanted to sag to the ground. "And yes, I will return home."

Victor cleared his throat and shifted his attention to the Honda Civic. "What happened to your car?"

"Something with the engine. The Check Engine light started blinking." Suleiman threw up his hands. "I do not know why."

"Let me check it." Victor took one look at the engine and the mess of oil that had run from underneath. "I think you threw a rod. It's toast. We'll have Butch tow it back to the shop, but most likely, he's going to say to give it up and get a new car."

"Sana will like that."

A ghost of a smile flickered across his mentor's face. "She will. Let's get your stuff to my Jeep. If we're lucky, you can be unpacked by the time she gets home. Which is when?"

"She said six."

"Then let's do it." Victor opened the back door.

Within minutes, Suleiman locked the Civic. "Thank you. For everything."

"You're welcome." Victor led the way to the Commander. He clapped him on the shoulder. "And Suleiman, welcome home."

32

Tori sat on her knees in the middle of her room. In front of her was a low play table that Deborah had brought from Gracie and Marie's room. A big hunk of clay rested on the wood surface. Deborah had suggested that being creative might help her push past the barriers that had seemed to exist for the past two weeks, and she couldn't have agreed more.

Tori took a deep breath and released it. Outside, the warm breeze rustled through the pines and brought its fresh scent into the room. Once more, she inhaled. The sharp, tangy aroma coursed over her. Ever so slightly, the tension in her shoulders eased.

Still, her mind remained a blank. From her concussion or her time as a hostage, she didn't know. Slowly, something began emerging. Not that her mind's eye could picture it. Like a projector with its focus knocked out of kilter, it remained a fuzzy image.

The door burst open, and the two youngest Fields girls bustled inside. Each held a bundle of white fur with a pink tail in their hands.

Tori offered a smile. "What do you have here?"

"Our rats." Marie settled on her knees by the table. She offered Tori the rat. "This is Cupid."

"And this is Valentine." Gracie placed the squirming white rat on the table in front of Tori.

Tori took Cupid from Marie. The rat's whiskers quivered as she sniffed her skin. She climbed up her shirt and onto her shoulders, where she ran her tiny paws along her hair. "They're cute. How long have you had them?"

"Since right after we got here."

Tori lifted Cupid off her shoulder and placed her on the table. The rat began investigating the clay.

"Miss Tori, Mommy says you're a doctor," Gracie said.

"I am."

"Can you look at Valentine? I'm worried about her."

"Why's that?" Tori peered at the other rat, who seemed plumper than her pal.

"She's getting fat, but I haven't been feeding her any more seeds than normal. I'm worried she might have a tumor." Gracie's blue eyes widened.

"Let me see." Tori stroked Valentine, who seemed content to rest in her hands. "She doesn't feel strange." She peered at Cupid, who had scurried up the hunk of clay. She stood on her haunches. Tori stared at her, and recognition suddenly dawned on her. "Um, I think Cupid might be a boy rat, which means that Valentine is going to have babies."

"Rat babies?" If it were possible, Gracie's eyes widened even further. "Like we're going to have baby rats?"

"I believe so."

"How do you know?" As if she were the skeptical one of the two, Marie crossed her arms and scowled.

Suddenly, Tori realized things had gone from simple to complicated in a second. Warmth flooded her cheeks as she struggled for an explanation suitable for a six-year-old. "Um, well, um, let's just say that Cupid has the right…the right equipment."

Now Marie grinned. "Cool. We're going to have babies, Gracie. Maybe we could start a rat farm."

"Or a rat ranch."

The girls began discussing names for the baby rats.

"How about Millie?" Marie asked.

"And we could have Vanilli." Gracie scrambled to where Tori had begun writing out thoughts about her ordeal in Somalia. She ignored the scribbles and flipped to a blank page.

She looked so much like an assistant taking notes that a smile began spreading across Tori's face.

"Or Mutt and Jeff."

"Or Bonnie and Clyde." They started giggling.

Before she realized it, Tori joined them. "Or Frank and Earnest."

"Gracie! Time to unload the dishwasher so we can start supper," Deborah called from downstairs.

Suddenly, the image she'd envisioned came clear in her mind. A rat. A mama rat and babies.

More than that, she recalled Captain Jameson's words from weeks before. "You have a heart for missions, but there are other ways to serve the Lord besides living like a nomad on a hospital ship."

Now she knew where her next calling would be.

She wanted to jump up and shout for joy. Instead, she said, "You two run along. Tell your mom I'll be downstairs in a few minutes to help."

Already chattering about how they'd build a miniature barn for the new rats, the two girls ran from the room.

Tori couldn't help it. Still chuckling, she rose and approached the nightstand. Her engagement ring rested on top of her Bible, which had remained closed since her arrival, save for when she'd pried the ring from it. She slid the marquis diamond onto her finger and read about how God would wipe away all tears. It was true.

She closed the book with a snap and picked up her phone. Tori punched in a number. When Jake answered, she said, "It's me. I'm ready to see you."

Friday, July 17, 2015, 1830 hours Pacific Daylight Time, Flagstaff, AZ

A dozen people crowded around the twelve-person table in the eat-in kitchen of the Chavez house. Silverware clinked on pottery. Laughter bubbled over. Rich smells of chicken and vegetables cooked by Deborah on the grill filled the kitchen. Contentment washed over Victor as he relaxed at the head of the table and gazed at everyone.

To his right sat Deborah with DJ and Anna to her right. Sana and Suleiman were beside them. To his left sat Gracie. Marie snuggled next to her Uncle Butch with Elizabeth Walters, Norm's wife, and Jake next to Butch. Tori occupied the other end. Her countenance, so downcast even as of this morning, had lifted as if a switch had flipped. Right then, he didn't care about why.

She'd turned a corner, and that's all that mattered.

This was how he'd imagined things when he'd taken the chance and married Deborah. Being surrounded by friends. Making an impact in people's lives. Seeing the children God had given him along with Deborah grow a little bit each day.

Butch rubbed his stomach. "Good as ever, Deb. Boy, I hope one day I'll have a bride who cooks as well as you."

"Keep eating like that, and she'll figure it out pretty quickly." Deborah winked at Victor's best friend.

Butch turned his attention to Suleiman, who sat across from him. "Hey, Suleiman, you going to finish that, or is the food contaminated since it might have accidentally touched each other?"

"You're a funny man, Butch Addison." Suleiman grinned.

Thankfully, any discomfort from their discussion alongside the interstate had vanished under the warmth of being with friends.

"I've got divided plates on your Christmas list already." Butch picked up the broccoli bowl. "Someone, please, take these last lonely pieces of broccoli. Marie?"

He offered it to the six-year-old.

She pouted and folded her arms. "No."

"No? And break Uncle Butch's heart?" Butch mock-sniffed. "Are you sure? Here."

She pouted some more and lifted her chin. "Nope."

Butch heaved a sigh. Then he grinned and dumped them onto his plate. "More for me."

"Daddy, Valentine's going to have rat babies," Gracie announced.

"What?" Victor leaned forward and gazed at the eight-year-old. "Sweetie, I don't understand."

He glanced at Tori. She began shaking her head and making shushing motions. Huh?

"Rat babies. I asked Miss Tori to look at Valentine for me since she's a doctor and since I was worried that Valentine had a tumor." Gracie already sounded grown-up. "She did, but then she said that Valentine's going to have babies."

"But...why?" Again, he gazed at Tori. This time, she pursed her lips, and she shook her head as if to say, *Don't ask*.

"Because she said Cupid's a boy," Marie piped up.

"Why did she say that?" Too late, Victor realized his blunder.

"Because she said that Cupid has equipment," Marie replied. "Daddy, do you have equipment?"

Uh, oh. He'd done it this time. "You're kidding, right?"

Opposite him, Tori hid her face, but he still saw the way her cheeks creased in a smile.

Time to learn from Deborah about how to talk about the birds and the bees.

At the other end, a muffled snort from Sana answered his question. She began giggling. That set off an explosion of laughter around the table. It was almost like the tension that had covered the ranch popped in one burst due to the innocent question of a six-year-old.

Tori banged on her glass with a fork. "I—we have an announcement."

Everyone calmed.

Victor cleared his throat. "What is it?"

"Are you having rat babies too?" Gracie asked.

Tori laughed. "No, no, no. But, Jake and I." She took her fiancé's hand in hers. "We're going to proceed with our wedding in October as planned. But, well, we may or may not stay in Charleston afterward. A lot has to come clear before we make that decision. And"—she fingered her silverware—"I've decided that I want to be involved in a women's ministry to rape victims, to share what happened and help women heal."

"Hear, hear. A toast is in order." Victor raised his glass. "May God bless you and keep you during this special time. May his face shine upon you and give you peace, both now and forever."

It could happen.

Peace had finally come.

Friday, July 17, 2015, 2200 hours Pacific Daylight Time, Flagstaff, AZ

"What a day. What a week. What a month." Suleiman held Sana close on the couch of the Women's Building. He gazed through the open screened door and picture window.

At the Big House, most of the lights were out save for a few in the den where DJ and Anna most likely hung out. The fire pit on the terrace blazed, and Butch, Victor, Deborah, Tori, and Jake lounged around it. Normally, he would have joined the group. Not tonight when it was his last night alone with Sana.

He rose. One by one, he shut off the lights. Closing the blinds and door sealed them from any prying eyes. "I want some privacy to be with you and you alone."

Mindful of her healing arm, he drew her close. His embrace tightened as he remembered how close he'd come to losing her today. At least now, he could bury his nose in her freshly washed hair almost any time he wanted.

"When you told me what happened, I got so scared."

"I know." He pulled away and cupped her cheek in his hand.

The firelight from the wood stove reflected off her brown skin in golden tones. It sparkled in those dark eyes he so dearly loved. He ran his thumb down her cheek. As soft and smooth as her hair. "But, as you say, God is good."

"He is indeed."

He kissed her.

One minute turned into two, and he pulled back, his heart pounding, and rested his forehead against hers.

"I guess you'll be needing a new car." A smile appeared on her face. Beneath his fingertips, she trembled slightly.

He felt it, too. It wouldn't take any effort at all to slide the strap of her tank top from her shoulder. He shouldn't. He wouldn't. He knew how the physical attraction flared, but he had already learned the importance of modesty for Sana. "Butch said he'd send a tow truck out there, but he said I should stop being a cheapskate and get one. Maybe an SUV?"

She shifted so she curled up in his arms. "What about the rest of the fee you got?"

"I'll probably bank it and keep working as a waiter. I need the schedule, after all. But I also want to save some of it for my education at University. What about you?"

For a moment, only the insects outside peeped. Did he detect the faintest of tension? "I have a dream."

"And what is that?"

She faced him and giggled. "Maybe it's my secret."

"Shall I drag it out of you?" He kissed her again. Slowly.

"Keep up that kind of interrogation, and you might get more than you bargained for." Her voice shook as she slipped into his embrace again. "Actually, I'd like to open my own coffee shop. I know there's already a lot of competition, but I want to try my hand at it. Pause Cafe and More. Put your life on pause for a bit. And for dog lovers, I'd like to open a patio called Paws at Pause."

"I like it. You could have Shelly do your website."

"True. Boy, it's a far cry from what Father had envisioned for me."

"Which was?"

"Compete in the Olympics. Earn a degree in business or computer science. Run his company." She snorted. "Fat chance of that now. No, nothing I do, no matter how good, would satisfy him now."

"Even...me?"

"No. But I don't care about his opinion. About anything." She stroked his arms. "Honestly, I want more than just a coffee shop."

"Oh?"

She wrapped her arm around his middle. "I...I want to be with you."

He kissed her on the hair. "I love you, Sana Jain."

And perhaps one day soon, we'll marry.

He held her as thoughts about Sana's strained relationship with her father raced around in his head. Then came the thoughts of Makmoud. Would his half-brother come after him? Did it matter at the moment? He shoved them away. No, peace had come. That's all that mattered.

ACKNOWLEDGEMENTS

It's hard to believe that this is my fifth book that I have produced as an indie writer. Through it all, I've come to realize how producing a novel is more of a group effort than anything else. Many thanks go to my beta readers. Rich Bullock, Phyllis McCutchen, Susan Patterson, and Pam Vashaw, your comments and wisdom made *Operation Peacemaker* stronger than it ever could have been without your help. I also want to thank Dafeenah Jameel of IndieDesignz for her great cover work. Dafeenah, your covers continue to amaze me.

I also want to thank those who have acted as my cheerleaders. Thank you to my fellow writers at Seven Serious Scribes and in my Heart and Soul of North Carolina Chapter of the American Christian Fiction Writers. I truly appreciate your support. Also many thanks go to my husband, Steve, and my other family who have supported this endeavor. Writing can be a lonely business, and it's nice to have that support network. Last, I give thanks to God for the many gifts He has given, including this gift of writing.